COLDHEARTED KING

EMPTY KINGDOM BOOK 1

L.M. DALGLEISH

Cover Design: Wildheart Graphics

Content Editing: Brittni Van—Overbooked Editing

Editing, Proofreading, and Formatting: Sugar Free Editing

To my readers, thank you for loving books and reading and romance and smut as much as you do. Your passion is what fuels mine!

CHAPTER ONE

COLE

I lean on the hotel balcony's railing, my forearms braced on top, my hands hanging loosely. A mild breeze cools my sweat-damp skin, which, along with the rumpled sheets of the king-size bed behind me, bears testament to the activity that's occupied me for the last few hours. This high up, the normal sounds of New York City—music, shouts, the occasional siren, the honking of car horns—are muted, much like the stars, which can barely be seen through the haze of illumination cast by the sprawling urban jungle below.

From here, I can see King Plaza, the fifty-three-story office tower which houses the global headquarters of the King Group. The lights glimmering in the windows reveal that many of our people are still at work, even this late on a Friday night. A glow from the corner of the highest floor shows that Roman, my older brother by five years—thirty-six to my thirty-one—is there too.

Hardly a surprise.

"Hey," a low, feminine voice purrs behind me. Soft breasts press against my shirtless back as slender arms wrap

1

around my chest. "How about you come back to bed so I can take your mind off whatever it's on?"

I don't bother turning. "I thought you'd gone."

The tension in Jessica's body says she isn't happy with what I've said. But she persists, trailing her fingers down my stomach toward the waistband of the black boxer briefs I'd pulled on after I climbed out of the bed fifteen minutes ago.

My dick twitches, but I've already come twice tonight, which means I can easily ignore my biological reaction to being touched by a naked woman. And it annoys me she's still here, because she knows how this works.

I keep my eyes on King Plaza. "I'll call you next time I need a date."

Jessica curls her fingers, her nails pricking my skin. "You're an asshole." Her tone has cooled, but she's holding back the anger she's so obviously feeling. I'm used to it. Since I'm one of the richest men in the country, people tend to disguise their true emotions around me.

Although, in Jessica's case, she has her own wealth. What keeps her from unleashing her anger on me is that she likes how I fuck her a little too much to piss me off.

Her arms drop from around me and she steps back. That's when I finally turn and take her in. Aside from the pout on her face, she's completely naked, and apparently unconcerned about being exposed on the balcony. This is one of the sub-penthouse suites hotel management keeps permanently available for the King family—one benefit of being the owners—so we're high up. But the paparazzi still occasionally manage to get a photo of one of us up here. Sometimes alone, sometimes not.

I'm sure Jessica won't have a problem if she gets her photo in a tabloid or two, even if her father would be less than impressed. She's gorgeous in a way only money can make you—every inch polished, styled, and enhanced to perfection. At this stage, I'm not even sure her personality is real. Not that I'm complaining. She made a very pretty picture as my date to the awards ceremony tonight, and an even prettier picture bouncing on my dick for the last couple of hours.

We're done now, though, and having her here is grating on my nerves.

I need her gone.

When I step forward, she must think I'm responding to the doe-eyed expression she's giving me, because a satisfied smirk curls her plump lips. It disappears when I reach for the tumbler of whiskey on the table behind her. "I have to get some work done."

A frown mars her perfect face for a split second before she gives a casual shrug and a fake smile. "Sure. I'll go back downstairs and find someone else who wants to keep the party going."

If it's an effort to make me jealous, she should know better—I'm not the type. I can't imagine why anyone is. And that goes for men *and* women. Maybe that means there's something intrinsic missing from my psyche, some fundamental aspect of human nature that I don't quite grasp. Or maybe jealousy is something that some people are simply more prone to than others.

"You should. The night's still young." I move past her, see her red lace thong hanging over a lamp, and hand it to her.

I'm not a complete asshole.

Jessica finally realizes I'm not about to change my mind. She takes her panties and slides them up her long legs. Her movements are jerky, but she quickly makes them smooth and seductive when she catches me watching. I might not

3

want her to stay, but that doesn't mean I won't enjoy the show.

She's soon dressed and combing her fingers through her long blonde hair as I walk her to the door. I open it for her, and she breezes past me, her perfume diluted from our long night but still strong enough to tickle the back of my nose. She pivots when she reaches the hallway leading to the private elevator. "Call me next time you need a date, or . . . anything."

I nod. "I will."

Once she's gone, I shut the door, stretch, crack my neck, and make my way to the shower. After stepping into the hot spray, I rinse the sweat and Jessica's perfume off me. My mind moves to the meeting with my father and brothers tomorrow. We're expanding our empire even more. After months of pre-development work, we've just publicly announced our latest project. We're known globally for our large-scale commercial developments and luxury hotels, and now we're moving into the more competitive mid-range accommodation sector. As chief investment officer for the King Group, it's something I've been pushing for over the last couple of years.

As I step out of the shower, my phone rings. It's Roman. I answer it with one hand while I snag a towel with my other. "To what do I owe this pleasure?"

I rub the towel over my wet hair while I wait to see what the emergency is. There must be something wrong. I can't imagine why he'd call me otherwise, since we mostly limit our contact to the office.

"Dad's been arrested," he says without preamble, his voice as cold and unaffected as it always is these days.

It takes a second for the meaning of his words to sink in. I stop toweling off. "What the fuck for?" My mind immediately goes to a DUI. Dad does like a drink or ten. But he has a driver. Why would he be behind the wheel?

"Insider trading."

Shock courses through me. "What the hell?" Dad has always been a risk taker, in business and in his personal life; I know that all too well. Insider trading, though? That's a whole new level of illegal.

"I've spoken to the lawyers. Allegedly, he's been using information from one of his government contacts to buy and sell stocks and putting the profits into a bank in the Caymans. He's been taken into custody and is being held until his bail hearing tomorrow. But the lawyers say it'll most likely be denied, since they'll consider him a flight risk."

Not surprising, considering he owns a fleet of private jets. "Did he do it?"

"He's pleading innocent. But if you're asking my opinion, let's just say I wouldn't put it past him."

"*Fuck.*" I throw the towel into the hamper. "We need to manage the situation before it goes public."

"Exactly." Roman lets out a harsh breath. "The SEC will be investigating, and the King Group is going to be under a microscope until they can determine if Dad used company funds and if anyone else was involved. I'll get in touch with Tate after this, and I want you both to come to the office straight away. We need to call an emergency board meeting. The three of us have majority shares, so we can take control and limit the damage . . . but we have to act now."

I make my way out of the bathroom and locate my clothes, putting the phone on speaker as I dress. My mind works over the implications. The King Group will be under fire, and the press will be all over us. Our reputation will take a serious hit, and our share value could plummet unless we get ahead of this.

"We'll get the lawyers to file the paperwork to make a change of leadership official," Roman continues. "I'll take over as CEO, and I need you to step into my position as COO. I plan to remove Peters and put Tate in his place as chief marketing officer so we can manage the narrative going forward."

"Makes sense," I say as I button my shirt. The next few weeks will be critical in ensuring the stability of the company and maintaining investor confidence once news of Dad's arrest becomes public.

"The lawyers are already on their way, so get your ass over here ASAP and be prepared for a long night. We need to make sure everything is in place by tomorrow morning." He hangs up without another word.

I stare at myself in the mirror as I shrug on the suit jacket I'd stripped off and thrown over the back of a chair only a few hours ago. Getting the company past this unscathed will require me and my brothers to work together more closely than we have in a long time. Considering how strained the relationship between the three of us has become over the years, I only hope we can manage it.

I grab my phone and head toward the door. It's time to put our differences aside and focus on protecting the company, whatever the cost. The King Group is the only thing that matters. And at this stage, our shared dedication to it is all that's holding this family together.

CHAPTER TWO

DELILAH

My fork clatters onto my plate. "What are you saying?"

Paul winces, his dark eyes darting around the intimate restaurant to make sure I haven't drawn anyone's attention. When he realizes no one is looking, he reaches across the table and clasps my hand. "I like you, Delilah. A lot. But things have changed, and I just don't feel as if we're in a position to progress our relationship."

"By things have changed, do you mean because I'm on your team now? Because you told me nothing would change when you took over as project manager."

He sits back in his chair. "And I didn't think it would. In fact, I thought it would be a good thing because we could spend more time together. It hasn't turned out that way, though. I see how hard you work, Delilah, and I know how driven you are. But even though we're working side by side every day, our relationship hasn't moved forward the way I wanted it to."

"Is it because we haven't had sex yet?" I say in a low

voice that wobbles only a little. "Because when I told you I wanted to wait, you said you were okay with that."

Frustration flashes across Paul's face, but he smooths it away. "And I *was* okay with it. I understand what happened to your mother, but it's been three months and I don't get what more you want from me before we take that step. You're twenty-four. You're not a teenager like she was, for god's sake." His voice has been gradually rising, and people's heads are turning. He lets out a slow breath before continuing. "If you were committed to this relationship, we would already be sharing that kind of intimacy. As it is, sometimes I think you're more passionate about your career than you are about me."

"That's not . . ." I shake my head, guilt tugging at my chest because I can't deny what he's suggesting. Mom conceived me when she was eighteen, and it's made me cautious. It's his other comment I choose to address, though. "I *have* to work hard, Paul. There are a lot of eyes on me in the office. I need to put in twice as much effort as everyone else because no one is sure they can trust me to do the job when I got my license at such a young age."

"I understand that." His voice is sharper now. "And I admire your dedication to architecture, I do. I want more, though. At this stage in a relationship, I *need* more. And I'm not sure you can give it to me. As much as I like you, I think it's better if we end things now when we're not so emotionally involved that we can't maintain an amicable working relationship. Particularly given my new position and how important the current project is."

Tears sting the backs of my eyes. "It's nice to know you're not emotionally invested enough to be bothered about our breakup."

Paul reaches forward to take my hand. "That's not what

I meant. Look, I really wanted this relationship to work. You know that. I even waited until you received your licensure before asking you out because I knew how focused you were." He squeezes my fingers. "I'm just as disappointed as you that things haven't worked out."

Part of me doubts that. Paul is—*was*, now, I guess—my first actual relationship. Which sounds crazy, considering my age. But becoming a licensed architect at twenty-four didn't come easy. I spent so many years focusing on my studies, interning every spare moment, then challenging myself to start my licensure exams straight after graduation. I didn't have time for a boyfriend.

When I received my license only ten months after graduating, I thought I could ease up. I thought I could start to enjoy more of the things other women my age did, like going out, dating, and, yes, finally having sex. But on top of still feeling the need to prove myself to my older, mostly male colleagues on a daily basis, letting go has been harder than I expected. Relaxing enough to step outside the comfort zone I've studied myself into and sleep with Paul has been . . . difficult.

The newly purchased teal lingerie I'm wearing under my best little-black-dress suddenly binds uncomfortably around my meticulously de-fluffed body. Tonight would have been the night I finally stopped overthinking things, but there's not a chance in the world I'll admit that to Paul now.

I make eye contact with the woman at the table next to me. She shoots me a sympathetic look, and I avert my eyes. Can everyone in the restaurant tell what's happening at this little table for two? A combination of hurt and humiliation swirls in my stomach, and I blink back tears as I stare down at my half-eaten pasta. "I can't believe you decided to break it off with me while we're out to dinner. Did you think I would make a scene? Was this your way of making sure I didn't?"

Paul's gaze darts around the room before reluctantly meeting mine again. "No, that's not why. I didn't plan this. But you were talking about your concepts for the project, and you looked so damn passionate that I realized I'm not okay with waiting for you to share some of that passion with me."

I swallow past the hard lump in my throat. "Right," I whisper.

"I am sorry, Delilah. Let's just finish our meal, and then I'll take you home. On Monday, we can both be adults about this and work together to get our proposal finalized."

The emotion bubbles up in my chest, made mostly of disappointment and frustration—with Paul *and* myself. "Actually, I'm not hungry anymore. You stay here and finish. I'll get a ride home."

"Come on, Delilah. Don't be like that. We can still be friends and have a meal together, surely."

"Maybe we can at some point, but not tonight. I just want to go home."

He huffs out a breath, which manages to make me feel like I'm being childish. "Fine. But the least I can do is drive you home."

Being stuck in a car with him is the last thing I want. "No, thank you. I'd prefer to be on my own right now. I have my phone; I'll call a rideshare." Before Paul can argue further, I shove back my chair and stand.

Paul's brow puckers, and he stands too, but I turn and rush from the table before he can say anything else. I push through the door of the restaurant, wondering if I should have paid before leaving. But it's only a fleeting worry. It's the least Paul can do, considering what just happened.

My heels clack at a rapid tempo as I make my way down the street, clutching my phone in my hand and dodging oncoming people. I want to get away from the restaurant so I don't have to stand outside and risk facing Paul while waiting for my lift. When I think I'm far enough to avoid him if he leaves, I raise my phone to open the app. A dark wooden door swings open next to where I'm loitering, and a couple bursts out of it, distracting me. They're laughing, and before the door swings shut, the sound of music and the murmur of conversation drifts out. I peer through the heavily tinted windows.

A bar.

Standing there in my sexy dress and my strappy heels and my beautiful lingerie, having just been dumped, I suddenly don't want to slink home like a dog with its tail tucked between its legs. I want to have a drink. If my room-mate Alex was home, I'd buy a bottle of wine and take it back to our cozy little apartment to drown my sorrows with her. But she's at a concert with her boyfriend, and I no longer like the idea of being alone.

Trying not to overthink it, I push open the door and enter the dim space. The first thing that hits me is the distinct aroma of beer and whiskey, with an underlying hint of wood polish and leather. When my vision adjusts to the limited lighting, I make out various individuals sitting at tables and clustered around a long wooden bar. That's what I make a beeline toward.

After finding a vacant high-backed stool next to a dark-haired man in a white business shirt, I throw myself down on it while fighting back my tears.

It's not that I'm heartbroken—Paul and I weren't dating

long enough for me to fall for him—but I *liked* him, and I thought that would eventually grow into more. That liking would be enough for now.

But I was wrong.

I get the bartender's attention, and perhaps seeing the expression on my face, he hustles over. Just as I'm about to order my customary glass of white wine, I catch myself. This situation calls for something stronger. "Whiskey. On the rocks."

One of his brows twitches upward. Probably because I don't look like the typical hard-liquor type of girl. And I'm not. But what the hell? Overthinking and caution are what got me here. Rather than questioning my decision-making skills, the man merely nods, grabs a half-full bottle of amber liquid from one of the shelves behind him, and pours an inch or so into a tumbler. He places it in front of me and I smile my thanks, pick it up, and down it in one go.

Oh god, it burns. I gasp and shudder, then cough a little. The bartender's amused gaze catches me off guard, but I don't care that he's laughing at me. "Another one, please."

This time, his brows shoot up. "Are you sure?"

"Sure, I'm sure," I say, then laugh. Damn, am I tipsy already? I drank a glass of wine at dinner before Paul decided we're better off as . . . friends? Colleagues? Who knows.

The bartender bites back a grin and pours for me. "You want me to set up a tab?"

I'm about to tell him what a great idea that is when a smooth, deep voice comes from next to me. "Not if she's here on her own."

CHAPTER THREE

COLE

F rom the corner of my eye, I see her turn to stare at me, but I don't bother to meet her gaze. I'm not even sure why I said anything. It's none of my business if a woman wants to get drunk at a bar on her own. After all, I'm drinking alone.

My mind flashes back to today's visit to see Dad in jail—the reason I'm here with a whiskey in my hand. Roman, Tate, and I, along with the King Group's head lawyer, had gone to inform him of the company's change in leadership. Seeing him sitting at the table in his orange jumpsuit had been a shock, yet any sympathy I might have felt for him had gone out the window a week ago when I learned the extent of what he'd done. And why.

It was bad enough he'd made money via inside info he received from his contacts within the defense industry, but then he'd used those profits to support at least three of his mistresses. He'd also passed his hot tips to several of his cronies. The stupidity—and selfishness—of his actions had stunned all of us, particularly considering how he'd spent our formative years drumming into our heads that loyalty to our family name and our company was the only thing that mattered.

But everything we'd learned from him also made it easy to do what we were there to do. Saying he was unhappy to hear what we had to say was an understatement. But considering his current situation, there was nothing he could do about it.

As soon as we'd finished our discussion with our team of lawyers, I'd headed home. Except, for the first time, the thought of being alone in my massive penthouse didn't appeal to me.

I'd come here instead and spent the last hour nursing a couple of glasses of their most expensive whiskey, trying to figure out why the hell my father had done what he'd done. I'd been going around in circles and was about to leave when this woman had thrown herself onto the stool next to me.

Now I'm interfering in her plan to drown whatever sorrows she's obviously suffering from, and instead of backing off like any self-respecting asshole, I double-down, turning to the bartender. "The next glass you give her should be full of water."

I can almost sense the outrage pouring from her. "Excuse me?" she says. "I don't know you and you don't know me, so I'm pretty sure you don't have a say in what I order or how much of it I drink."

I finally tip my head in her direction to fully take her in, and fuck, she's gorgeous. A tight black dress encompasses a petite but perfectly curved body. Hair almost as dark as my own tumbles around her shoulders in loose waves. But it's her face I can't tear my attention away from. The striking green of her eyes, and the way they tilt up at the corners, gives them an almost feline appearance. Her nose is small and straight, and her mouth makes me think of only one thing: how those lush, pink lips would look wrapped around my dick.

Normally, if a woman looking like her sat down next to me, I'd know immediately how the night would end, but there's a glassiness to her gaze that doesn't come solely from the whiskey she's downed.

She blinks those cat-like eyes at me and turns away, looking down at her drink. I almost laugh as she visibly steels herself, picks it up, and throws it back. She reacts the same way she did the first time, with a gasp and a shudder. It sends a hot surge of lust through me when I imagine her making that same sound as I bury myself inside her.

She looks up at the apparently entranced bartender. "One more, please."

His eyes dart toward me, but before I can shake my head at him, she raps her knuckles on the bar to get his attention. "Hey!" she says. "He's not ordering. I am."

"Another one of those is going to hit you like a Mac truck," I say, and I still don't know why I'm engaging in this. Far be it from me to dissuade anyone from drowning their sorrows. But there's something about her that seems to trigger a protective instinct in me I didn't know I had. Which is ridiculous. She looks young, but she's an adult and can do whatever the hell she likes.

And yet, I keep going. "I'm going to guess the reason for your sudden need for hard alcohol is a man. Probably a man who's recently broken your heart. And if I can tell that, so can every other man in here. Which means one more whiskey and every asshole that's watching you right now will try to pick you up—particularly looking like that." I let my eyes drift over her dress and back up again. I know what the other men in here are thinking, because I'm thinking exactly the same thing. Luckily for her, taking advantage of young, drunk, heartbroken women isn't my thing, so I let her hear the amusement in my voice, just to make my point. "But hey, if you're looking for a quick, dirty revenge fuck, drink away."

She stares at me, pouty lips parted in shock, and I almost feel bad.

Almost.

"Wow," she says, and those pretty eyes narrow. "First of all, I thought I was in a bad mood before, but you're just the icing on the cake. And second, it doesn't matter how much I drink or how many guys try to pick me up, I'm not really the *quick, dirty revenge fuck* kind of girl."

She probably isn't, but it would do her more good than getting wasted on whiskey. "Maybe you should be," I say before I can stop myself. And do I really want to, anyway? This conversation is a distraction, and after the last week, I could use a distraction. Especially one as appealing as her.

She turns to face me. "Why? Do you think that will make me feel better tomorrow when I'm doing the walk of shame?"

"Why would there be any shame in it? Sex is about feeling good in the moment. Getting out of your own head by getting absorbed in someone else's body for a few hours. It doesn't need to be some deep, meaningful connection. You feel bad, sex feels good. Why not do it?"

Her eyes slide away from me, but they wander back a few seconds later. Her teeth press into her lower lip, and I can almost see her brain working overtime.

I smirk. "You're considering it, aren't you?"

Even in the bar's dim light, the pink of her cheeks is visible. "I'm not sure that's any of your business."

She turns away, and I laugh quietly to myself. I should

go home. I've got an early-morning video conference with the heads of our European offices. Instead, I gesture to the bartender for another whiskey. When it arrives, I take a sip, then turn to face her. "So what did he do?"

She cocks her head and frowns. "Who?"

Yeah, she's definitely had too much whiskey if she's already forgotten whoever screwed her over tonight.

"Your boyfriend," I clarify.

She looks down at her empty glass. "Ex."

"Well, that seems obvious, but I didn't want to assume."

She gestures a little too broadly with one hand. "Assume away."

"You still haven't told me what he did." I signal to the bartender again, and he knows what I'm asking for. He pours some water from a pitcher, throws in a slice of lime, and places it in front of her. She doesn't protest this time, just picks it up and takes a sip.

She steals a glance at me from the corner of her eye. "Don't tell me you're really interested in my sob story."

"Normally I wouldn't be. But I need a distraction right now. And you're it."

She turns to face me fully, those expressive eyes filling with what looks like sympathy. "I'm sorry. We've been talking about me. Is everything okay with you?"

Surprise flashes through me. When was the last time someone asked me if I was okay? I ignore her question, though. There's no way I'm telling a random woman about the shit hitting the King Group thanks to my dear old Dad. "Tell me what this asshole did to make you contemplate having quick, dirty revenge sex with someone tonight."

"I didn't say I was."

"You're right. My apologies." I hold my hands in the air and fight a smile.

17

She frowns. "Are you mocking me?"

"I wouldn't dare."

She stares at me for a second before a laugh bubbles up from her throat. "I'm sure you would."

She's even more gorgeous when she laughs.

Over the top of her head, I catch a couple of suited businessmen watching her from the other end of the bar. Barely concealed hunger flashes like a warning light in their eyes, and I let the smile fall from my face, giving them the full weight of a stare that has intimidated far more powerful men than them. They take a sudden avid interest in the beers in front of them, and I turn my attention back to the woman sitting next to me.

"Do you really want to know?" she asks, and I take a moment to realize she's responding to my question about her ex.

I don't really have a burning desire to hear about what this guy did to disappoint her. "Disappointing" sums up most relationships, as far as I'm concerned. But I want to keep her talking, even if it's only until those two assholes pay up and leave. Not to mention the other men in this place that have been eyeing her since she sat down. So I nod. "Might as well get it off your chest." By some miracle, I stop my eyes from dropping to the swell of her breasts as I say it.

She takes another sip of water. "Okay. Well, I work with him."

I raise a brow, and she grimaces.

"I know. Not the smartest move. But I interned there during my final year of college, and we got to know each other then. He'd flirt with me, and I was flattered because he's handsome. And older."

"Is that your type?" I ask with a smirk.

A small crease forms between her brows, and her gaze wanders slowly over my face. "Maybe."

Her response isn't what I expect. Heat surges through me, arousal creating an urgent pulse in my veins. I shove it down with more difficulty than I'm used to. I didn't come here to pick up a woman. I came here to have a drink in a place where people probably wouldn't recognize me. Not that I think she's looking to be picked up—not seriously, anyway. She's just a woman who's sexy without even trying.

Her eyes drop and she traces a line of condensation on the glass in front of her. "Anyway, when my internship ended, Paul asked me out for a drink, one thing led to another, and we kissed."

"Just kissed?" I ask. "How very Hallmark of you."

This time, she glares at me. "Yes, just kissed. It was . . . nice. I liked him, but I was focused on finishing college, so that's how we left it. After I graduated, I was offered a job back at the company. Paul was working temporarily in our London office when I started, but not long after he moved back, we started dating."

"How long ago was that?" I ask.

"Three months."

"So, it only took three months for your scintillating love affair to fizzle out?"

She offers me a cute little scowl. I shouldn't make fun of her, but I enjoy seeing the sparks flashing in her green eyes when she gets offended. She reminds me of a little kitten when you rub its fur the wrong way—tiny, all fluffed out, and hissing and spitting as if her irritation might actually scare me away.

I bet she'd purr like a kitten if I stroked her the right way, too.

"I never said it was scintillating."

"So the guy was boring."

"I didn't say that, either." She shakes her head then laughs, her irritation already passed.

It's fascinating to me how changeable her emotions are. And how easily she expresses them. It says something about the world I live in. Honest emotion is hard to come by. "What went wrong?"

She's quiet for a beat, staring down at her glass of water. "He just said things weren't working out."

"Sounds pretty standard," I say.

This time, her laugh is humorless. "I suppose it is. Nothing special about me or my story."

I rake my eyes over her lush body. "I wouldn't say that."

A sharp indrawn breath proves she isn't immune to me.

I rest my elbow on the bar. "So, what are you going to do?"

She drags her gaze away from me. "Nothing, I guess. My job is great and I love the company I work for, so it's not as if I would leave. I just don't like how I feel right now. I don't like thinking it was something I did wrong. That I should have tried harder. That if I'd just . . ." She trails off, then takes another sip of water.

I lean back and study her. The water she's been drinking has cleared the alcohol haze from her eyes. I linger on the length of her thighs, exposed by her short dress, and I make a decision. "You should forget quick, dirty revenge sex, then."

"I should?" She sounds breathless after my slow perusal, and I can't wait to hear her begging me to fuck her in that same breathy voice.

I nod, unable to tear my gaze away from her. Drinking alone wasn't taking my mind off things. She might be exactly what I need to forget about everything I've got going on, and it will help to distract her, too. "I'm thinking you should go for downright filthy revenge sex that lasts for hours. And I think I should be the one you do it with."

Her cheeks bloom with heat, and my dick is already half hard as I imagine pressing my lips against the warmth of her skin as I move inside her.

"Wh-Why you?" she asks.

I tilt my head toward her, a hint of her scent reaching me as I do—a heady mixture of wildflowers and something more sensual. "Because I can guarantee I'll make it good for you. Because I think we can both do with getting out of our heads tonight. And because I haven't stopped thinking about peeling that dress off you since the moment you sat down."

She actually squirms on her stool, and I've officially gone from half hard to fully hard. How wet is she right now? I can't fucking wait to find out.

She tucks some of her hair behind her ears and tries to pull herself together. "Wow, you work fast, don't you?"

"I can go slow when I need to." I cross my arms and lean back on my stool as I wait for her to answer.

"Well," she says, her eyes dropping to my forearms, where my shirtsleeves are rolled up. "I might need you to go a bit slower right now."

It's not a yes. But it's not a no, either.

I could just go back to drinking. I could pick up one of the other women in here, some of whom have already lingered next to me as they ordered drinks, casting hopeful glances my way. I could even give Jessica a call, although the last thing I want is to give her the impression I'm interested in expanding our arrangement. But when it comes down to it, this woman has caught my attention in a way few do these days. And after today's shit show, the thought of losing myself in her body is a temptation I can't resist.

"Let's do slow then," I say.

She's silent for a moment, then her delicate jaw firms. "Actually, I've changed my mind."

Disappointment hits me harder than it should, but before I can say anything, she surprises me again.

"I'm sick of going slow. For once, I don't want to over-think everything."

"So you're saying . . ."

She takes a deep breath. "I'm saying, yes."

CHAPTER FOUR

DELILAH

My hands start to shake when his blue eyes heat. But he doesn't move, even though it feels as if his big body is suddenly coiled tight. Maybe he senses my nervousness.

"Yes? You don't have any more questions for me? You're not curious about the man you're planning to leave with? Who I am, what I do?"

I lick my lips. I should be more curious. Those are the things I should want to know before doing anything with this guy. But unless he confesses to being a serial killer, will any of it make a difference? At this stage, I'm sick of thinking about it. I just want to have sex with this man who, from the way he talks and acts, seems like he knows exactly what he's doing. Then I can get past this hurdle and move on with my life. "Let's not pretend we'll ever see each other after tonight. You don't strike me as the more-than-one-night kind of guy."

He inclines his head. When he looks up at me through his dark lashes, there's an almost mischievous glint in his eyes. "Does that bother you?"

"No." I let out a shaky breath. "Yes. I don't know." I guess I'm not as unconcerned as I thought. "I'm sorry. I'm not used to this."

One corner of his mouth tips up. "I can tell." A slow, seductive smile blooms on his face. "Do you need me to convince you?"

The rasp in his voice sends a full-body shiver through me. I lick my lower lip and nod, because maybe hearing precisely what he plans to do to me will calm my nerves.

"You want me to tell you why you should come back to my hotel room right now?"

"Yes." It's a breathless whisper.

I gasp when he reaches for my stool and drags it closer to him so my knees end up between his thighs. Then he leans forward, tucks my hair behind my ear, and whispers into it, the heat of his breath causing goose bumps to scatter over my skin. "Because when we're alone and I've already made you come twice, once with my fingers and once with my tongue, when I've buried my cock inside you and I'm driving you toward your third orgasm, I'm going to tell you exactly how sexy you are, exactly how hard I am for you, and exactly how incredible your pussy feels when it's squeezing me. You'll forget there was ever another man inside you, and when I finally let you, you're going to come, screaming, all over my cock."

He leans back so he can see my eyes, and I imagine they're dilated enough to expose how much his words have affected me.

He smiles, drifts his knuckles over my burning cheek, and says, "Convincing enough?"

My mouth is so dry I can barely speak, and my heart is flinging itself against my rib cage. This is the craziest, most reckless thing I've ever contemplated in my life. I can tell myself I've had too much to drink, but that's not it. I'm totally clear-headed now. But I'm tired of being responsible and doing the right thing all the time. I'm sick of over-thinking this. Mom always told me to concentrate on my studies, get a good job, and not rush into a relationship or let a man change the course of my future. Well, I took her advice and more. I'm one of the youngest licensed architects in the United States, and that's proof enough, but I still have a lot I want to achieve. I don't need the added pressure of determining which man to share my body with for the first time. I could just do it already, get it over and done with, and move on without it hanging over my head.

So yes, tonight I'll be reckless for once. I'll let my hair down, stop thinking, and give this man, this stranger, something Paul apparently wasn't willing to wait around for.

And I get the feeling he'll make sure I enjoy every second.

I meet his gaze. "Very convincing."

A flare of satisfaction brightens his icy blue eyes.

"What's your name?" he asks, reaching out to tuck another stray tendril of hair behind my ear. His fingers drift down the column of my throat, and butterflies erupt in my stomach.

"Delilah. What's yours?"

"Cole," he says, studying me with an odd intensity, as if learning his name might make me change my mind.

Strangely enough, I'm reluctant to carry on with our small talk after agreeing to have sex with him. Like most things in my life, once I've decided I want to do something, I'm committed to making it happen as soon as possible. I'm still nervous, but there's a sense of anticipation swelling within me I can't ignore. A need to fulfill a part of me I've been holding back.

So when he asks if I'm ready to go, I nod, take a final sip of water to wet my dry throat, and slip off my stool.

Cole puts his hand on my lower back and guides me toward the exit, and I can't stop thinking about what else his hands will soon do to me. I can't stop the vision of his sweat-slicked body moving over mine.

My feet stutter to a halt and I can't go any further without confessing the truth to him. This might be more than he bargained for. It's possible my virginity could be a deal breaker for him, and he has a right to know what he's getting into. "Wait. There's something I need to tell you first."

Wariness tightens his features, and his brows rise as he waits for me to explain my hesitation.

"I . . . um . . . I actually haven't done this before."

"I think it's pretty obvious that going home with a man you've just met at a bar isn't typical for you."

I lower my voice. "No. I mean, I haven't done . . . it . . . before. At all."

A crease forms between his brows.

"I'm a virgin," I hiss when he fails to respond.

Surprise flares in his eyes. "How old did you say you are?"

His obvious disbelief makes me raise my chin. "It's not like it's that uncommon." I hold my breath, wondering if he'll change his mind.

His eyes run over me, and something I can't identify glimmers in them. A hint of a smile curls his lips. "Uncommon enough." He shakes his head, still with that half smile on his face, then takes my hand. "Let's go."

IT'S ONLY a short walk to his hotel, one of the King International chain of luxury accommodations. I'm too nervous to take in all the architectural details or the expansive foyer the way I normally would, but when he guides me to the elevator, swipes a card, and presses the button for the second highest floor, shock hits me. "A suite?"

His lips curve up. "Perks of the job."

"What do you do?"

"I'm in . . . hospitality."

I smile at him. "Wow, I should have kept my waitressing job."

I wait for him to ask what I do, but he doesn't. He just watches me out of those gorgeous, darkly lashed blue eyes because we're here for one reason and one reason only. Getting to know each other isn't a part of that.

When I realize my mistake, I laugh at myself. "Okay," I say. "I'll get the hang of this soon."

He shakes his head, a crooked smile on his lips, as if I amuse him. And I probably do. I'm sure he's used to being with far more experienced women. That thought rattles me far more than I expect it to. Before I can dwell on it too much, the elevator dings as it reaches his floor, and the doors slide open.

Cole ushers me down a short corridor that looks like it's tiled in marble. He waves his card in front of the door and swings it open, standing back to let me walk through first.

"Oh my god." My feet glue themselves to the floor as I take in the massive space. I've never been in such a luxurious hotel room before. There's no other word to describe it but opulent, with its high ceilings, hardwood floors, and expensive-looking furniture. It even has a crystal chandelier hanging over the dining table.

But what catches my eye is the unobstructed view of the

New York City skyline. "Wow," I whisper. The floor-to-ceiling windows draw me forward, and I stand in front of them, my fingertips resting lightly on the cool glass as I look over the city spread out beneath me.

Unease flickers in my chest. Cole's employer might be paying for this hotel suite, but he's obviously wealthy himself. And I know what wealthy men are like—relentless when going after what they want, whether that be possessions or people, and with no regard for the repercussions of their selfishness.

Am I making a mistake?

I shake my head. I'm overthinking it. After tonight, I'll never see Cole again, and I've done all I can to protect myself from any unintended consequences. As soon as I started dating Paul, I got a birth control implant. Assuming I'd be doing this with him tonight, I even brought a condom in my purse. If for some reason a man like Cole doesn't have one handy, I'm covered.

"Would you like a drink?" Cole asks from behind me.

I drag myself away from the view and focus on him, where he's standing in front of an extensive wet bar. As tempting as it is to have a big glass of wine to help with my courage, I want to know exactly what happens between us.

"I've probably had enough alcohol tonight. I'll just have water, thank you."

He cracks open a bottle, pours it into a glass, adds a slice of lemon, and walks over to me. Our fingers brush as I take the drink, and my gaze flits to his, my heart rate speeding up.

I take a sip, and then another. Cole hasn't bothered with a drink for himself. Instead, he's watching me, his eyes darkening as I lick a stray drop from my lips.

He doesn't wait for me to finish, reaching for the glass

and taking it from me. "You didn't come here to hydrate and admire the view, did you?"

My pulse hammers in my throat. "I—Uh, no, I didn't."

His gaze lands on my mouth again, and he reaches up and brushes his thumb over my lower lip. Is he going to kiss me now?

"Turn around," he says, his voice low and firm.

I blink, let out a shuddery breath, and do as he says. I only jump a little when he grips the zipper of my dress and drags it down. He takes his time, as if he's enjoying the anticipation, then he slips the straps off my shoulders. The material slithers over my body and pools on the floor.

Oh my god, this is really happening.

"Walk to the bedroom. Slowly," he commands, and when I shoot a look at him over my shoulder, he gives me a wolfish smile. "Come on, kitten. If you want to do this, we do it my way. And I want to see you."

Kitten? Really? I don't question it, though. I've got more important things on my mind. "This isn't quite how I imagined this happening."

His knuckles drift down my spine, and goose bumps ripple out from beneath his touch. His eyes pierce me. "You chose me for a reason," he says, "and it's not because you thought I would be soft and gentle. I'm sure you've been around plenty of very nice men that would have gladly sweet-talked you out of your clothes and into their beds, but you didn't want them, did you? You want me. And that's because a part of you knows exactly how this is going to go. You're done overthinking, and now you want to let go and feel. But I could be wrong. Maybe what you really want is sweet words and spooning afterward. If that's the case, feel free to walk back out that door. I'll even call a driver to take you home."

Maybe I should leave. Maybe I should take up his offer and put this night behind me as a moment of insanity. But standing here in my lingerie in front of a man who's basically a stranger, I don't want to leave. I have to put my faith in myself and my own judgment. To learn to trust my instincts instead of overanalyzing. And right now, my instincts are telling me I need what this man is offering me. I want him to take control so I can let go.

I let out a breath, all my muscles loosening as I step away from my discarded dress and walk to the bedroom.

CHAPTER FIVE

COLE

F*uck me*. Delilah is a fucking vision. She may be petite, but her slender shoulders and narrow waist flair out to curvy hips and a round ass I'd love to see bent over the back of the couch.

As much as that image tempts me, I'm not so much of an asshole that I'd take her virginity that way. Doesn't mean I can't fantasize about it, though.

Her body sways enticingly, and I follow behind her, loosening my tie as I go. I rub the silky material between my fingers, imagining wrapping it around her wrists as I hold them above her head. But no. Not for her first time. Fuck. There are so many things I want to do to her, but I'll never have the chance to experience them. Not when the next few hours are all we have.

She reaches the bed and looks over her shoulder at me again. She doesn't turn around, just waits for my next instruction, and hell if that isn't a huge fucking turn on.

One last step and I'm behind her, so close my painfully hard dick brushes her ass. She inhales sharply as I flick open the clasp of her bra, ease the straps off her shoulders, and let the lacy material drop to the floor. With one hand, I tilt her head to the side so I can brush my lips against her neck, tracing my tongue over the rapid flutter of her pulse point. She trembles against me, and I can't help but smile.

"Turn around." My voice is a low rasp, and as she pivots, my eyes are immediately drawn to her full breasts and the pale-pink nipples that form hard little points. I can't wait to fucking taste them.

Reaching the end of my patience, I circle her waist with one arm and cup one of those gorgeous breasts, bending my head to take the tight peak into my mouth.

Instinctively, her hands go to my head and she clutches at my hair, moaning as I swirl my tongue around her nipple. I transfer my attention to her other breast, scraping my teeth over it and nipping at the tender tip.

"Cole," she gasps. "I need . . . I need . . ."

I straighten. "I know what you need and I'll give it to you soon, but first I want you to get on the bed, crawl up to the top, then sit with your back against the headboard."

She hesitates again, but I step back from her and wait with my arms crossed, giving the appearance of having far more self-control than I do.

When she complies and crawls toward the headboard, I'm presented with that luscious ass again—the tiny strip of material between her cheeks the only thing covering her— and I have to press my hand against my erection to relieve some of the aching pressure.

Once she's sitting at the top of the bed, leaning back against the black leather headboard and looking at me with a mixture of nerves and need, I drop my hand. "Now I want you to pull those little panties to the side and touch yourself."

Her cheeks redden, and she gives a little shake of her head. "I don't think I'm comfortable doing that."

I slowly unbutton my shirt. "If this is your first time, I want to make it as good for you as possible. Knowing how you like to touch yourself will tell me what I need to know to make that happen." Which is true, if not the whole truth. I'm not sure she'll react quite as well if I say I also want to get off by watching her finger that tight little cunt. "Unless you're telling me you're so innocent you've never even touched yourself before?"

She's tracking my every movement as I strip off my shirt. The way her eyes darken as they drift over my chest tells me she appreciates the time I spend in the gym.

But when she registers what I said, her gaze darts back up to my face. "Of course I'm not."

I let myself smirk at the spark of annoyance flaring in her eyes, and I can't stop myself from provoking her further. "Maybe I should find out just how innocent you are. How far have you gone? Have you put anything inside that pretty pussy? Has a man? Has anyone ever had their tongue in you? What am I dealing with here?"

The spark of annoyance flares hotter. "Yes to all of that. And I'll have you know, I have a drawer full of toys at home, so you don't have to worry about getting blood on your sheets. In fact, I'm not sure if what you're packing is going to compare to my favorite. It's *big*."

I laugh. I can't help it. This little kitten has claws. "If I didn't know what I'm *packing* is going to have you screaming my name very soon, I might be nervous. But unless you've got one of those fucking monster dildos, I'll be the biggest thing you've ever had inside you. And since you're so experienced at self-care"—I smirk as her cheeks redden with the realization of what she's admitted—"then you shouldn't mind showing me exactly how you do it."

I palm my cock and watch her eyes widen at the visible bulge in my pants. "If it will make you more comfortable, I'll show you just how hard you're making me while you do it."

Her teeth press into her bottom lip for a moment. "Okay," she whispers.

"Good girl," I growl.

The way her gaze jumps to my face and her tongue darts out to wet her lips is intriguing. She likes me calling her that.

Watching her closely, I unzip my jeans, pull out my aching shaft, and wrap my fingers around it. Delilah's eyes widen as they fixate on the way my hand slowly works my dick. "Your turn," I say.

With an audible swallow, her hands move downward. Her fingers pull aside the lace of her thong, revealing the prettiest pussy I've ever seen. The fingers of her other hand tentatively brush over her clit, then circle it.

Fuck.

I tighten my grip on my cock. "That's it, kitten. I'd tell you to keep going until you're wet enough to take me, but from the way you're already dripping, it looks like you're almost there."

She sucks in a breath, but like the good girl she is, she keeps going, her eyelashes fluttering.

I slow the movement of my hand because I'm getting too close too fast as I watch her pleasure herself. The urge to crawl between her thighs and fuck my way into what's bound to be the tightest little cunt I've ever been inside has heat searing through me. "I was going to have you see how many fingers you can fit inside you, but I'll be greedy and find that out myself."

The bed dips under my weight as I climb onto it and make my way between her spread legs. I can't stop staring at her already slick, pink flesh, and the urge to plunge myself into her is so strong I have to close my eyes and suck in a deep breath. I haven't felt this much anticipation about fucking a woman since . . . I don't know.

With Delilah, I get to be the one who shows her exactly what her body can do with a man's. I get to be the first to make her come on my cock. I'll be the man that every other man has to measure up to. And as it turns out, that's a damn heady feeling.

"Hands off. Your pussy's mine now," I say, but before she pulls her fingers away, I grab her wrist, bend down, and slide her fingers between my lips. I groan. My dick leaks pre-cum, smearing it against her inner thighs as I push over her, savoring the taste of her arousal, knowing she's ready for me.

"Oh my god, that's so . . ." Her fingers twitch against my tongue, her gaze is fixed on my mouth, and fuck, I'm going to *wreck* this girl.

But first she needs to come. I want her dripping and desperate for my cock.

I grip her hips and pull her until she's flat on her back, then I lean down and swipe my tongue over her clit as I dip a finger into her. God, she's so tight. She's going to feel it when I push into her.

I alternate flicking that sensitive bundle of nerves with swirls and sucks while I ease my finger in and out of her until I can fit another inside. Her tight muscles give a little as I work my fingers into her, but it's only a few moments before her inner walls tighten around me again. Her breathy moans come faster. She's almost there. I suck hard on her clit, then gently bite down on it, and she explodes with a loud cry. The orgasm rips through her, and she clenches hard around my fingers. I can't fucking wait to experience the same thing when I'm inside her.

"Cole, oh my god. That was . . . I can't even . . ."

One glance at her flushed face, her parted lips, and her dilated green eyes and I'm done. I told her I'd make her come twice before I fucked her, but once will have to be enough because I need to be inside that tight little body right now.

I reach for the bedside table and grab a condom from the drawer, ripping it open with my teeth and rolling it over my erection. Bracing myself with one hand next to her head, my eyes lock with hers. Her needy expression is one of the sexiest things I've ever seen. Her pupils are flared so wide there's only a small ring of emerald surrounding them, and her lips are parted to let out breathless little pants as she looks up at me.

A tiny crease forms between her brows. "You're, um, bigger than I was expecting."

Even though I'm only barely hanging on to my restraint, I huff out a laugh. "Bigger than your *biggest* toy?"

She laughs too, the sound unexpectedly trickling like honey over my inflamed senses. "Maybe a little."

And fuck, when was the last time I laughed during sex? Have I ever? The thought is fleeting, but it lingers in the back of my mind. At least until I press the head of my cock to her entrance, and then I'm not thinking about anything except filling her.

I pin her hands with mine as I press forward, because having them on me right now is a distraction I don't need.

Not when her needy little cunt is already squeezing around the tip of my dick.

She's tight. So fucking tight. And she gasps as I push in, working my way into her with shallow thrusts, pausing now and then to give her a chance to breathe and adjust to my size. She's making soft sounds, little gasps and whimpers that brush over my skin like the fingers I haven't let touch me yet.

A bead of sweat trickles down my forehead as the strain of holding back builds in my shoulders and biceps. With one last thrust, I'm fully seated inside her. Her pussy is like a heated vise around my dick, and my balls are already drawn tight.

"Are you okay?" I ask through gritted teeth.

She doesn't answer right away, her beautiful green eyes searching mine in fast, dazed flicks. I don't know what answers she's looking for in my gaze, but if she's waiting for me to say something poetic, she'll be disappointed.

"Kitten, unless you tell me to stop, I'm going to fuck you, and I won't stop fucking you until you come all over my cock. Got it?"

She licks her lips. "Yes." She shifts her hips experimentally, making both of us groan. Then those mesmerizing eyes are back on mine. "I want you to fuck me. I want to come with you inside me. But . . ." She twists her hands in my grip and I release her. Immediately, she brings them to rest on my chest, fingers tracing my pecs, traveling to my shoulders and down my biceps. "I need to touch you."

I close my eyes. The urge to fuck hasn't gone away, but I like her touch, the brush of her fingertips leaving little sparks in their wake. When she pulls on me, tugging me down to her, I don't stop to think. I press my mouth to hers, slide my tongue inside, and capture her gasp as I pull out of her body. The moment I thrust back in, I'm lost to the roaring, crackling hunger within me, deafened by the thunder of my blood in my veins.

I rear back, grip her under her hips, and angle her so I can slide in deeper. She cries out, but it's not in pain, so I keep going. With every stroke, I'm pushing her closer to the edge. Her moans get louder, her body gripping me even tighter. I reach up to her mouth and slide my thumb between her lips. "Suck."

She does, curling her tongue and lapping at the pad, and fuck if this girl isn't a natural. Whoever she ends up with after tonight is going to be damn lucky.

The thought has my jaw clenching—a ridiculous, animalistic response to the idea of another man having her. I pull my thumb from her mouth and roll it over her swollen clit.

"Cole!" Delilah cries out as her back arches off the bed. I keep up the movement of my hips and thumb while I bend down and swirl my tongue over her nipple before drawing it into my mouth. Pleasure coils at the base of my spine, like a snake about to strike, and I want her to get there before I do. I want to feel her clenching around my dick, forcing my cum from me.

I suck hard on her nipple, pinch her clit, and angle my thrusts to hit the spot that will make her come apart. A few seconds later, she does, her hands fisting in the sheets, head thrown back, as her internal muscles clamp down around me.

"*Fuck*. That's it, Delilah," I groan. "You're such a good girl, coming with my cock inside you."

She cries out as I withdraw between pulses, then slam back in. My climax claws at me. *Shit*. I won't last any longer, "You're going to make me come. *So. Fucking. Hard.*"

Every muscle in my body tightens as heat and pleasure scorch up my shaft. I grab her hips, thrusting in as deep as I can go, my release filling the condom in wrenching spurt after wrenching spurt. I have a sudden irrational urge to pull out, rip it off, and sink back into her so I can see my cum spilling out of her when I'm done.

What the fuck is wrong with me?

Instead, I give in to a different urge, taking her mouth in another kiss, our tongues twining together, her moans vibrating against my lips. It's only when I'm completely spent that I tear myself away from her and pull out, rolling off her and onto my back.

I stare at the ceiling and try to catch my breath. It's a damn lucky thing I'll never see her again after tonight, because sex that good would be all-too easy to get addicted to.

CHAPTER SIX

DELILAH

One Month Later

My fingers tremble as I smooth down my navy-blue pencil skirt with one hand, my paperwork and notebook clutched in the other. The team is gathered outside the large wooden doors of the meeting room, waiting to be summoned. This is our big day, and the pressure is weighing on all of us. Paul has reassured us we've refined our proposal to perfection, and I know he has faith in me for my part, but that doesn't stop my nerves from taking over.

As we wait for our turn to present, Philippa, our project liaison, sidles up and inserts herself between Paul and me.

"I just heard that the COO is here," she whispers, more to Paul than to me. "He's sitting in on all the presentations."

Paul frowns and rubs his chin. His gaze meets mine over the top of Philippa's blonde head. "I know I said you could do the section on sustainability, Delilah, but if the COO's in the room, it might be better if I do it all. You understand, right?"

"I can handle it," I protest. "I've been preparing for the last three weeks."

"I understand that, but in this situation, I'm sure the partners will expect me to do the whole presentation."

Disappointment fills me, but I nod. He's the project manager, after all, and it's likely that the COO of the King Group is a man who will relate more to Paul's seasoned professional demeanor and seniority than my youthful enthusiasm—even though I specialize in sustainable design.

I ignore the slightly smug tilt to Philippa's smile. I don't know what I've done to annoy the icily beautiful English woman, but she seemed to take a dislike to me from the moment she transferred from our UK office two months ago. At least she won't be with us full time if we get this job. She'll be busy coordinating with other teams and projects within the firm.

This isn't the time to worry about her, though. I've got more important things to think about. Like helping Elite Architecture secure this project.

The doors open, and a man sticks his head out. "They're ready for you."

My pulse leaps and I smooth down my skirt one more time. Years of non-stop study and interning at multiple architectural firms haven't quite prepared me for my first big proposal, and this is one of the biggest out there—a hotel chain with initial development sites in ten major US cities.

I trail Paul into the room, which is bright and spacious, with large windows showing off the incredible view from the fifty-third floor of King Plaza. Nerves squirm in my stomach as I look around at the serious men and women surrounding the massive table.

My gaze reaches the far end and all my muscles lock up, the air freezing in my lungs as I jerk to a halt. A pair of cold blue eyes stare back at me. Eyes that were seared into my brain only a month ago.

It can't be him. It can't.

One of my team members jostles past me, and I jolt into motion again, forcing my feet to continue moving toward the table. I frantically glance at the man, searching for some discrepancy within his features. Something, *anything*, to tell me this isn't the person who took my virginity during a night I'm not sure I'll ever forget.

But the way his eyes narrow on me tells me I won't find it.

The intensity in his gaze floods me with memories: the things he said to me as he made me come with his mouth and fingers; his low, dark voice murmuring filthy words in my ear as he thrust into me; his mouth between my legs afterward, giving me another orgasm; the lazy stroke of his tongue soothing the sting his body had left behind.

After that third orgasm, when I'd been lying there exhausted and wrung out, I realized I had no idea how a one-night stand was supposed to end. I'd thanked him, my cheeks blazing as I tried to figure out the etiquette for that kind of thing. Then I'd rushed out of his suite and down to the foyer of the hotel to call a rideshare, even though he'd offered to call a car for me.

Now I'm seeing him again in the very last place I ever expected. My throat dries and I wrench my attention from him and focus on finding an empty seat as another harsh blush burns across my skin.

I can't believe this is happening. How is it possible that I slept with the King Group's chief of operations and didn't know it? Maybe I'm jumping to conclusions. After all, when we first got word we'd be putting a proposal together for this project, I'd looked up both the CEO and the COO of the company, and it wasn't Cole's picture I saw. Although . . . now that I think about it, I can see a resemblance between him and the man I remember from the photo.

I steal another look at him as I make my way down the table, pull out a chair, and sit. The older, far more portly man beside Cole keeps him locked in conversation, so I take the opportunity while he's distracted to observe him more closely.

And now my throat is dry for another reason.

If I thought the Cole who lived in my memory was gorgeous, seeing him in his impeccably tailored suit at the head of this enormous table is absolutely panty-melting. Everyone focuses on him, either overtly or covertly, and he's all power and control. He exudes the confidence you'd expect from a man in charge of thousands of people and numerous multi-million-dollar real estate projects around the world. Based on what I know about the King Group, Cole has to be a billionaire.

I'm in hospitality. That's what he'd said that night.

I huff out a breath. While he wasn't outright lying, considering his actual position within the company, he definitely stretched the truth.

Cole's eyes flash my way, a bright blue that sears into me and sends a jolt of adrenaline through my veins. I jerk my gaze away. It's only when I focus on Paul, sitting several seats down from Cole, that my stomach clenches. The true horror of this situation hits me. I'm stuck in a room with Cole . . . and my boyfriend. The same boyfriend who'd been an ex when I told Cole—*god, I have to make sure to call him Mr. King now*—all about being dumped. Except not a week after that night, Paul had turned up at my apartment, asking for a do-over and saying he hadn't known what he was thinking.

I wasn't sure if I wanted to give him a second chance, but his sincere regret had eased some of the hurt I'd felt at his rejection. Of course, then there was the matter of telling him I was no longer a virgin. He'd pouted for a while, but I told him he had no choice but to take it or leave it, and I guess he came to terms with it because he asked me out to dinner, and a few days later, he stayed the night.

But since I didn't even know who Cole was until now, there's no way Paul has a clue. And that's how it has to stay.

I turn away from them, reaching for the glass of water that's been set at each position at the table and taking a desperate gulp. Even though I'm not looking at Cole anymore, his intimidating presence almost has a weight of its own. Like the heavy air that precedes an approaching thunderstorm, it makes my skin tingle, raising goose bumps along my arms and the back of my neck.

Needing something to do with my hands, I square my notebook and paperwork in front of me, place my pen on top of the pile, then take it off and position it alongside. A moment later, I pick it up and put it on top again. Only when I have nothing else to fiddle with—and I'm certain his attention will have shifted elsewhere—do I dare to glance up the table.

He's still staring at me, even while the man next to him leans forward and talks earnestly at him. But that hard, blue gaze doesn't leave mine.

I swallow and look away. Why does he seem so angry?

I certainly hadn't been expecting to run into him again. I'd all but forgotten about him.

No, that's a lie.

Fantasies of that night have continued to run through my head, and they only get worse after Paul rolls off me and goes to sleep. Then I lie awake, trying to work out why my body doesn't respond to him the same way it responded to Cole.

But that's just what they are—fantasies. The memory of a moment when I let go of my overthinking and just experienced.

And what an experience it was.

I shake my head to clear it. I can't think about that. Not now, and definitely not here, when the man in question is sitting only feet from me.

And unhappy about it, apparently.

Whatever his problem is, I hope it won't affect our proposal. I can't imagine someone like Cole letting a meaningless physical encounter—which is what it most likely was to him, if not to me—influence his decision making.

Conversation around the table stops as Cole—*Mr. King*—rises from his seat. "Thank you for coming today." The deep, shockingly familiar voice sends a shiver through me. As if every one of my nerve endings remembers when that dark, silky tone was whispering dirty things in my ear while its owner drove my body to heights of pleasure it hadn't experienced before—or since.

I clench my pen in my fist. *Stop it.*

"This development is a priority for the King Group," Cole continues, "and we'll be assigning significant resources to it. The team of whichever architectural company we partner with will relocate to this building for the duration of the project."

I twitch in my seat. Maybe it won't be a good thing if

our proposal is chosen. The thought of running into him on a regular basis is less than appealing.

But I can't think like that.

This is a huge opportunity for the firm and for me personally. Very few architects have the chance to work on such a prestigious, high-profile development at my age. Having this on my résumé would be a major boost for my career. I won't let what's now looking like a colossal mistake on my part ruin this opportunity.

Cole finishes his opening words and nods at Paul, who smooths down his tie and rises to his feet.

I keep my attention fixed on him as he runs through our presentation. The whole time he's listing our firm's qualifications and the key features of our proposal, my eyes fight to slide to the right. The side of my face heats, as if I can sense Cole's gaze on me. Which is ridiculous. I'm sure he's riveted by Paul's polished delivery.

But after a few minutes, my focus slips and my eyes are once more drawn his way. A spark sizzles through me as our gazes collide again. This time he has one arm folded across his chest, the elbow of the other resting on top of it as he rubs his thumb slowly back and forth over his lower lip. His brows are pulled low over his narrowed eyes, and I'm worried he's too busy glaring at me to absorb the details of our proposal.

Knowing how much we need this deal, and also knowing I can't keep staring at my potential boss's boss, I turn my attention back to Paul, who's wrapping up his speech by stating that the team is happy to answer questions.

Silence competes with the too-loud ticking of the clock that hangs above Cole's head. My heart drums in my chest. Have we completely screwed this up?

Cole lifts his pen and taps the end on the table in front of him. "You've added quite a few sustainability features that weren't included in the original design brief. Whose idea was it to focus on that for the project?" he asks.

At least he was paying attention.

Paul hesitates, and I know why. It's unclear from Cole's tone whether he's pleased or annoyed about it. After clearing his throat, Paul gestures in my direction. "Sustainability is Delilah's area of expertise. She's a—"

"Is that so?" Cole says. I shift uncomfortably in my seat as he looks down at his notepad before leveling me with an inscrutable look. "Can you explain your thinking with some of these choices, Delilah? Making those kinds of customizations for each build will add significant cost to the project."

I've prepared for these questions, and I know what I'm talking about. I take a second to compose myself, then meet his steely gaze. "Sustainable hotel architecture might carry some capital expense, but as I'm sure you're aware, stronger infrastructure also brings the highest return on investment. Along with internal elements, such as low-flush toilets, aerators on faucets, and smart showers, the external systems we're considering for this project include solar panels, water recovery systems, and HVAC systems that can customize air flow, heating, and cooling in response to various factors." I sort through my notes in front of me. "Using your Chicago hotel as a case study for installing an intensive water recovery system, my projections predict it could be paid back in full in less than a year. And if we incorporate a solar panel system into the hotel's design, it would not only contribute to its LEED Platinum certification, but it could offset up to fifty percent of total electricity consumption with a six- to eight-year projected payback."

"Interesting." He leans back in his chair, his gaze locked on mine. "Keep going. I want you to *convince* me."

I don't miss the emphasis he puts on the word, and I almost choke, remembering how I'd asked him to convince me that night at the bar. Before I can embarrass myself, I take a sip of my water. "Yes, of course, Co—Mr. King. These big-ticket items will fundamentally change the way your hotels operate, reducing your footprint without sacrificing comfort. This will bring you into line with the future of sustainable design and improve your sustainability ratings." A bead of sweat trickles between my breasts under the pressure of Cole's scrutiny. "Hotels that invest in sustainable practices generally have higher occupancy rates, guest satisfaction, and revenue per room compared to nonsustainable counterparts. So although the initial capital outlay may seem expensive, I'm confident that the savings they incur will offset the expense within only a few years."

Several heads around the table nod, but not Cole's. I can't read his expression at all.

"Okay," he says eventually, turning his attention back to Paul. "I think we've heard everything we need to hear from your team. Someone will be in touch to let you know our decision once we've made it. Thank you for your time today." He pushes back his chair and stands. The rest of his team follows his lead.

Obviously dismissed, we stand too. I gather my pen, notebook, and papers and turn to leave, not daring to look in his direction again.

As we walk to the door, Paul's hand brushes my lower back, and he leans down to whisper in my ear. "That bastard is impossible to read. I have no idea how that went."

I nod. It's only when I'm passing through the door that I

risk a glance over my shoulder. Cole is watching us, the hard angle of his jaw and cold eyes sending my stomach plummeting.

I have a horrible feeling that the incredible night I shared with him a month ago is about to bite me in the ass.

CHAPTER SEVEN

COLE

"So, how have the presentations been going?" Roman asks from across his large mahogany desk.

When I got back to my office after Elite Architecture's presentation, I'd had a message from my brother, asking for an update. I decided to give it to him in person.

Roman's question sends my mind back to the moment Delilah walked into the conference room. The second I'd recognized her, I'd been taken back to that night in my hotel room—to her moans, the way her body had writhed under mine, her almost startled sounds of pleasure once I began to move inside her. My dick had immediately stood at attention, begging for another round.

I force the memory from my thoughts, leaning back in the deep leather chair and crossing my ankle over my knee. "Fine. There are a few good proposals."

"When do you think you'll decide?"

I rub my chin. Although there are several proposals which meet our requirements, there's only one that stands out. But Delilah's involvement has me reluctant to choose it.

I didn't trust the look of shock on her face when she saw

me. In a city the size of New York, what are the odds that my one-night stand and her team would end up bidding on our project?

Back when we met, they would have already been working on their proposal. Which means she probably knew exactly who I was. If she actually thinks I'd give her team preferential treatment because I've screwed her, she's mistaken. In fact, now I'm doubting everything about her. It surprised me when she told me she was still a virgin at twenty-four, but that was more believable than having her architecture license at that age. It doesn't add up. The whole thing must have been a ploy to get into my bed. After all, this project isn't only worth a fortune to her company. It's an opportunity that would make a young architect's career.

"Cole!" Roman snaps, and I jerk my attention back to him. That's right, he'd asked when I would decide.

"Soon," I answer. "Just doing some final calculations. I'll make a decision by the end of tomorrow."

He gives a curt nod, then returns his focus to his computer screen.

I roll my eyes, leave his office, and head toward mine, stopping by my PA's desk before I get there. "Samson, I need you to compile a report for me on the LEED certification status of other hotels near our sites. That's L-E-E-D. Leadership in Energy and Environmental Design. You'll find details on the U.S. Green Building Council website."

Samson nods. "Absolutely, sir. When do you need it?"

"By the end of the day."

"I can do that. Just to clarify, are you looking for information on all the hotels around the future developments, or just those similar to those we're planning to build?"

"Let's focus on the similar ones for now. Can you also

gather some data on any other sustainability initiatives they have in place? And include any notable certifications or awards they've received."

He nods again and jots something down on a notepad by his keyboard. "Got it. I'll get started on that right away."

I thank him and enter my office. As soon as I sit at my desk, I give in to curiosity and search for Elite Architecture. The King Group hasn't worked with them before, but they have an excellent reputation, with offices in multiple countries. I'm more interested in learning how someone Delilah's age gets to be where she is, though. She mentioned interning for them, but how is she already on a team handling a proposal of this size?

I find an employee list and locate her photo and bio at the bottom. It's short, and it's obvious she's new. Unlike most of the other architects, she doesn't have any major projects to her name. Landing this one would be huge for her.

I shake my head. There's no way she didn't deliberately seek me out.

Then there's *Paul*. Her ex, I'm assuming, since she'd said she worked with him. He seems like a smug asshole. I noted the way he touched her lower back as they left the conference room, and the way he leaned down to whisper in her ear. It seems a little too familiar, considering they're no longer dating.

Or was that part of the lie?

I frown, then shake my head. None of it makes any difference. I'll wait for the report from Samson, but a part of me already knows I'll give the job to them. Emotions have no bearing on this decision. Business is business, and they seem to be the best fit, but I'll make it abundantly clear I will not tolerate any attempts at manipulation.

And if she's harboring any delusions that I'll invite her back into my bed, she'll soon discover how wrong she is.

CHAPTER EIGHT

DELILAH

My ringing phone wakes me from a restless sleep. I fumble around on my side table until I find it. "Hello?" I mumble, squinting against the fingers of light finding their way past the edges of my bedroom curtains.

"We got it!" Paul's loud voice makes me wince.

I sit up and rub my eyes. "Got what?"

"The King Group project," he says, and now I'm wide awake.

"Really?" I'm simultaneously shocked, delighted, and wracked with nerves. Delighted that all our hard work has paid off, and excited at the knowledge that something I'll have a hand in designing will feature prominently in major cities around the US.

But my stomach twists at the thought of being in the same space as Cole for an extended period.

From the way he looked at me during our presentation, it's obvious he was less than happy to see me. And I guess I understand why. Cole doesn't seem the type to be interested in mixing business with pleasure, particularly not when the pleasure was only ever meant to be a one-night thing. Luckily, there'll be more than a few floors separating us, and he'll probably be dealing mostly with Paul.

Which reminds me . . .

I tune back to Paul's voice, hoping I haven't missed out on anything important.

"They'll have the space ready for us by Monday, so we can start then. I'll have my own office, but you and the rest of the team will have desks on the main floor."

"Okay."

"Cole has also asked to meet with all of us individually on Monday. I suggest saying as little as possible at this stage. Answer his questions, tell him you're looking forward to working with him, and leave it at that."

My stomach flips again. Oh god, why do we have to meet him on our own? It would be so much easier if the entire team was with me. Still, disregarding what Paul just said about not saying much, this might be an opportunity to clear the air with Cole. Let him know I won't go blabbing about our previous . . . interaction to anyone.

"And Delilah," Paul continues, "I don't need to remind you how important this project is. You're the youngest and newest member of the team, so you have to appear professional at all times. Also, I think we should keep quiet about our relationship. There's no reason to discuss personal details like that with anyone outside of our firm."

I roll my eyes. I know Paul is angling for promotion to partner, and having a project of this scale go smoothly will improve his chances, but when am I ever unprofessional? Or prone to spontaneous PDAs at work? Or running my mouth to people about my personal life?

It's not worth saying anything about it now, though. Not when I'd rather get off the phone and digest the news than get into an argument. I just make a general sound of acknowledgement, and he carries on for a few more minutes.

When we eventually say goodbye, after arranging to have dinner tomorrow night, I sink down on the bed. My nerves from before have dissipated and now excitement zips through me.

When the sound of our coffee machine reaches me, I realize Alex must be awake. I immediately throw back my covers and climb out of bed. After using the bathroom, I make my way to our small-but-neat kitchen, which is filled with the delicious aroma of fresh coffee.

"Any left for me?" I ask, smiling at my very tousled-looking roommate, whose long auburn hair is half falling out of its ponytail.

She passes the mug she's just finished pouring and reaches for another. "Ugh, why are mornings so hard?"

I sit on one of the chairs in our little breakfast nook and pull my knee up to my chest. "They're only hard because you were sexting your rock star boyfriend all night."

"Fiancé," she corrects with a wink as she fills a cup for herself.

I laugh. "I'll start remembering soon, I promise." Alex's boyfriend, Jaxson, is an up-and-coming rock star, whose band Lightning Strikes was recently signed by Hazard Records. A week ago, just before he and his band flew to LA for two months, they'd gotten engaged, and I keep forgetting to call him her fiancé.

I take a sip of my coffee as she comes over and sits opposite me. "So, have you found somewhere for you guys to live yet?" I ask. Alex has started looking for an apartment for her and Jaxson to move into, since Alex isn't keen on moving into the bachelor pad he lives in with his bandmates. The thought of her moving out makes my chest feel a little hollow.

Alex and I are close friends, despite being opposites in just about every way. When I'm not working late, I'm either reading a good book or binge-watching cheesy television shows, while she loves going out to clubs and socializing. Despite our differences, we bonded over our shared interest in design during our internship at Elite Architecture. When we were offered permanent positions after graduation, we decided to share an apartment. That was almost a year and a half ago. I'll miss living with her, but I'm happy that she's happy.

"No," she says. "To be honest, I'm not looking too hard. There's a lot going on with the band at the moment. They're talking about permanently moving to the West Coast now. Not much point in finding somewhere here if they have to move."

My eyebrows shoot up. "What will you do if that happens?"

She bites her bottom lip. "There's Elite's LA office. That might be an option. Or Jaxson and I can do the long-distance thing until we figure out what's going on."

"Mmm," I say, noncommittally. Alex and Jaxson's relationship seems to be super strong, but long-distance isn't easy, especially for a newly engaged couple. Hopefully it will all work out.

"Paul called just before," I say, to change the topic.

"Oh yeah?" She eyes me over her coffee cup, and I wince internally. She isn't exactly a fan of Paul. Then again, he isn't a fan of her either. I try to keep them apart as much as I can. Still, after a week of bad-mouthing Paul when we broke up, she made sure not to make too many comments about him when we got back together. But what I have to say isn't about Paul, anyway. It's about his news.

"Yes, and guess what? We got the King Group job!"

"That's fantastic, Dee!" She puts down her coffee cup and half stands to reach across and give me a hug. "Not that I'm surprised. You worked so hard on it. And wow, it's going to be amazing for your résumé."

"I know." The thought sends a thrill through me all over again. I worked long hours and multiple weekends, helping to perfect the proposal. Now all that hard work is going to pay off with . . . more hard work. But it's what I love doing, so I'm more than happy.

"When do you start?" Alex asks.

"Monday. We'll be moving into King Plaza for the duration. And Cole . . . I mean, Mr. King, wants to meet with us all individually, too."

She nods. "Makes sense to welcome you and make you all feel like part of the same team."

"Yeah, um, there's only one thing . . ." I'd told Alex about losing my virginity after my breakup with Paul, but I never told her Cole King was the man I slept with. Maybe because I'm still trying to wrap my head around it myself. But now I could use some advice. "I've met Mr. King before. About a month ago."

Alex cocks her head to the side. "Okay. So, you've met before. What's the big deal?"

I take a deep breath. "It was when Paul and I had broken up. The night we broke up, actually."

Her brows hike skyward and her mouth drops open. "Are you saying you lost your virginity to Cole King? One of the King Group Kings? Billionaire and basically your new boss?"

I cringe. "Yes. I didn't know at the time, though."

"Holy shit," she breathes. "I can't believe it." Then she laughs, her big brown eyes tearing up. "Oh my god, Dee. When you finally decide to let your hair down, you go full throttle and hook up with one of the richest, most eligible bachelors in the country."

"Stop laughing. It's going to be so awkward. Particularly during our one-on-one meeting."

She wiggles her eyebrows. "Maybe it will turn into a literal one-on-one meeting."

The sip of coffee I've just taken almost chokes me. "Paul and I are back together. Plus I work for him, so that would be completely inappropriate." I think back to Cole's icy expression during our last meeting. "Not to mention, I'm pretty sure he has no interest in a repeat performance."

"From the minimal juicy details you gave of that night, it sounds like it was pretty intense. Why wouldn't he want to repeat that? He's a man, isn't he?"

"You should have seen the way he was glaring at me. He was *not* happy to see me."

"Hmm." She purses her lips. "Could he be worried you'll tell everyone you screwed the boss?"

"When we have our meeting, I should probably let him know I won't say anything to anyone."

"Have you considered pretending you don't recognize him?" She lets out a laugh. "I'm sure that would drive him nuts."

A smile tugs at my lips, but I shake my head. "I'm pretty sure he knows I recognized him."

Alex taps her nails on the table. "Take this with a grain of salt, since I've never been in this situation, but I wouldn't say anything unless he raises the topic. You don't want to make it out to be a bigger deal than it was, and if you say nothing and act completely professional, you'll show him you're only interested in doing the job he's hiring you for."

I scrunch up my nose. "You think?"

Alex shrugs. "You should do whatever you feel is right. After all, if it were me, I'd dump Paul ASAP and give Cole King the best one-on-one meeting of his life."

I laugh, even as I shake my head. "I don't have any interest in him like that anymore. It was a great night, but Paul and I are really trying to work on things right now."

"Mm-hmm," Alex says. "Have you told Paul?"

"No. And I'm not going to. It was bad enough telling him I'd had sex with someone while we were broken up. I can't imagine his reaction if he knew who the man was. He'd hate it, and I don't want to jeopardize their working relationship."

"Yeah. Probably a good call. I'm sure having to sit across a meeting room table from the man who screwed his girl-friend's brains out before he had a chance to wouldn't sit well with him. I don't have a problem with him getting himself into trouble by trying to one-up his new boss, but I'd hate for it to affect you."

"So, you won't say anything to Paul?"

She shakes her head, miming locking her mouth shut and throwing away the key.

I stand and round the table to give her a hug, since I'm not tall enough to reach across it the way she did. "Thanks, Alex."

"That's what friends are for, right?" she says. "Keeping scandalous secrets from each other's boyfriends."

"Something like that," I say with a laugh. "Come on. Now that you know, you can help me find something professional to wear to my meeting."

"By professional, you mean sexy, right?"

I roll my eyes at her before heading to my bedroom, with Alex trailing behind me.

But yeah. It wouldn't hurt to look at least a little sexy when facing down the man who gave me the best night of my life.

So far, anyway.

IT'S Monday and I'm sitting on the beautiful, uncomfortable leather couch outside Cole's office, trying not to fidget. My heart raps against my ribcage and a nervous sweat dampens my skin. Cole's PA, a young man who introduced himself as Samson, eyes me from across the space, and I wonder if he can tell how nervous I am.

He picks up his phone, glances at me, says something, and hangs up. "You can go in, Miss West."

I smile my thanks at him, then stand, smoothing down my gray pencil skirt. With Alex's help, I paired it with a cream sleeveless blouse with delicate little buttons running down the front of it. Black strappy heels finish off the look. As Alex put it, the outfit is classy, while still doing a fantastic job of highlighting my curves.

Professional with a hint of sexy. Perfect to give me the confidence I need to face this uncomfortable situation.

Samson gives me a slightly concerned look, and I realize I've ground to a halt, standing frozen in front of the wall of frosted glass encasing Cole's office door. Shaking off my temporary paralysis, I cross the last few feet and knock.

"Come in." His curt tone stiffens my spine. Whatever his problem is, I haven't done anything to be ashamed of. I refuse to let him intimidate me more than he already does.

The onyx door effortlessly swings open under my hand,

and I step into the enormous office, my eyes sweeping the room to put off looking at the man sitting behind the large mahogany desk.

It's a corner office, so the expansive windows make up almost all of two sides, and I'm immediately struck by the stunning view of the city's skyline. Twin couches face each other across a low table at the other end of the office, with a bar and a coffee station alongside. A few artsy black-and-white prints hang on the far wall, and there's a second door, which probably leads to a private bathroom.

With no more excuses, I finally focus on Cole.

God. He's still so good looking. Even though he appears far more like the stern businessman he is than he did the night we first met. His suit jacket fits like a dream across his broad shoulders, and as he stands, my eyes drift over the well-tailored lines that only emphasize his stature.

I drag my attention back to his face, my lips twitching up in a nervous smile.

He doesn't return it, merely rounds his desk and leans against it with his arms crossed, his cool gaze running over me.

After taking a deep breath, I walk toward him and hold out my hand. "It's nice to meet you . . . uh, again, uh, Mr. King." My cheeks warm as memories of that night force their way into my head.

He hesitates for a second, and my stomach sinks. Surely he won't leave me hanging.

He doesn't. He steps forward and clasps my hand in his big, warm grip.

My palm tingles.

"Is it?" he says.

My brows jump, and as soon as he lets go of my hand, I pull it back. "Um . . ." God, this is embarrassing. I'm a professional, for god's sake. This situation is awkward as hell, but I should at least be able to string a sentence together. "Of course. I'm very excited to work with the King Group." There, that sounds professional and upbeat.

His eyes narrow as he studies me. "How long were you working on this proposal?"

I shift my feet and look at the deep leather chairs in front of his desk, wondering if I'm expected to stand here the whole time while he interviews me. Cole notices my gaze but doesn't invite me to sit.

I bite back a sigh. "We've been working on it for about two months."

He nods, rubbing his hand over his jaw. I have a sudden memory of when that same jaw, rough with five o'clock shadow, rubbed deliciously on the sensitive skin of my inner thighs. My nipples tighten, and I hope my reaction isn't visible.

"So you knew who I was when you sat next to me at the bar?"

What? I shake my head. "No, I didn't know who you were."

One dark brow lifts. "You're saying you sat next to one of your most lucrative potential clients, dressed to kill and with a ready story about your broken heart, and it wasn't on purpose?" His voice betrays nothing—he sounds like he doesn't care what my answer is—but the hard angle of his jaw belies his nonchalance.

"What are you asking me?"

"I'm asking if you planned this. What are the odds you'd turn up next to me at the bar that night, end up in my bed, then walk into my office last week?"

Who does this guy think he is? My shoulders stiffen. "I

don't know the exact odds. I imagine they're low. But I didn't plan this. It's just a crazy coincidence."

"I don't believe in coincidences."

Anger whips through me. What sort of cold, empty life would allow him to see a simple coincidence as some subterfuge to manipulate him? "Are you insinuating that I used my body to get this job for my firm? Because if you are, it sounds very much like you're suggesting I prostituted myself."

He stalks closer and my breath catches. I hate that even though I'm furious with him, my body reacts to his proximity. He's the only man who's given me such intense pleasure, and apparently my body doesn't care that he's insulting my integrity. It just wants to relive the feeling of his head between my legs and the way he filled me so thoroughly.

My gaze snaps back to his as I realize it's drifted down to his lips.

My nipples tighten even more, and I'm sure by now they must be visible. I cross my arms as if I'm bored with this conversation.

Only the smirk curling his lips lets me know I haven't succeeded.

He's standing so close that I need to angle my chin sharply to keep my eyes locked with his.

"I'm not calling you a prostitute," he says, "but I've met plenty of men and women who are prepared to do whatever it takes to get something from me. I want to know if you're one of them. This job is worth more than a lot of money. It comes with a significant amount of prestige."

This time *my* lip curls. "I don't know what sort of people you spend time with, Mr. King, but that sounds like a *you* problem. I'm telling you the truth. I didn't know who you were the night we met. If I had, I absolutely would never have . . . done what I did." His eyes darken, and I have to swallow past my dry throat before I can continue. "When we were first notified about the project, I looked up the company and the only photos I saw were your father's and, I'm assuming, your brother's. So unless your face is plastered all over social media—which, by the way, I don't follow—I wouldn't know you from the next guy. I worked my ass off over the last few months on our proposal, and insinuating we couldn't win this account from merit is a slap in the face. Not to mention you're basically saying that I, as a woman, would rather use my body than my mind and talent to get a job."

I raise my chin, doing my best to rein in my temper. As much of a jerk as Cole is, I don't want to be responsible for our firm losing this job. "But if you still have a problem with me, I suggest you ask for my removal from the team. Otherwise, let's just act like professionals and maintain our distance from each other until this project is done."

Cole's eyes flick between mine, and I can't tell what he's thinking at all. Even though I've given him the option, I really hope he doesn't ask for my removal. Not only will that be a professional disaster for me, but explaining the why of it to Paul would be difficult, to say the least. But he just gives an abrupt nod and steps back. He returns to his desk, settling into his chair.

"You can stay on the team, Miss West. Far be it from me to cast aspersions on your character or your talent. Since we'll have very little to do with each other during your time here, I can assure you, keeping our distance won't be hard. But let me be very clear, just so there are no misunderstandings. There won't be any repeats of that night."

I gasp. The absolute nerve of him. I know I should just

turn and go, but I can't leave it at that. "Of course there won't be a repeat of that night. After all, I can only lose my virginity once. Now that Paul and I are back together, what would I need you for?"

Something dark flashes in his eyes, but he merely raises his brows. "He convinced you to take him back, did he? Or were you the one who did the convincing with your newfound sexual confidence?"

My head starts to pound at the base of my skull, and I glare at him. "Not that it's any of your business, but Paul apologized and asked if we could try again."

Cole doesn't say anything, just scrutinizes me as I stand there. Do I need to wait for him to dismiss me, or can I just make a move for the door? Before I can decide, he's out of his seat again and stalking toward me.

He steps right into my personal space, lowering his head until his face hovers just above mine. "So let me make sure I'm clear on this. Now that you're back with Paul, you have no more need of me?"

"N-No." My voice comes out shaky and I curse myself, even more so when his lips tilt up in a smile that isn't a smile at all. He steps closer again and his woodsy, masculine scent brings back memories of that night.

That's a good girl.

I'm going to come so. Fucking. Hard.

A shiver works its way through me, and he glances down, then up, triumph flaring in his eyes. I look down too, only then noticing that my nipples are clearly visible through my blouse.

And that they're brushing against his shirt with every rise and fall of my chest.

"Seems like your body disagrees with you," he says.

"That's just a biological reaction. It doesn't mean anything."

"Keep telling yourself that, kitten. You might actually start to believe it."

I can't believe he thinks he can get away with calling me kitten again. In a moment of insanity, I reach out and wrap my fingers around his dick. His very hard dick.

He freezes, eyes flaring wide, and I know I've surprised him.

"See? You have no interest in me, but you're hard. It's a biological reaction."

When he speaks again, his voice has gone low and gravelly. "If you don't stop stroking my cock, you'll find out exactly how this reaction ends, and I can guarantee it will involve you screaming my name."

A return to sanity has me snatching my hand away, and a blush sears its way over my whole body. I can't believe I just fondled him in his office. That's so far out of line it's not funny.

He steps back calmly, as if I didn't just have my fingers wrapped around his erection a few seconds ago, and returns to his desk. "You can go."

I blink, shocked by the sudden dismissal, even though I'm more than ready to get out of here.

"Now, Miss West. My time is valuable."

I grind my teeth but turn on my heel and reach for the door handle. My neck prickles as I leave the office, and I can almost feel his eyes on me as I let the heavy door swing shut behind me. I give Samson a tight smile as I hurry to the elevator. I want to put as much distance between me and Cole as I can.

The meeting hadn't gone at all the way I'd wanted. With

the way things escalated, I forgot to mention that Paul doesn't know about him and that I'd like to keep it that way. Not that I think Cole is likely to talk about me to anyone. I'm sure I'm just another notch on his bedpost. One he'd probably completely forgotten about before I walked into that meeting room.

I reach the elevator and press the button. While I wait, I cross my arms and stare absently at the huge black-and-white print showing King Plaza during its construction.

Thinking of Cole and what he suspected me of tightens my chest, a dull ache spreading through me. It's hard to believe the man who gave me such an incredible experience could turn out to be such an asshole. The memory of the night we'd spent together, which I'd been holding close to my heart ever since it happened, is now tarnished.

The elevator doors whoosh open, and I step inside, trying my hardest to suppress the hurt. I have a job to do, one which could make my career. Letting a man like Cole derail my dream would be an insult to me and Mom.

I punch the button for the forty-ninth floor, the location of my team's temporary office space, and watch the numbers tick down.

With any luck, that's the last time I'll ever need to get up close and personal with Cole King.

CHAPTER NINE

COLE

"Are you listening?" Roman's voice brings my attention back to the discussion. My brothers and I are sitting around a table in his office, analyzing the King Group's financials for the last quarter, as well as the projections for the next six months.

"Of course," I say. And I am, despite the memory of my meeting with Delilah this morning taking up most of my attention.

She'd surprised me. I'm mostly convinced that our original encounter and what happened between us was a coincidence. The shock and horror on her face when I suggested otherwise was believable enough that a part of me—a tiny part—actually feels bad about accusing her. But there are women out there who would do exactly that. Outside the bedroom, there have been plenty of people over the years who've orchestrated meetings with me and my brothers to try to get something from us.

In our position, trust is scarce. I'm not sure there's anyone in my life I trust completely. I know my brothers won't screw me over, because that would mean screwing the family and the company over, but it isn't because of any fond feelings we have for each other. It's because our power and wealth depend on our united front. That's the only thing that keeps the jackals at bay.

But trusting them with anything else is a different matter. Delilah may have been offended that I suggested she arranged our meeting, but I'd have been stupid not to ask.

The only problem is, once I got the answer out of her and she was standing there staring up at me, cheeks flushed, eyes sparking with anger, my own had evaporated, replaced by something different but just as heated.

My mind had flashed back to a time when her smooth skin flushed with arousal rather than anger. My dick had hardened in my pants at the memory of the thrust that buried it in her pussy, and the way she let out a breathy gasp when she was completely filled for the first time. Remembering how she'd come for me had sent a hot surge of lust flowing through my veins. Would she come as prettily if I were to fuck her again?

I'd shut that down fast, returning to my desk and dismissing her before my thoughts became too obvious.

But that memory and the scent of her perfume that lingered in the air had taken over my mind. The minute she'd left my office, I'd been out of my seat and in my private bathroom, stroking my dick to the visions replaying in my head. I'd never fucking done that before. Sure, I'd occasionally relieved some stress during the day, but never because of a specific woman.

Afterward, I'd stared at my reflection in the mirror and told myself I needed to get past this. I vowed to put Delilah out of my mind. She's my employee and nothing else.

And yet here I am, thinking about her again. In the

middle of a business meeting.

Completely un-fucking-like me.

I grit my teeth. Roman's gray eyes bore into me, but I calmly return his gaze. *I'm focused.*

Tate, my other brother, leans back in his chair, raking his hand through his blond hair. "I talked to Dad's lawyer yesterday," he says, breaking the tension and changing the topic from the numbers we've been discussing for the last hour. "He's still resisting the idea of a plea bargain."

I tap my pen impatiently on the table. "He's too damn arrogant for his own good. He actually thinks he can win if he goes to trial."

"He can't," Roman says flatly. "The lawyers need to keep pushing him. We don't need any more hits to the King Group's reputation. And a long, drawn-out trial won't do anyone any favors."

I nod in agreement. "Let's focus on what we can control. The hotel project is our top priority right now. If we can deliver on that, it'll go a long way in restoring confidence in the company."

"The board and our investors are expecting us to break ground on the first three hotels in twelve months," Roman says. "Can the architects have the final designs and all the planning permissions completed so we can meet that deadline?"

"I met with them this morning," I say. "They seem motivated. The initial concepts they've presented are sound. It might be tight, but I'll make sure we meet the target."

Tate takes a sip of water, clearing his throat before speaking. "We need to look at boosting investor confidence in the meantime. There are some rumors flying around that Berrington's weighing his options."

I frown. Kenneth Berrington is one of our largest

investors, as well as an old friend of our father's. His opinion carries weight in the business world and losing him could influence other investors who are watching to see how the company performs.

Berrington is also Jessica's father. After she and I kept running into each other at social and industry events over the years, we developed a mutually beneficial arrangement: when we can't be bothered organizing another date, we attend together, reinforcing the relationship between our respective families' companies—and more often than not, finishing the night with a good fuck. She's one of the few women I've had sex with more than once. Not because there's any emotional attachment between us, but because it's convenient. The sex is good, and we both know exactly who the other person is and what we do and don't want from each other.

Although, recently, she's become clingier. If she carries on the way she did the last time we were together, I might have to rethink our arrangement. The last thing I need is the complication of Jessica wanting to deepen our involvement.

Roman drums his fingertips, his eyes narrowing. "He's been with us for a long time, but the situation with Dad's arrest has thrown everyone's confidence. Berrington wants assurances we can maintain our profit margins. We may not have the relationship with him that Dad did, but we need him. If he pulls his investments, others will consider jumping ship as well."

Tate has been tapping away at his laptop as we speak. "Unfortunately, I don't think Cole regularly screwing his only daughter is enough insurance for us." His golden-brown eyes, so different from mine and Roman's, lift from the screen, and he smirks at me. "Maybe you should think about putting a ring on it."

The idea sends a chill down my back. Marriage is the last thing I'm interested in. I'll eventually have to find a wife and have children—it's expected, after all—but I could happily hold out for another ten years.

"No one's going to be putting a ring anywhere," I reply.

"Not even a cock ring?" Tate throws back with a smirk. "You're missing out."

I ignore him. "Berrington is more than happy to have me and Jessica put on a show now and then. He likes that everyone thinks he has an in with us. But that's all it is, a show."

Tate's about to say something else when Roman interrupts. "Our current aim is getting the hotel project underway as quickly as possible and meeting our milestones. That will convince the investors that Dad's removal as CEO won't impact our operations. Cole, I want you working closely with the architects to make sure they stay on track. I trust you to get this done for us."

I give a curt nod, brushing aside the hint of pride his words spark in me. It's just a holdover from years ago, when I actually cared about my older brother's approval.

"Tate. We need to make sure our messaging is on point," Roman says.

Tate leans forward, resting his elbows on the table. "I've been holding weekly meetings with the marketing team. They're launching a public relations campaign next week to highlight our commitment to transparency and ethical business practices. They'll focus their social media efforts on our philanthropic efforts and environmental initiatives." His gaze finds me. "It might be worth being seen out and about as much as possible. Attend a gala or three—the more charitable the cause, the better. Make sure you're seen throwing cash around. It'll reassure shareholders and investors that we're operating as usual, and the public will see that we're actively giving back."

I glance at Roman, then focus on Tate again. He's already chuckling. Probably because my face is reflecting my thoughts. "You're suggesting I'm the one who'll do all of that?"

Roman crosses his arms and gives me a pointed look. "You're the best choice. You're better at charming investors than I am, but not so charming that you're likely to end up with their wives' ankles around your ears."

Tate snorts out a laugh. "That's only happened twice. And to be fair, one of them was in an open marriage and the other was already getting divorce papers drawn up."

I can't quite stop my lips from twitching, but Roman's scowl says he's less than amused. Looks like I'll have to suck it up and start accepting more of the invitations we always seem to receive.

Even as I resign myself to that, my mind is already back on the hotel project. I need to take a more hands-on approach than I typically would. Follow Tate's example and hold weekly meetings with the architects. Make sure everything stays on track.

Of course, that means weekly meetings with Delilah as well. I refuse to acknowledge that part of me might actually look forward to that. She may have a way of getting under my skin, but there's too much at stake to let myself get sidetracked by a woman.

With that thought, I turn my attention back to the meeting and focus on what's important: making sure the King Group stays on top. It's the only thing that matters, and I'm more than willing to do whatever it takes to ensure it happens.

CHAPTER TEN

DELILAH

I tap my pen on my notepad as I study the concept design I've drawn for the roof of the Chicago hotel. After doing some calculations, I turn to my other computer screen and scroll through the U.S. Green Building Council website, checking over the information on their certification requirements. I take a few notes, then put my pen down and stretch.

It's Friday, and I've made it through my first week with the King Group. Aside from the confrontation with Cole on Monday, it's been great. I scan my surroundings and smile. They've given us an impressive office, filled with sleek, modern workbenches, ergonomic chairs, and several drafting tables. Large windows line two walls, allowing natural light to flood in and giving the space an airy, open feel. A small kitchen area with a fridge, microwave, and coffee machine is located at the far end.

My desk sits in the corner, facing the rest of the room. The double computer screens block most of my view, which is great for preventing distractions. Although it also blocks me from seeing who's approaching. It's only when the familiar waft of Paul's aftershave—which he always applies a little too liberally—reaches me that I'm alerted to his presence.

He peers at me over the screens, and I smile up at him. "Hey, what's up?"

"Cole's asked for a status meeting in ten."

My stomach twists. "With all of us?"

He nods. "I offered to give him a rundown myself, but he wants the entire team there."

Not seeing any sign of Cole since Monday has given me a false sense of security, but at least he won't make any more insulting accusations if there's a room full of people.

I hope not, anyway.

I stand, grab my notepad and pen, and follow everyone as we file into the elevator to take us to the executive floor. After shuffling to the side to let in a straggler, my attention is caught by Philippa, who's been in the office this morning in her liaison role. She's standing close to Paul, and as I watch, he leans down to her so she can murmur something into his ear.

A spike of unease hits me at their easy familiarity. And not for the first time, I wonder if there might have been something between the two of them while Paul was in the UK. It would explain her barely veiled animosity toward me. I asked Paul once, not long after she joined our office. He denied it.

The thought gets pushed to the side as we enter the conference room, and I can't stop myself from looking toward the head of the table. The chair is empty, and the tension in my shoulders loosens. I make my way to the seat furthest away. There's no point in making this situation more uncomfortable than I need to.

While we wait, I open my notepad and sketch out some ideas that have been running through my head since I saw the updates to the USGBC website. I don't look up as the conference room door opens again, although my body is all-too aware of his entry. I wish it wasn't. Having my pulse automatically speed up as soon as I sense his presence—and not just from nervousness—has guilt washing over me. Particularly with Paul sitting only a few seats away.

When Cole speaks, I force myself to turn and face him. The last thing I need is to be called out for unprofessional-ism. Thankfully, his eyes aren't on me. Now that he's figured out I didn't attempt to con my way into this job—or his bed—he'll pay no more attention to me than any other of the hundreds of people working in this building.

"We're facing a tight deadline," Cole says. "I intend to have regular meetings to make sure the timeline doesn't slip. During these meetings, I expect progress updates from each of you." He turns his attention to Paul. "I also expect a written update from you on the overall status of the project, and I want it in my inbox every Friday morning."

My brows draw together. Am I imagining it, or did his tone become curter when he spoke to Paul? If Paul notices, he doesn't show it. He just nods his acknowledgement.

We spend the next hour going around the room, and everyone shares their updates. I'm not as prepared as I should be when his steely eyes land on me. "Miss West," he says, and this time I'm sure I'm not imagining the coolness of his tone.

"I'm working on the concept for the Chicago property. I'm on schedule and have completed several preliminary designs and conceptual sketches, but . . ." I pause and out of the corner of my eye, I see Paul's head swing toward me. Should I say anything? I haven't discussed any of this with him yet. My plan was to feed this information up the chain through him, but since I can't avoid interacting with Cole, I might as well mention it now.

"What is it?" Cole sounds impatient, and I almost lose my nerve.

But then I straighten in my seat. This is where my expertise lies. He doesn't get to make me doubt myself just because he's a rich, entitled asshole. I look him straight in the eye. "I've been checking the USGBC website, which provides the LEED certification requirements, and I've done some calculations."

He doesn't say anything, just picks up his pen and rolls it between his fingers while he leans back in his chair and pins me with his gaze.

I clear my throat. "My initial thoughts were to install a solar panel array on the roof, but I think there'll be significant value in installing a green roof as well. It will help reduce the urban heat island effect and provide natural insulation, reduce energy use for heating and cooling, and help to manage stormwater runoff and improve air quality. Besides the solar panel array and the other sustainability systems we're already looking at incorporating, a green roof will result in a higher LEED certification."

"Delilah—" Paul starts, but Cole cuts him off.

"Won't the solar panels take up all the space on the roof?"

"Yes, but there are ways we can have both. In fact, we can design it so that the two systems complement each other. For example, we can install solar panels that generate electricity from both the top and bottom, which will take advantage of the reflected sunlight from the green roof. In turn, the panels provide shade for the plants. A green roof reduces the heat absorbed by the building, which can actually improve the efficiency of the panels."

"And how much extra will this cost?" Cole asks, his expression inscrutable.

I wince internally but aim to keep my face as expressionless as his. "I haven't finished calculating the cost estimates, but with the modifications needed, it would add a significant amount of upfront costs. With the higher LEED certification, however, you'll be eligible for additional incentives, potentially including government grants."

Cole's eyes fix on mine, and my cheeks heat under the intensity of his gaze.

I wet my lips. "The preliminary plan I originally drew up is ready to go, but it only includes the solar panel array. Paul has it at the moment. But if you're interested in considering the green roof, I can send those to him as well, and you can discuss them together."

Cole rocks forward on his chair and places his pen in front of him. "I would prefer you talk me through it."

My eyes dart to Paul, and I catch the scowl on his face. We might have words about this later, but it's too late to worry about that now.

"I'm sure Paul can—"

"Don't hide behind your . . ." His infinitesimal pause has me wondering if he'll say boyfriend. Thank goodness he doesn't. "Project manager. If you're asking the company to take on additional expenses, I expect you to be able to justify it. Contact Samson and organize a time to meet with me this week."

I swallow. Great, another meeting with Cole. "Yes, Mr. King."

Something flickers across his face, but before I can identify it, he looks down at the tablet in front of him. "I think that wraps things up, so I'll see you all next Friday. Miss West, I expect to see you before then."

I nod, then push back my chair and stand with the team. Paul's presence looms behind me as we leave the room, and I try to avoid the coming confrontation by making a beeline for the elevator. Before I can get there, he grabs my arm.

"Delilah, when we get back downstairs, I'd like to see you in my office."

My shoulders slump and I turn, my gaze catching on a pair of icy blue eyes. They drop, then narrow when they reach Paul's hand clamped around my arm. Instead of saying something, Cole turns and strides toward his office.

I follow Paul to the elevator. Everyone else has already gone down, so we wait together for its return.

"What was that?" he hisses. "You should have raised your proposal with me before presenting it to Cole."

"This is an update meeting, isn't it? If he doesn't like the idea, he can say no."

"It's not your place. I'm the project manager. Cole isn't going to appreciate a junior architect making suggestions that will cost his company a lot of money. Plus, I don't appreciate you going over my head like that."

The elevator arrives, and Paul steers me in.

As soon as the doors close, I tug away from him. "Well, Cole wants to talk about it, so he can't have hated the idea that much."

"Don't go around calling him Cole, either. It's Mr. King to you."

I stare at him, wondering why he's being so pompous. He's right, though. I shouldn't be so familiar. A flush warms my cheeks as Paul eyes me. "Let's not argue about it. From now on, I'll make sure to go through you first."

He looks a little appeased. "I'll join you during your meeting and we can all discuss it together."

I nod, my irritation with Paul's attitude offset by my relief at not having to face Cole—*Mr. King*—alone.

Another one-on-one encounter with him is the last thing I need.

CHAPTER ELEVEN

COLE

Samson buzzes me. I look up from the email I'm reading and answer. "Yes?"

"Miss West and Mr. Donovan are here for your meeting."

What the hell is Paul doing with her?

"Keep them there," I bark. I push back my chair and stride to the door, jerking it open and stepping out.

Delilah and Paul are waiting to come in. Rolls of paper fill Delilah's hands, and her green eyes lock on mine, a hint of pink tinting her cheeks.

I shouldn't like that I make her nervous, but I do. A little too much.

My attention shifts to Paul hovering close to her. I wonder if the man senses something. If he's somehow picking up on the memories that ripple between Delilah and me whenever we're in the same room together. The idea almost makes me smile.

But I don't. "Paul, I'm sorry you wasted a trip here, but I asked to meet with *only* Miss West."

Paul's eyes dart between Delilah and me. Oh yeah, he senses something all right. But I doubt he knows what. Would she have told him she slept with someone while they were apart, or did she act the role of the blushing virgin the first time he sank his dick into her?

I've never cared about taking a woman's virginity, but there's something about Paul believing he's the first man to have her that sets my teeth on edge. Some primal urge to make sure every other man knows she was mine before she was anyone else's.

And as much as I'm disinterested in repeating our encounter, imagining Paul touching her has my back clenching with a spike of irritation.

"But as the project manager, I feel like I should—"

I pin him with my gaze. "If I wanted you here, I would have asked you to take part."

A muscle tics in Paul's jaw, but he knows better than to argue. He just nods and turns to Delilah. "Come by my office on your way back."

Delilah throws him a look that I can't interpret. Annoyance? Nervousness? I can't tell, and that frustrates me. I'm used to being able to read people.

With one last frown in our direction, Paul moves off.

I step back and gesture for Delilah to enter my office. As she passes, her soft wildflower scent drifts to me, and all my senses go on high alert. I'm not even embarrassed about my eyes dropping to her heart-shaped ass swaying in front of me in one of those fitted skirts she likes to wear.

She stops in front of my desk as I circle it and sit down, leaning back in my chair and rubbing my chin as I watch her. She glances uncertainly at the two leather seats next to her, obviously wondering if she's allowed to sit this time.

I raise my brows as I wait to see what she does. Without looking at me, she smooths her skirt and sits, crossing her legs.

I let my eyes linger on the exposed skin of her thighs, and when I meet her gaze, her cheeks are flushed again.

"Um," she says. "So, would you like me to run through my thoughts on the green roof?"

I tip my chin at her. "I want to hear about feasibility."

"Okay." She stands and unrolls a schematic, placing it on the desk in front of me. She leans forward and my gaze is drawn to the neckline of her blouse, which is gaping just enough to show a hint of creamy cleavage.

I force my attention back to where she's pointing out the details of her preliminary design.

Delilah's eyes light up as she talks about the green roof, her hands making graceful movements over the plan. I'm watching her as much as listening to what she's saying.

"Do you have an idea of what the additional costs might be?" I ask.

"I'm estimating it will be in the ballpark of an extra two hundred thousand on top of the one and a half million we're looking at for the solar panel array. But considering the additional savings from increased energy efficiency, decreased water runoff, and that, theoretically, the green roof will also improve the solar array's efficiency, the payback period of installing both systems is the same as installing the solar panels on their own."

"And how long will that be?"

"Approximately eight years."

I nod slowly, impressed with her diligence.

"Plus," she adds, "you can use the increased LEED rating to one-up your competitors."

My lips quirk up. The cost benefit is obviously in our favor. I'd liked the idea when she'd floated it in our team meeting earlier in the week, but I'd wanted to make sure she wasn't increasing the spend without considering the return on investment. Clearly, she knows what she's talking about.

"Is this something we can use for all the hotels?" I have a good idea what her answer will be, but I'm interested in what she has to say.

Or do I just want to keep her here longer?

Delilah straightens. "We can use it on several, but we'd need to do a cost analysis based on the climate of the various cities. A green roof might not be the best solution in some of the drier states. Although, there is always the option of using drought-tolerant plants."

I study her design for a moment longer, then flip to a few waiting underneath. There's a site plan showing the proposed hotel's relationship with the surrounding topography and other buildings, as well as what looks like her original concept design with just the solar panel array on the roof.

It's a delaying tactic more than anything. I already know what I'm going to tell her. "Okay." I flip back to the plan on the top of the pile and look up at her. "Give the numbers to accounting and get them to get back to Paul with the approvals."

She blinks at me. "Just like that?"

I shrug. "It makes good financial sense."

"Right. Okay then. Uh, thank you." She pulls the plans toward her and begins rolling them up, having to start over again when she rolls them crookedly. She's flustered. Is it because she wasn't expecting me to accept her proposal so quickly? Or because she's alone with me in my office?

I want it to be the latter.

"Well, thank you for listening to me. I appreciate it," she says.

I stand and walk around my desk, and she lifts her chin as I stop in front of her. Shoving my hands in my pockets, I ask, "So how are things with Paul?"

Her eyes widen. "Paul? Um, they're fine."

"No problem working on the project together?"

She hesitates, probably wondering where I'm going with this. "We've worked together before."

I take a step forward. "And does he always treat you that way?"

"What do you mean?"

"Like a child instead of a very competent architect."

Delilah blinks, her lips parting. The next moment, her expression shutters. "I don't know what you're talking about. This is a high-profile project. It's Paul's job to make sure everything runs smoothly."

I suppose it's hardly a surprise she doesn't want to discuss her boyfriend with me.

"Paul and Philippa seem to have a good working relationship." I don't know why I say it. It could be because I sense some undercurrent between Paul and the beautiful blonde. Or maybe it's because I'm an asshole and I recognize a kindred spirit when I see one. And there's no doubt in my mind that Paul's an asshole. After all, he's broken up with her once already—which I should probably thank him for—then come crawling back.

Delilah stares down at the plans in her hands. When she raises her gaze again, there's a spark of anger in the deep green of her eyes. The sight sends a flare of heat through me.

"I'm not sure what you're trying to insinuate," she says,

"but my personal relationship with Paul and his *professional* relationship with Philippa aren't any of your business."

"I'm not trying to insinuate anything. Just commenting."

"Well, how would you like it if I commented on your girlfriend's relationship with another man?"

A smile curls my lips. "That's not really an issue for me."

Something shimmers in her eyes. Is it relief? I can't tell for sure because she tilts her head and it's gone. "Let me guess. You're one of those men whose relationships consist of multiple one-night stands because they're afraid of emotional intimacy?"

I raise my brows and she presses her lips together, probably remembering who I am and where she's standing.

She gives a little shake of her head. "I'm sorry, that was completely—"

"Accurate. Except for the *being afraid* part. Replace that with not being interested in, and you've got it."

"Right," she mutters. "Well, lucky me to be one of the many, then." She pivots as if she's about to leave.

"More memorable than most," I say, and she jolts to a stop, looking at me over her shoulder. I don't know why I'm poking her. Or why I enjoy seeing her cheeks turn pink with either embarrassment or anger—both options being equally appealing. I'm not interested in her as anything more than an employee and a very pleasant memory. Not to mention she's another man's girlfriend. So why can't I leave this—*her*—alone?

Her nose wrinkles. "Should I be flattered that if you line up all the women you've slept with, I'll be one of the few you can pick out?"

"Most women would."

She puts her hand on her hip and angles her head to the side so her dark hair tumbles over one shoulder. "I doubt that. But if that's what you need to tell yourself to sleep at night, then you just go ahead. While those women are chasing you around, begging for a night in your bed, I'll be with my very attractive, very intelligent boyfriend, having some very enjoyable emotional intimacy."

I casually cross my arms over my chest. "Not long ago, you were the one begging for a night in my bed. You were more than happy to have a one-night stand so I could give you what you needed." Baiting her like this is crazy. If I'm not careful, I could end up with a sexual harassment suit. And yet, I can't seem to stop.

The urge isn't helped when she curls her lip and says, "I should have waited. If I'd known who I was spending the night with, I would have realized what a big mistake I was making. Now at least I've got a man who takes care of my needs and has an interest in me as a person."

Her eyes spit fire, and I find myself standing way too close to her, taking in her wildflower scent and basking in her anger.

Even though I brought up Paul in the first place, I don't particularly like her thinking about him while I'm standing in front of her. Though she says she should have waited, she'd loved every second of the hours we'd spent together. The scratch marks down my back had proved it. That needling irritation is what makes me keep going. "Does Paul know? Did you tell him about that night, or did you keep your little indiscretion to yourself?"

Her chin rises. "I was honest about what happened."

"Exactly how honest? Does he know it was me? Have you shared that truth with him?"

Her delicate jaw clenches, but her gaze darts away—proof she hasn't. "There's no point," she says. "It would only make the working relationship between the two of you uncomfortable."

"If that's what you need to tell yourself to sleep at night." I throw her words back at her.

Her nostrils flare and those bright green eyes flash. "Surely you can't believe it's a good idea for him to know?"

"You don't think he deserves to know that the man sitting across the table from him is the man who took his girlfriend's virginity?" Her lips part on a gasp, but I keep going. "That a month ago, you were screaming my name as you came on my cock? Tell me, Delilah, when you look at me, do you remember my mouth between your legs? Do you touch yourself and think about how you did it for me that night?"

Her breaths are fast and choppy. "No."

"No what? No, you don't think he deserves to know? No, you don't remember? Or no, you don't play with yourself and think of me? How honest are you, kitten?"

Her eyes narrow. "You seem to remember an awful lot about that night for someone who's probably screwed any number of women since then. How often have you touched yourself thinking about me?"

She's not trying to be seductive. She's angry. And sick bastard that I am, I like it just as much.

"Too many times to count," I admit, savoring her sharp inhale. "So next time you and your boyfriend are sitting across the table from me, you'll know I'm remembering your sweet pussy wrapped around my dick and I'll know you're remembering my fingers and tongue in you, and how hard I made you scream. You might be with Paul, but I have no doubt you'll be thinking about me the next time you fuck yourself with your fingers."

Hectic patches of red bloom on the arches of her cheekbones. My eyes dip to the jut of her stiff nipples through her thin blouse. I would give anything to bend my head and suck one of those hard tips into my mouth.

But I can't.

I wouldn't, even if she didn't have a boyfriend.

"Vibrator," she says shakily.

I raise my brows. When she speaks again, her voice has strengthened, and she meets my gaze head-on.

"I'll be using a vibrator. And when I come, I'll be thinking about whatever the hell I *want* to think about. Now, if you'll excuse me," she says, and pushes me away from her.

I let her, stepping back so she can slip past me. Without another glance in my direction, she leaves, not even giving me the satisfaction of attempting to slam the door behind her.

A few seconds later, I'm unzipping my pants in the bathroom. Exhilaration pings through me, and I'm so fucking hard it hurts. I enjoy it far too much when she talks back to me. Seeing the anger snapping in her eyes makes me desperate to bend her over the nearest desk and remind her how much she'd loved having my dick in her.

I bare my teeth in a smile as I stroke myself. Because she *is* honest, and she was very careful not to say what—or *who*—she'd be thinking about. Which tells me everything I need to know.

The mental image of Delilah playing with her tight little pussy while she thinks about me is the only thing running through my head as I groan out my release a few hard strokes later.

"HOW'S THE PROJECT GOING?" Tate asks.

"It's moving along. We're almost ready to sign off on several preliminary designs." It's late at night and Tate, myself, and Roman are probably the last people in the building. Roman is still in his office, but Tate and I encountered each other on the way to the elevator, so we're heading down to our cars together.

"How's marketing?" I ask.

He shrugs his shoulders and scowls. "We're doing our best to offset any new press about Dad's arrest by replacing it with everything positive we're doing, but it's an uphill battle."

I frown at him. "Why is that?"

"The press is more interested in our private lives than what the company is doing. At yesterday's interview, the woman spent more time asking me about my reputation than our current projects and the effort we're putting into making our developments more sustainable."

"What did you do?"

"Took her into the bathroom and fucked her."

I shake my head. "That's not helpful, Tate." I don't know what the hell we were thinking, putting him in charge of marketing. All we've done is give him access to more women who are obsessed with finding out if the youngest King brother is as kinky in the bedroom as he's rumored to be.

We exit the elevator and make our way out the front. Our cars are waiting there for us, and I nod a farewell at Tate and climb into the back of mine. While my driver, Jonathan, waits for a gap in the traffic, I look out the window, my gaze caught by a familiar couple standing on the corner—Paul and Philippa.

I narrow my eyes as I watch them. They seem to be arguing. Philippa gestures wildly while Paul rubs his hand over his face and attempts to respond. Then he grimaces as if he's frustrated, tucks a strand of hair behind her ear, and wraps her in his arms.

Well, fucking, well. Looks like my senses are on point. The guy is an asshole.

I don't get to see anything else as Jonathan accelerates away from the curb, obscuring the couple from view. But I don't need to see anything else. It might not have been a kiss, but there was far more intimacy in that interaction than there should be between colleagues.

My mind jumps to Delilah, and I rub my thumb across my lower lip. Despite what I said in my office, her relationship with Paul is none of my business. There's no reason for me to insert myself into the situation. Yet, the fact that Paul is screwing her around sends a surge of anger through me. I'd bet anything he started fucking Philippa when he broke up with her—if not before. He probably regretted it soon after because compared to Delilah, Philippa comes across as a cold fish. So either Philippa doesn't want to let go, and he's too weak to make her, or he's stupid enough to believe he can juggle both women without getting caught.

I lean back in my leather seat. As much as Delilah deserves to know, and as much as having Paul out of the picture would give me incredible satisfaction—and I'm not thinking about why that is—telling her won't end well for anyone. She'll just have to open her eyes and see the man for who he is.

I try to turn my thoughts elsewhere. After all, I have far more important things to worry about than the relationship of a woman I screwed once, even if she does work for me now.

And yet, it's the flash of fire in Delilah's beautiful green eyes I see as I stare out the window, not the lights of passing cars.

CHAPTER TWELVE

DELILAH

"Why are we doing this again?" I ask Alex as our Uber pulls up in front of the club. A long line of people snakes its way down the block. Not surprising, considering the hype behind this place. Tonight is its grand opening, but it's already being touted as the next big hotspot —where the rich, famous, and beautiful will go to be seen.

"Because you've been working hard for weeks, first on your proposal, and now on the project, and you need a break. We both do."

I pat her knee sympathetically. Things have been a bit rough for her since Jaxson left for LA. She's been struggling with the temporary separation. She's even started teaching interior design classes at a community center a few evenings a week to keep herself distracted. I guess a night out on the town will do us both good.

After paying the driver, we climb out. I smooth down my sparkly green minidress, the one Alex says matches the color of my eyes. With bare legs and a pair of strappy nude stilettos, I feel sexy tonight. Alex is wearing black skintight leather pants and a red halter top, and she looks amazing.

I smile as I take in the bright lights and all the dressed-up people. As someone who wasn't exactly a party girl during my high school and college years, the novelty of going out like this is still fresh and exciting.

Although the line to get in is long, we don't have to join it. Jaxson has somehow gotten our names on the list because of his connections in the music scene. After Alex talks to the bouncer, he unhooks the red rope and we're ushered straight in.

My eyes widen as we enter the two-story club. A circular bar stands in the middle of the large open space. Tables and booths with plush velvet seating line the outer wall, and there's a crowded dance floor with a raised stage at one end for live performances. A second level with a balcony allows people to watch those mingling and dancing below.

My gaze catches on the mountain-sized, black-suited man standing at the bottom of a staircase across the room. I guess that's where the VIP section is.

"Drink first?" Alex asks, and I nod. I'm looking forward to having a couple of cocktails and doing some dancing. The last few weeks have been both exhilarating and tense because of my interactions with Cole. I want to let go and relax.

Once we have our drinks in hand, we make our way to the outer edge of the club and score a booth when a group of people leaves. A sigh gusts out of me as I sink into the plush red velvet seat.

"It feels as if you and I haven't had a chance to catch up in ages," I say. Even though Alex and I live together, the two of us have been like ships passing in the night for the last few weeks. With Alex spending her evenings teaching at the community center, and me alternating between doing long hours at work and attempting to have more quality time with Paul, it's been a while since we've had time to hang out.

Alex takes a long sip of her drink, then grins. "Tell me about it. And I haven't even had a chance to ask how things are going with you know who."

I raise my brows. "Paul?"

Alex snorts. "Your sexy, virginity-stealing boss."

Even though there's no way anyone around us can hear what she's saying, I wince. "Please don't refer to him that way. How about my arrogant asshole boss? That works."

Alex laughs. "I mean, it's all accurate, right? And I've seen photos of him. He's definitely sexy, despite being an arrogant asshole. Maybe even more sexy because of it."

I roll my eyes and shake my head. "Believe me, there's nothing sexy about being accused of trying to sleep your way into a job—which he's never apologized for, by the way—and having your memory of the night you lost your virginity cheapened. Not to mention him asking whether I think of him when I masturbate. In the middle of his office."

"What?" Alex leans forward, an avaricious expression on her face. "You didn't tell me about that."

I fill her in on what had happened with Cole earlier this week. When I finish, she sits back in her seat, her brow furrowed. "That's unprofessional."

"Tell me about it."

"He doesn't really strike me as the type to do that kind of thing. Which makes me think you've gotten under his skin."

I sip my cocktail. "I doubt it. I'm pretty sure he dislikes me as much as I dislike him."

"Mmm. You know what they say about love and hate. It's a fine line, baby."

"I'm not sure he's the kind of man who feels love."

She smirks. "Lust, then."

"He's a billionaire that can have his pick of any number of gorgeous women, and you think he's secretly lusting after me?"

"Didn't he admit that he's been jerking off because of you?"

I scoff. "I'm sure he was just playing mind games with me. He wanted to get in my head."

She taps her finger against her pursed lips. "What if he's one of those guys who assumes by taking your virginity, he's claimed you as his?"

I let out a laugh. "I very much doubt it. He was obviously unimpressed when I turned up in his building. Not exactly the behavior of someone who thinks I belong to him."

"Okay, then maybe seeing you with Paul has his competitive drive running at full speed."

"That's the most likely scenario out of a series of unlikely scenarios, but personally, I think he's just a sadistic bastard who likes to make people squirm."

She waggles her eyebrows. "I'm sure he'd like to make you squirm."

I shake my head, suppressing my smile. "Okay, enough about my bosshole. How are things with Jaxson?"

Her mouth pulls down in a frown. "It's been harder than I expected, being away from him." She looks down at her left hand, where she's fiddling with her engagement ring. "It seems like every time I call, he's out partying with the guys. I mean, I know it's part of the lifestyle, but it's not exactly easy being the one left behind."

After putting down my drink, I slide closer to her in the booth and give her a hug. "I'm sorry it's been hard for you, but I bet he's missing you lots. Hey, how about we take a selfie now and send it to him so he can see it's not just him going out and living it up?"

Alex grins. "Good idea." She holds her phone and we smile for the photo. Then she taps away, composing her message, and I take the opportunity to do some people watching.

The dance floor is packed, and the rhythmic beat of the music has my body itching to get out there and let loose. I look up at the second-floor balconies and see quite a few people looking over the crowd. Then my eyes drop and catch on the VIP entrance.

A familiar form snags my attention, and I squint to see better. No, it can't be. Surely Cole wouldn't deign to bring himself to a nightclub. But as he turns to talk to the man behind him, I know it's him for sure. He's with a couple of other men, and a bevy of beautiful women jostles to stand next to them.

I sink down in my seat, hoping he doesn't glance over. Although, even if he does, I'm sure his icy gaze will pass right over me without a second thought.

"What are you doing?" Alex asks, amusement threading her voice.

"It's him," I whisper-shout over the loud music.

"Who?" She scans the surrounding area.

"*Him*. About to go up to the VIP section."

She peers in that direction, and a grin stretches across her face the moment she spots him. "Oh, this is perfect."

"Why is it perfect? I'm here to relax and forget about work and him. Isn't that what you're always telling me to do?"

"No, you're here to have fun. And what's more fun than seeing your ex—"

"He's not my ex."

"Your ex-*hook-up* when you look like a million dollars and are bound to have men vying to dance with you?"

"No one's going to be vying to dance with me. And I doubt Cole will even notice me in this sea of people. Particularly not when he's surrounded by what looks like a bunch of supermodels."

"*You* noticed *him*, didn't you? And you underestimate how hot you are, Dee. Anyway, you're right. Cole King can have his supermodels. Tonight is about you letting go and living a little. So, come on. We're both looking as sexy as fuck. Finish your drink and let's get out on the dance floor and enjoy ourselves."

I really do want to dance. Cole will be up there with his women and his friends, completely self-absorbed, and will never know I'm here. Why not forget about him and have fun?

I down the rest of my drink, scoot from the booth, and hold out my hand for Alex. We wind our way through the tables and people until we reach the dance floor.

Turns out Alex was right. We soon have a bunch of guys dancing around us. And she's right about something else, too. When I imagine a pair of icy blue eyes looking down from above, I smile and sway my hips even harder.

After all, pretending never hurt anyone.

CHAPTER THIRTEEN

COLE

"When was the last time the three of us were out together?" Tate asks, raising his voice to be heard over the pounding beat.

I swirl the whiskey in my glass. "It's been a while."

While Tate often attends our club openings, I only do occasionally, and Roman rarely ever does. I'm sure he considers it beneath him to fraternize with the commoners, let alone his brothers.

But putting on a united front is more important than ever now, which is why we're all making an appearance at the opening of one of our recent investments. I have no clue if Roman's enjoying himself or not. He reclines in his chair, drinking top-shelf whiskey, his cool gaze scanning the crowd while a hot blonde chatters in his ear about something I'm sure he doesn't give a fuck about.

Even with the dim lighting in the VIP section, I can see shadows under his eyes. For the first time, I feel a pang of sympathy for him. It can't be easy, helming a vessel as large as ours while trying to stop all the rats from jumping ship.

Crystal, the woman who plastered herself to my side as

soon as we arrived, puts her hand on my thigh and squeezes. "Would you like to dance?"

"No thanks," I say, barely glancing in her direction.

Her hand trails further up. "How about after this, you show me your penthouse?"

This time I look at her. I run my gaze from her silky blonde hair to her plump tits and small waist. She's a knock-out. I could do far worse than take her to bed tonight. If I do, it won't be to my apartment, though. It'll be to the hotel.

I give her a lazy smile but don't confirm either way.

"How's Jessica?" Roman asks me out of the blue.

I frown. "Jessica? I'm sure she's fine. It's been a couple of weeks since I saw her. Why?"

"Just wondering if she's said anything about her father."

"He isn't our normal topic of conversation when we're together. Is there something I should know?"

Roman shakes his head, then without saying anything more, he stands and strides to the bar.

Tate and I share a look. Roman has always been the more serious brother. Even when we were kids. Now he's practically unreadable.

A dark-haired woman drapes herself over Tate. "You want to dance, sexy?"

Tate runs his hand up the length of her thigh, his fingers disappearing beneath the hemline of her short dress. She gasps and then giggles. His hand reappears and he stands, pulling her up and tugging her to the small VIP dance floor.

Sitting alone, and now the sole focus of the remaining women, I start to get irritated. After finishing my drink, I stand as well, telling my blonde companion that I'm going to the men's room. When she offers to come with me, I shake my head. I'm not in the mood for bathroom sex tonight. Even if the bathrooms here are first rate.

Thinking of bathroom sex makes me think about Delilah. I remember when I first met her. Before we'd even spoken more than a few words, I'd imagined taking her to the bar's bathroom and fucking her. It had been a strangely compelling urge. With her breasts spilling over the top of that little black dress and the way she shivered as she drank the whiskey, the idea of sinking my dick into her had overtaken my brain.

Considering she was a virgin, I'm glad I didn't make that suggestion.

The crowd of women has grown in the last few minutes, so I don't return to our table after using the men's room. I wander to the balcony overlooking the dance floor instead.

I lean against the railing, watching the writhing masses below, wondering if Tate will care whether I leave and take blondie with me. I'm just about to return to the group and make my excuses when a woman wearing a shimmery green dress draws my focus. Her dark hair swirls around her shoulders as she moves her hips to the pounding beat. For some reason, I can't look away.

Men hover around her and her friend in a hopeful swarm, and I narrow my gaze on her. Would they come up here if I send someone to invite them? It's only when she throws her head back and raises her arms in the air as she dances that I recognize her.

I straighten.

What are the fucking odds?

My hands grip the railing as one of the men moves closer to her. I scan the area for Paul, but I don't see him. Either he's not dancing or he didn't come with her. Or perhaps she found out about Philippa and dumped him.

The man sidles closer, his gyrating hips almost brushing against her ass, and a burst of aggravation has me clenching my teeth. I wonder how she'll react if he makes contact. If she's broken up with Paul, she might welcome his touch.

My eyes fix on the man as, growing braver, he slides up behind her and wraps his arm around her waist. Delilah jerks away from him and spins around. With a shake of her head, she moves away, but the guy doesn't seem to get the message, following her as she tries to avoid him. Delilah's friend looks like she's about to intercede, but I'm already on the move. I'm down the stairs and stalking toward them.

Shoving my way through the crowd, I spot Delilah and her friend facing the man, who's now wearing a scowl. Guess this asshole isn't a fan of rejection.

With one stride, I'm in his face, bending down to growl in his ear. "I suggest you leave these ladies alone or security will be escorting you from these premises."

He steps back. "Who the fuck are you?"

I tower over him, so he's ballsy, I'll give him that. "The owner. So if you don't want to find yourself permanently banned, I suggest you leave. Now."

With a sneer in Delilah's direction—which has me contemplating throwing him out anyway—he disappears into the crowd.

I turn to face her, taking in her wide eyes and flushed cheeks.

When she doesn't say anything, her friend steps in. "You're the new boss, I presume?"

I spare her a glance, noting the slight curve to her lips. "Temporarily."

Finally Delilah speaks. "You didn't need to intervene. I had it handled." There's a stubborn tilt to her chin.

"I'm sure you did, but this is my club and we don't tolerate harassment."

"And I guess all cases of harassment get personal attention from the owner?" She's had a bit to drink, otherwise I don't think she'd be talking to me like this. Or maybe she would. All I know is that her attitude gets my blood boiling.

And my dick hard.

"I need to talk to you, Miss West," I say through gritted teeth.

She tosses her hair. "I'm dancing."

"I'm not asking."

"What was that you were just saying about harassment?"

"This isn't harassment. I'm your boss."

"Not after hours."

She's so defiant. I want to fuck it out of her. "If you were at home and I called you to discuss the project, you wouldn't answer? Are you telling me you're not willing to put in the extra hours?"

She gives me a dirty look. "Fine."

She turns and walks toward the edge of the dance floor, but I wrap my hand around her arm and guide her the other way, further into the mass of dancers.

When we get to a dark corner, I turn her to face me, moving closer until she's backed against the wall.

"Did you know I'd be here tonight?" I ask.

Her mouth falls open. "You have got to be kidding me. Do you still think I'm stalking you? I didn't know this was one of your clubs. I didn't even know you owned clubs."

The glittering strobe lights reflect in her eyes, distracting me from her reply, and we stare at each other for a heartbeat that seems to last too long. Then she wets her lips. "What do you want to talk to me about, Cole?"

"You know, your attitude leaves a lot to be desired," I say.

"So does yours."

I move closer, tipping my head toward hers and enjoying the way her eyes flare and her pulse flutters in her throat.

"What attitude is that?"

"Constantly accusing me of trying to manipulate you. And never saying you're sorry."

"You want an apology?"

Her chin tips up. "It would help."

"Why?"

She blinks at me. "Because . . . you're wrong. And because . . ." Her gaze dips, then rises to meet mine. "Because you hurt me." Emotion threads through her voice.

I brush my thumb over her cheek, then press it to the tender skin under her ear as I slide my fingers around the nape of her neck. "How did I hurt you?"

Her eyes dart between mine. "Does it matter?"

"Yes." And strangely enough, it does.

She releases a ragged breath. "That night we spent together might not have meant anything to you, but . . . it did to me. I was happy that you were the one I had my first time with. I thought I was lucky to have been with someone who made it so good for me. And then . . . then we met again and you accused me of trying to use you, and you ruined it all. You made me regret something that I'd held close to my heart."

What she's saying shouldn't bother me. I'm sure it isn't the first time I've hurt a woman's feelings. But they usually don't tell me. If they did, I couldn't guarantee I'd care. In the sphere I live in, admitting to being hurt is admitting to weakness. No one operating at our level will admit to that.

So why does the vulnerability in Delilah's eyes trigger a tightness in my chest? Why does knowing she regrets our time together make me want to strip her down and give her a new memory to hold on to?

My dick throbs behind my fly, and all I want to do is press her against the wall, slide my hand under the little dress she's wearing, and thrust my fingers into her. Make her pant and writhe and come for me, right here in the club, in front of everyone.

Make her feel good again.

The urge is so strong, I have to curl my free hand into a fist to stop myself from touching her. Instead of walking away, which is what I should do, I grasp a tendril of her hair, curling the silky lock around my finger.

"Where's Paul tonight?" I ask.

She stiffens, as if I've reminded her she shouldn't stand this close to a man who isn't her boyfriend. "He was too tired to come out. He wanted to have an early night."

The memory of Paul with his arms around Philippa flashes through my mind. I'd bet my Bugatti he's balls deep in the blonde woman, not having an early night at home. Though why any man would want to be with that ice queen instead of the woman standing in front of me is beyond me.

Paul's stupidity is irrelevant, though. I've already decided not to interfere with their relationship, regardless of how much I'm craving another taste of her. Risking the project by indulging in my desire would be stupid, and that's not something anyone's ever accused me of being.

So why the hell do I lean forward, pinch her chin between my thumb and forefinger, and tip her face toward mine? "I very much doubt Paul is having a quiet night at home."

Delilah jerks away from my hold and glares at me. "I don't know what game you're playing, but you don't know what you're talking about. Why don't you go back to your supermodels and leave me alone?"

Irritation rips through my veins, and I step back. "If you want to be willfully blind, that's your choice. It's nothing to me. As you said, I've got better things to do than care about whether my employees are being taken advantage of by their boyfriends. Crystal has already told me she's more than happy to bounce on my dick for the rest of the night. I think I'll take her up on her offer. Have a good night, Delilah. I hope you enjoy the club."

I turn and stride off, annoyed that I let her get to me. If she wants to place her trust in Paul, that's her choice.

I return to the VIP section and drop into my seat. Roman has disappeared somewhere, probably back to the office. Tate has his dance partner pressed against a wall. It's a little too reminiscent of how I just had Delilah.

A waitress brings another glass of whiskey and I take it from her, downing half of it in one go, relishing the fiery burn in my throat. Crystal appears by my side and flings herself onto my lap, grinding on my still-half-hard dick.

"Mmm," she purrs. "Feels like you're ready to take me back to your place."

I run my eyes over the breasts spilling from her dress and imagine peeling the material down so I can suck her nipples while she rides me. I'd been considering taking her back to the hotel before. The picture I'm painting in my mind should seal the deal.

Infuriatingly, the image in my head morphs—blonde hair to brunette, blue eyes to green. And it's Delilah riding me. Delilah throwing her head back and gasping my name as she clamps down on my cock and milks my orgasm out of me.

My half-hard erection, that remained unmoved during

Crystal's gyrations and my thoughts of fucking her, swells and jerks under her ass.

Crystal rolls her hips, thinking it's for her, but any interest I had in sleeping with her, if I ever really had any in the first place, has died. The desire to relive my night with Delilah has overtaken my thoughts. She's off limits, though. Not to mention she hates me. Maybe I just need a good fuck to reset my brain, remind me that sex is sex, and it feels damn fantastic no matter which woman it's with.

My eyes drop to Crystal's curves again, and I cup one of her breasts, flexing my fingers and making her moan. It's a sound worthy of a porn star, and I've barely done anything. It irritates me, particularly when my memory taunts me by replaying Delilah's breathless gasps and needy whimpers as I took her for the first time.

I drop my hand and reach for my drink again, my attention drawn to Tate as he leads the woman toward the private VIP bathrooms.

I throw back the rest of my whiskey and lift Crystal off of me, ignoring her confused frown. "Not tonight."

She scowls for only a split second before a fake smile fixes in place. "Another time, then."

She sashays away, and I let my head drop back against the seat. Shit, looks like I'm going home alone tonight.

...nstri...
...at him.

...ning deeply to ho...

They're facing away f...
Philippa on her hands and kne...
slapping rhythmically against h...
gasping like his dick is the best t...
her. All I can think is that she's ob...
dick in her.

That thought is enough to pus...
sting my eyes. I stiffen my spine, ...
throw my keys at the back of Paul's h...
any more of my time and energy on him...
won't give Philippa the satisfaction of...
while she sits there and watches with a sm...
face. As far as I'm concerned, the two of them...
to each other.

I return to the living room. Looking aroun...
white-marble-topped coffee table. The one whe...
wineglasses sit. There's also a small clutch tucked...
corner of the couch. I pick it up, rummage around, a...
what I'm looking for—a tube of lipstick. I uncap ...
scrawl a big, red Fuck You over the table, which give...
more satisfaction than I expect. Then I take his apartm...
key off my chain, drop it between the two wineglasses, gr...
my nice leather jacket that I'd left here last time I stayed th...
night, and walk out.

I'm not quiet when I close the front door behind me.
Even if he hears it, I'll be gone by the time he figures out
what's happened. It's only when I hit the foyer that my
hands begin to shake.

111

CHAPTER FOURTEEN

DELILAH

I scan the crowd for Alex. When I spot her at the bar, I rush over. "Hey, do you mind if we leave?"

Her brows draw together. "Are you okay?" She scans the surrounding area. "Did he do someth—"

Things blur a little as I shake my head. Maybe I drank more than I thought tonight. Regardless, my head is all mixed up after what just happened with Cole.

What *had* just happened with Cole?

I don't know, but any buzz I was feeling has gone, and knowing he's upstairs in the VIP section, ready to screw whatever model he was talking about, makes me want to get as far from here as possible. Not that I want to be the one he's screwing. I've got a boyfriend, after all. I just don't want to have the image of the two of them together in my head. "I'm not feeling it anymore. Do you mind?"

"Of course not. Let's get out of here."

We head toward the door, and I refuse to look up at the second floor. After we fight our way through the stream of people entering the club, Alex calls for a ride. A few

minutes later, after fillir
down with Cole, we're he

I should feel relieved,
around my head. Why we
Paul? Was he trying to mess
might know something I a
through my stomach.

As much as I hate to lend cr
stop the suspicion from taking ove.

I turn to Alex. "Do you mind i
for a minute?"

She studies me with her dark eyes,

I give the driver the new address,
my seat. I'm sure Cole is just full of shit
genuinely tired when he called from his
he wouldn't be coming tonight. Surely he w
me. Not after just getting back together.

My nerves are shot by the time we pu
Paul's building. After assuring Alex I'll only b
minutes, I climb out of the car and use the key he
to enter instead of ringing the buzzer.

I run up the single flight of stairs, my pulse pou
my ears. I don't know how I'll explain myself when
in on him unannounced. In fact, considering how la
he's probably already asleep. I reassure myself with
thought as I quietly turn the key in the lock and swing
door open.

The lights are on in the living room, but there's no or
there. I tiptoe through the room, and my heart stalls at the
sight of two wineglasses sitting on the table.

A pit forms in my stomach. Already knowing what I'll
see, but unable to stop myself, I make my way to the
bedroom. The sounds emanating from the slightly ajar door

I run back to the car and slide in next to Alex, trying
steady my racing pulse.

"What's wrong?" she asks, automatically putting her
arms around me as the driver shifts the car into gear and
pulls away from the curb.

"Paul was there with Philippa. H-He was screwing
her." Hurt starts to break through my veneer of anger.

"That fucking asshole," Alex seethes, voice dripping
venom. "Just let me go back there and rip his balls from his
body."

I let out a wobbly laugh. "He's not worth it. He's a piece
of shit. I just can't believe I didn't see it. I even gave him a
second chance. I feel like such a fool."

She brushes a few strands of hair away from my cheek.
"You trusted him."

I nod, and she rubs her hand up and down my back.
"What did you say? What did he say?"

"They didn't see me. He was fucking her doggy style
with his back to me." Bile rises into my throat at the thought
of the nights I've slept in that bed. How many times has he
screwed her there?

"So he doesn't know you know?"

"I left a pretty clear message."

I tell her what I did, and she shakes her head and
laughs. "You've got more restraint than me. I would have
thrown something at the back of his head."

"Believe me, I considered it." A new emotion joins the
anger and hurt. Humiliation. Cole had known. Or at least
strongly suspected. Which means he's seen things I haven't.
How many other people know? The whole team? Am I the
laughingstock of the office?

The car drops us off and I march for the door. I fumble

while trying to get the key in the lock, so Alex gently takes it from me and lets us in.

I drop my purse on the table. "I'm going to take a shower."

"I'm sorry, Dee. I really am." Alex gives me a long hug.

I let out a ragged breath. "You never liked him."

"Because I didn't think he was good enough for you," she says, pushing my hair away from my face.

I nod, hating that tears continue to burn the backs of my eyes every time I think back to what I saw. Also hating that my mind keeps going to Cole and the fact that he knew. That he practically spelled it out for me, and I told him he didn't know what he was talking about.

I turn the shower on as hot as I can bear and let it cascade over me. Paul hasn't called, which either means he hasn't seen my message yet or he has and is too chicken shit to talk to me.

A sudden rush of nausea hits me. How the hell can I face him and Philippa on Monday with the image of what I saw running through my head? How can I walk into our weekly meeting and look Cole in the eye?

And why do I keep thinking about Cole?

I turn off the shower and dress in my pajamas. I'm just coming out of the bathroom when the door buzzer sounds. The air evacuates my lungs, and I stand frozen.

"Dee, it's him," Alex calls. "What should I do? If you want, I can go down and give him hell."

As tempting as it might be to curl up on the couch and let her rip him a new one—something the glitter in her eyes tells me she'd enjoy far too much—this is something I need to do myself.

I march to the living room and snatch up the intercom. I

don't say anything. He'll have heard me pick up and know someone's listening.

"Delilah? Is that you?"

"Yes." It's all I give him.

"Delilah, baby, please let me up so we can talk."

My hand tightens around the handset. "No thank you. I'd prefer you don't step foot in this apartment again."

"Well, can you come down here? I really need to talk to you."

"I won't be coming down. If you have something to say, you can say it like this."

He lets out a heavy sigh. "I'm so sorry, baby. I don't know what you saw, but you have to know that I care about you so much. I would never want to hurt you. What happened tonight was just a lapse in judgment. That's all. And if you'll forgive me, I promise it will never happen again. Just . . . Just come down so I can see you."

Anger is a hard stone in my chest. "You can't be serious. A lapse in judgment? I saw you fucking her, Paul. And not just a random woman, someone I have to work with. How could you do that?"

"Baby, please—"

"Don't call me baby. You don't have the right anymore. Plus I never liked it."

"Delilah—"

"You know what? I've heard enough. You disrespected me in the vilest way possible, and I have nothing more to say to you. At work, I'll appreciate it if you limit our interactions to only those necessary for the completion of this project. And tell Philippa to stay the hell away from me."

I hang up and Alex immediately wraps her arms around me, holding me as the tears I've been holding back finally spill over—more from anger and humiliation than heartbreak. "You'll be all right. It hurts now, I know, but you'll get over it and find someone so much better. I promise."

I nod, even as tears continue to drip down my face.

I'll take this moment to cry and let out all my hurt and disappointment and anger. And then on Monday, I'll go to work with my head held high.

I CHECK the time on my computer screen, then take a deep breath, pick up my phone, and connect to Cole's PA line.

"Cole King's office," Samson answers.

"Hi. It's Delilah West from the architectural team. I was wondering if I could get a quick meeting with Mr. King sometime today?"

"Hold on for a second." The faint clicking of keys makes its way across the line. "He has fifteen minutes available this afternoon at one o'clock. Does that work?"

"Yes, that's fine. Thank you."

I lower the receiver and clench my fists. I do not want to do this. I really don't. But I will.

This morning, I'd done what I promised myself. I walked into the office with my head high, even though my stomach was in knots. Paul was waiting by my desk, and the anger that surged through me at the sight of his face took my breath away.

"Delilah—" he started, reaching for me.

I jerked back. "Don't touch me."

His hand dropped, but he kept talking. Repeating the same things he said to me Friday night.

And I gave him exactly the same answer.

Eventually realizing I wasn't going to change my mind, he sighed heavily and walked away.

I'd sunk into my seat, shaking, and tried to take my mind off him by throwing myself into my work, but I kept flashing back to Friday night at the club. I kept remembering Cole leaning into me, telling me about Paul, and then what I'd said to him after.

That's when I picked up the phone and made the appointment to see him.

And that's why I'm sitting outside his office now, my pulse racing.

"You can go in," Samson says.

With a deep breath, I stand and smooth my skirt, then knock.

"Come in."

I enter and close the heavy wooden door behind me. Cole is sitting at his desk, leaning back in his chair. I swallow hard, taking in the breadth of the shoulders encased within his impeccably tailored suit jacket. His icy blue eyes bore into me, and a little shiver works its way down my back.

"I wasn't expecting to see you today, Miss West. To what do I owe this pleasure?"

I take a few steps closer and clasp my hands in front of me. "I want to apologize, and . . ." I inhale a shaky breath. "To thank you."

His dark brows arch high, and he leans forward, resting his elbows on his desk. "For what?"

"You were right about Paul."

He stares at me for a moment, then stands and walks to the front of his desk. "And what was I right about?"

Taking a deep breath, I steady myself. "After we left the

club on Friday night, I stopped by his apartment. He wasn't alone." There's no need to say more.

Something flickers across his face. "I can't say I'm surprised. But I am sorry."

I suck my bottom lip between my teeth and nod. With his unreadable expression, it's hard to tell how sincere he is.

He paces forward, stopping when he's close enough to tip my chin. There's a faint line between his brows. "Are you okay?"

My mouth opens, but nothing comes out. I don't know how to answer that question. I'm hurt and angry and humiliated, but I don't want to talk to Cole about it. "I-I'm fine."

He searches my face, then abruptly walks back to his desk, reaches across it, and presses his intercom.

"Yes, sir?" Samson answers.

"Please call Paul from the Elite team and ask him to come to my office immediately."

"Of course, Mr. King."

My eyes widen as I watch him. Why is he having Paul come in?

"And Samson," he continues, "don't notify me when he arrives. I'll let you know when I'm ready for him."

"Yes, sir."

"Why do you want to speak to Paul?" I ask as soon as he disconnects.

Cole regards me steadily. "He's causing problems on my team."

I shake my head. "This is a personal matter. I didn't come here to get you to fix this for me."

"I'm not fixing anything."

I frown.

"I told you. I don't appreciate people messing with my

projects, and if Paul is messing with you, he's messing with my project."

My shoulders sag a little. Of course his concern is for the project, not me. I don't know why I would have imagined otherwise.

He moves closer again. "You know you deserve a better man than him," he says.

I square my shoulders and raise my chin. "I know."

"You would never have been happy with him in the long run."

"I know." It comes out a little quieter and more shakily this time as I stare up at him, my heart pounding in my chest.

He takes one more step, and now I have to tilt back my head to meet his gaze. His eyes sweep over my face, and the woodsy, masculine scent of his aftershave takes me right back to the night we spent together. That's a dangerous memory to dredge up right now.

I lick my lips, and he focuses on them. I remember what it felt like to have his mouth on mine. I remember his hands against my skin, his fingers inside me, and my body pulses with sudden need.

Cole grips my chin between his thumb and forefinger. "You would never have been satisfied with him."

I say nothing, frozen as I stare up at him. The heat rolling off his body warms me.

His thumb drags over my lower lip. "Did he make you come like I did, Delilah?" The rasp in his voice causes my nipples to pebble.

I don't answer.

"Did you cry out for him, beg him to fill you again and again? Did you writhe and moan for him?"

The imagery is too vivid, affecting me too much. I can't

let him get to me. I can't let myself fall under his spell. It won't end well for me.

But I hesitate, even though I know it's a bad idea, because he smells so good and I remember how incredible he made me feel.

He senses my weakness, a smile curving his seductive lips.

Then he takes one more step.

CHAPTER FIFTEEN

COLE

I back her against the door, looming over her and bracing my hands on either side of her head.

She tilts her face toward mine, eyes flashing. "What do you want, Cole?"

"You know what I want."

She exhales shakily. "Why?"

"Why what?"

"Why do you want that from me? You have your choice of women. Why risk our professional relationship for this?"

I lower my head, my nose grazing against her cheek until I reach her ear. "Because I want another taste. I want to see if you'll come as sweetly for me now as you did then."

Her breath hitches, and I turn so my lips brush against the soft skin of her cheek. "Just think. By now, Paul will be up here, right outside this door. He'll be sitting out there waiting patiently for me while I'm making you come. If that isn't revenge, I don't know what is."

"I'm not having sex with you in your office." There's far less conviction in that statement than she probably thinks.

My lips travel down until they're hovering just over hers. "I'm not offering to have sex with you in my office."

"Then what—"

"I'm not going to fuck you, but I am going to make you feel good. You only have to trust me and keep quiet like the good girl you showed me you are the night we met. Can you do that?"

I'm almost sure she'll turn me down, but I hold my breath as I wait.

A few seconds pass before she says, "I can do that."

Fuck yes.

I'm being reckless. I know that. But I don't care. Right now, I'm not thinking about anything but Delilah and making her come. I'm not thinking about my father and what he did. I'm not thinking about the investors doubting what my brothers and I can achieve.

She's the only thing on my mind.

I reach down with one hand and run it up her thigh, snagging the hem of her skirt and dragging it up to her ass. Pulling back, I watch her face as I brush my fingers over her panties. Her lips part and her eyes go glassy. My thumb finds a damp spot and when I press against it, her hips twitch and a whispered moan drops from her lips. Triumph rockets through me. She's wet. She's standing in my office with wet panties.

The need to pull out my cock and sink into her is so strong my pulse pounds with it. But that can't happen. This is all I'll allow myself. One more momentary taste of her.

I ease my hand underneath the silky material, my knuckles brushing over the smooth, soft skin of her pussy.

"Cole," she breathes, and I bare my teeth at her in a smile which probably looks more than a little feral.

Pressing deeper, I slide into her slick heat, and my

mouth goes dry as I anticipate replacing my fingers with my mouth. The flutter at the base of Delilah's neck steals my gaze. I want to press my lips against it, scrape my teeth along her throat, suck the delicate skin until it leaves a mark so that when I send her back out, Paul will know exactly what happened in here.

But I won't because it makes no sense. I couldn't give a fuck about Paul and his screw ups, except that it allows me to do this again. I don't have a fucking clue where the desire to mark her comes from.

Shaking the thought away, I press my thumb against her clit, then slide my finger deeper before pulling it out and repeating the process.

She moans, and I nearly do too. I'd forgotten just how tight she is, her body wrapping snugly around my fingers thrusting inside her.

Delilah's hips begin to move in rhythm with my hand. Her lids are half-closed, lips parted as she watches me watch her. "More, Cole. Please."

If she thinks finger fucking her to orgasm is my end goal right now, she's mistaken. She lets out a little cry when I pull my hand out of her panties, her wide eyes searching mine. A flash of doubt crosses her face, as if she thinks I'm done with her. As if she thinks I'd make promises about making her feel good and then leave her hanging.

She has a lot to learn about me.

I drop to my knees, my fingers hooking in her underwear and pulling them down her thighs as I go.

Her gasp lets me know she isn't expecting it.

"Off," I say, tapping her ankle, and she lifts each foot in turn, stepping out of her panties. I stuff them into my pocket. "Hold your skirt up for me."

Her eyes are dilated, her cheeks flushed. But she does as

she's told, gathering her skirt, shimmying her hips to get the tight material over her ass, and then clutching it at her waist.

She's already glistening with desire, and lust pounds a heavy beat in my blood. My hard dick strains against my fly.

But it will have to wait.

I use my thumbs to part her, my mouth watering as I see how wet she is. Then I lean forward and run my tongue from her entrance to her clit in one long swipe. Her taste almost has my eyes rolling back in my head. She's fucking delicious—like the finest wine. How have I had her in this building for the last month and not done this before?

Then I remember.

Paul.

He's been the one tasting her, making her whimper and tremble. The thought has my shoulders knotting. Not anymore. The asshole screwed up, and now I'm the one with his mouth between her legs.

I alternate sucking and flicking her clit, then slide a finger back into her. Her breaths are coming fast now, but so far, she's kept quiet. That changes when I thrust another finger inside her. Her head falls back against the door. It doesn't rattle, because it's a solid fucking door. But it makes a thump.

I graze her clit with my teeth, then look up at her. "Quiet, Miss West, unless you want the entire office to find out you were in here with my tongue in your pussy."

"Cole!" she gasps, her hands clutching my hair as I go back to licking and thrusting into her. I know she's close when her hips begin rocking against me. "Oh my god, Cole. I'm going to come."

Before she can, I swap, my thumb going to her clit, rolling over that swollen bundle of nerves in a fast rhythm while my tongue spears into her.

Delilah sucks in a sharp breath at the sensation, and the dual stimulation is too much. Her hands tighten in my hair, her pelvis jolts forward, grinding on my face, and then she's coming. She makes little panting moans as her internal muscles spasm around me, and I groan against her slick flesh as I savor the arousal seeping from her.

When she sags back, I swipe my tongue over her one last time, then stand. I bring each finger that was inside her to my mouth and lick them clean, then rub my hand over my lips and chin. I'm not rubbing her off me. I'm rubbing her in. When I lean forward, my mouth hovering over hers, her eyes widen, probably thinking I'm going to kiss her. But I don't. Because that's not what this is about.

At least, that's what I'm telling myself.

Instead, I swipe my tongue against her lips, groaning when hers darts out to follow the trail of mine. "Now when you walk past Paul, you'll have the taste of us on your lips," I growl.

I straighten, stepping back from her. She's a glorious sight. Her cheeks flushed, eyes slightly glazed, skirt still clutched at her waist. I want to bend her over my desk and fuck her. But I close my eyes and breathe deeply to push the urge aside.

"Can I have my panties back?" she asks.

"No."

She stares at me, but instead of arguing, she eases her skirt down her thighs, smoothing out the wrinkles. Then she fusses with her hair a little, avoiding my eyes.

I won't let her get away with that, though. "We seem to be making a habit of revenge."

Her gaze meets mine, and I'm not sure what I see in it. It better not be fucking regret.

"It won't happen again," she says. "I don't want

anything to do with Paul anymore. Not outside of work, anyway."

I nod, satisfied to hear Paul is out of chances. Less satisfied that she's stating this will be the last time I get to touch her. Having had another taste, I'm not sure I'll be happy until I've fucked her again. Completely gotten her out of my system. But we'll cross that bridge when we come to it.

She finishes straightening herself out, and rather than lingering and letting her know that I'm not quite on board with her declaration, I return to my desk.

She watches me with a frown. "Aren't you going to . . . uh, clean up?" Her eyes flick to my mouth, then my hand.

I smirk. "When Paul comes in, I want the hand he shakes to be covered in you."

Her mouth drops open and her cheeks redden even more, but something flashes in her eyes, and I wonder if my little kitten doesn't have a more vengeful side after all. Instead of protesting, she just rolls her bottom lip between her teeth and nods.

Sooner than I expect, she's turning, opening the door, and slipping out. As much as I would love to watch her walk past Paul with no panties on, her face still flushed from her orgasm, that's not how I do things.

Instead, I wait a few minutes, then push the intercom, asking Samson to send Paul in.

When he comes through the door, I'm waiting for him, my hand extended.

I hide a smirk as he shakes it. "Sit down, Paul."

I gesture at the chair in front of my desk. After he sits, I round it to take my seat. Before I say what I need to say, I lick my lips, closing my eyes for a second to savor Delilah's taste. I don't care if it makes me an asshole. After all, it takes one to know one, and I knew Paul was an asshole from the moment I met him.

My silence must be making Paul nervous, because he shifts in his chair and fiddles with his tie. Then he clears his throat. "I'm not quite sure why you called me here today, Cole—" My raised brows make him choke. "Uh, I mean, Mr. King. If you're looking for an update on the project, I don't have anything prepared."

"I'm not after an update from you. Delilah gave me everything I wanted."

If only he knew.

A flash of anger crosses his face at the mention of his ex-girlfriend. I almost lick my lips again, but refrain.

"I've called you here because I've been made aware of something that I believe needs to be addressed."

Paul looks a little confused. "If you have concerns with one of my team—"

"Not one of your team. You."

Surprise twists his face, but he clears it quickly. "Me?"

"Yes. It's come to my attention that you've been having a personal relationship with two of your team members. At the same time."

His lips pinch, and he adjusts his position again. "I'm not sure what Delilah has said to you—"

"Delilah was not the source of my information."

His brow furrows as if he can't imagine any other way I could have found out.

"Uh, okay. Well, whoever passed on this information, that is not the case."

I narrow my gaze and lean back in my chair. Hopefully Paul realizes he's on very shaky ground right now. "That's not the case?"

From the flare of panic in his eyes, he does. "Yes, well.

Not currently. I'm not sure if you're aware or not, but I ended . . . I mean, my relationship with Miss West has ended." Anger burns in my gut. He was going to say he ended his relationship with Delilah, but obviously changed his mind when he remembered I just met with her.

"That may be, but during your time with Miss West, you were also seeing Miss Grant, correct?"

"I'm not sure this is any of your business," he says.

"Ah, but that's where you're wrong, Paul. My company is investing a serious amount of money in this project, and we chose your firm based on your designs and the under-standing that you and your team would behave in a profes-sional manner. My project manager having an affair with not one but two of his team members is a situation that could easily result in significant emotional upheaval and therefore affect the smooth operation of the team. That's one hundred percent my business."

Paul goes white. "Uh, yes, I see your point. Well, the situation has now resolved itself, and I can promise nothing like it will ever happen again."

"I hope not. Because if I hear of you acting unprofes-sionally while contracted to the King Group, I will be forced to reassess your position in the team handling our project."

Part of me wants to do it anyway. To teach him a lesson about screwing with Delilah. But my more logical side real-izes that letting emotions influence my business decisions is ridiculous. Outside of his bad decisions regarding Delilah and Philippa, he's a decent project manager. There is some-thing I can do that won't have as big an impact on the project, though.

I lean forward. "I expect you to organize a replacement liaison for Miss Grant immediately."

Paul stammers. "B-But Elite assigned her to this position. I can't—"

"Yes, you can. Because if you don't arrange it, I will. And I don't think you want your senior partners to receive a call from me. I don't care what you tell them to get the change made, but if it falls to me to do it, I'll tell them exactly what the issue is. I can guarantee that won't end well for you or Miss Grant."

Paul's swallow is almost audible. "I understand, Mr. King. I'll organize it immediately. And you have my promise that I won't do anything to jeopardize the project."

I give him an assessing look and can't resist running my finger across my bottom lip as if I'm considering his words. Really, I'm just enjoying knowing he has no idea that finger was recently buried in Delilah's pussy.

I've had enough. I want him out of my office. Not only because I have no interest in talking to him anymore, but because I need to take care of the throb in my pants.

I nod as if I've made a decision. "Make sure you don't."

Relief drops his shoulders from around his ears, and only when I stare at him silently for a few more seconds does he realize he's been dismissed. He rushes to stand. "Thank you, Mr. King."

As soon as he's gone, I'm out of my chair and heading for my bathroom. Again. This is getting ridiculous. Somehow, I have to get her out of my head so I can concentrate on business. This company is the only thing tying my brothers and me together, and I can't let one little architect, enticing as she may be, distract me from it.

Not bothering to lock the door behind me, I have my fly undone and my cock in my hand within seconds.

I just need to figure out how the hell to do it.

CHAPTER SIXTEEN

DELILAH

For more than one reason, I can't look at Paul as I pass him. What I just did plays over and over in my mind. What I let Cole do to me. In his office. In the building I work in. With Paul sitting outside.

What the hell came over me?

This is not me. I'm the girl who puts her head down and works hard and achieves what she wants to achieve. I'm not the girl who lets her boss go down on her in his office. What is it about Cole that makes me act so out of character?

On shaky legs, I make my way back to my desk. If I thought I couldn't concentrate before, it's nothing compared to how scattered I am now.

Every time someone passes, I jump, imagining it's Paul and he's somehow found out what I did. Not that it's any of his business anymore. Because it's so unlike me, it feels as if any minute now, someone will point their finger at me and accuse me of reprehensible behavior.

But Paul doesn't come. And neither does Cole. Although, why would he? He's playing games with me. With Paul. I don't know why. Maybe he's bored?

The only thing I know is that this job is important to me and I'm on very shaky ground at the moment.

By forcing myself to focus on my CAD model, I make it through to the end of the day. I glimpse Paul around the office, but thankfully he doesn't approach me. I haven't seen Philippa at all, which isn't that unusual since she's only here sometimes. Regardless, it's a relief. When five o'clock hits, I log off, grab my purse, and head out.

After getting home, I get into the shower and wait for the hot water to relax my muscles. As much as I try, I can't stop thinking about what happened in Cole's office. My nipples tighten, my skin sensitizes, and I groan. Why can't I get him out of my mind? Yes, the sex I had with him was far better than anything I had with Paul afterward. And in his office this afternoon . . . Well, that was beyond anything any man has ever done to me.

But he's still a coldhearted, arrogant asshole, even if he knows how to make my body sing.

After drying myself, I dress and head to the kitchen to make dinner. I've eaten, washed up, and am sitting on the couch with my laptop when a key turns in the lock and Alex comes in.

"How was work?" she asks, walking over, bending down, and giving me a hug. "Did you see Paul?"

"He was waiting for me at my desk when I showed up."

She scowls. "The asshole. He was never interested in giving you what you needed."

I throw her a grateful smile. "I told him to leave me alone, and he did."

"So that was the last you saw of him?"

I bite my lip. "Well . . . I saw him outside Cole's office in the afternoon."

Her brows shoot up. "What were you both doing outside Cole's office?"

Heat flares across my cheeks.

"What did you do, Dee?"

"I just went to apologize for what I said to him Friday night, and to thank him for telling me about Paul."

"Okay, so what happened? Obviously, something did. Otherwise your face wouldn't be as red as a tomato."

I cover my face with my hands. "He went down on me. While Paul was outside waiting to meet with him."

I drop my hands to see Alex's mouth hanging open. "Are you serious?"

I nod, not sure whether to laugh or cry.

A huge grin spreads across her face, and she barks out a laugh. "I hate to say it, but I like the guy's style. Paul deserves it, the selfish asshole." Then she notices my face. "What's wrong? You can't tell me you feel bad for him?"

"No. I almost feel bad because I don't feel bad about it."

"Good. I hope you strutted past him on your way out."

My lips twitch up in a smile, but it soon fades. "I think it was the most unprofessional thing I've ever done. I don't know how I'm going to face Cole again."

Alex sits down next to me. "Who instigated it?"

"He did."

Alex nods. "Do you think Cole is wasting any time worrying about whether he acted professionally? Do you think he's sitting at home right now, worrying about facing you tomorrow?"

"Probably not."

"Not a chance in hell, actually. The man's probably jerking off and planning what he'll do to you the next time he gets you in his office."

"There won't be a next time. He even said it was just a revenge thing."

Alex tips her head to the side and smirks. "Ah, my poor, naïve friend. You actually believe Cole went down on you out of the goodness of his heart? Because he's some kind of sexual good Samaritan?"

I snort out a laugh.

"No, my dear. That man's probably been dying to get another taste of you since you walked back into his life."

"You mean after he stopped believing I'd only slept with him to gain an advantage with our proposal?"

"Well, yes, after that. But he obviously wants you. And if I were you, I'd take advantage of it. Next time he gets you alone, tell him you want the full meal, not just the appetizer."

"I honestly don't think that's going to happen. He has access to the most beautiful women in New York. Why would he risk a secret workplace hookup with me?"

"You doubt yourself too much, Dee. And any man who doesn't think you're worth the risk is a fool you don't want to be around anyway." Her voice softens. "Don't let the assholes in this world impact your opinion of yourself, okay?"

I give her a grateful smile, knowing she's not just referring to Paul. A few months after we moved in together, I confided in her about my father—small-town royalty, whose family company owned most of the businesses in town. Mom fell for him, believing he felt the same way about her, until a faulty condom proved otherwise. He walked away, telling her she'd been fun, but he didn't want a kid, especially with someone he was "slumming it" with. Not that Mom said it quite that way, but it wasn't hard to read between the lines.

He rejected her *and* me, then went on to marry a woman from an equally wealthy family and have two sons—half-brothers I doubt even know I exist.

Not that I care about my father. After all, why would I want anything to do with a man who would leave an eighteen-year-old girl to raise his baby all on her own? At least, that's what I told myself when I was growing up. But every now and then, when I saw how tired Mom was and how hard she worked to provide for me, I wondered why he hadn't wanted us.

Alex's voice snaps me back to the present. "I guess we'll just have to wait and see what happens, but I bet Cole will call you to his office first thing tomorrow for a repeat performance."

I shake my head, but Alex just grins and walks away. I look down at the schematic on my screen, but my mind isn't on work right now. Could Alex be right about Cole? And if she is, what exactly will I do about it?

The next day at my desk, my pulse leaps at every email notification, every ring of my phone. I half expect to be summoned to Cole's office, and I'm not sure if I'm dreading it or anticipating it. I get a few emails from Paul, including one letting me know the King Group has nominated our concepts for the H+ Architectural Design Awards, which, even with my current emotional turmoil, has me feeling a swift rush of pride. His correspondence has been completely impersonal and related to the project, so he must have finally accepted that I'm not interested in anything he has to say.

When the end of the day arrives and I haven't heard or seen anything from Cole, a chaotic mix of emotions swirls inside me. Apparently, Alex was wrong. I should be happy about it, so why does disappointment sit like a lead weight in my chest?

That evening, when Alex gets back from teaching her classes, she asks me what happened at the office. When I tell her nothing, her face falls. Then she says he probably doesn't want to appear too eager, and she's sure he'll come looking for me tomorrow.

But she's wrong again.

I don't see him or hear from him all week. By the time our Friday team meeting rolls around, I don't know if I'll even be able to look him in the eye. I'm embarrassed, angry, and—stupidly—hurt. I let Alex's words get to me, and now I'm questioning if that's because a part of me *wants* Cole to want me.

When I walk into the conference room for the meeting, I keep my eyes away from the man sitting at the end of the table, determined to conceal how much his radio silence has bothered me. I sit as far from Paul as I can, noticing Philippa's absence once more—she hasn't been here all week, much to my relief—and open my notebook, pretending to jot notes until he starts the meeting.

My eyes jerk toward him when he finally starts talking, because it's not Cole's voice. The man addressing us is Cole's brother, Tate.

"Good afternoon, everyone. Cole has asked me to take today's meeting since he's unable to attend. We'll proceed the same way you usually do, beginning with a rundown of your individual projects. We'll start with you, uh . . ." He looks down at his notes. "Robert."

I'm distracted while Robert speaks. Where is Cole? Surely he's not avoiding me. I can't imagine a man like Cole would ever stoop to avoiding a woman, especially since he probably hasn't spared a thought for what happened in his office on Monday at all.

I release a quiet breath. I'm thinking about this way too much, which is just a sign that I should never have let that happen. It's messing with my head and making me lose track of my priorities.

By the time Tate gets around to me, I've pulled myself together and I give a clear, concise report. Tate nods, his eyes lingering on me longer than comfortable. I squirm internally under his scrutiny. Is it possible he knows something?

He finally continues, and I breathe a sigh of relief.

I need to put Cole out of my mind. What happened was an aberration, and nothing else is going to happen between us. Alex was wrong, and I'm happy about that because now I can move on and forget it.

After leaving the meeting, I return to my desk and finish the plan I've been working on. I stay a little later to apply finishing touches so I can move to the next one on Monday.

It's dark by the time I finish, and I hurry out of the almost empty office, eager to get home and switch my mind off for the weekend. As I exit the elevator into the foyer, my feet stutter to a stop. Cole and his brothers are standing outside the expansive glass doors, all three of them dressed in tuxedos, obviously preparing to attend some kind of formal event.

A lump forms in my throat, and my resolution to forget what happened comes crashing down. Cole made no effort to see or talk to me this week and he didn't come to our meeting today, but he's available to attend some party or other with his brothers.

I'm such a fool. For all my protestations to Alex—and to myself—I'd convinced myself that Cole's actions meant something when they obviously didn't. For all I know, he puts his tongue in women on a daily basis.

I hover away from the glass doors, waiting for them to leave—too embarrassed to walk out and see him, particularly with his brothers around. A black limo pulls up and the three of them get in. Cole climbs in last, and as he turns, he looks back into the building, his gaze colliding with mine.

I flinch, humiliated he's seen me lurking here, obviously watching him. His eyes bore into me for a second before the driver swings the door shut, severing our connection.

I swallow hard as the big black car pulls away, my cheeks burning and tears pricking the backs of my eyes. This last week has been one of the worst of my life. First Paul and Philippa, then Cole. I just want to go home and pour myself a glass—or several—of wine and forget the last seven days ever happened.

CHAPTER SEVENTEEN

DELILAH

I walk into the office on Monday, refreshed and ready to be productive. After drinking wine with Alex on Friday night, then going out for another night of dancing on Saturday, I'm determined to put everything to do with Paul and Cole behind me.

When my phone rings midmorning and I see it's Cole's PA, my pulse leaps, even as my stomach twists.

"Hello," I answer.

"Good morning, Delilah. Are you available for a meeting with Mr. King?"

My mouth goes dry, and I need to clear my throat before I answer. "Yes, of course."

"Come on up, then."

I hang up, then stand, wiping my sweaty palms on my skirt. When the elevator deposits me on the top floor, I smile at Samson, hoping my nerves aren't showing on my face.

"He's expecting you. You can go right in." He nods toward the office.

When I knock and hear his deep voice telling me to

come in, butterflies take flight in my stomach. I enter and close the door behind me, then quickly step away from it. I don't need a reminder of being pressed against it a week ago. Stopping in the middle of the office, I interlace my fingers, hoping my face is as expressionless as his.

"Good morning, Miss West," Cole says, his vivid blue eyes sweeping over me.

"Is there something you want from me, Mr. King?"

His gaze flashes to mine, and my breath hitches. Why did I say it that way?

"Yes," he says, nodding to the chairs in front of his desk. "I want you to sit."

Letting out a silent sigh, I take a seat in one of them.

He surprises me by asking, "How are you doing after . . . ?"

I blink at him. Is he asking me how I am after he made me come last week? A blush creeps over my cheeks.

His brows draw together. "Has Paul bothered you at all?"

Oh. He meant how am I after finding out my boyfriend cheated on me. Of course he doesn't care about how I am after orgasming in his office. If he'd cared about that, he might have been in touch sooner.

"Paul's kept to himself. He's been professional."

Cole nods, then stands and walks around to my side of the desk, leaning back against it and crossing his arms as he regards me. I stop my eyes from dropping to his broad chest. Why does he have to look so incredible in a suit?

"I'm flying to Chicago at the end of this week to represent the King Group at a black-tie benefit gala. I plan to visit the hotel site while I'm there. Since you have a site visit scheduled soon anyway, it makes sense for you to come with me. And since we'll be there together, I'd like you to attend the gala as my plus one."

I stare at him. This is not what I expected at all. He has nothing to say about what happened between us or ignoring me for the week after, but he wants me to accompany him for a night or two, away? "I'm not sure . . . I mean, I do need to see the site, but . . ."

He frowns. "What's the problem, Miss West?"

I stand, needing to gain some kind of equal footing. "Do you think it's a good idea, after . . . after last week."

He drops his arms. "I think it's a very good idea. That's why I suggested it."

I swallow past my dry throat. "If you're asking me because you think we're going to repeat—"

His brows slam down. "I'm asking you because you are the architect working on this site and having you travel with me on the company jet rather than flying out separately makes good logistical sense. I'm asking you to attend the gala because I need a plus one, and I don't want to worry about organizing someone else. And since there will be plenty of people there from the industry, it will do you good to attend." He shakes his head, his scowl deepening. "Do you honestly think I need to manipulate a woman into having sex with me?"

My jaw tightens. "No. I'm sure you don't."

He regards me with a frown. "Do you have an issue with me, Miss West?"

"No," I automatically reply, but then everything that's happened overwhelms me, and I fling my hands in the air as it all comes pouring out. "Except maybe it would have been nice if you hadn't disappeared off the face of the earth after making me come last week. What we did was completely unprofessional, and I had no idea what to think about it. Paul had cheated on me, we did . . . that, then I didn't hear from you or see you for the rest of the week. You didn't even come to the team meeting. And I saw you—" I cut myself off, not wanting to remind him of how I'd been lurking and watching him and his brothers get ready to go to some kind of event. "Anyway. You may be used to screwing employees in your office then forgetting they exist, but that's not the kind of thing I'm used to. I felt . . ."

He stares down at me with inscrutable eyes. "What did you feel?"

It's too late to go back now. A shaky breath rushes out of me. "I felt alone."

His gaze locks on mine, and I cringe inwardly at everything I've admitted. Without a word, he turns and heads back to his side of the desk. But he doesn't sit. He leans forward and braces his hands on the surface, his eyes boring into mine. "I had to fly out to our California office Monday night. I was there all week, putting out fires. I flew back Friday afternoon, in time to attend the engagement party of a long-time associate."

I wet my lips. "Oh."

"And I didn't know making you come went along with the need to update you on my whereabouts at any given time."

He sits down and rubs his hand over his mouth and chin, and I remember how he did the same after making me orgasm. Heat pools low in my core, and I mentally slap myself.

I'm so out of my depth with this man. Everything in my life has gone off the rails since I slept with him all those weeks ago. Although, admittedly, what happened with Paul had nothing to do with Cole.

Regardless, I have to stop letting my emotions get away from me around him. He's obviously used to this kind of thing, so making a big deal of it is just going to make me look immature. If he can act as if nothing happened between us, then so can I.

"I shouldn't have said anything. It won't happen again." I keep my gaze level and fixed on his, even though all I want to do is walk away and pretend none of this happened.

"Don't worry about it." He watches me, his eyes dark. "Now that we've cleared that up, I expect you to be ready for an overnight trip to Chicago. The jet leaves at eight a.m. on Friday, and we'll fly back on Saturday. I'll pick you up."

He doesn't say anything more, just continues to look at me. I brush my damp palms over my skirt. "I'll be ready. Is that all?"

"That's all."

I make for the office door as quickly as I can while maintaining some kind of dignity, but he stops me just as I'm about to turn the handle. "Delilah."

I look at him over my shoulder.

His jaw works and he looks uncomfortable for the first time since I've known him. "I'm sorry that I made you feel alone."

My brows arch high. I doubt he's used to apologizing to his employees. I can't help but give him a tiny smile. But I just murmur, "Thank you," then leave.

As I wait for the elevator, I reassure myself that I can move forward from what happened between us. And I'm excited to visit the site. As much as photographs and 3D terrain models are usable for the initial designs, I'll have a much better understanding of the space once I've seen it in person. I'm not as excited about attending the gala since I have no idea what to expect and don't have anything to wear. I'll have to ask Alex if she can help me with that. We're a similar size, and she has some great dresses. Hopefully she'll have something to lend me.

Except, I don't have to ask Alex to borrow a dress, because when I come back from my lunch break, there's an envelope on my desk. Inside is a note from Cole, and a black-and-silver corporate credit card with his name on it. At least, I think it's a corporate card. I flip it over, but there's nothing on it except Cole's name. I shake my head and laugh at myself. There's no way Cole would give me his personal credit card. This must just be how VIP corporate cards look. I place it on the desk and read the note.

Miss West,

Use this card to purchase a dress and shoes for the gala on Friday night, as well as anything else you might need. Please remember you will be representing the King Group, so make sure you take advantage of the unlimited budget.

Cole

I stare again at the card. Wow. Okay. This is the kind of thing I've only ever seen in the movies. It's like something out of *Pretty Woman*.

Maybe I should be more reluctant to spend his company's money, but considering Cole is worried about how I might look while I'm representing them, I'm happy I get to spend more than I could afford myself. Even one of Alex's dresses probably wouldn't meet their requirements.

I quickly message her.

> Any chance you're up for a shopping trip sometime this week?

> ???

> I have to buy a dress to attend a gala on Friday night.

> What? Where? With Who?

> In Chicago. With Cole.

My phone rings in my hand and I look around, not wanting anyone to make a fuss about a personal call during work hours. But there's no one close enough to worry about, so I answer.

"You can't just tell me you have to buy a fancy dress to go on a date with Cole in Chicago and not give me all the details about what happened between you two today. Last I heard, you were going to pretend nothing happened and move on."

"Well, first, it's not a date. And second, that's kind of still the plan. I'm just going to be in Chicago pretending nothing happened."

"But what happened today? How did he ask you? I need to know everything!"

I laugh. "I'll fill you in tonight. All you need to know is that he summoned me to a meeting this morning and then said he wanted me to come with him on Friday."

"Did he say anything about why he ignored you for the last week?"

My cheeks heat with remembered embarrassment. "He's been out of town. He only got back Friday afternoon."

"Do you believe him?"

It hadn't even occurred to me to doubt him. "I don't think someone like Cole needs to lie to anyone about his whereabouts. If he didn't want anything to do with me, I'm sure he'd have been quite happy to tell me to my face."

She laughs. "True. So, are you going to sleep with him?"

"What?" I realize I've raised my voice and duck down a little in case I've attracted anyone's attention.

"Come on. The two of you alone together in another city for a night, probably sleeping in adjoining rooms. And you've already told me how good the sex was with him. Why not give him another go?"

"Because things are different now. The situation is different."

"It wasn't that different when he had his mouth between your legs last week."

"Alex!" I whisper-shout.

She sniggers. "I'm just saying."

"Well, don't say. I'll be completely professional, and so will he."

"Mm-hmm. Well, let's go shopping at lunchtime tomorrow and find a dress that will have him panting. Even if you don't plan to do anything about it, it's nice to know you have the option." She lets out a groan. "I can't believe this is happening the weekend I'm flying to LA to see Jaxson. I won't be there to hear all the juicy details when you get back. You have to call me as soon as you're home, okay?"

"I'm not going to interrupt your weekend with Jaxson just to tell you nothing happened."

She manages to get me to promise to call her anyway, and then we hang up.

I sit there, staring at the schematic on my screen for a moment. Alex is right. I want to look good for Cole—and I'm not sure what that says about me. Despite that, I can't afford to let anything else happen between us. My career and feelings are at risk, not his.

And that's what I need to remember.

CHAPTER EIGHTEEN

COLE

Jonathan pulls the car up outside Delilah's apartment building, where she's waiting. She barely has time to pick up the bag at her feet before he's out of the driver's seat to take it off her and open the rear door for her. She smiles at him, then slides in to sit opposite me. I drink her in a little too avariciously. Her long dark hair is tied back in a ponytail. The green V-neck shirt she's wearing deepens the color of her eyes, and her jeans fit like a second skin. It's all very suitable for attending a future building site, and yet it's still as sexy as hell on her.

Her gaze flits over me, probably taking stock of my clothing as well since this is the first time she's seen me dressed casually. I hide my smile as she takes in my fitted gray T-shirt and jeans, her bottom lip caught between her teeth.

Realizing she's been staring a little too long, her eyes dart to mine, then out the window, a slight blush warming her cheeks.

"Did you purchase a dress?" I ask, forcing her to make eye contact with me again.

"Yes. And thank you for arranging a card for me to use. I gave it back to Samson on Wednesday."

I nod. Samson had returned it to me immediately after she'd dropped it off, looking just as curious as when I asked him to take it down to her in the first place. He knows better than to ask any questions though. The truth is, I didn't have a good reason for giving her my personal card to use, except that the idea of her wearing a dress I bought for her, even if she's not aware of it, appeals a little too much.

We pass the rest of the drive to the airport in silence. I answer emails on my phone, including one from Roman that has me firing off a reply straight away. Rumors that Berrington is considering pulling his investments are circulating again. We'll need to meet and discuss how to handle it when I return to New York on Saturday.

After I finish replying to my urgent emails, my focus returns to the woman across from me. Delilah has her tablet open and she's making quick, efficient marks on the screen with a stylus.

I watch her for a few moments, admiring the curve of her cheek and the fullness of her pink lips. A vision of those lips wrapped around me soon invades my mind, and I turn away, spending the rest of the trip looking out the window and thinking.

I need to restrain myself around her. Yes, I want to fuck her again. I'd be more than happy to spend every minute of our spare time in Chicago in bed with her. But I told the truth when I said I wasn't inviting her for that reason. In a rare moment of conscience, I realized she might not be in the headspace to spend all night fucking her boss. Not so soon after Paul's betrayal, anyway. And considering her reaction to me after what happened in my office, it's obvious she isn't comfortable with the idea of casual sex, despite what happened when we originally met.

I doubt I could sleep with her tonight and then send her on her way. I respect Delilah as a professional and I want to explore her body for as long as it takes to get her out of my system, but I don't want to get involved in anything that will be hard to extricate myself from, and I get the feeling it would be hard to extricate myself from her. I want more time with her, even though I've already had her once, which means she's piqued my interest more than any other woman I've been with. And that's not something I'm comfortable with.

Even knowing all that, it's hard to resist the urge to touch her when she's so close. I curl my fingers around my phone to stop myself from doing anything stupid.

When we get to the airport, Jonathan drives us to the private airfield where the company jet shines bright white in the sunshine.

Delilah peers out the window, then turns to me. "This is an upgrade from what I'm used to."

"Not having to fly commercial is definitely a perk."

She quirks a brow. "Have you ever flown commercial?"

"Only first class."

"You mean you've never experienced the thrill of fighting for overhead luggage space or dealing with the person next to you who doesn't believe in personal boundaries?"

"No. Only the joys of massage chairs and a fully stocked bar."

I don't miss the little eye roll she gives before turning away, and I let a smile slip out. I bet she won't be rolling her eyes once she gets a look inside the jet.

I follow her up the stairs, my eyes fixed on her ass in

those tight jeans, and almost bump into her when she stops inside the door. She turns to look at me with her mouth open and I actually laugh. It's impressive—all pale carpet, cream leather, and wood accents.

The flight attendant, Marigold, stands to the side with a wide smile on her face. It broadens when her gaze lands on me. "Good morning, Mr. King. It's nice to see you again." The familiarity and suggestion in her tone has Delilah's gaze bouncing between Marigold and me.

Despite what Delilah is obviously thinking, I haven't slept with her. She's made it known she's up for it, but I'm not interested in seeing a woman I've had sex with every time I need to fly somewhere. I just give her a polite good morning and usher Delilah through to the seating area with a hand on her back.

She sits down in one of the leather window seats and buckles herself in, doing her best to avoid my gaze. Small, bright patches burn on her cheeks, and I wonder if they're from anger or embarrassment.

I'm looking forward to finding out.

Even though there are several seats available, I buckle myself in opposite her. The jet is spacious, but our legs are still within touching distance. Delilah looks over at me, then out the window, and I rub my hand over my mouth to hide my smile.

Now that we're on board, the engines start to warm up. Marigold appears at my side, putting her hand on my shoulder. "What can I get you to drink, Mr. King?"

I glance up at her. "Just a tonic and lime this morning."

She nods and looks at Delilah. "Anything for you, ma'am?"

"An orange juice would be nice. Thank you." She smiles at Marigold, who nods and heads to the galley to get our drinks. Delilah meets my gaze and tilts her head. "What's that look for?"

"You're very polite."

Her brows arch. "Aren't most people?"

I shrug. Not the people I spend my time with. The competition to always be on top—to be the richest, the most powerful, the most beautiful—means they can be vicious if they think someone is vying for whatever it is they have or want. Not that Delilah seems to want me that way. Maybe that's the difference. But I don't miss the hitch in her breath when the plane jolts forward and my leg presses against hers.

"Are you looking forward to seeing the site?" I ask.

"I am. 3D models are all well and good, but there's nothing like being on the ground and seeing how the building is actually going to exist in its environment."

Her enthusiasm is obvious and infectious, and her smile is bright. I'm only visiting the site because I need to be in Chicago for the gala anyway. Otherwise, I wouldn't have bothered. I certainly don't have time to visit all future development sites. Although it might also have something to do with it being a good excuse to have Delilah come with me.

She's like an itch I can't scratch. I can only hope that more time with her will ease that itch, make me stop lusting over her. Or maybe it will only make things worse.

Who the hell knows?

Marigold brings our drinks, passing Delilah's juice with a warm smile. When she meets my gaze, the smile she gives is perfectly professional and polite. She must think Delilah is my girlfriend.

As the engines spin up and the jet roars down the runway, Delilah closes her eyes, her fingers tightening around the armrests. I wasn't expecting this reaction from her. "Are you scared of flying?" I ask.

She blinks a couple of times, then focuses on me. "A little. It's manageable. Just the takeoff and landing, really." A minor bump as we rise through an air pocket has a gasp falling from her lips.

It bothers me that she's scared. "Our pilot's an ex-naval pilot. He's incredibly experienced."

The corners of her mouth lift. "That's reassuring. Thank you for telling me." But her fingers don't relax until the plane levels out and the engine noise drops.

"Better?" I ask.

She gives me a smile. "Better."

I relax as well. "So tell me, why did you decide to become an architect?" I find myself genuinely interested in her answer. In my experience there are very few licensed architects of Delilah's age. I'm curious about what's behind that level of hard work and commitment.

"I was always good at math and art in school. Architecture seemed like a natural combination of those two things. And there's something amazing about imagining a structure in your head, putting it on paper, then seeing it converted into a reality that will hopefully last long after you've gone. Knowing your work has a long legacy is an incredible thing."

I nod. I can understand that.

"Plus it pays well," she adds.

"Always an important consideration." I tap my fingers on the leather armrest. "How did you get your license at such a young age?"

She laughs lightly. "It's called not having much of a life."

"So explain why a smart, young, beautiful woman would put her life on hold to achieve that."

She looks down at her glass and runs her finger around the rim, then lifts her gaze to mine. "My mom had me when she was young and raised me on her own. She had to work multiple jobs to earn enough to keep a roof over our heads and food on our plates. Growing up, seeing how hard she worked, how she put aside her own dreams to take care of me, all I wanted was to take care of her. The sooner I could become licensed, the sooner I could start earning the money to do that."

Her upbringing is the complete opposite of mine. It takes me a moment to realize that the sharp tug in my chest is another surge of regret over accusing her of trying to manipulate me. "That's admirable." I take a sip of my drink. "Do you mind me asking what happened to your father?"

Her expression shutters. "He didn't want to be in the picture."

It's obviously an uncomfortable subject for her, so I change back to safer topics. "How did you manage to pay your way through college?"

"I was lucky and received a scholarship. That meant I only had to work part-time to cover my remaining expenses. I interned the rest of the time so I could get a head start on logging my practical hours."

"I'm impressed." And I am. Very few people surprise me, and even fewer impress me. Delilah's just done both.

She puts down her empty glass. "Anyway, that's enough about me. Why did you decide to go into the family business?"

I may have peppered her with questions, but I'm not particularly interested in answering any about me. Still, I guess I owe her the same honesty she gave me. "It wasn't really a decision. We were born and raised into it."

She nods, her eyes intent on mine. "Do you enjoy it?"

The question gives me pause. Do I enjoy it? It's not really something I've ever asked myself. "I enjoy making decisions, being in control. I enjoy having power, and I enjoy having money."

Her eyebrows rise and a smile flirts with the corner of her lips. "That sounds like something a rich and powerful man would say."

I shrug. "It works for me."

She laughs quietly, and it hits me then. This is the most relaxed I've seen her since we met. The two of us have spent every meeting either rubbing up against each other or rubbing each other the wrong way. As much as I enjoy seeing the sparks flash in her eyes when she's angry, I like this side of her too.

"I guess I could get used to this," she says as she runs her fingers over the seat's soft cream leather. "If you have to fly, this is the way to do it." Her eyes wander to the back of the plane, to the closed door behind me. "What's back there?"

"The bedroom."

Her eyes shoot back to me, and a faint blush tints her cheekbones. "Oh."

I give her a lazy smile as I picture taking her into that room and making her cheeks flush for a different reason.

She looks down at where she's fidgeting with her seatbelt.

Marigold returns to take our empty glasses and ask if we want something else. Delilah looks from Marigold to the bedroom door, then back to Marigold again, before her gaze lands on me. I can almost see the wheels turning in her mind. She's making an assumption. Probably a logical one, but in this case, incorrect.

We both decline another drink, and after Marigold leaves, neither of us seems inclined to continue the conversation. Delilah pulls out her tablet again and goes back to work. I decide to join her, taking out my phone and answering the new emails that have come in. They never seem to stop.

Two hours later, the pilot lets us know we're about to descend into O'Hare. Delilah stashes her tablet and gives me a self-conscious smile as she grips the armrests. I distract her by asking questions about her work. It seems to be effective, her shoulders relaxing and her expression becoming animated as she tells me about the first building she worked on and what her favorite design has been so far.

I'm so absorbed in watching her that the mild jolt of the plane's wheels bumping down onto the tarmac surprises me.

Delilah also starts and looks around. "We landed?"

"I told you he was a good pilot."

"You did. Thank you again for that." Her lips curve up, and her green eyes sparkle. Something tightens in my chest. I can't recall the last time someone smiled at me with such genuine happiness.

I look away, watching the airport pass through the window as the plane taxis off the runway. I'm not used to feeling something for the women I'm with, or have been with, in Delilah's case. It's . . . disconcerting. When we halt at the terminal, I unbuckle my seatbelt and wait for Delilah to unbuckle hers, then follow her out of the jet and down the stairs to the waiting car. We slide in next to each other and the driver starts the car, heading out of the airfield.

"We'll go to the hotel and drop off our bags, then head straight to the site," I say.

"Okay." Her gaze skitters away from mine. Probably because I've avoided looking at her since she smiled at me on the plane.

When we get to our hotel, and I mean ours as in it's a King-Group-owned hotel, we head straight to our adjacent rooms. After settling our things, we return to the car. As soon as we reach the site, Delilah is out the door.

There's not a whole lot for me to get excited about—it's an empty space between two other buildings and when I look at it, all I see are numbers, the potential for profit—but Delilah's face glows as she turns around, looking up at the surrounding buildings, her eyes rising to the roofline.

"Can you picture it?" I ask.

She turns to me and the brightness of her smile sparks through me like a static shock.

"Yes. And I already have an idea to make the design even better."

"What sort of idea?"

She points at an angle across the street. "The buildings on the diagonal are smaller. In that direction, the lower floors will get a better view. I'd like to try curving the north-eastern corner of the hotel to maximize it."

"And that's going to cost me more money."

Her face falls. "Should I stop making structural changes? I—"

I let my smile escape. "I'm kidding, Delilah. Why do you think you're here? Draw up any modifications and send them for estimates."

She stares at me, then lets out a short laugh. "I think that's the first time you've made a joke. I mean, it was an awful one. But I like that you tried." She throws a smirk over her shoulder as she turns to walk further onto the plot.

The curve of her lips and the sway of her ass merge

together to make me want to bend her over the hood of the car and fuck her. Apart from the company not needing its COO getting arrested for public indecency, if I get the chance to have Delilah again, it won't be on the hood of a car in the middle of a busy street.

But the way the urge to touch her is taking over my mind, I'm not sure how reckless I might get.

CHAPTER NINETEEN

DELILAH

I check my reflection in the mirror one more time, smoothing my fingers over the silky material of the floor-length red dress I'm wearing. Hopefully with an outfit this gorgeous, *and* expensive, I should fit in with all the other guests at the gala.

I turn away from the mirror and check the time. Cole will be here soon to collect me. The thought has a whole kaleidoscope of butterflies beating their wings in my stomach. I haven't seen him since we got back from the hotel site. He'd told me I could do whatever I wanted for the rest of the day, then disappeared into his room for a conference call with his brothers.

I spent a couple of hours wandering around and indulged in a delicious deep-dish pizza for lunch, then returned to my hotel room and distracted myself by sketching out my ideas for the hotel's revised design.

I've tried hard to forget about what happened in his office, but it's been on repeat in my mind since I slid into the car this morning and saw him looking so gorgeous. Images of what could happen tonight flash through my head at high speed, and heat pools low inside me.

Not that he's suggested anything of the sort to me, but the way his eyes lingered on me this morning tells me he probably wouldn't say no if I offered. I just don't know if offering is something I should do.

The rap of his knuckles on the door startles me, and I take a deep breath before opening it. Cole's brilliant blue eyes take a long, slow sweep down my body and back up again, catching on the plunging neckline of my dress. He doesn't even bother to hide the desire that sharpens his gaze.

Part of me wants to grab him by his crisp white shirt and drag him into my room. Make him remind me how his body feels moving with mine. But the more sensible part holds me back. The risk is too high, and despite recent evidence to the contrary, I'm not someone who regularly throws caution to the wind. While the reward would be great, it would also be fleeting. I have to be smart and keep my focus on my long-term goals, and they don't include ruining my career by sleeping with my company's biggest client.

Again.

I step out to join Cole, pulling the door firmly shut behind me. Before I can ask how the rest of his day was, his hand goes to my back, his fingers sliding around to my waist.

He leans down, his breath fluttering the tendrils of hair at my neck. "You look beautiful, kitten."

Goose bumps erupt over every inch of me, and I let out a shaky breath. "You look very . . . uh, handsome, too."

It's a gross understatement. I've seen Cole in a business suit, but this is the first time I've seen him up close in a tuxedo, and he is the definition of a sexy, powerful, rich man. His black jacket is perfectly tailored to show off his height and broad shoulders. The heat of his gaze scorches over my exposed skin, and the curve of his seductive, masculine lips reminds me exactly what he can do with them.

When I lick my own suddenly dry lips, his fingers tighten on my waist, sending an excited little quiver running through me. God, why is it so hard for me to ignore him? After all, I managed to ignore plenty of men during college, and those men were far more my type than Cole—kind, considerate, respectful.

Exactly the way Paul was at first.

I turn away from Cole's too-hot perusal and make for the elevator.

The gala is being held at the Lakefront Plaza, another King Group property, so a limo is waiting outside to take us there. The driver opens the door for us, and I slide in first, Cole following me.

During the drive, tension swirls in the air. Neither of us speaks, but instead of it being awkward, the temperature only rises. All I can seem to think about is the way he's touched me, the feel of his muscles under my fingertips, how hard he's made me come.

The spacious car isn't big enough to give me the distance my body needs. I can almost feel his gaze burning into the side of my face, but I refuse to look at him. If I do, there's a chance I might decide to embrace the previously undiscovered reckless side of me—the side that only seems to come out around Cole—and unbuckle my seatbelt so I can straddle him. There's no mistaking how damp my panties are already. I close my eyes and take a deep breath.

"Delilah, look at me." Cole's deep voice is commanding enough to get me to turn toward him. "I told you back in New York that I don't have to manipulate women into having sex with me, and that's true. I brought you here because it made sense for you to join me. But I'm not going to lie, either. I want to fuck you again. I haven't been able to stop thinking about it since you walked into the meeting room that first day, and I'm tired of fighting it."

I inhale sharply, my nipples immediately hardening under the thin material of my dress.

He notices, and a muscle leaps in his jaw. "I want you tonight, Delilah. Tell me I can have you."

My heart hammers. My mouth opens to respond, but nothing comes out. I'm frozen, torn between wanting to experience what I know he can give me and my awareness of just how horrendously wrong this could go.

Cole reaches out and brushes his thumb across my lower lip. "I want to see this lipstick smeared all over my cock. I want my tongue deep in your pussy. I want to make you come until you physically can't anymore. And I want it tonight. Just one night and then we go back to New York and the way things are now. But if you agree, you're mine until morning. And Delilah," he says, gripping my jaw and forcing me to focus on his words over the pounding of blood in my ears. "If you say yes, I plan to make you forget Paul ever existed."

That last bit makes me flinch, and his hand drops away.

"Think about it and give me your answer before we leave the gala tonight. If you say yes, I won't wait until we get back to the hotel to start. Do you understand?"

I am way out of my league with this man. I want to scream at the driver to pull over right now so I can get naked and rub myself all over him. I want to unbutton his pristine white shirt and kiss a trail down his skin until I can unzip his pants and take him into my mouth. I want to pull my dress up my thighs and slide onto him. I want to experience everything my body and his can do together. After having a taste of just how amazing sex can be, then being disappointed with my physical relationship with Paul, I just want to feel it all over again.

But instead of doing any of that, I force out two words. "I understand."

Cole stares out the window and I sit in stunned silence, trying to figure out exactly what I should do. I could whip out my phone and message Alex, but I don't want to interrupt her time with Jaxson. Plus, I already know what her advice will be. Something along the lines of, "Ride 'em, cowgirl."

I'm mercifully distracted from the overwhelming chaos in my mind when we approach the hotel. The building is lit up, with an honest to goodness red carpet out front. Photographers stand on each side, snapping photos of the people walking on it.

"I didn't realize this was such a big event," I murmur.

"Some of the richest people in the US are here tonight," Cole says. "And people with that kind of wealth and power want to make sure everyone sees them."

I turn to look at him. "Do you go to many of these?"

"Usually it's Roman or my father." The line of his jaw sharpens. "Or it used to be, anyway."

I consider asking him about his father, about how he feels about what happened, but I don't have the time—or probably the courage—because our car is pulling up to the red carpet.

The driver gets out and opens the door on Cole's side.

"Ready?" Cole asks.

I'm not, but I nod anyway. He steps out, then turns to hold out his hand for me. I take it, feeling completely overwhelmed as he tucks it into his elbow, and we start down the red carpet. Camera flashes from both sides dazzle me, and I hear voices calling out to Cole.

"Mr. King, who's your date tonight?"

"Mr. King, who's your date wearing?"

"Mr. King, how do you respond to rumors that investors have lost confidence in the King Group following the arrest of your father?"

What the hell kind of question is that at this kind of event?

The muscles in Cole's arm tighten, and I peer at the group of mostly photographers standing to the side. Two or three people hold microphones, attempting to ask the attendees questions, but I can't tell which of them asked about his dad. Cole doesn't answer anyway. His expression appears completely inscrutable, but I'm close enough to detect the faintest tic in his jaw.

Curling my fingers around his bicep, I squeeze it reassuringly. He looks down at me, surprise lightening his eyes. One corner of his mouth kicks up for a millisecond, and then he's looking straight ahead again as we approach the large open doorway.

Now that we've mostly finished with the photographers and reporters, I can relax and take in the lobby as we enter. It's beautiful, with gleaming marble floors and soaring ceilings adorned with sparkling chandeliers. The ballroom where the gala is being held is equally impressive. It's a huge space, featuring intricate moldings, mirrored accents, and even more extravagant chandeliers. A table with various objects placed on it runs down the side of the room. Cole had mentioned a silent auction, so it must be for that.

"It's an amazing space," I murmur, my gaze roaming over the ornate ceiling.

"It is."

I smile up at him. Does he actually seem . . . relaxed?

The tension from before seems to have gone, and something akin to a spark of warmth resides in his gaze.

"I like watching you looking at architecture," he says.

I cock my head. "Why?"

"Your eyes light up, and your whole body becomes animated."

"Oh." Warmth unfolds in my chest. That was the last thing I expected to hear from him.

His gaze holds mine. "Your passion is a beautiful thing."

My breath catches in my throat as something shimmers in the air between us—a connection I never would have believed possible. And yet, it's there.

Maybe I should have known my relationship with Paul was doomed. He'd never once bothered to share his appreciation for me the way Cole just did. Any time we went somewhere with amazing architecture, he was too busy lecturing me about his expert opinion to care about my response to it.

"Thank you." I don't know what else to say, so I force my gaze away from him and look at the people filling the vast room.

Cole was right. Everyone here is rich and powerful, and they're not shy about showing it. Expensive suits and designer dresses, jewels dripping from necks, wrists, and ears, laughs that sound a little too loud, as if only uttered to draw attention. It's completely different from anything I'm used to.

Cole leans down and whispers, "Stay by my side or you'll have all the unmarried men trying to take you home tonight. Probably half of the married ones as well." When I glance up at him, there's no humor in his expression. "Let's find our table." He urges me forward, his large hand spanning the small of my back.

We weave our way through the crowd until Cole spots

our designated table at the front of the room, and I wonder if the positioning is deliberate. Do the big billionaires sit at the front and the little billionaires get relegated to the back?

I stifle a laugh, then quickly straighten my face when Cole glances at me with a raised brow.

He pulls out my seat and I try to sink into it as gracefully as possible. Then he sits next to me.

A server materializes by our side. "Can I get you something to drink this evening?"

Cole turns to me. "Would you like champagne or something else?"

Champagne would be nice, but the bubbles are bound to go to my head, and I need to keep my senses about me tonight. "I'll have a glass of white wine, thank you."

Cole orders two glasses of white and the server rushes off, dodging and weaving his way through the crowd. He's soon back with our glasses, and I thank him with a grateful smile, getting a grin and a wink in response. Cole mutters something under his breath and casually rests his arm along the back of my chair.

We're soon joined at the table by some other couples, mostly older than Cole and me. They greet him familiarly, and Cole introduces me as his colleague, which isn't really true. He probably says it to ensure people don't think I'm his date, or God forbid, his girlfriend.

The final couple joins the table, and although there's no obvious physical reaction from Cole, I swear tension seems to roll off him as they sit opposite us. His greeting seems pleasant enough, however, as he nods in their direction. "Jessica, Tom."

The couple seems about Cole's age. The blandly good-looking man reminds me of a Ken doll, and the woman is a complete knockout. She's blonde, tall, and curvy, and her black dress shows off every single one of those curves. Her pale blue eyes fix on Cole.

"I wasn't sure you were coming tonight," she says to him. "You usually let me know."

"Roman originally accepted the invitation, but he has other business to attend to."

He doesn't say anything about why he didn't let her know he was coming. And what does that mean, anyway? Surely she's not his girlfriend, considering they're both here with other people.

I look at Cole, but he keeps his attention fixed on Jessica.

She shifts in her chair, her gaze briefly flicking to me. "Who's your date tonight?"

"This is Delilah. She's an architect working on the new hotel chain. I brought her to look at the Chicago site."

I smile at Jessica, and although she smiles back, it's brittle around the edges.

"How convenient," she murmurs.

We're spared further conversation with Jessica and her date when the emcee takes to the stage to talk about the schedule for tonight, which includes numerous courses of food and a lot of mingling, followed by the silent auction and then dancing. A casual Friday night for billionaires.

Once everyone is seated, the first course is brought out. It's caviar, artfully dolloped on some fancy-looking lettuce leaves. I try it because I've never had it before, then do my best not to screw up my nose. I quietly panic. Is it considered rude if I don't eat it?

Cole's thigh presses against mine as he murmurs in my ear, "Don't eat it if you don't like it. It's an acquired taste."

"Let me guess." I tilt my face up to his. "You've acquired it?"

He shrugs. "I wasn't given much of a choice when I was a child."

I look down at the pile of shiny black fish eggs. "I can't believe your parents gave this to you as a kid. I used to kick up a fuss when Mom made me eat my beans."

The corners of his mouth turn up. "My brothers and I were expected to gain an appreciation for the finer things in life early on, whether we wanted to or not."

I try to picture Cole as a child, forcing down caviar at the dinner table because it was expected. A pang of sadness hits me. I don't know anything about his upbringing, so I'm probably making a huge assumption, but somehow it doesn't seem like the act of loving parents. I touch his arm. "I'm sorry. That doesn't sound very nice."

He looks down at my hand, then up at my face. The strange intensity in his eyes has my stomach flipping over. Then he shakes his head and gives me a tilted smile. "Only you would pity me for my childhood of eating incredibly expensive food, Delilah."

My cheeks heat, but the way he's still looking at me makes my breath catch in my throat. As I turn away, Jessica catches my attention. Her eyes are on Cole, and she's frowning. There's definitely something going on there, but what? Is she his ex? Or does she want a relationship with him, and he's not interested?

I'm distracted by a server who whisks away my mostly untouched plate. It's soon replaced by something far more appetizing: a small serving of salmon ravioli with a saffron cream sauce. It's delicious and I hum with approval as I lick the sauce from my lips.

Cole leans toward me again. "Keep that up and I'll demand an answer sooner." His low, raspy voice sends a thrill through me.

I throw him a wide-eyed look. Then, and I'm not sure why I do it, I hold his gaze and deliberately lick my lips again.

I almost laugh at the look on his face, but the way my body reacts to the dark, sinful expression that takes hold of his features is anything but funny. It promises retribution of the darkest, most decadent kind. And suddenly, I wonder why I'm hesitating about this.

We're here for one night. I'm dressed up and looking as good as I'll ever look, and Cole is . . . Well, Cole is Cole. He always looks incredible. But right now, he's looking at me like he wants to eat me alive, and I'm pretty sure I'm looking at him like I want him to.

I lean toward him, and the flare of his pupils causes breathless excitement to radiate through me. "What if I'm ready to give you my answer now?"

He lets out a slow, controlled breath. "Don't."

I blink. "But I thought—"

"Don't tell me until I'm in a position to do something about it. If you tell me now, I'll pull up your skirt under the table, bury my fingers in you, and make you come in front of all these people."

A shudder wracks me and I close my eyes for a beat because a small, hidden part of me wants him to do just that —to claim me in front of all these people. But I sink back in my chair. A fantasy is one thing. The reality would be quite different.

"I'll tell you when you can answer me," Cole says, and I nod. I'm sure my arousal must be visible to everyone at the table, and I stare fixedly at the remains of the food on my plate until that too is whisked away.

Two more courses come and go before the emcee tells us there'll be a short break to allow for mingling.

Cole is immediately out of his chair, taking my hand to pull me behind him.

"Cole, I want to talk to you about . . ." Jessica's voice trails off behind us as Cole tugs me away from the table. I only glimpse the hard expression on her face from the corner of my eye as I try not to stumble in my heels.

"How do you know Jessica?" I ask.

Cole's hand tightens around mine, but he doesn't turn his head. "She's the daughter of one of our biggest investors."

My feet start to drag. "Did you two have a relationship? Because I get the impression she's annoyed you're here with me."

This time he meets my gaze over his shoulder. "I've never had a relationship with Jessica. We've spent a lot of time together at these kinds of events, though."

Tension at the base of my neck eases. She must just be annoyed that I'm monopolizing the person she would normally pass the time with.

Cole leads me through a door set in the side of the ballroom. "Where are we going?" I ask as the crowd noise fades behind us. "Are we allowed down here?"

"I am," he says, and I almost roll my eyes.

He drags me into an alcove and spins me around, pressing my back against the wall and bracing his hands on either side of my shoulders. "You have something you want to tell me." The grit in his voice has tendrils of need tightening into a hot knot inside me.

He said he only wanted to hear my answer when he could do something about it. So what exactly is he planning to do here, in this semi-public place?

My heart thrashes in my chest, my nipples pressing hard and tight against the thin material of my dress.

Throwing caution to the wind, I tilt my head back and look him straight in the eye. "Yes."

He doesn't misunderstand me or ask for clarification. He knows exactly what I'm saying.

His lips crash against mine as he takes possession of my mouth, and I'm consumed by the flash fire of heat that flares between us.

I arch into him as one of his hands leaves the wall and smooths down my back to my ass, cupping it and jerking me toward him so I'm pressed against the long, hard ridge in his pants. I shamelessly rub against it, making him groan deep in his throat.

He inches his hand down and gathers up my dress, dragging it up my legs and bunching it in his hand until it's high enough that he can slide his fingers underneath it and into the tiny scrap of lace that makes up my thong.

He pulls back to watch my face as he makes contact with my clit, already swollen and pulsing, waiting for his touch.

I gasp and shudder as he rolls his thumb over it, and I know it won't be long until I'm coming apart under his touch. I should be embarrassed, but I'm not. And considering how blown his pupils are—the blue of his irises nothing but a thin ring around the black—he doesn't mind at all that I'm already hovering on the edge.

One long finger thrusts into me and I almost cry out, but thankfully he covers my mouth with his own, muffling the desperate sound.

His fingers and thumb move in tandem, and my hips roll into the movement as I race to find my release. Sparks shimmer behind my closed lids and I'm so close—

"Cole?" a female voice calls from down the hallway.

"Cole, are you down here? One of the servers told me he saw you come this way."

I freeze, blinking up at Cole. Anger rolls off him in icy waves, and his hand slows but doesn't stop. I'm caught, hanging on the edge. If he speeds up his movements, it will fling me over. Considering the woman calling out to Cole is coming closer, I'm not sure I want to be flung right now.

The last thing I need is some stranger watching me orgasm on my employer's fingers.

"Cole? I really have to talk to you about my father." The voice is closer now.

For the briefest moment, Cole works his fingers faster and I think he's going to do it. I think he's going to make me come anyway. My body tightens in involuntary pleasure, squeezing his fingers, and I widen my eyes, shaking my head.

He growls but pulls his fingers from me, reaching up and smearing them over my lips before taking my mouth in another fierce kiss.

"A little appetizer for later," he mutters into my ear.

Then he's stepping back, and I'm frantically straightening my dress, trying to put myself back together.

Apart from the dark dilation of his eyes and the flush on the arches of his cheekbones, he looks just as put together as before, although I notice his fingers still glisten with my arousal. He hasn't wiped them off—probably unwilling to smear bodily fluids onto his expensive suit or my dress.

It's too late to say anything, though, because he tugs me out of the alcove, and we come face to face with Jessica.

She smiles, but it stops short of her eyes. "There you are. I need to talk to you about something I overheard my father discussing."

She can't be oblivious to what she interrupted, and I

should be alarmed that any mention of what Cole and I were doing might get out, but at the moment I'm just frustrated and horny. I don't know this woman, but right now, I'm pretty sure I actively dislike her.

"I'm not really interested in talking business right now, Jessica," Cole says. "Can it wait until we're back in New York?"

She lives in New York too?

"Oh, I suppose so," she says. I wonder if it was all just an excuse to hunt down Cole and interrupt what he was doing with me. They might not have had a relationship, but it feels like she wishes they did, regardless of the man she left at the table.

"Let's get back then," Cole says, gesturing for Jessica to lead the way.

She gives me a look that rakes over me as if it has claws of its own before heading back the way we'd come. With her back turned, Cole takes the opportunity to run his tongue over the fingers he just had inside me, holding my gaze the whole time. "Who needs dessert?"

My stomach swoops. Even more so when he takes my hand and leads me back to the main room.

Interruption aside, I've just had a small taste of what I'm in for tonight.

And I think I might be in trouble.

CHAPTER TWENTY

COLE

I wait for as long as I can—until I've bid on, and won, a weekend in Aspen—and then I get us out of there. I messaged our driver to tell him to meet us out the front, and he's waiting when we come out. I glance at Delilah out of the corner of my eye. Her cheeks are beautifully flushed, and it's not the heat that's causing it. She knows exactly what will happen as soon as we're in the car.

After getting her so close to orgasm earlier, she's probably been feeling every bit as frustrated as I have.

Fucking Jessica. I don't know what game she's playing, but I'll have to talk to her when we get back to New York. I've dismissed the signs I've noticed recently—the reluctance to leave after we've finished fucking, the attempts to make me jealous. Either she's started to get attached or she has some other ulterior motive. I need to find out which it is and address it either way.

But it's not something to think about now. Not when the driver is opening the door and Delilah is sliding in, looking up at me with desire-hazed eyes.

My dick is already hard and throbbing. I've been

waiting for this moment for a long time—since she stepped foot in my office. Before that even. In the weeks after our night together, I'd stroked one out several times, closing my eyes and remembering how fucking good it had been to make her fall apart for me. I'd even found myself searching the streets for dark hair and green eyes. It was ridiculous. I've never done that in my entire fucking life.

But it was the completely irrational urge to return to the bar where we met that jolted me out of my strange obsession. Chasing after a woman, stalking her, isn't something I have ever—or will ever—do. So I'd deliberately put her out of my mind.

And then she'd walked right back into it, with her long legs and her pretty smile and those cat-like eyes. And those fucking skirts she wears. Not too short, but tight enough to cup the gorgeous curve of her ass.

I flex my fingers. It won't be a skirt cupping that ass tonight.

I climb in behind her and the driver closes my door.

Before I raise the privacy barrier, I tell him to take the scenic route to the hotel. His eyes meet mine in the rearview mirror. He acknowledges me with a nod, and I press the button to raise the partition. It doesn't make the car soundproof, but it should muffle some of the sounds Delilah is about to make.

"Come here," I tell her.

She only hesitates a second before sliding toward me. I wrap my arm around her waist and pull her onto my lap, then tug down the bodice of her dress. She's braless, and the shadow of her hard little nipples has been distracting me all night long. Now I'm going to get a taste.

I bend down and take one of the tight pink peaks into my mouth, rolling my tongue over it and groaning as it immediately hardens enough that I can tease it with my teeth.

"Cole," she breathes, her hands going to my hair to hold me against her. I pinch her other nipple, enjoying her sharp gasp as her hips buck upward. I'd bet money that shot straight to her clit.

After lavishing attention on her breasts, I reach for the hem of her dress and pull it high around her hips so I can slip my hand underneath. Her barely there thong is saturated, and I inhale deeply to slow myself down. We have the whole night. Right now is just about getting her primed and ready for what will happen when we get back to my hotel room.

My knuckles drift along the seam of her sex, and she bites back a whimper.

"No need to be quiet," I tell her. "The driver knows exactly what's going on. If you moan loud enough, you'll probably make his night."

Her cheeks burn, and she shakes her head at me.

I give a low chuckle. "Have you been on edge all night, kitten?"

"Yes," she breathes.

As annoyed as I am with Jessica, a part of me takes twisted joy in the fact that Delilah has been sitting next to me, desperate and needy for the last few hours. Thinking about this moment. Wanting my fingers and mouth on her, my cock working its way into her.

I kiss her. Hard. I want her lipstick smeared over both our faces. Our tongues tangle together, and she wriggles her hips. The friction of her ass against my erection makes it swell even more.

With my thumb on her clit, I slide a finger inside her. Her hands drop to my shoulders and clench as she lets out a moan. Her little cunt is so wet and ready for me that I add another finger, working it into her while I increase the pressure of my thumb.

I look down, drunk on the sight of her splayed out on my lap, her full breasts bared, legs parted and my hand disappearing under her red dress. I add a third finger. She's so damn tight. I know she's feeling the stretch, but I'll stretch her more once we're back in the hotel room, so she might as well get used to it now.

"C-Cole," she moans louder, and her eyelids flutter shut.

"Look at me." I want to see it in her eyes when she comes. There'll be no hiding her pleasure from me.

Her lids fly open again and from her unfocused gaze and tightening body, I know she's close. I bend over her, taking one pink tip in my mouth again and sucking hard. Her whimpers grow louder, but I need her to give in and let go. I want that gorgeous mind of hers to shut down so she can stop thinking and start feeling.

Curling my fingers and pressing against her front wall, I simultaneously stroke my thumb over her clit and bite down on her nipple.

"Yes, Cole!" she cries as her pussy spasms around my hand and her arousal practically gushes out of her.

I slow the movement of my hand and tease the hard peak in my mouth with my tongue to bring her back down. She breathes heavily and turns her face into my neck, trembling against me, and I'm overcome by an unexpected surge of tenderness. I fight the urge to stroke her hair away from her face and press a soft kiss to her lips. Tonight is about enjoying each other's bodies, not sharing affection.

I pull my hand from her panties and bring my wet

fingers to her mouth, drifting one along her soft, lush lower lip. "Suck."

Her eyes flash to mine, a crease marring her brow before she opens for me. I slide my fingers inside. Her tongue laps against them as she sucks, making my cock jerk under her ass.

Fuck.

I let her savor her own taste for a few more seconds, then despite my resolve from before, I pull my fingers away, cup her head and brush a kiss against her lips. It starts out slow, but soon I'm tilting her head to get deeper, my hand tightening in her hair as I lose myself in her.

When I finally ease away, she's not the only one breathing heavily.

The driver's voice comes over the intercom. "We're approaching the hotel, sir. Do you want me to keep driving?"

There's no doubt that even with the privacy screen up, he heard Delilah come. He probably assumes it's safe to ask the question.

"You can take us back now, thank you."

Delilah tries to slide off my lap, her gaze suddenly dipping away from mine.

I grab her chin. "Uh-uh. You said you were mine for the night, which means you do what I want. And what I want is for you to stay right where you are."

She swallows. "Okay." The word is little more than a faint breath, and I smile.

If Delilah thinks our first encounter is an indication of what will happen tonight, she's wrong. She was a virgin then. I'm not a complete asshole, so I didn't push any major boundaries. But she's not a virgin anymore. She's been with another man.

My muscles tense at the thought. I shrug my shoulders to loosen them, dismissing my reaction. I'm not someone who's ever cared whether a woman's been with someone else. I only care that Delilah's with me right now and I have no plans to take it easy on her.

As soon as the car pulls up outside the hotel, I'm hustling her out and up to my room. Even as the door swings shut behind us, my hands are cupping her ass and I'm taking her mouth again. I can't seem to stop. The way she moans has me deepening the kiss. She tastes so sweet. If I were any other man, I might get addicted.

I lift her and press her against the wall, rocking into her, pressing my cock against her pussy. She whimpers and bucks against me. Her dress is pushed up, and she wraps her legs around my hips. My need to devour her flames higher as her nails dig into me, holding me close. If she's worried I'm going somewhere, she shouldn't be. There's nowhere else I want to be.

I lower her to the floor, letting the silky material of her dress fall around her legs. "All the way down," I growl as I unzip my pants and pull myself out.

She looks at where my fingers are wrapped around my aching shaft and understanding flares across her face. As does something else.

Want.

Her eyes rise to meet mine, and I'm lost in their green depths, my heart thundering an erratic rhythm in my chest. She breaks the spell by dropping to her knees, the red dress pooling around her on the floor. I'm not sure I've seen anything sexier than Delilah looking up at me with pink-stained cheeks, her full lips a mere inch from my already leaking dick.

I press my thumb into her mouth, a fierce tension

building low and deep inside me when she sucks on it. I let myself enjoy the sensation for a few seconds before tugging her jaw open and sliding the swollen crown of my cock onto her tongue. When I release her, it's only to tangle my hand in her hair. "Show me how much you can take."

Without breaking eye contact, her lips wrap around me, and she slowly sinks down until I hit the back of her throat. She laps at the underside of my shaft, sending flames scorching across my skin. But I want more from her. I want to push her past her comfort zone.

I stroke my thumb across her cheek. "I'm going to go deeper, kitten. Breathe through your nose for me."

She nods, and I use my hand in her hair to hold her still as I drive myself deeper, only stopping when she gags and her eyes begin to water, tears beading on her lower lashes. She hasn't taken all of me, but the way her throat reflexively tightens around the head of my cock triggers an almost unbearable pleasure.

Cupping her jaw, I angle her face up to mine, admiring what a pretty picture she makes. I rub my thumb over her cheek again. "Such a good fucking girl, swallowing my cock so well," I murmur.

Her lashes flutter, and as her moan vibrates through me, I jerk in her mouth, swelling even more.

Fuck. The sensation is so intense that a warning flare shoots up my spine and my abdominal muscles clench. I'm too damn close already. I breathe deep, holding on to my fraying restraint and resisting the urge to pump my hips and fuck her mouth until I spill down her throat.

I'll save that for later. When I come this time, I want to be buried deep inside the pussy I've been craving for way too long.

I pull out, taking in her beautifully disheveled face, her

cheeks damp and her lips red and swollen. As soon as I help her to her feet, I'm shoving my fingers into her hair and tilting her head back so I can lick and nip my way along her jaw. "I'm going to fuck you now, Delilah. Take off that dress and get on your hands and knees on the bed."

Her eyes widen at the demand in my tone, but I'm too impatient to wait any longer.

"Go," I growl.

She takes a few steps away from me, then stops and looks over her shoulder, her lower lip caught between her teeth. God, she's still so fucking inexperienced when it comes to sex, and I know I shouldn't, but I fucking love it.

At least Paul did one thing right—for my purposes, anyway. There's no way that asshole did a damn thing to satisfy her needs or help her explore the latent sensuality that emanates from her with every look and movement and touch. Instead, I'm the one who gets to do it. Even if it's only for one night.

Delilah faces forward again and reaches behind her to unzip her dress. After she slips the straps off her shoulders, she does a little shimmy and lets it fall, leaving her in nothing but her thong and heels.

I press my hand against my cock to ease the ache, but only sinking it into her will help me now. "I hope you're not attached to that tiny scrap of lace you're wearing," I say, "because I'm about to rip it off so I can taste you again."

She freezes and a shiver visibly works its way through her. Then she keeps going, crawling onto the bed and stopping on her hands and knees, just the way I commanded.

After stripping out of my clothes, I stalk toward her. I can't take my eyes off her ass, the material of her saturated thong a thin line between her cheeks. It's still too much covering her, and I hook my fingers in the fabric at her hip and twist, snapping it. Delilah gasps, and I do the same with the other side, crumpling the fabric in my hand. I'll be keeping these, but for now, I let them flutter to the ground by the side of the bed.

I run a finger up the seam of her sex. She's wet, dripping, and when I slip the tip into her opening, my greedy girl clenches around me.

I lean down and run my tongue from her clit all the way to the tight rosette of her ass. She jolts forward, but I don't let her go, wrapping my arm around the top of her thighs to keep her still as I do it again and again.

"Cole," she cries out as I lap at her and spear my tongue into her pussy. God, she tastes fucking incredible.

I rear back, stroking my erection from root to crown. "Do you want me?" I ask.

"Yes." It's a breathless gasp.

"You want me to fill that perfect little cunt of yours with my cock?"

She shudders again. "Yes."

"Beg for it."

She twists her head to look at me over her shoulder, the arousal in her eyes shadowed by doubt. "God, Cole," she says, her voice wavering. "You can't . . . I can't . . ."

I stroke my hand up and down her back. "It's okay to like it, beautiful. This isn't about humiliating you. You begging for my cock doesn't change how I see you, but it does turn me the fuck on, and"—I slick a finger through her wetness, which is practically dripping down her thighs—"I think it turns you on too. So stop thinking and do whatever the hell makes you feel good."

The tension in her body eases under my touch, and she nods. I grip my erection again, sliding the head between her soaked folds until it nudges her clit. She lets out a moan, rocking on her hands and knees to force me to keep moving.

"Beg me." I push her to take the step.

She licks her lips. "Please, Cole." Her voice breaks on my name. "I need your cock. I need you to fuck me. I need you to make me come."

Music to my fucking ears.

I quickly roll on a condom, then grip her ass and flex my fingers. I'm torn. I want to fuck her this way, but I also want to look into her eyes the first time I take her again. The sheer strength of that uncharacteristic urge makes me resist it. Instead, I slide my cock between her legs one more time to coat myself in her arousal, then wrap my hands around her hips. With one hard thrust, I bury myself to the hilt.

"Oh my god," she cries as her body seizes around me.

Blood pounds in my ears as her pussy grips me so tightly I can barely move. I grit my teeth and pull back before pumping into her again, fucking her with long, sure strokes.

Her internal muscles clutch my cock and she's moaning now, clawing at the sheets and pushing back against me. I grip her ass cheeks and spread them so I can watch the way she's stretched around me as I drive into her. The tight ring of muscle between her cheeks captures my attention, and I can't resist the urge to press my thumb against it.

Delilah sucks in a sharp breath and turns her head, her startled gaze meeting mine. Judging by her reaction, she's never been touched here before. I swipe my thumb through her wetness and use it to let me press a little deeper. Her eyes widen. "Cole?"

"Tell me it feels bad, and I'll stop."

She hesitates briefly, then shakes her head. "It doesn't feel bad."

To reward her, I slide my hand around to her front and

tease the swollen bundle of nerves between her legs. The added sensation makes her clench even tighter around me, and my balls draw up. Fuck, I won't last long this first round. Luckily, this is only the first of many tonight.

With my fingers working her clit, and my thumb pushing a little deeper into her ass with every thrust of my hips, I give Delilah no choice but to come. Her body goes rigid, and she lets out a cry as she clamps down hard around me. My fight to hold back is over. I slam into her, closing my eyes and throwing back my head with a low groan as fire races from my balls, along my shaft, and erupts from me. My hips continue to work, and I can't seem to stop coming.

When I finally stop pumping into her, my chest is heaving and even my fingertips are tingling.

Delilah West just fucking wrecked me.

CHAPTER TWENTY-ONE

DELILAH

The limo pulls up outside my apartment, and I look over at Cole. He's been distant throughout our return trip, and I'm not sure why. It's not like I've been a chatterbox, but that's because I'm not used to this type of casual affair and I'm trying to wrap my head around what comes next. Nights like last night must be familiar territory to someone like Cole.

It had been hard for me to slip out of his bed in the early hours of this morning. Harder than I thought it would have been. I probably should have left after he gave me my fifth orgasm of the night, but I'd been so relaxed, filled with the gentle hum of residual pleasure, that I'd fallen asleep with my body still draped over his.

When I'd woken up a few hours later, I'd been shocked to find myself on my back with Cole's hand spread over my stomach as he slept next to me. I expected he would have woken me and told me to go back to my own room. I really didn't want to have that conversation, so I slipped out of the bed, put on my dress, and quietly left—sans panties, of course.

Heat suffuses my skin as I remember the way Cole ripped off my thong last night, but I take that hit of lust, package it in a little box in my mind, and file it safely away under things I'll never forget.

Since Cole still hasn't spoken and appears to be deep in thought, a line etched between his brows, I guess it's up to me to end this. "Well, thank you for, uh, for the opportunity to, uh, visit the site and the gala and . . ."

God, could I be any more awkward? Do I thank him for all the orgasms? Pretend it never happened?

His eyes are on me now, and I'm not sure if the glimmer I see in them is amusement or something else.

"You're welcome, Miss West."

Miss West? I guess we're going with the pretend-it-didn't-happen option. I try to ignore the disappointment that wells in my chest. I knew what this was when I agreed to it.

I nod and put my hand on the door handle.

"I'm not finished with you, Delilah," he says in a low voice.

"I'm sorry," I say. "Do you have something you want to talk about before the team meeting on Friday?"

He nods. "I do." His gaze moves slowly over my face, dipping down to my breasts, then back up. "I want you again."

My lips part and I blink at him. "What?"

"I want to fuck you again. I thought last night would get this out of my system, but there are still things I haven't had a chance to do to you yet."

Considering what he's done already, I'm not sure what else he has in mind. But considering how my pulse has accelerated, my body really, really wants to find out. "So you want us to do this again? Another night?"

He doesn't reply for a moment, just stares at me, a muscle pulsing in his jaw. "More than one night."

I take in a shuddery breath, trying to get my head around what he's suggesting. "You want to date me?"

I wince at the small snort that escapes him.

"I don't date. But I don't want last night to be it. I want us to work this thing out of our systems, and that takes however long it takes."

I shake my head, unsure whether to be offended or flattered. He doesn't want to date me, but apparently one—no, *two*—nights aren't enough.

I can't deny a large part of me wants more too. More of what we did last night, more of how he made my body come to life, more orgasms. But it's not just the sex. He intrigues me. Most of the time he comes across as an arrogant asshole, but then there are those rare flashes of humanity. A glimpse of the man behind the coldhearted-billionaire persona. The man who told me my passion was beautiful, who made me feel more seen in a few words than Paul had in the months we were together.

But I know better than to romanticize this situation. Cole isn't the kind of man to let people in. I need to be okay with that if I decide to go ahead with this arrangement. I can't read more into it.

Not like Mom did with Dad.

"What would that mean for our working relationship?" I find myself asking.

"It doesn't mean anything for our relationship at work. We'll remain professional—"

"Professional?" I eye him as the memory of being pressed against his office door and made to come flows through me.

I see the memory hit him too, a small smile curving his

lips. He dips his head and looks up at me through his lashes, suddenly appearing far younger than he is. "Exactly as professional as we've been so far."

His playful expression is so unexpected that a laugh escapes me, and for a second we're smiling at each other as if whatever this is between us is the start of something sweet and beautiful, not an office fling where my boss gets to fuck me out of his system.

The same thought must occur to him because his expression sobers. "Do you have an answer for me?"

There's a sudden tension in his voice, a snap to his tone that sets my teeth on edge. I wonder about it coming so soon after that moment of boyishness on his part. Does he regret letting me see that side of him?

That glimpse pushes my decision over the line. I need some assurances from him, though. I won't be blind to what this arrangement entails. "I have some stipulations."

Satisfaction flares in his eyes as he realizes what my statement means, but his only reaction is to lean back against his seat, his seeming relaxation offset by the way his hands curl into fists where they rest on his thighs. He inclines his head for me to continue.

"I know this is casual and temporary, but it has to be exclusive. If you decide you're done, you need to tell me before you move on to someone else."

Understanding flits across his face. "The same goes for you," he says. "I don't want you letting another man touch you while you're mine." There's the barest hint of gravel in his voice, and those words and that tone cause heat to curl low in my stomach and my nipples to tighten. Crossing my arms will only draw his attention to my physical reaction, so I will him to remain blind to the way they're pushing against the thin material of my shirt.

It's useless though. Cole's eyes drop to my chest and narrow before rising to focus on my face.

"So we're agreed," he says, and the gravel that was barely there before is in full force now.

I swallow, wondering if I really have any clue what I'm doing, but I nod anyway. Apparently, a night of incredible sex has made me reckless.

Cole works his jaw from side to side. "Come here."

I move toward him, a gasp falling from my lips as he hooks his arm around my waist and hauls me to him so that my knees are on the seat and I'm straddling him.

"What are you—"

"Sealing the deal," he growls, and the next moment, his lips are on mine in a rough and demanding kiss, his teeth tugging on my lower lip, tongue thrusting deep to claim my mouth.

I moan as his hands find my hips and he drags me down until I'm centered over the hard ridge of his cock. My eyelids flutter shut as he uses his hold on me to rock me against him. Little sparks of pleasure ricochet out from my core.

Too soon, he pulls back, his lips curving up at the little sound of protest I make. "As much as I would love to have you ride me right now, kitten, I don't want Jonathan hearing you scream."

"You didn't mind the driver last night." I don't know why I'm arguing the point, since I'm not particularly comfortable with Jonathan hearing me either.

"You'll never see the driver from last night again. I don't want Jonathan thinking about how you sound when you come every time he looks at you."

I bite my lip to hide my smile. It's not exactly the most

romantic thing to say, but somehow it still makes my heart flutter.

I climb off him and straighten my clothes so what I've just been doing isn't obvious. I watch him from under my lashes, but his expression is unreadable again.

Once I'm a bit more put together, I clear my throat, completely unsure how to proceed. "So, I'll see you next week?"

"Yes," he says, and his voice has lost the heat that filled it only a few minutes before.

I guess that's that then. I nod and open the door, but before I can get out, he stops me.

"Delilah."

I turn back to him.

"I'm looking forward to it."

I smile. "Me too."

CHAPTER TWENTY-TWO

COLE

First thing Monday morning, Roman asks me to come to his office. I drop into one of the chairs on the other side of his desk and grab a chocolate chip muffin from the tray his assistant lays out for him every morning. He never eats any of it.

"I'm assuming you want to know how the trip to Chicago went?" I say when he doesn't look up from the papers in front of him. It's a classic Roman power play that he learned from Dad. I became immune to it long ago.

He finally looks up. "Among other things, yes."

"The site is good," I say. "Delilah had some thoughts on maximizing the view."

His cool gray eyes take me in. "She did, did she?"

I meet his gaze unflinchingly. "Yes. She's a very talented architect."

"I'm sure it's her architectural talents you're interested in."

I won't confirm I'm sleeping with her, even if he suspects it, but I won't let him disparage her skills, either.

"She's excellent at what she does, and you'd know that if you bothered to look at any of the plans."

He looks down at his paperwork. "I don't need to anymore. That's your job. And I trust you to do it well."

"I don't think—" I stop when what he said sinks in. I never thought I'd hear those words from my older brother.

"Just make sure you're thinking with the right head on this one, Cole. We can't afford any mistakes, and we can't afford to lose investors. Not unless we want to be the ones saying the company went down on our watch." He pierces me with his gaze.

Ah, that's more like the Roman I know. Still, I can't help but question myself. Delilah already has me doing things I wouldn't normally do. Am I letting myself get distracted from ensuring the company remains strong?

No. I have everything under control. Delilah and I are on the same page. There's nothing to stop us from enjoying each other's bodies while still focusing on doing our jobs, and I'm not just saying that because I can't wait to get her alone again.

"I understand your concerns. But you have nothing to worry about."

He studies me for a few seconds longer, then nods. "There's something else. We need to bring the timeline for submission forward by two weeks."

"Why?"

He leans back in his chair and rubs a hand over his eyes. "I've just heard from legal. There are new requirements for environmental impact studies, which will affect the Dallas and Phoenix sites. I don't want to announce a delay if we apply and then need to make adjustments post-application. So—"

"So, we apply early and get feedback with enough time

to make adjustments and still resubmit in time to make our original timeline."

Roman nods. "Can you do it?"

The team is good. I have no doubt they can pull it off. "I'll call a meeting this morning and let them know. I don't anticipate a problem."

"Good. Let me know if any issues crop up," he says.

I stand, straightening my cuffs as I do so.

"Don't forget, there's the Manhattan Philanthropy Gala the weekend after next. It wouldn't hurt to turn up with Jessica. There'll be a lot of press there, and being seen with Berrington's daughter will send a message to anyone harboring concerns about the company's stability."

If he's worried I'll turn up with Delilah on my arm, he should know better. The past weekend aside, what she and I are doing will remain strictly behind closed doors. "I know what's required," I say, then I stride toward the door, leaving his office and returning to mine.

I stop off at Samson's desk and ask him to organize a meeting with the architects. Then I sit at my desk to start addressing various issues that flared up while I was gone. Five minutes later, Samson buzzes me to let me know he's scheduled the meeting for after lunch. While I wait for a call from our UK office, I take a second to think about seeing Delilah today. I hadn't planned to. The last thing I want is to set up an expectation that this is anything more than a casual physical relationship. And yet I can't deny that the thought doesn't exactly make me unhappy.

Visions of Friday night and Saturday morning invade my head, and arousal simmers in my blood. Luckily, my phone rings, distracting me. As I pick up, I have a smile on my face, and it's not in anticipation of talking about market conditions in Europe.

I've got a lot planned for Delilah over the next few weeks. I hope she's prepared.

AS I FLICK through the messages Samson forwarded to me, I sense Delilah enter the meeting room. I glance up to see her gorgeous green eyes land on me. She looks as sexy as hell in a white silk blouse that's unbuttoned just enough to reveal a hint of cleavage, and a pencil skirt that emphasizes her slender waist and the curve of her hips. Her lips tip up before her attention darts away, as if worried someone will catch her smiling at me.

Paul walks in next and decides to sit next to her. My eyes narrow. Delilah doesn't look at him and deliberately angles her body away. I sweep the room and find Bruce, Elite's new project liaison, sitting at the end of the table. Luckily for Paul, he did what he promised, and Philippa quietly disappeared from the office. I was half-expecting to get a call from one of Elite's senior partners about the request, but none came, so he must have thought of a convincing enough reason for her removal.

I would have thought he was smart enough to leave Delilah alone, though. I don't know why he thinks sitting next to her is a good idea. Surely he doesn't think he can win her back. The idea of him trying should make me laugh. After all, Delilah is far too smart to give him any more chances. And yet, as he shifts closer to her, my fingers tighten around my pen, and I have a sudden urge to stalk over there, rip him out of his chair, and throw him out of the room. See him try to explain that to his senior partners.

Where the hell are these irrational thoughts coming from? I shake my head. I need to concentrate on this meeting, not the strangeness of my reactions when it comes to Delilah.

I clear my throat, and all conversation at the table dies. I start the meeting, updating everyone on the revised project timeline. Looking directly at Paul, I mention the visit Delilah and I made to the Chicago site on Friday. By the way his jaw clenches, I get the feeling he suspects something more than work went on during the trip.

He's right, of course, but I don't give a fuck if he suspects something. There's nothing he can do about it except regret his actions. I just give him a cool smile that makes his fist clench on the table before he looks down at his legal pad and picks up his pen as if he's taking notes.

After I get a rundown from everyone on their plans for the week ahead, I open the floor to questions. Once that's wrapped up, I end the meeting and stand, making my way to the door as the team gathers their notes and follows me out.

Using the excuse of pausing to fire off a quick email to Roman on my phone, I wait for Delilah to exit the room. When she emerges with Paul walking next to her, his head bent to talk directly in her ear, my muscles tense. I'm not sure what he's saying to her, but from the stiff expression on her face, she doesn't seem happy about it. I resist the urge to intervene. After all, despite my new and disconcerting feelings of possessiveness, Delilah is more than capable of looking after herself.

She stops and faces him, putting a hand up and pushing against his chest, forcing him to give her some space. I can't see what she's saying, but her chin is up, her delicate jaw firm as she talks. Paul scowls and rubs his hand over his mouth, but he nods and takes a step back. Delilah continues toward the elevator.

"Miss West. Can I see you in my office?" I say.

She looks startled, as if she hadn't even noticed me standing there, but she nods and changes course.

My eyes meet Paul's, and I can tell by the anger simmering there that he knows—or at least strongly suspects —that I'm fucking her. It shouldn't give me so much pleasure, but it does. And I let it show on my face.

I'm still smirking as I turn my back on him and follow Delilah to my office. I can almost feel the daggers he's shooting into my back, but I couldn't give a fuck if he's pissed or not. He screwed up with Delilah. Twice. He doesn't deserve her.

I catch up with her as she stops outside my door.

"What do you want to—"

"Inside," I say, pushing the door open and ushering her in with a hand on her back. I don't bother to check whether Paul is still watching.

As soon as I close the door, I turn and press her against it, swallowing her gasp as my hands roam over her curves.

"Cole, what are you doing?" she breathes as my lips skim over the smooth skin of her neck.

I wrap her hair around my fist and tilt her head so she's looking up at me. "What was Paul saying to you?"

She blinks. "He asked what happened while we were in Chicago."

"What did you tell him?"

She presses her full lips together. "I told him that considering he didn't think I had a right to know he was sleeping with Philippa when we were together, he doesn't have a right to know who I'm sleeping with when we're not."

That's my girl.

I tug her head back and brush my lips over the pulse

point fluttering at the base of her throat. "What time are you finishing today?"

"I'll probably work until six."

"Come home with me tonight." I wince, even as I hear myself say the words. I don't take women back to my penthouse. It's my private sanctuary. But now that I've said it, I can't take it back. If I take her to the hotel where we shared our first night, she'll have questions.

Turns out I don't have to worry about that, though.

"I can't tonight. I'm having dinner with Alex. I'm going there straight from work."

She's blowing me off to have dinner with another man? "Who's Alex?" Even to me, my voice sounds rougher than usual.

"My roommate. We have a standing dinner date every Monday. She's missing her fiancé, so I don't want to skip it."

I didn't know my muscles had tightened, but they relax now. Although I'm not particularly happy that I won't have her tonight, it's the visceral response I had to the thought of her having dinner with another man that's concerning. Even though I agreed with her stipulation to keep this arrangement exclusive, I wasn't expecting to be bothered by who she spent her time with.

"Okay," I say curtly, letting her go and making my way to my desk.

She's still standing by the door when I sit down. She's tucked in her blouse and looks put together again. As gorgeous as she is, I prefer seeing her with signs of my touch all over her.

"I'm free tomorrow night," she says, her head tilted as she studies me.

"I have plans." It's true. It's also something I could reorganize, but my irrationally possessive reactions coupled with Roman's earlier words of warning have me suddenly needing to rein in my desire for her—to prove to myself that I have this thing under control.

She stands there for a moment, watching me, and even now I'm fighting the urge to go over there, shove my hand up her skirt, and push my fingers into slick heat.

"I have to go," she says.

"Okay."

She hesitates another second, but when I don't say more, she turns and slips out the door.

I lean back in my chair and pinch the bridge of my nose.

What the hell is going on with me?

CHAPTER TWENTY-THREE

DELILAH

Alex puts down her wineglass. "You turned down a night in a billionaire's penthouse for me? I'm flattered, but you shouldn't have."

"Yes, I should," I say, taking a sip of my wine. "He's very . . . overwhelming, you know? I mean, doing something like this in the first place is not like me. I can't let myself get completely sucked in by him, because he'll just chew me up and spit me out. I also really can't afford to screw up this job."

Alex's brow crinkles. "Then why are you doing it?"

I run my finger around the rim of my glass and let out a sigh. "I'm not sure. I've never felt anything like this, you know? I've never been . . . swept away by anything or anyone. I've always done the smart thing."

I've spent my life achieving one goal after another, but there's a price for that level of commitment. One I wasn't sure I'd thought twice about paying until the first night Cole touched me. He showed me another side to life I'd been missing in my single-minded drive to secure financial futures for my mother and myself.

"Yeah, I get that. You've been so focused on work ever since I met you, so I don't hate the idea of you doing something that gets you out of the office. But . . ."

I brace myself. "But what?"

"As hot as he is, and as much as I've been pro having the sexy billionaire give you multiple orgasms, I can't help but wish someone other than him had swept you off your feet. After everything you've said, he doesn't sound like the most emotionally available man around."

"If it's just a casual fling, does it matter if he's emotionally available?"

Alex's smile is gentle. "If I thought it would stay just a casual fling, I'd agree with you, but you know how these things go. Usually someone catches feelings, and from what you've told me, it doesn't sound like it's going to be Cole."

I pause as the waiter brings out our meals, placing the pasta-filled dishes in front of us. As delicious as it looks, I don't dig in straight away. "I was with Paul for months and I didn't fall for him."

Alex swallows the mouthful she's already taken and raises her brows at me. "I wouldn't exactly compare Paul to Cole."

I laugh. "Good point."

Alex reaches across the table and squeezes my hand. "As long as you're having fun and guarding your heart."

I squeeze back. "I am. I'm doing both things."

"Good." She goes back to eating. "So, what's the plan? You've turned him down for tonight. Will you accept his next offer? Or maybe you should go into his office tomorrow, lock the door, and take him for a ride."

I snort. "That might be a bit more advanced than I'm capable of at the moment."

"Learn by doing, Dee. Learn by doing."

I swirl strands of spaghetti around my fork. "I might work my way up to that lesson."

"Fair enough." She raises her wineglass with a smile. "Well, here's to having fun with a hot, hung billionaire."

I laugh again and clink my glass against hers. "Cheers to that."

And to living life more fully than I ever have before.

THE NEXT MORNING I'm putting the finishing touches on a revised exterior 3D visual when Paul saunters up. He places one hand on my desk and leans over me. "We need to talk."

I look up at the face that I used to find handsome. "Is this about work?"

"Of course. Those were your instructions, weren't they?"

I don't like the snide tone of his voice, but he's still my project manager, and I need to be mature about this. "Okay," I say, standing and smoothing my skirt down my thighs. He leads me to his office, which is in the corner of the otherwise open office space.

He ushers me in, and I take a seat. Instead of sitting at his desk, he leans against it and crosses his arms, looking down at me.

"What are you playing at, Delilah?"

I frown. "What are you talking about?"

"Cole King," he hisses. "Are you crazy, or is this just your way of getting revenge?"

I stand in a rush. "I thought you said this was about work?"

"It is. If you're screwing the biggest client this firm has

ever had, you're risking our reputation. And that means you're risking your job."

My mouth drops open. "Is that a threat?"

"No, it's not a threat. I'm just saying, it's not like you to make such reckless decisions."

"Well, maybe it's about time I started making reckless decisions," I say.

"It sounds like you've been making those since the first time we broke up. For god's sake, Delilah, you screwed some random at a bar. Maybe if you'd given me what you gave him, we wouldn't be in this situation."

I'm shaking with anger. "What situation are you talking about? The one where you're an asshole who cheated on me and now can't stand the thought that I might have moved on with someone a hundred times better than you? How is Philippa, by the way? I was surprised when Bruce took over the role."

He clears his throat. "I decided it would be better if she weren't here, and she was due for some leave anyway." His tone changes, becoming softer. "I was thinking of you, Delilah. I didn't want to hurt you anymore than I already have. Can't you see? I'm sorry for what I did. It was a terrible mistake and I regret it. Don't risk your job just to get back at me. You know the type of man Cole is. He'll break your heart worse than I ever could. All I want is a second chance with you. To show you how I've changed."

"You already had a second chance—after you broke up with me because I didn't jump into bed with you."

"You didn't have trouble jumping into bed with someone else, though, did you? Does Cole know you're the type of woman to go out to bars and pick up strange men?"

I'm so angry, I almost blurt out that Cole knows very well that I'm that kind of woman, and he definitely didn't have a problem with it. But I refuse to be as unprofessional as Paul. Instead, I ask the burning question. "Is that why you cheated on me? Because I slept with someone else after you ended it with me? Was it supposed to be some kind of punishment?"

He crosses his arms and looks out the window for a moment, and at least he has the grace to look embarrassed.

"You owe me the truth," I say.

He turns back to me and his shoulders sag. "It didn't start out that way—to punish you."

"So what then?"

"When I was in the London office, Philippa and I hooked up. It was only ever meant to be casual, and it ended when I came back home. Then you and I started dating. But when she came over from the UK, she let me know she wanted to continue our relationship. I'd hoped things would progress between you and me, but obviously they didn't. Since Philippa made it clear she wanted us to pick up where we left off, I decided breaking up with you was the best thing to do."

"So while we were broken up, you and Philippa . . ."

"Yes, but Delilah, what Philippa and I had was only physical. After you and I split up, I missed you."

I cross my arms over my chest. "And that's when you decided to apologize and ask me to take you back? And what, you just forgot to let Philippa know?"

"No." He scrubs his hand over his face. "I broke it off with her, but then you told me you'd slept with someone else while we were apart, and . . ." He shrugs helplessly. "I tried to be okay with it, I really did. But I was angry. Philippa and I were working late one night, and. . . Well, you know how things like that can happen."

"No. I don't know how things like that can happen. Because I would never cheat on someone."

He scowls. "Of course not. You'd just screw your company's client. How very conscientious of you."

I've had enough of his pettiness. I have an answer about what happened, and I don't want to look at his face anymore. I push my way past him and into the main office, only to grind to a halt when I see the figure standing by my desk.

What is Cole doing here?

Paul follows me out of his office, and obviously not expecting me to have stopped just outside of it, he runs into me, grabbing my hips to steady us both.

Cole's eyes drop to Paul's hands, and it's as if every muscle in his body draws tight—like a predatory cat that's about to strike.

I step forward, pulling out of Paul's hold. When I shoot a glance at him over my shoulder, I can see he's trying to stare Cole down.

This isn't good.

I walk briskly to my desk. "Mr. King, can I help you with something?"

He's staring over my head at Paul, but at my words, he looks down at me. His eyes narrow slightly. "I came to see how the new plans for the Chicago build are tracking?"

I'm not sure if I believe him. This is the first time he's come down to the office since we've been here; normally we're summoned if we're needed. A part of me is ridiculously thrilled at the idea he might have come down here just to see me. The other part is nervous about how it might look to everyone else in the office.

Still, I smile at him, hoping to ease the tension around

his eyes. "Of course. I have them here if you'd like to see them."

He gives a curt nod, and I shuffle through the pile of plans on my desk until I find the ones I'm modifying. Cole stands beside me, his arm brushing mine. Paul loiters nearby, but when he catches my gaze on him, he scowls and returns to his office. The rest of the team sneak glances, but no one is openly staring.

As I point out the changes, there's a light brush of fingertips against the back of my thigh. I suck in a breath, my voice faltering for a moment. Luckily, my desk is against a wall and my computer screens block the view from the office.

"Continue," he says, and I clear my throat and talk about the structural changes I've made to the building so it can bear the green roof's extra weight, as well as the modifications I'd suggested during our trip to Chicago. And as I do, his hand slides under my skirt, his knuckles brushing across my panties.

"Cole," I whisper, even as his fingers slip under the material. I let out a shuddery breath. "What are you—"

"What were you doing with Paul?"

Before I can answer, he spears a finger inside me, and it takes everything I have to hold in the gasp that rises to my lips. My gaze flies around the room, and I'm relieved to see everyone's gone back to their work and no one is looking at Cole and me.

I close my eyes for a second, wondering if it's wrong that I should enjoy what he's doing to me in an office full of my colleagues. Especially since I can hear the thread of accusation winding through his words.

His finger moves in and out of me as we stare down at the plans in front of us. I struggle to form words. "He was . . . uh . . . wanting to know why I would be reckless enough to sleep with you. And then . . . And then . . ."

I let out a little whimper as he adds a second finger.

"And then what, kitten?" His tone is dark, seductive.

"And then I asked him to explain why he cheated on me."

"Did he give you a good reason?"

I narrow my eyes at him. "Is there ever a good reason?"

He doesn't answer the question, only studies me, his eyes dipping to my lips. "Are you looking for an excuse to take him back?"

I start to straighten, but he pushes his fingers into me, and I'm forced to brace my hands on the desk. "No, of course not."

His fingers stop moving inside me, and he leans closer. "Good, because I'm not done with this sweet little pussy yet." He leans a little closer. "And I have plans for her."

He pulls his fingers out, smoothing the material of my panties over me.

"Can you show me the estimates?" he asks, as if he wasn't just knuckle deep inside me.

With shaky hands, I pull out the sheet and place it on top of the plans. But he doesn't care about the cost. It's just an excuse for him to bend down and murmur in my ear. "You're coming back to my place tonight. Stay late. We'll leave straight from work."

"I thought you had plans tonight."

"I did. Now I don't."

"What about work tomorrow?" I ask.

He chuckles darkly. "Don't worry. I won't keep you out too late on a school night."

Well, that answers the question I didn't ask. I obviously won't be staying the night. And while I can't help the instinctual hurt I feel because he only wants me for one thing, I'm well aware that's what I signed up for. Not to mention, I'm still tingling from the illicit feeling of having his fingers inside me in front of my co-workers, and I need him to finish what he started.

"Say yes," he mutters in my ear as another feather-light touch grazes my thigh.

"Yes, Cole."

I glance at him in time to see the corners of his lips twitch up, his eyes glittering, sending a delicious shiver down my spine.

He's not using me. We're using each other.

And who knew it could feel so good?

CHAPTER TWENTY-FOUR

COLE

When I walk into the architectural team's office space that evening, it's late enough that the place is empty. Except for Delilah. She's sitting at her desk, and I pause for a moment to watch her.

Her long, dark hair is drawn back in a ponytail, with a few loose tendrils falling forward to frame her face as she looks down at what she's doing. Her lower lip is caught between her teeth and her brow is slightly furrowed as she concentrates.

She's fucking gorgeous, and my dick stirs in my pants as I anticipate the hours to come, but I don't move from where I'm loitering at the doorway. My behavior this afternoon is confusing me. I decided to rein in my attraction to her, but after not seeing her last night, the urge to see her today had taken control of me. I canceled my planned dinner meeting with one of my old college associates and did something I hadn't done since her team moved into the building. I went down there to see her.

The looks I received when I walked in reminded me why I rarely mingle with the workers. Everyone stiffened at my presence, then rushed to look as busy as possible. I made my way to Delilah's empty desk, wondering where she was and what I should do now that I was there and she wasn't.

It was then that she walked out of an office near the end of the room, looking like a fucking fantasy in a skirt that hugged her hips before flaring out to flirt with her thighs, and a pale-pink blouse which revealed the barest hint of lace beneath it.

But when Paul walked out and stood behind her, with his hands gripping her hips, a tidal wave of possessiveness crashed over me.

I've rarely felt the urge to punch anyone. In my position, people don't often dare to cross me. But seeing Paul touching her—touching what I'd already claimed as mine, even if only temporarily—made me see red in a way I never have before.

And now here I am, watching her work like I'm some kind of crazy person.

Enough.

I stalk to her desk. She jumps when she notices me, her hand fluttering to her chest. Then she lets out a light laugh. "You scared me."

"Maybe you should be scared," I say.

She looks up at me, a playful expression on her face. "Should I? Why is that, Mr. King?"

I lean over her, bracing one hand on her desk, the other on the back of her chair. "Because before the night is out, I'm going to make you scream."

Her lips part and her pupils dilate, her voice dropping to a whisper. "Should I run, then?"

I lean even closer and growl. "I wouldn't recommend it."

She blows out a breath. "Y-you're good at this."

I straighten with a smirk. "I'll show you just how good I am when we get back to my place. So let's go, before I bend you over this table and fuck you right here."

She stands in a rush. "I'd say you were joking, but at this stage I wouldn't put it past you."

"Smart girl."

She throws me a smile which will get her in trouble, but I don't say anything. I just wait for her to gather her things together, then put my hand on the small of her back and guide her toward the door.

Jonathan has the car waiting for us outside. Delilah glances around as he opens the door for her, as if she's worried someone might see us. I understand her concern, but it's unlikely anyone aside from my brothers and their PAs will be loitering this late, and I'm not worried about their opinions.

But luckily for her, she doesn't try to change her mind, sliding into the back seat and looking up at me as I follow her in.

As Jonathan pulls the car into traffic, my gaze is still tangled with Delilah's; I can't seem to tear it away. Visions of her laid out before me on my bed—and the things I can do to her—tumble through my mind. A smorgasbord that I get to choose from. Surprisingly, the thought of having her in my own bed doesn't disturb me as much as I expected it to.

The thought of seeing her spread out over my black silk sheets, or her face buried in one of my pillows as I take her from behind, has blood surging south. I'm about to reach for her when a ringing from her purse breaks the connection between us.

She rummages around and pulls out her phone, her eyes darting to me.

I raise a brow. "You can answer it." At least that way I'll know if it's a man or not.

"Thanks." She swipes her screen and holds it to her ear. "Hi, Mom."

I relax, even though I didn't know I was tense to begin with.

"Oh . . . I'm just . . . on my way to a . . . friend's place," she says, her eyes darting to mine again.

I smile to myself and turn to face the window, giving her as much privacy as I can, but I can't help overhearing her conversation in the close confines of the car. I give up trying to avoid listening.

"You know me, I like being busy," she says. Then she laughs. "I might not go out and party every night, but I'm not exactly confining myself at home. . . . No. I'm not dating anyone else yet," she says, and she's lowered her voice. "Look, Mom, I'm almost at my friend's place, so I should probably go. I'll call you later this week." She's silent for a second. "I miss you too. I'll organize a flight home as soon as I can, and we can spend the weekend together. Okay. I love you too. Bye, Mom."

I'm struck by the genuine warmth and affection in her voice. Have I ever spoken to either of my parents that way? Maybe when I was young. Before I realized they considered my brothers and me as mere pawns in their genetic legacy.

"I'm sorry about that," she says as she slips her phone into her purse.

"No need to be sorry." I clear my throat. "You and your mom are close?"

She smiles, her eyes soft. "Yes. It's only ever been her and me. We're each other's best friend."

"You mentioned before that your father wasn't in the

picture." I don't frame it as a question—even though it is—so I'm surprised when, after a small pause, she answers.

"Mom got pregnant with me when she was eighteen. He was older than her, but he wasn't interested in starting a family. Not with us, anyway." Her voice is casual—almost flippant—but the shadow in her eyes tells me her tone is a lie.

"Do you see him at all?"

"I occasionally saw him around town when I was growing up, but not since I was sixteen."

"What happened when you were sixteen?"

She shrugs. "Nothing in particular. He just walked past me in the street."

Rising anger tightens my ribs. "Did he talk to you? Acknowledge you?"

She looks away before meeting my gaze again. "He saw me, but he just kept going. Climbed into his Mercedes and drove off. I didn't expect anything different."

I consciously loosen the fists my hands have tightened into without me realizing. I don't have a lot of good things to say about my father, but I have even less to say about Delilah's. "I'd say you were better off without him."

"I like to think so," she says, flashing me a small smile that has my heart doing something odd in my chest.

"What does your mom do?"

"She's a hairdresser." Delilah absently touches the end of her ponytail, and I imagine her mom probably cut her hair for her when she was younger.

I nod, but instead of continuing the conversation, I look out the window. I'm not used to asking this many questions of the women I'm with. My interest in Delilah is . . . unusual. Maybe because she's different from the women I normally sleep with. Considering most of them are part of a social sphere where appearance is everything, vulnerability is considered a lethal weakness. And love . . . Well, love is a transaction.

Tonight isn't supposed to be about getting to know each other, though. It's about one thing and one thing only. The less we share regarding our private lives, the easier it will be for her to keep that straight in her mind.

We ride the rest of the way in silence. My penthouse isn't far from the office, and I'm glad because I'm itching to strip her out of that outfit and finish what I started in her office this afternoon.

When we pull up outside my building and Jonathan opens the door for Delilah, she steps out gracefully and stops to look up at the building, then to the trees of Central Park looming on the other side of the street.

Her gaze meets mine. "I knew you were rich, but . . ." She glances away again, up at the huge steel-and-glass building that reaches skyward. "Sometimes reality outstrips imagination."

I picture this through her eyes. From what she's told me, her mom struggled to give her the things she needed, to keep a safe, comfortable roof over their heads, and now I'm about to take her up to my multi-million-dollar penthouse apartment that I purchased without a second thought.

I'm not ashamed of my wealth—why would I be?—and yet I feel something right now I've never felt before. Not shame, but maybe the wish that someone had been there to help support her mom and her when she was growing up.

Someone like her father.

I'm hit by the urge to find out who he is and what he does, to learn if there's any way I can make his life just a little harder. I make a mental note to get Samson to look into it tomorrow. It won't hurt to find out his name and see what business he's in.

The doorman has been watching us keenly, waiting to leap into action, so I start toward him. I've only taken a couple of steps before I realize Delilah isn't next to me. She's looking across at Central Park again, a faint smile on her face as she watches a couple walk past, arm in arm, heads tipped together as they laugh at something.

I reach back and grab her hand, threading my fingers through hers. Her focus switches from the couple to where our hands are connected, then up to my face. The curve lingering on her lips and the way her fingers curl around mine send a strange pulse of warmth through me.

I clear my throat. "Let's go," I say, brusquely.

As expected, the doorman jumps forward, opening the door and tipping his hat at us. "Good evening, sir, ma'am."

I give him a nod. "Good evening, Jeffrey."

"Hello." Delilah gives him a smile that has his grizzled cheeks reddening.

I grumble to myself and tug her after me.

We ride up to my penthouse in my private elevator, and when the doors open directly onto my foyer, I hear her indrawn breath. It's only when I lead her out that I realize I'm still holding her hand.

I use the excuse of shrugging out of my suit jacket to let go of her, but she doesn't seem to notice. The foyer opens directly onto the open-plan living area, and she's focused on the view over the park and the glitter of the city skyline, both visible from the floor-to-ceiling windows that line the room.

"I can't believe you get to look at this view every day," she says.

I stand next to her. "You get used to it after a while."

She tips her head up to me. "That's a shame." When I don't respond, she walks past me and her mouth drops open. "Oh my god."

The main living room is huge, sleek, and modern, with high ceilings, hardwood floors, and expensive art hanging on the walls. The kitchen is visible at the other end of the room. It's a spotless white, with state-of-the art appliances that never get used because cooking isn't one of my skills.

Delilah turns to me. "Your home is beautiful, Cole."

"Then my interior designer earned her pay." I don't bother to mention that this place has never felt that much like a home. But then, I'm not sure if any place I've lived in has felt that way.

Delilah rolls her eyes at me, then laughs softly. The sound does things to me that are anything but soft.

I reach for her, pull her close and drop my head so my lips brush the curve of her neck and I can breathe her in. My already hardening cock swells even more at the feel of her against me.

I don't want to talk about my apartment. Or her family. I definitely don't want to talk about *my* family. I just want this. Her body and mine. Together.

And I'm not waiting another minute.

I TIE a knot in the condom and drop it into the trash. As I turn to leave the bathroom, I glimpse myself in the mirror. A fine sheen of perspiration coats my body, and the satisfied gleam in my eyes has everything to do with the orgasms I've had over the last two hours. And even more, the ones I've given Delilah.

Although I came only a few minutes ago, the thought of

her lying stretched out and naked in my bed has me hardening.

It's late and she's probably tired, but I think I can drag another orgasm out of her before I send her home. I exit the bathroom, only to stop when I see Delilah standing by the side of the bed, pulling her skirt over the curve of her ass.

She already has her bra on, and as I watch, she reaches for her blouse.

I cross my arms and lean my shoulder against the door-frame. "Going somewhere?"

She glances at me over her shoulder, a tentative smile playing on her lips. "I think five is probably my limit. And I didn't want to . . ."

"What?" I ask.

She turns away. "Overstay my welcome."

I want to go to her, strip her naked again, and throw her back on my bed. But I don't. Because it is late. And she's right. I should have had enough of her by now. The goal might be for me to fuck her out of my system, but it obviously won't happen all in one night.

So instead of doing what I want to do, I just nod and go to my dresser to fish out a pair of pajama pants.

We dress in silence. While I usually don't have a problem with the part of the night which involves sending a woman home, something about this feels off, and not knowing what it is or why I'm feeling it is irritating.

"Okay," Delilah says, breaking me from my reverie. "Is it still all right to get a ride home, or would it be better to call for an Uber? It's pretty late. I'd hate to wake Jonathan."

"Don't worry about Jonathan. I pay him a hefty salary to be available whenever I need him. And besides," I add, "I wouldn't trust a rideshare with you. Particularly at this time of night."

A soft smile curves her lips. She walks over to me, goes up on her toes, and brushes her lips over my jaw. "Thank you."

Something hot and potent rushes through my veins, and I band my arm around her waist and haul her into me, molding her body to mine. I want to kiss her, but I don't. The emotions Delilah brings out in me are unfamiliar. They make me feel out of control, and I don't like feeling out of control. So I drop my head and breathe in her scent—the faint aroma of the wildflower perfume that still lingers on her skin. Then I let her go. "I'll call Jonathan and tell him to meet you outside."

"All right. I'll wait down there for him."

I reach for a shirt, but Delilah stops me. "You don't have to come down with me. I'm okay waiting on my own." She turns away and walks out of the bedroom.

After a moment's hesitation, I toss my shirt back in the drawer and follow her out. We walk through my huge apartment until we get to the foyer and my private elevator.

I press the button for her, and the doors sweep soundlessly apart. She faces me and gives me a slightly wonky smile. "Thank you. For tonight. I had . . . um . . . fun."

An honest to god laugh slips past my lips. "I think you need more practice at this part."

She groans and covers her face with her hands, then laughs too. "You might be right."

I cave to the urge that's clawing at my chest and grab her by the waist, pressing her backward until she's against the wall next to the elevator. Then I curve my hand around her slender neck and use my thumb on the angle of her jaw to tilt her face to mine. I take her mouth the way I wanted to before. The doors of the elevator whoosh shut beside us, but I ignore it.

Her taste is intoxicating. Like the finest vintage in my wine cellar, and if I could, I'd spend the rest of the night getting drunk on her. But before I can do something I'm bound to regret in the morning, I tear my mouth from hers and smack the button next to us, causing the doors to open again.

I step back, eyeing her as she stands with her back pressed against the wall, chest rising and falling, mouth swollen from the intensity of my kiss. Then she blinks, licks those swollen lips, and lets out a shuddery breath before peeling herself off the wall and stepping into the elevator.

Her gaze holds mine. "Good night, Cole."

"Good night, Delilah." My voice comes out gruff.

And then she's gone, and my apartment is suddenly empty.

CHAPTER TWENTY-FIVE

DELILAH

"What are you doing this weekend?" I tuck my phone between my cheek and shoulder as I drop the tea bag into my cup and pour in the hot water. It's Friday night, and with Cole having plans, I decided to leave the office at a normal hour, relax at home, and give Mom a call. Considering how distracted I've been with work and Cole over the last two weeks, we haven't spoken as often as usual.

"A book I've had on hold for weeks at the library has finally come in, so I'm going to pick it up tomorrow morning and spend all weekend devouring it," Mom says.

I laugh. "Sounds perfect."

She sighs happily. "Doesn't it? One day, when I have my dream house, I'm going to make sure it has its very own library. One with a ladder to reach the top shelves."

"And a window seat?"

"Of course. A window seat is essential for any home library. Oh, and it needs to be a bay window looking out over a beautiful garden."

This is a game my mom and I play. It started when I was young and one of my friends pointed out a big, beautiful house behind a black wrought-iron gate and enviously listed all the fancy things that must be inside it. She didn't know the house belonged to my father's family, but I did. Mom had always been honest with me, and that included answering my questions when I started asking about my dad.

When I saw Mom that afternoon and mentioned it to her, she'd sat me down and told me that a house can be big and beautiful and full of expensive things, but that doesn't mean it's full of love. And then together, we'd started dreaming up all the wonderful things we'd put into our own dream house. One that would be full of everything that gave us joy.

And we still do it today.

After chatting for a while longer, I say goodbye to Mom and immediately go to my little desk in the corner of the room. I pull out the plans I keep rolled inside a document holder and spread them out over my desk.

Mom doesn't know it, but describing our dream house that day ignited my desire to be an architect. I wanted to be the one to design my mom's perfect house. Throughout high school, I used to doodle ideas in the backs of my schoolbooks. Once I started college and learned the proper skills, I began drawing them up. The thought of surprising her with the plans one day, and eventually having enough money to build it for her, was the dream that kept me going through years of study. And after that, the hard work to get my license.

Imagining her happiness when she finally got to live in her dream house—one that would far surpass the house my dad had lived in when I was young, because it was full of everything she loved—always made me happy.

I make some changes to the plan in front of me. I've already added a library, since it's something she's mentioned before, but now I want to make it larger and add in the bay window. This isn't the first iteration of Mom's house I've created. I've gone through quite a few variations throughout the years. As my skills increased and I had different ideas, or when Mom mentioned something else she'd like that I hadn't already thought of, I'd make changes.

I'm so caught up in perfecting Mom's library that I don't realize Alex is home until she speaks behind me. "Working on your mom's house again?"

I put down my drafting pencil and stretch before turning to face her. "I want it to be perfect by the time I finally have the money to build it for her."

She peers over my shoulder. "It looks pretty perfect to me."

"It's getting there." I roll up the plans and store them back in the corner. Then I get up and wander to the couch while Alex rummages around in the small kitchen, putting together a dinner of leftovers. Pretty much what I had done several hours ago.

"Not spending the evening with lover boy tonight?" she asks as she shoves some Chinese food from a couple of days ago into the microwave.

"No. He has some kind of event he has to attend tonight."

"It's been a few weeks since we've had a Friday night together," she says.

I grimace. "I know. I'm sorry. I've been a bad friend."

"No, you haven't. I'm only joking. It's good that you're getting some so regularly. At least one of us is." The microwave dings and she pulls out the steaming bowl of food, then comes over and plops next to me on the couch.

"Does Jaxson have plans to visit?" I ask.

She sighs. "Not for a while. He's busy attending PR events and then they'll be in the studio to record their album."

"Has he said anything more about their plans? Are they still considering moving to LA?"

Alex's shoulders slump a little. "They're still debating it. It makes sense for them to be there, but all four of them have lived in New York their whole lives. It's a big choice."

"And there's you. Don't forget, you're his future too, not just his music. Have you told him how much you're missing him?"

Alex bites her lip. "I've tried to hide it. I want Jaxson to do the right thing for him and his band without worrying about how I'm feeling. But honestly, just this little taste of having a long-distance relationship has been harder than I expected."

"What about your idea of getting a job in the LA office?"

"I asked about it, but they don't have any positions available. Something might open up in the future, but nothing at the moment."

"Would you consider joining another firm?"

"If I have to. I suppose I'm waiting until the guys make up their minds about what they're going to do. And then I'll decide."

I reach over and give her a hug. "I'm sorry. I know it's hard and you miss him. I shouldn't have left you here all by yourself so often."

Alex waves her hand in the air, her usual smile returning. "You haven't. And it's not like I'm curled up in bed crying. Yes, I miss him, but we talk every night and I've got my classes. And it's not like you're my only friend." She pokes me in the stomach. "I go out with my other friends plenty. That doesn't mean I won't monopolize your attention and get you to update me on what's happening with tall, dark, rich, and handsome when you're here."

I stretch my legs in front of me. "I don't know if there's much to update you on. I go over to his place. We have sex. I come home."

Alex looks at me skeptically. "In the last two weeks, you've been at his place almost every second night. There must be more to it than just sex."

"I don't know. I mean . . . you know what I said about him being overwhelming? Well, he is, and sometimes it's hard to separate what's him being the man that he is from him feeling something more than just lust. Every now and then he does something that makes me think there might be more between us. The next minute he does something that reminds me that this is just casual sex for him."

Alex slurps up a noodle. "Maybe he's still working out how he feels."

"Or maybe I'm reading too much into things, and this is just how he is with the women he sleeps with—intense."

"Well, how do you feel about him?"

That's a loaded question and one I've deliberately avoided asking myself. I want to believe I can keep this thing between Cole and me only physical. That I can enjoy what he's offering, knowing it will end one day and he'll walk away without a second thought. But what I said to Alex is true. He is intense, and his occasional hot-and-cold attitude gives me whiplash.

He's all over me when I'm there with him, doling out orgasm after orgasm until my legs shake so much I can barely walk, but the minute it comes time for me to leave, he goes cold. Since that first night, he doesn't kiss me when I go. He kisses me plenty while we're naked and writhing around together on his bed or his couch or his dining table, but when I'm dressed and standing at the elevator doors, all I get is a cool farewell.

That should be more than enough for me to keep my heart under wraps, but there's something in the way his gaze lingers on me right up until the elevator doors close that makes my heart do crazy things. And there are other moments too. When I see one of his rare smiles or hear one of his even rarer laughs. When he runs his lips tenderly down my neck or traces the outline of my mouth with his fingertip, as if he's memorizing the shape of it.

It's confusing. *He's* confusing. "I think if we keep this up, there's a chance I might fall for him," I admit.

Alex stops eating, a line forming between her brows. "So maybe you should break it off, then? Especially if he hasn't given you any sign he might want this to turn into something more."

"It's only been a few weeks, and I'm not sure I'm ready to give this up yet. If I feel like I'm approaching the point of no return, that's when I'll tell him I think we should stop."

Alex's frown reveals her concern, but she doesn't push me on it. "When are you supposed to see him again?"

"I'm going to his place tomorrow night, but I was thinking maybe you and I can go out for lunch before that?"

She nods. "I'd like that."

We switch on the television and get caught up in a new rom-com that's on. But eventually, my mind drifts to Cole, as it does so often these days. I find myself smiling as I think about tomorrow night and how good he'll make me feel. I'll just enjoy the incredible sex while I can because I know very well that giving my heart to a man like Cole is a risk—a risk I can't take.

Although, from the way butterflies whirl around my stomach at the thought of being with him again, there's a chance I may have already started down that slippery slope.

CHAPTER TWENTY-SIX

COLE

As I step out of the limo, camera flashes explode in my face. I extend a hand back into the car to help Jessica out. Her cool fingers wrap around mine and she smiles at me as she emerges, looking stunning in a dress cut nearly low enough to be indecent. She tucks her hand in my elbow and sweeps along at my side as we make our way to the entrance.

"It's good to know you remembered my phone number," she says as we finally get inside. I knew she was stewing about something. Jessica has never been the warmest person. It's not something that's ever bothered me before, but the ice coming off her in the limo was palpable.

Considering there has never been anything between us —apart from the benefit of convenience—I don't know why she's pretending to be upset about it.

"Is there something you want to say?" I don't hide the boredom in my voice. She's been pushing things lately, and she knows I'm not interested.

She pouts, but all I do is raise a brow,

A breath huffs out of her. "It's just that it's been a

while," she says. "I was disappointed we didn't catch up when you were in Chicago. I had some plans for that beautiful hotel room and big bed of yours. I thought you weren't going when I didn't hear from you, but then you turned up with that . . . architect . . . of yours."

Irritation flares. "Delilah is working on the Chicago hotel. I brought her along to view the site. I wasn't about to leave her in her hotel room while I went out."

"I get it. She's cute. I hope you took advantage of that big bed like Tom and I did."

I don't want Jessica getting her claws into Delilah. I know how vicious she can be. If she's somehow misunderstood the reality of our arrangement, the last thing I want is for her to view Delilah as a potential rival.

I pierce her with my stare and say nothing. She gets the message. "Anyway, Tom and I had a great time."

"Good to hear. Shall we?" I usher her toward our table.

The speeches last forever, and my mind drifts. Images of Delilah find their way into my thoughts. What is she doing tonight? Is she thinking about the things I plan to do to her the next time I get her alone? If I leave early enough, Jonathan can drive past her place after we've dropped Jessica off, and I can take her back to my penthouse, spread her out on my bed, and have my fill of her.

I shift on my chair as my dick hardens. This isn't the best place to get an erection. Not when I'm slated to give a speech soon.

A hand lands on my thigh and skims upward. I grab Jessica's wrist just as she reaches the spot where I'm straining the material of my tuxedo pants. I pull her away from me, but when I look at her, she has a coy smile on her face.

"Are you thinking about what's going to happen after this is over?" Her voice is a husky whisper in my ear.

I am. But not the way she thinks. "Nothing's happening after this is over."

Her eyes flare. "What's going on, Cole? It's not like you to turn down a no-strings-attached fuck."

"Nothing is going on. You and I aren't in a relationship. We haven't made any promises to each other. If I want to fuck and you want to fuck, then we'll fuck. But that's all there is to it. And tonight, I'm not interested."

Her eyes narrow to icy blue slits. "Does this have to do with—"

My hard stare is enough to silence her. The man at the podium is wrapping up his speech, so I push back my chair and stand, then make my way to the front of the room. As soon as I'm done here, I'm leaving. I'll check with Jessica to see if she wants me to drop her off or if she wants to stay here and mingle—maybe find some other man to scratch her itch tonight. And then I'm going to get Delilah, take her home, and give in to my craving.

It's that thought that has a smile on my face when I take the stage. My speech is about the King Group's commitment to social responsibility and our dedication to making a positive impact on the world through our charitable trust. Considering recent events, however, I need to address the elephant in the room before I launch into the core of my speech. I acknowledge the seriousness of my father's arrest and highlight that despite the previous CEO's actions, the King Group is committed to operating with transparency and integrity.

Twenty minutes later, as applause rolls through the room, I nod to the crowd, walk off the stage, and wind my way through the tables until I reach Jessica and her unreadable expression.

Instead of sitting, I lean down and murmur in her ear. "I'm leaving. Do you want me to drop you off, or are you going to stay?"

She studies me, dabs her lips with her napkin, and rises. "I'd appreciate it if you could drop me off."

I'm not sure I trust this more subdued version of Jessica, but I'm too busy thinking about what I'll do to Delilah to care what's going on with her. It sounds coldhearted, but there's never been any emotional intimacy between her and me. I won't start indulging her now that she's annoyed because I don't want to sleep with her.

When we get outside, there are still a few die-hard photographers lingering around, probably hoping to get a photo of some debauchery on behalf of the rich and famous filling the ballroom. I stride toward where Jonathan is parked waiting for us, only slowing when I notice Jessica is taking her time, making sure the photographers get plenty of shots.

We finally get to the car, but before I can open the door for her, Jessica stops me with a hand on my shoulder. Impatiently, I turn, only for her to wrap her arms around my neck and slam her lips against mine.

My hands go to her waist. I'm conscious of the camera flashes going off around us, so I don't immediately extricate myself, even though anger boils in my veins. When I eventually ease her away from me, I know she can see the fury in my eyes, but like any good businessman, I don't let it show on my face. "What the hell was that for?" I say through clenched teeth.

She smooths her hand down my lapel. "I just wanted to remind you what you'll be missing out on."

"I don't need a reminder. I'm not interested."

She steps back, and I reach for the door and hold it open for her.

"Get in the car."

She slips past me, and I follow her inside. As soon as the door closes behind us, I press the button and tell Jonathan to take us to Jessica's building.

I fix her with a hard glare. "Never pull a stunt like that again."

She pouts at me. "It's not like we haven't done far more than kiss before."

"Not like that. And never in public."

"What does it matter? It's not like you have a girlfriend. Everyone knows Cole King doesn't have girlfriends. So what's the big deal?"

"It matters because it's unacceptable. If you try anything like that again, you'll find out just how little I appreciate it when people cross boundaries."

"Fine." She smooths her hands down her skirt. "I just hope you get whatever this is out of your system before you do something you'll regret."

I don't bother responding. What I'm doing with Delilah is none of Jessica's business.

We spend the next few minutes in silence. Jessica's apartment building isn't far away, and it's not long before we're pulling up outside the expansive glass foyer. Jonathan opens the door for her but just before she climbs out, she turns to me. "It's not too late, you know. You can still come up to my place."

I merely arch a brow, and she huffs out a breath and slides out. Jonathan closes the door behind her, then gets back into the driver's seat. "Am I taking you home, sir?"

I think about my plan to swing past Delilah's place and

pick her up, but now I'm not so sure. I've been seeing her a lot lately—maybe too much. It might be better to have a break. I briefly consider telling her about Jessica kissing me, but it was meaningless on my part, so I don't see the point. It's unlikely she'll ever see the photos that will probably be printed in the tabloids. I doubt she reads the gossip columns.

"Yes, thank you, Jonathan."

The car glides into traffic, and I lean back in my seat and stare out the window. I'm supposed to see Delilah tomorrow night, but I might need to take a step back. Give us both some breathing space. Seeing each other so often isn't a good idea. I don't want to give her the wrong impression about what's going on between us.

Even though I'm not overly happy with my decision, I force my mind to other things. There's always plenty of work that needs to be dealt with.

I pull out my phone and start reading emails.

CHAPTER TWENTY-SEVEN

DELILAH

I put the finishing touches on the interior plan I'm working on and try to keep my mind off the fact Cole canceled on me this weekend. After all, as I told Alex, this is only meant to be casual. I need to take things as they come instead of investing too much time and effort on trying to figure out what's going on in his head.

Still, disappointment followed me around for the rest of the weekend after he called on Saturday morning and said something had come up. I'd been looking forward to seeing him.

I draw one final line on the plan and click print. I'm unpleasantly aware of Paul lingering on the far side of the room. I can sense his eyes on me, and I'm not sure why. He's mostly kept his distance since our meeting in his office, apart from when he's had something work-related to discuss with me.

My stomach rumbles and I check the time. It's well past lunch and I haven't eaten anything since breakfast. I head to the kitchen to get the salad I made this morning, but just as I close the fridge door, Paul corners me. When I try to sidestep him, he puts his hand on my arm and holds me back. I look down at his hand before returning my attention to his face. He smiles, but there's an edge to it I don't like.

"I need to talk to you about something," he says.

"Can we do it at my desk?"

"I don't want anyone else around when I show you this," he says, holding up his phone.

I can't help but look, and when I do, my heart does a painful stutter. It's a photo of Cole kissing a blonde woman. He's dressed in a tuxedo and his hands are circling the woman's slender waist, while she has her arms wound around his neck. I keep my expression neutral, not wanting Paul to get a reaction from me, particularly since I've never confirmed that Cole and I are spending time together. And after all, there are lots of photos out there of Cole with various women. "I don't know why you're showing this to me."

"Don't you?" he says, a nasty smile flitting at the corners of his lips. "That's funny. I got the impression there was something going on between you two, so of course when I saw this photo from Friday night, I thought I should let you know. My mistake, I guess."

My stomach drops. From Friday night? It couldn't be. Cole didn't say anything about taking a date to the event, and we had an agreement. We're meant to be exclusive while we're . . . doing whatever it is we're doing. Is this why he canceled on me? Was he with her instead?

Paul swipes his screen casually. "She's quite the looker." He flashes his phone in front of my face again, and this time the photo is of the woman about to climb into Cole's car. He has his hand on her back, but that isn't the only reason pain slices through me. It's the woman's face. Because it's one I recognize. Jessica. A woman Cole had assured me he didn't have a relationship with before I slept with him for the second time.

I'm so stupid. Of course he said that. If someone asked him about me, he'd probably say the same thing. Because we're *not* in a relationship. We're screwing. Fucking. Scratching an itch. I'm sure that's how he sees it, anyway.

I force my lips into an unconcerned smile. "Even if there was something going on between Cole and me, you'd be the last person I'd want help from. So if that's all . . ." I push past him and head back to my desk, but nausea swirls in my stomach and I no longer feel like eating the salad I'm holding.

My food sits uneaten next to me as I grab my phone and navigate to the website Paul showed me. Like some kind of masochist, I flick through the photos. There aren't that many, just four, but what they show is damning. The two of them arriving together, Cole's hand possessively on her back. And then their departure and the kiss before he helps her into his limo. If I know Cole, he probably fucked her in the back of it or took her back to his penthouse to screw the hell out of her there.

I put my phone face down on my desk, heat prickling the backs of my eyes. I'm not sure if it's worse that he didn't try to hide it. At least Paul hid his cheating from me because he didn't want to lose me. Apparently, Cole doesn't care if I find out.

Unable to sit there one more second, I shove my container of salad into my bag and log off my computer. Paul loiters nearby, probably waiting to see what chaos he's caused. Unfortunately, there's no leaving without talking to him, so I make my way over. "I'm not feeling well. I'm going to work from home for the rest of the day."

The fake sympathy on his face turns my stomach, but I hold myself together.

"No problem. I hope you're feeling better tomorrow." He's all toothy smile, and I picture slapping it off him even as I hold his gaze with my chin high.

I turn and walk away as calmly as I can but as soon as I get into the elevator, my shoulders slump. I can't believe I was so stupid. Men like Cole—like my father—are all the same. Once they get what they want, they discard you without a second thought.

The elevator dings and I step out, taking only a few steps before I see who's standing there with a group of men. Outside of meetings or when he's sought me out, I can count on one hand the number of times I've seen Cole around the building. I close my eyes. Of course it would be him.

He catches my eye and frowns, but I turn away and continue walking to the entrance.

"Miss West." His voice comes from behind me, and I curse to myself. I don't have a choice but to stop. He's still my boss and I'm at my place of work.

I take a deep breath, then turn to face him. He says something to the group of men, then walks toward me. Anger wars with hurt in my chest as I wait for him.

He comes to a stop in front of me, a frown furrowing his brow. "What's going on?" he asks in a low voice.

I finally meet his gaze head-on, the intensity of his stare hitting me like a punch to the chest. "What do you mean?"

"You barely looked at me as you passed, and it's not like you to leave early."

"I'm not feeling well. I'm going home."

My pulse hammers, and I want to yell at him. To ask him how he could do something like that to me when I thought . . . Well, I thought wrong. Saying something like that is bound to be the quickest possible way to get fired, so I bottle it all up and push it down where it has to stay until I can be alone. Because I won't lose everything I've worked for over this man.

His frown deepens. I glance over his shoulder to find the group of men he was with eyeing me with curiosity. One of them looks at his watch, then says something to the others.

I take a step away from Cole, hoping he'll let me go, since his group is waiting for him.

"Delilah," he growls. "Tell me what's going on."

The awareness glimmering in his eyes makes me think he knows exactly what's going on. How can he not imagine there was a chance I'd see the photos?

But suddenly I want him to know. To realize it's not okay to hurt people just because there are no repercussions for him.

The elevator behind him dings, and the men board it, holding the door open. "Cole?" one of them calls out.

I take another step backward. "I'll see you later, Cole. I'm glad you and Jessica had a good time on Friday night."

His jaw clenches, but he says nothing as I spin on my heel and make for the front door. My mouth is dry, and I need to get home so I can drown my sorrows. It's mid-afternoon, but I'm giving myself permission to crack open a bottle of wine.

I step outside and take a deep breath. I can't bear the thought of catching the train home, so I hail a cab. My phone beeps in my purse and I pull it out to see a message from Cole.

We need to talk.

234

I stuff it back in my bag and blink back tears. What was I thinking? Honestly, how had I ever thought sleeping with him was a good idea? I'm such an idiot. Tears blur my vision, but I can't be that woman crying in the back of a cab over a man. I won't.

For all my determination, the moment the door of my apartment closes behind me, the dam bursts. Hot tears splash down my cheeks and I sink into my couch. Why am I this hurt? This wasn't a real relationship. It was just sex. We were just enjoying each other's bodies. Yes, he lied to me, but being stupid enough to believe him, to let myself feel more than I should . . . That's on me.

More tears leak out and I wipe them away. God, this is ridiculous. I want to think it's humiliation, and that's definitely a part of it. No one likes being made a fool of, and this is the second time it's happened to me. But the truth is, I've done exactly what I promised myself I wouldn't.

I let myself start feeling things for Cole, and this is the consequence.

My phone beeps again, and when I see his name, I can't stop myself from reading the message.

Don't ignore me, Delilah.

I huff out a breath. I'll need to talk to him at some stage, to officially end this thing between us, but I want to be calm and in control when I do it so I don't say something stupid and end up off the project and potentially out of a job. If I speak to him now, I won't be anywhere near calm and in control.

My phone lights up with Cole's name on the screen, but I decline the call. I don't understand why he's bothering. He hasn't lost anything that he can't easily replace. Why can't he just leave me alone to take a breath and work through these emotions?

Another message notification and my eyes automatically drop to my phone's screen.

Answer your phone, Delilah.

Anger dries my tears. *What is his problem?*

A minute later, my phone rings again and I stare at it, a pulse throbbing in my temple as my temper rises even more. It feels good to let the anger take over. He's rich and powerful and I'm technically working for him at the moment, but that doesn't mean he gets to treat me like this. Like someone he can discard with thoughtless cruelty.

Before I have time to overthink it, I answer.

"Delilah," he says.

"What is it you want to say, Cole?" I'm glad my voice is steady. Steadier than I feel, anyway.

"Why haven't you responded to my messages?"

"Because I don't want to talk to you."

He lets out a sigh that seems to be made up of sheer irritation. "Obviously you saw the photos."

His tone fuels my anger. "Yes." It comes out through gritted teeth.

"It isn't what you think." There's no apology in his voice. He doesn't believe he's done anything worth apologizing for. Or maybe it's that I'm not worth apologizing to.

"Really? Do you mean it's not you kissing another woman when you told me you wouldn't be with anyone else while we were together? Or do you mean it isn't you kissing Jessica, who you told me you weren't involved with?"

"I told you that Jessica and I aren't in a relationship, and we never have been."

236

"I'm not stupid, Cole. You're either straight up lying to me, or you're lying by omission. I may not be that experienced with men, but I can guarantee that's not how you kiss a woman who's just an acquaintance."

There's a pause on the phone. He knows he's been caught. "I have a shareholder meeting in half an hour that I can't miss, but I'll send Jonathan to get you tonight, and I'll explain it to you," he finally says.

"I'm not interested in seeing you."

"Being immature about this isn't helping." His tone lowers. "At least give me the respect of listening to what I have to say."

A bright flash goes off behind my eyes. "Respect? You're talking to me about respect? You guessed I saw the photos, which is why you've been messaging me. Which means you already knew exactly how seeing them would make me feel, and you know that because it's how most normal human beings would feel when they realize they've been played. So don't make me out to be childish for reacting exactly the way you expected me to. My lack of response to your messages and phone calls should have told you I needed time to deal with my emotions, but you refused to give it to me. Instead, you've decided the best way to handle this is to harass me, then when I answer, you tell me I'm being immature."

My fingers tighten around my phone. "I asked you straight to your face about Jessica, Cole. I wanted to know what I was getting myself into if I said yes to you. To protect myself from getting hurt. But rather than tell me the truth, you said what you needed to say to get what you wanted. You humiliated me. And you h-hurt me." I was doing so well, but I lose it at the end as more tears well up.

"Delilah—"

I gather myself together. "No, Cole. I'm not done. You're obviously used to getting what you want when you want it. You obviously don't care what you have to do or say to get it. So, if what you wanted when you kissed Jessica Friday night was a quick and easy way to get rid of the immature workplace hookup that's been hanging around a little too long, congratulations. You got it."

With a trembling finger, I end the call, then slump back on the couch and let the tears fall.

CHAPTER TWENTY-EIGHT

COLE

I barely stop myself from flinging my phone against the wall. This. This is why I'm not interested in relationships. I tried to do the right thing, and look where it's gotten me. I shove my chair back and stand, striding to the window and looking out at New York spread below me.

Maybe it's better if she ends it anyway. I've got too much going on with work at the moment, and spending so much time with one woman might be a novelty, but that was always going to wear off eventually.

So why the hell does my chest feel so fucking tight? The way her voice wavered when she told me I hurt her had sliced right through my ribs and into my heart. When was the last time anything had reached that frozen organ?

I brace one hand against the glass and stare down at the streets below. Looking down on everyone from up here normally makes me feel alive. It makes me feel in control. But it's not working now.

I need to get my mind off Delilah and back where it belongs. As Roman already hinted, she's become a distraction I don't need. It's better for both of us if it's over.

I sit down, but instead of preparing for my meeting, I open a browser and search for the photos from Friday night. They flash in front of me, and I wince. I'd put on a good act when Jessica kissed me. With the rumors of her father's wavering support, I didn't want to reject her publicly. While we won't go under if Berrington pulls his investments, I don't want his pack of cronies following his lead. The last thing we need is a panicked exodus for no reason other than I embarrassed his daughter.

Unfortunately, my lack of negative reaction to her kiss comes across in the photos as enthusiasm.

I frown and lean back in my chair, scrubbing my hand over my face as regret pulls at cords inside me that haven't been pulled in a long time.

Just then, my door swings open and Tate saunters in. He stops, his eyebrows rising as he takes me in. Then he grins and continues into the room, taking a seat and stretching out his long legs.

"I'm not used to you looking so out of sorts," he says. "What's the occasion?"

I click away from the website. "What do you want, Tate?"

"I can't shoot the shit with my big brother?"

Tate might be just the distraction I need right now. "I don't know if we've ever shot the shit, but if you're saying you've got something to discuss with me, then please, go right ahead."

He smirks, leans forward in his chair, and rests his elbows on his knees. "The marketing department is reporting decreased engagement and more negative comments on social media. Dear old Dad's indiscretions are circulating more widely and confidence in our brand appears to be declining. We need a quick win to improve public perception and keep everyone happy."

"I'm assuming you have an idea."

He nods. "The team has been brainstorming and they want to run some press campaigns on the hotel development. Early stages, preliminary concept plans, with a heavy focus on the sustainability aspects."

"Okay, get what you need from the architects." Which makes me think about Delilah. Once again, something tugs painfully in my chest.

"They're also thinking about filming our contractors smiling and looking competent, that kind of thing. Maybe that sexy little architect of yours could be our star."

"She's not mine," I snap.

His brows arch up again. "A little defensive, aren't you? I just meant she's part of your team."

I force myself to relax, and he watches me with a twisted smile.

"Is she who had you all out of sorts when I came in? I don't blame you. If she were working for me, I would have bent her over my desk in—"

"Don't," I growl, and he lets out a laugh.

"Oh, that got a reaction. So you *are* tapping that fine piece of ass?"

I don't know why he's being so chatty. Or why I haven't kicked him out of my office yet. Maybe it's because right now, with thoughts of Delilah trying to take over my mind, I don't hate having him here.

I drum my fingers on the desk. "We may have had a . . . thing."

"A thing? What type of thing are you talking about exactly?" His cunning eyes scrutinize me before they widen. "You weren't dating her, were you?" The look of shock on his face would be funny if the subject of Delilah wasn't such a sore spot right now.

"It was just casual," I say. "Just a few weeks."

He runs his pointer finger over his bottom lip as he watches me. "So you ended it, then? Did she get clingy? Or did you get bored?"

I pick up a pen and spin it between my fingers, debating whether to say anything. He's just sitting there, looking relaxed, his golden-brown eyes bright with curiosity. It takes me back. To a time when the three of us were closer. When we'd been friends, instead of . . . whatever we are now.

So I tell him. "She ended it. Just before you came in."

His brows shoot skyward. "She ended it?"

I clench my jaw and nod.

"I'd ask you when was the last time a woman ended a relationship with you, but since I can't remember when you last had a relationship, it's a moot point."

When I don't say anything, a slow smile spreads across his face.

"You like her."

It's a statement, not a question, but I answer him anyway. "I enjoyed spending time with her, that's all."

"What happened then?" he asks.

My gaze drops to my computer, and my chest tightens as I picture the photos that had been on the screen moments before. "I hurt her."

"Was she in love with you?"

I focus on him. "I don't think so. She never said anything to indicate she was."

"Well, she obviously feels something for you if she was hurt enough to end things."

I'm supposed to be taking my mind off Delilah, not being forced to confront my mistakes. I wave my hand in the air. "It doesn't matter now. It's over. She can move on to someone who can give her the kind of commitment she's after. And I can go back to—"

"Screwing random beautiful women and making a fuck ton of money?"

I raise my brows at him. "It's the family business, isn't it?"

"Not sure Mom would agree," he says.

"No. In Mom's case, it's having semi-discreet affairs and taking advantage of the money we make for her." Tate is silent and I shake my head. "Sorry."

He shrugs, but the amusement in his gaze has dimmed. Considering he's the result of one of Mom's affairs, they're a sensitive topic for him. It's hardly a secret. His blond hair could have come from Mom, but those startling copper eyes of his don't come from anywhere in our family tree. It explains why Dad has always been the hardest on him too, even if Tate is still his son on paper. Like most things in our world, it's all about outward appearances. People can whisper whatever they want behind closed doors, and as long as it doesn't affect our wealth and status, we don't care.

Except, I remember a time when Tate cared. A lot.

I also remember the times when Roman and I got into fights with the boys who thought it was a good idea to taunt him about his parentage. That was before things changed, anyway. Before we grew apart, becoming strangers to each other.

Maybe working together like this will give Tate and me a chance to reconnect. I make a mental note to catch up with him about non-work-related issues on a more regular basis.

"Are you planning to get her back?" Tate asks.

I've lost track of our conversation. "What?"

"Your architect. Are you going to make it up to her?"

"I think we're both better off if we just leave it." A pit forms in my chest at the realization that my last time touching her happened without me even knowing it.

"Are you sure about that?"

I look away from Tate's too perceptive gaze. The best way to distract myself from Delilah is to concentrate on what's important—work. "I've got to prepare for this meeting. Feel free to go directly to the architectural team if you want to use them in any promos."

"That's it?" Tate protests. "That's all you're going to give me?"

"You're lucky you got that much. Now let me get back to work."

He huffs out a breath, slaps his hands on his thighs, and stands. "Fine. Leave me hanging, then."

I grunt and return to my notes, not bothering to watch him cross to the door.

"So if she's single now, you won't mind if I ask her out?"

My eyes shoot to his, rage bubbling up in my chest. He's more of a playboy than any of us. "Keep your fucking hands off her."

He's still laughing when he shuts the door behind him.

CHAPTER TWENTY-NINE

DELILAH

"Are you going to be okay?" Alex asks as I gather my purse and get ready to head out the door. When she returned from work last night, she'd immediately known something was wrong. Probably because my eyes were red from crying. When I explained what had happened, she wrapped me in her arms and told me Cole was an asshole who didn't deserve me. Then she ordered in dinner and put on a thriller with absolutely no romance in it, and I managed to turn my mind off for a couple of hours.

This morning, I'm prepared—if not exactly ready—to face Cole and Paul. The former I probably won't even see, and the latter, well, I'll just have to put up with his smugness.

"I'm going to be okay. I won't let a man as self-absorbed as Cole King get me down. I just need to finish this project and then I'll never have to see him again."

She comes over and gives me a hug. "Good for you. Just keep your head held high and ignore those assholes. You're worth twice the both of them put together."

I smile and return the hug. "Thank you." After a bracing breath, I pull my purse strap higher on my shoulder and head out.

When I get to the office, I quickly scan the foyer before I press the button to the elevator. The last thing I need is to get caught in a metal box for multiple floors with either man I'm trying to avoid. Thankfully, I don't see them, and I ride up with several people I've never met before. When I get to our floor, I slip past them and hurry to my desk.

I log on to my system and start on my plans. I really want them signed off by next week. As far as I'm concerned, the faster this project is completed, the faster I can get out of this building and away from Cole. I just want to put what's happened behind me.

I manage to get absorbed in my work, tuning out everything around me, until the phone on my desk rings. I don't recognize the name on the screen, but I answer the call. "Hello?"

"Hi, Delilah? This is Sophie. I'm Tate King's PA."

"Oh, hi," I say tentatively.

"Tate would like to have a word with you in his office. Do you have a spare moment?"

"Yes, of course."

"Great. And if you have any finished schematics or 3D renderings, can you bring some of those as well?"

I blink, immediately looking down at the plans neatly laid out on my table. "Okay. Can I ask what this is for?"

"He'll discuss it with you when you get here," she says pleasantly enough.

"Okay, thanks. I'll be up straight away."

I hang up, then stand, smoothing the wrinkles out of my dress. I don't know what the head of marketing might want to discuss with me, but Tate's timing has me wondering if it has anything to do with what happened between Cole and me. Surely not. Billionaires have more important things to do than involve themselves in each other's failed flings.

After gathering several of my plans, I make my way to the top floor, hating that I both hope to avoid Cole and wish for a tiny glimpse of him. I steel my spine as I exit the elevator, doing my best to keep from turning my head toward his office door as I pass. From my peripheral vision, I can see it's closed anyway. I continue down the hallway until I reach Tate's office, then approach the woman sitting at the desk outside, who I assume is Sophie. "Hi, I'm Delilah. I'm here to see Mr. King."

She offers a warm smile. "Nice to meet you, Delilah. You can go in. Tate's expecting you."

I nod my thanks, knock on his door, and enter once he's invited me inside. I give the large room a quick glance before focusing on Tate sitting behind his desk. The office isn't too different from Cole's. It has the same big windows with the same incredible view. Similar elegant prints adorn the walls, and beautiful wooden furniture dominates the floor space.

Tate is leaning back in his chair and smiling at me. My breath catches. I've never seen Cole's younger brother up close before. Unlike Cole, who's usually always in a three-piece suit at work, Tate has his jacket off and his shirtsleeves rolled up to reveal his muscular forearms. Like his brother, he's gorgeous, even though he looks quite different from both Cole and Roman. Where they're all dark hair and icy eyes, Tate is golden-blond and tawny. Just as beautiful and just as deadly to women's hearts, I imagine. I'm sure he uses his good looks and charm to make women fall for him just as easily as Cole.

"Good morning, Miss West," he says.

"Please, call me Delilah," I say.

He nods. "Feel free to call me Tate. With multiple Mr. Kings in the building, it gets confusing."

I give him a small smile, then turn to close the door behind me.

"You can leave that open," he says, stopping me.

That's weird. Does he think I'll take advantage of him if the door is closed? Has Cole told him about us, and now he thinks I'll make a move on him too?

That thought has me lifting my chin as I take a few steps closer to his large desk. "I brought some of my plans, like you asked."

"Great, I'll take them." He stands and holds out his hand. I walk closer and pass him the rolled-up schematics, which he opens and lays flat on his desk.

"Can you show me what these are specifically?" he asks.

I'm still confused about what he's after, but I move closer and slightly lean over the desk as I point out the different plans I brought with me. "These are the initial concept designs. These are the modifications I made post-site visit." I glance up at him, just in time to catch him looking over my shoulder. Before I have time to turn and see what's caught his attention, he's returned his focus to me.

"Do you have interior schematics?"

I flick through the sheets and pull out one showing an internal section and place it on top. "These aren't complete yet. It's what I'm working on at the moment."

He glances over my shoulder again, and this time I turn to look. I can't see anything through the open office door, and I'm a little annoyed. I still don't know what I'm doing here, and now Tate doesn't even seem interested in what I'm showing him.

"Can I ask what it is you're looking for?" My tone is slightly curter than warranted, considering who he is and who I am, but today is definitely not my best day. I just want to get back to my desk instead of loitering on this floor.

Tate leans back in his chair and smiles at me, and I blink a few times because his smile is equal parts charming and wicked.

"The marketing team wants some of the CAD drawings, the interior plans, and 3D renderings for some marketing ideas they're putting together."

My brows shoot up. "Okay."

His mouth quirks. "Is there something wrong with that?"

"No, not at all," I say. "I guess I'm wondering why me? And why you? Why didn't this go through Paul? And why isn't someone from the marketing team handling this? You seem a bit . . . senior to be the one taking care of this."

He chuckles. "You're right. This isn't something I'd normally handle. But I had an ulterior motive for asking you up here."

I tilt my head and study him as I wait for him to elaborate.

"Let's just say I wanted to meet the woman who had my brother in a less than pleasant mood yesterday."

Cole was in a bad mood yesterday because of me? I'm surprised he cared enough to let it affect him. And oh, god, Tate knows I was sleeping with his brother. My cheeks heat, but I don't look away. I made a choice, and I won't be ashamed about it.

I lean over his desk and start gathering my sheets. "So I guess you don't really need to see these, then."

Once more, his gaze goes over my shoulder, and this

time a broad grin spreads over his face. I straighten and check behind me, but there's still no one there. What is going on with him?

"Do you want me to take these to the marketing team? Or was that just an excuse to get me up here?"

"It wasn't an excuse. The team really does need copies of these."

"Okay," I say. "I'll just—"

His ringing phone cuts me off, and he smiles as if he's expecting it. He holds up one finger and I stop what I'm doing, feeling awkward about listening in on his conversation.

"To what do I owe the honor of this phone ca—"

He stops, catching my eye and winking as he leans back in his chair.

I frown and fidget with the sheets I'm holding as I do my best to ignore his private call.

"Uh-huh. Uh-huh. I'm sensing some aggravation from you, Cole."

My gaze jerks back to his as I realize who he's talking to.

"I was merely talking to Miss West about the marketing plans." He listens for a moment. "I agree. That's not my job. Which is why Delilah is going to drop them down to the team now." He pauses again. "I don't know what you're talking about. This meeting is completely professional. My door stayed open the whole time. As you obviously saw when you walked past."

Was that why he kept looking over my shoulder? Had he wanted Cole to see me in here with him?

My anger is rising now. I'm not sure what's going on between these two, but I'm not interested in being involved in the games billionaires play with each other. I've worked too hard to get where I am. I may have let myself get distracted by sex, but I've learned my lesson. Getting swept up in a man, especially a man like Cole, isn't doing me any favors. Just like it didn't do Mom any favors.

I reach across Tate's desk and gather the rest of my plans. He eyes me as he continues to listen to whatever Cole is saying to him. I strangle the urge to walk out. Regardless of how irritated I am at whatever he's doing, he's still in a position of authority over me and I'm in a precarious situation as it is with what's happened with Paul and Cole. So I stand there stiffly until he finally hangs up.

As soon as he does, I say, "If we're finished here, I'll run these down to marketing."

Whatever he's reading in my tone or on my face has the corners of his lips tilting up. I'm obviously not doing a very good job of hiding how I'm feeling, but he doesn't say anything about that. Instead, he studies me, and I do my best to keep still under his scrutiny.

The humor simmering under the surface of his expression fades. His gaze gets distant, and he nods. "Thank you, Delilah."

I get out of there, giving Sophie a small smile as I pass her desk.

To get back to the elevator, I have to pass Cole's office. I hope I can sneak past without him knowing. My heart sinks as his PAs desk comes into view and I see a tall, broad-shouldered figure standing next to it.

I lift my chin and keep my pace even. I'll give him a polite nod and continue to the elevator.

But as soon as his eyes lock with mine and his gaze narrows, I know it won't be that easy.

"Miss West," he says, and I swallow at the dark tone of his voice.

I come to a stop a few feet from him, aware of Samson's gaze bouncing between us. "Yes, Mr. King?"

"I'd like to talk to you for a moment, if you don't mind."

I consider saying that yes, I do mind, but I have to face him eventually. So I just nod, take a deep breath, and follow him into his office.

CHAPTER THIRTY

COLE

When I walked past Tate's office after my meeting and saw Delilah leaning over his desk, her ass cupped by her fitted dress, my jaw had clenched so tight I'm surprised the people walking next to me hadn't heard my teeth grind together. What the fuck was my brother playing at? I'd been clear with him yesterday that he wasn't to touch her, and the very next day he has her up in his office with her long legs and her tight skirt and her pretty green eyes.

As soon as I'd gotten off the phone with him, I'd been out my door and making an excuse to talk to Samson about something, just waiting for her to come down the corridor. I should probably question why I'm acting so irrationally about this when I've already decided it's for the best, but I won't. If Tate thinks I'll let him have Delilah, he's sadly mistaken.

She follows me into my office, and her sweet sunshine-and-wildflower scent teases me. A vivid image grows in my mind. In it, I turn and press her against the door, running my nose down the column of her throat and sucking on the tender skin at the base—marking her so that if Tate calls on her again, he'll see my claim.

Which is fucking ridiculous. Delilah's already made it clear that our arrangement is over.

I stalk to my desk, but I don't round it to take my seat. Instead, I stand in front, with my arms crossed, while Delilah hovers near the doorway.

"Close the door," I tell her.

She complies, her shoulders stiff, then she turns back to me.

"What did Tate want?" I ask.

Her brow furrows. "Didn't he tell you on the phone?"

"I want to hear it from you."

She tilts her head. "Do you think he was lying? Why would he? He's your brother."

I lean against my desk. "He and I don't have the closest relationship. I'm not sure I trust him to tell me the truth," I say, then wonder why I've divulged that to her.

"Well, that's sad." Genuine sympathy flashes across her face. She's close to her mom, so maybe she doesn't get what it's like to be distant from your family members. But that's how it is in families like ours. Love, affection, trust—they aren't part of the equation.

"It's just the way it is." I try to get back on track. "So, tell me—"

"What about Roman?"

I stare at her. "What?"

"Are you closer to him?"

"No."

"Maybe that explains it," she says, almost to herself.

"Explains what?"

She shakes her head, as if realizing we've gotten

distracted. She squares her shoulders. "What did you want to talk to me about?"

Her beautiful eyes are on mine, but there's a shadow in them that wasn't there before. Regret tugs at me again. *I* did that to her. Because she was right. I withheld the truth to get what I wanted. And what I wanted was her. If I'm honest with myself, I still want her. Against all of my personal fucking logic.

I was angry when I called her in here. Angry that Tate had her attention—that he was the recipient of her pretty smile when I wanted it directed at me.

But what did I expect? She'd called me on it yesterday. I'd hurt her, and I hadn't even apologized. I'm not used to saying sorry, and it's not something I particularly relish doing, but I've been less than honest with her when, as far as I know, she's always been honest with me.

I force down my irrational anger and approach her slowly, as if she's a wild creature that might leap away from me before I get a chance to touch her. Her throat moves in a swallow as I come to a stop in front of her, but she stays where she is as I invade her personal space.

I take a strand of her silky hair and let it slide through my fingers. "I'm sorry," I murmur. "I should have told you the truth about Jessica."

Her eyes widen. "Uh," she says, clearly taken aback. "Y-yes, you should have."

"It's no excuse, but I don't consider what Jessica and I have had in the past to be a relationship."

"It didn't look to me like it was in the past."

I scowl as I remember Jessica's behavior on Friday night. "That was all her. I didn't invite it, and I didn't want it. She was annoyed because I turned down our usual arrangement, and decided it was a good idea to force my hand."

Her smooth brow furrows. "Your usual arrangement."

Fuck. I really don't want to get into that, but if I plan to be honest with her, I have to be completely honest. "What Jessica and I had was a matter of convenience. Our families move in the same circles. Her father is one of the King Group's biggest investors, so we're often at the same social events. Since neither of us is interested in relationships, it made sense for us to attend those events together, and afterward . . ." I shrug, not sure how much detail Delilah wants me to go into.

She presses her lips together, but only nods. "Thank you for telling me."

She doesn't look happy, or even relieved, and I realize what I've told her might not have cleared things up adequately. "I didn't sleep with her Friday night. I haven't been with her since I met you."

She lets out a little sigh, and some of the tightness in her shoulders loosens. "Okay."

I'm getting frustrated now. "I didn't stop her when she kissed me, because I didn't want to be photographed publicly rejecting the daughter of our major investor. But she knows not to do it again."

Delilah nods and clasps her hands in front of her. "I'm glad we've cleared that up. If there isn't anything else, I need to get back to my desk and finish my work."

I narrow my eyes at her. I've apologized, but it doesn't seem to have fixed anything. What does she want? She's acting as if the last few weeks didn't happen. Maybe this is another reminder of why I don't do relationships. Maybe now that I've apologized and gotten it off my chest, I can walk away and stop thinking about her. "That's all I had to say."

It might only be in my imagination that she hesitates

before she turns for the door, but it's that possibly imaginary hesitation, coupled with the sway of her hips and the tumble of her dark hair down her back as she walks away from me—hair that I can all too easily recall fisting in my hand as I took her from behind—that has me striding forward.

Before she can swing the door open, I'm slamming my hand against it, holding it shut. I stand close behind her, caging her in, my chest brushing her shoulder blades and my rapidly hardening cock pressing against her ass.

She inhales sharply, her body stilling.

"What do you think you're doing?" I growl.

She angles her head toward me, just enough so I can see the curve of her cheek and the dark length of her lowered lashes. "What do you mean?" Her voice isn't as steady as before, which sends a surge of satisfaction through me. She isn't as unaffected as she's acting.

I skim my hand over her hip until my fingers curve around her waist. "I apologized. I explained what happened. I told you I haven't been with her since before I met you. And you're giving me nothing." With my other hand, I brush her hair off her neck so I can run my nose along the soft skin, breathe in her scent. "Do you want me to believe you're done with me—with *this*—because I made a mistake?"

A breath shudders out of her as my hand slides up her waist to cup her breast, and I smile to myself as I feel her hard nipple pressing into my palm.

Her head falls forward. "You hurt me, and that's not what this was supposed to be about. I think it might be better if we just let things go."

Shock rattles through me, followed by a swift sting behind my ribs. "What if I don't want to let things go?"

She turns, pressing her back against the door and looking up at me. "Why wouldn't you? What am I giving you that the Jessicas of the world can't? You don't want a relationship with me, so if all you want is sex, why not get it from someone who won't care when you lie to her?"

Because there's no comparison between Jessica and her. Because she brings something out of me I didn't even know was there. That's why I can't seem to walk away, even when I know I should. I cup her neck, rub my thumb along her jaw. "I don't feel anything when I'm with Jessica. Sex between us has always been . . ." I shake my head. "Fucking cold and empty. It's different with you. When I touch you, it's pure fucking heat, and I haven't had enough. I want more with you."

Her breath flutters between her parted lips, her eyes searching mine. "More of what?"

"Everything. More time. More of your body." I dip my head and feather my lips across hers. "More of this." I hesitate for a heartbeat, then force myself to continue. To give her some of the truth she deserves. "I want your warmth, Delilah. You're about the only source of it I have. I don't want to give it up because of Jessica."

Her eyes soften at my admission. I've never said anything like that to anyone, and part of me wants to take the words back. They're too intimate. Too close to revealing a weakness I thought I'd buried a long time ago.

Her gaze is direct, but shadows linger in her eyes. "I don't know if I can trust you."

"I'm not usually a liar. I won't take Jessica to any more events. And I promise you, I won't let her kiss me again."

"You mean until this thing between us is over?"

She wants me to contradict her, but I just assured her I wasn't a liar. I can't make her a promise I'm not sure I can keep. "Maybe not even then." It's all I can offer, even though for the first time in my life I wish I had more than emptiness inside me to give to someone.

She's still searching my face, and I raise my hand and brush my knuckles over her jaw. "I'm sorry," I say again, lower this time. Then I tilt her chin, my lips hovering just over hers. "I don't like that I hurt you, and I'm sorry. Do you accept my apology?"

"No more omissions? No more half-truths?"

I shake my head. "No more."

She still doesn't give me what I want, and urgency pumps through my veins now. I use my thumb on her jaw to angle her head further back, so that our lips are only a breath apart.

"Delilah," I growl. "Do you accept my apology?"

Her pupils flare, and a hint of a smile plays on her lips, sending relief surging through me. "Maybe you should show me how sorry you are," she whispers.

Even as the tension in my chest loosens, my cock swells. "You want me to get down on my knees and grovel, kitten?"

Her pulse flutters against my palm, and she nods slowly.

If any other woman asked me to do that, I'd laugh and show them the door. Like so many things with Delilah, my reaction is different. "Before I do that, I need to kiss you."

She wets her lips. "I'll allow it."

I fucking love that she's playing with fire. I grip her ass and jerk her against me so she can feel exactly what she's doing to me. She gasps and I use the opportunity to close the distance between our lips so I can taste the sweetness of her mouth again.

With my hand tangled in her hair, I groan as she presses into me. Fuck, she's like a drug I've gotten far too addicted to. And right now, I can't bring myself to care.

I slide my hands around her waist, then turn her, maneuvering her backward across my office until she's pressed against my desk. "I'm going to show you exactly how sorry I am," I rasp, lifting her and setting her ass on top of it so I can run my hands up her legs and part her thighs. "I'm going to eat that gorgeous pussy until you come on my face. And then I'll know you've forgiven me."

"I didn't lock the door behind me," she says, breathlessly.

"I don't care. The only people who will walk in here without an invitation are my brothers, and if they see you spread out with my mouth buried in your pussy, they'll know you're mine and they better do the polite thing and walk the fuck out again. Now lie back."

With only a second's hesitation, she does as I command. I shove her skirt over her hips and drop to my knees. Her panties are a tiny scrap of fabric that I rip from her without a second thought. She inhales sharply, but I just shove them into my pocket.

And then she forgives me.

Twice.

CHAPTER THIRTY-ONE

DELILAH

I'm in my pajamas on Friday night, sitting in front of the television with a glass of wine and my tablet on my lap. Alex invited me out with her and her other friends, but I wanted to finish some work, so I declined.

It's been a week since Cole *apologized* to me in his office, and we haven't been together physically since. I'd expected him to ask me back to his penthouse that night, and I was fully prepared to say no. Not only because of my standing dinner date with Alex, but because I just wasn't ready to jump back into bed with him straight away. He hadn't asked, though. He'd kissed me at the door to his office, said he hoped Alex and I enjoyed our dinner, then told me he'd see me soon.

I was grateful he was giving me some breathing space. But unfortunately, he's been gone most of the time since then for work. And even though space was what I needed, I've had more than enough now. He's due back late tonight, but we won't see each other until tomorrow night. I'd be lying if I said I'm not looking forward to it.

I don't know what it is about Cole, but when I'm with

him, I feel . . . free. I do things I wouldn't have considered before, and I like it.

I like *him*.

The flash of vulnerability in his eyes when he told me he didn't have any warmth in his life made my heart hurt. Maybe I still should have walked away, but I couldn't bring myself to do it. Just like him, I want more of whatever it is that burns between us. Even if it will probably flame itself out all too soon.

I take a gulp of wine to ease the pinch in my chest. Casual and temporary is what I agreed to. And when it comes to Cole, it's all that's on offer. That's okay, though, because it's the best thing for me too. We've cleared the air, so we can keep enjoying our physical connection, and I can continue focusing on my career. Soon I'll have enough money to start saving for Mom's house. That's the goal I've worked toward for years, and letting myself get distracted by a complicated relationship would be silly. Cole will never want anything more than this with me, and that's perfect.

As long as I keep reminding myself of that, then I won't be disappointed when it ends.

My phone rings on the coffee table, and I put down my wineglass to answer it. Cole's name is on the screen and my chest deflates a little. He might be canceling tomorrow night.

I accept the call. "Hey! How was your trip?"

"I'm outside your building," he says, ignoring my question.

"You are?" I stand, walk to the window, and spot the big black car parked below. "Do you want to come up?"

"No. I want you to come down." He sounds tense.

"Okay, I'll be down in a minute."

"Leave your panties up there," he says.

I stop what I'm doing, since I know what that means. "I thought I was going to your place tomorrow?"

"You were. Now you're coming tonight."

It seems like arrogant Cole is back. His attitude rankles me, even though I was just thinking how ready I am to see him again. "I'm finishing some work."

"It's ten in the evening on a Friday. Why the hell are you working?"

"You're just getting back from working," I point out.

"And now I want to stop working and fuck you. So get your ass down here."

As much as I'm dying to see him, I sit on the couch. "You really know how to sweep a woman off her feet, don't you?"

He exhales a harsh breath, and when he speaks again, his tone is softer. "Delilah, I've had a long three days of meetings, our investors can't seem to accept the numbers I'm showing them, and all I want to do is fuck you with my tongue, then have you ride me until we both come. Is that too much to ask?"

Exhaustion threads through his words and I frown, particularly because his concern over the investors seeps through the phone. It's not like I haven't done a full week's work. There's no reason I shouldn't indulge in a couple of orgasms while helping Cole relax.

"Okay," I say. "I'll be down in five minutes."

I brush my teeth, splash some water onto my face, and finger comb my hair so I look presentable. Then I lock up behind me and head downstairs.

Jonathan is waiting for me when I get outside, and I smile at him. He tips his chin, but his expression remains inscrutable as he opens the door for me.

I slide in, my attention immediately caught by Cole's blue eyes. I give him a smile. "It's good to see you," I say, taking him in.

He looks as gorgeous as ever. He's without his jacket, and he's rolled up his shirtsleeves. I eye the corded muscles of his forearms, images of them wrapping around me flickering through my head.

Then, I really look at him, noticing the shadows under his eyes. "Are you okay?" I ask.

He doesn't answer my question. "Come here," he says, holding out his arm for me.

I cross the car and slide onto the seat next to him, but he wraps his arm around my waist and pulls me onto his lap as Jonathan starts the car. Cole presses his lips to my neck and groans. "Fuck, I've thought about nothing but tasting you again for days."

His teeth scrape across my pulse point. "I've been thinking about you too."

"What exactly have you been thinking about?" he says as his hands skim under my T-shirt.

"This." I feather my lips across his, barely touching.

Cole's fingers tighten on my waist, and he groans, deepening the kiss. He tastes like the whiskey he must have had on the plane. The hard length of him presses against my core, and since I'm not wearing panties, I half expect him to take me right now. Surprisingly, he seems content to kiss me as his hands roam over my skin. This slow, sensual molding of our mouths is something new. By the time we get to his building, my blood is simmering in my veins and I'm sure I've left a wet patch on his pants.

He continues his methodical assault on me in the elevator on the way to his penthouse. As soon as the doors open on his foyer, I'm dropping my purse on the floor and he's stripping my shirt over my head while my fingers fumble with his buttons.

True to his word, he has me flat on my back on the plush rug in front of his fireplace within moments, and his mouth is busy making me pant and moan. Seconds after I come, he's rolled on a condom and buried himself inside me. It's not the smooth seduction I'm used to from him, but I love it just the same. It makes me feel like he's been wanting me as much as I've been wanting him.

I close my eyes and lose myself in the sensation.

COLE IS PRESSING kisses down my stomach on his way to giving me a third orgasm when my stomach grumbles loudly. "Oh my god," I say, throwing my hand over my eyes in embarrassment.

He chuckles against my skin—a low rumble that has me looking down at him in surprise. I'm not used to such good humor from him.

He meets my gaze, and there's a sparkle in his eyes that wasn't there when he picked me up. "Do I need to feed you before I can eat again?"

I laugh and prop myself on my elbows. "It couldn't hurt. What do you have in the house? I could make something for us?"

He nuzzles his nose against my stomach. "I don't cook, so there isn't really anything. I'll order something."

I reach down and tug on his hair until he looks up at me. "You don't have a single thing in that massive fridge of yours?"

He crawls up my body and presses his lips to mine, then says, "Some wine, bread, possibly a block or two of cheese.

Nothing you can make a decent meal out of." He sucks a nipple into his mouth and tugs on it sharply, forcing a gasp out of me.

I lie back on the rug as he sucks and licks his way across my chest to my other breast. "Cole." I laugh, threading my fingers through his hair again. Then I roll him over and sit astride him. His eyes go dark as he grips my hips. I shake my head, and when he scowls, I lean down and brush my lips over his. "I'm going to make us dinner, and then I'm going to ride you like a pony."

He stares at me for a second and then bursts out laughing. "Like a pony?"

I'm secretly delighted to see him so relaxed. "Okay, I'm not good at dirty talk. Would it have been better if I'd said like a stallion?"

"Marginally," he says.

I climb off him and look around for my T-shirt, but his hands encircle my waist. "Wear my shirt," he murmurs in my ear.

He fishes his button-up from the couch and I slip my arms into it, my heart thumping rapidly in my chest.

His knuckles graze across my breasts as he slowly smooths the material over me. I shiver, my nipples peaking against the luxurious material. I reach for the buttons, but he brushes my hands aside. "Leave it."

I glance at the floor-to-ceiling windows surrounding his massive apartment, but he just shakes his head, trailing his fingers down over my abdomen and moving them lower until they slide between my slick folds.

"Someone might see in if they're looking. And if they're looking hard enough, they might catch a glimpse of this pretty pussy." He slides his fingers into me and I go up on my tiptoes, bracing myself on his shoulder and rolling my forehead against his chest as I pant. "If they do, they'll be fucking jealous, knowing it belongs to me tonight." He pulls his fingers from me and brings them to his mouth, sliding them between his lips. His eyes drift shut as he licks them. My cheeks flush, and when his eyes meet mine again, they glitter darkly. "My favorite appetizer."

"God, Cole," I breathe, and he gives me a slow, seductive smile that has me squirming. But then my stomach grumbles again, breaking the tension swirling between us.

Cole chuckles. "Come on. Let's see what wonders you can create from whatever's rattling around in my fridge."

He pulls on his boxer briefs, follows me to the huge double-door fridge, and hovers behind me as I look through what he's got in there. He was right. There's not much. Some expensive-looking cheeses, butter, some condiments, a bottle of white wine, and about a thousand bottled waters. I glance over my shoulder at him. "You said you have some bread?"

"I think so. Although I don't know how fresh it is."

He pads on bare feet to a cupboard. When he pulls open, it's actually a walk-in pantry. Curious, I peer in. It's huge, but once again, there's hardly anything in there.

Cole pulls out a brown paper bag and hands it to me. I look inside and see a half-loaf of crusty white bread. I pull it out and he's right. It is a little stale, but that's okay. It won't be an issue for what I have in mind.

I ask Cole for a cutting board and a knife, which he pulls out of various hidden compartments around his massive kitchen.

"Can I help?" he asks as I cut four slices.

I tuck a tendril of hair behind my ear and smile at him. "Can you get the wine and a jar of mustard?"

He collects the bottle and jar and deposits them on the

counter next to me. "What are you making? Grilled cheese?"

"A variation of it." I glance up at him. "Do you like grilled cheese?"

He shrugs. "Don't most people?"

"Well, I wasn't sure what billionaires eat at home. And you don't exactly seem like the comfort-food type."

"Is that what it is for you? Comfort food?"

"Yeah." I smile to myself. "My mom used to make it for me whenever I had a bad day. When I got older, and Mom was working two jobs, I started making them for her when she got home too late for dinner. When I was a poor college student, I experimented. This is my favorite variation. Although"—I hold up the cheese and wine he's given me— "I never had ingredients this expensive."

The corner of his mouth twitches. "I suppose not. That bottle cost five hundred dollars."

I freeze. "Oh no, I can't use—"

"Use it."

I bite my lip, then nod, and continue what I'm doing.

He watches quietly as I melt the cheddar and brie in a saucepan, then add in some of the wine.

Cole fetches two glasses, then takes the bottle and fills them. I accept the one he hands me and take a sip. The cool, tart flavor explodes on my tongue. "Mmm, that's good."

And now I know what a five-hundred-dollar bottle of wine tastes like.

Cole hasn't drunk any of his yet. He's watching me with an inscrutable expression on his face. It makes me a little nervous, so as I combine the butter and mustard in a small bowl, I ask, "Did your mom ever make you grilled cheese when you were growing up?"

He doesn't answer, and I look up at him. His jaw is tight, but he just shakes his head. "We had a chef. Sometimes if we harassed him enough, he'd make us one. He didn't like doing it, though. It was beneath his culinary talents."

Right. I guess caviar was more his thing.

"Well, we're the chefs tonight," I tell him. "So, here." I pass him a plate with two slices of bread on it, along with the bowl of butter and mustard. "Spread the melted cheese on, then butter the top with this."

He does, and I do the same with mine. When we're finished, I find a skillet and fry the sandwiches until the bread is a crispy golden brown. When I slide Cole's plate over the counter to him, he looks at it, then back up at me, something shifting in his gaze.

"Thank you," he says in a low voice.

When was the last time someone other than a professional chef made him a meal? I smile. "You're welcome."

I'm still standing on the other side of the bench, but he uses his foot to push the stool next to him out and nods at it. "Come here."

I carry my plate and wineglass around the bench and slide my butt onto the stool. The tension on his face relaxes, and he smiles at me. Once again, that expression has my breath catching in my lungs. He really is unbelievably gorgeous, even more so with that look on his face rather than the stern one he normally wears. Although, the stern expression he gets when standing at the head of a conference table, controlling a room full of people with a single look, isn't too bad either.

I pick up my sandwich and take a bite. The mix of sharp cheddar and creamy brie goes beautifully with the mustard and the hint of wine. I watch him as he bites into his and chews, and I'm more nervous than I should be to hear what he thinks.

His eyes meet mine. "This is delicious," he finally says, with a hint of what sounds like surprise in his voice.

I can't help the grin that crosses my face, and I take a sip of my wine. "Now that you know how to do it, you can make one of these whenever you get the urge for a snack."

"I'll probably just call my favorite restaurant and tell them how to make it, then get them to deliver it."

I stare at him with my mouth open. His expression is deadpan, and I don't know if he's serious or not until he cracks a smile and chuckles.

I laugh too. "Wow. There's that sense of humor again."

"It comes out on occasion."

I take the last bite of my sandwich and then, with a hum of contentment, I lick the last bit of greasy goodness off my fingers.

I look up in time to see Cole's eyes focused on my mouth. They've gone dark. He puts the rest of his sandwich on his plate, pushes it away from him, hooks his foot around the leg of my stool, and drags me closer, forcing a gasp out of me.

"Cole, I—"

He shakes his head, cutting me off before reaching for the wine and raising it to his mouth. He takes a sip straight from the bottle, then he tips it toward me. "Drink."

Relaxed Cole is gone. Intense Cole is back. My belly twists in anticipation, and I reach for the bottle. He shakes his head again, then presses the rim to my lips. When I part them, he tilts it until a trickle of delicious liquid fills my mouth. I barely have a chance to swallow before he's gripping the back of my head and dragging me to him. His tongue meets mine with an urgency I match.

It's almost one a.m. I should be tired after a long week at work and already having sex with him once. But I'm not. Instead, I'm filled with a strange energy that traces its fingers along my nerve endings, waking my body in a way only he has ever done.

I thread my hands through his hair, rubbing the tips of my fingers along his scalp, and he groans against my lips. Before I know what's happening, he's slipped his shirt off my shoulders and I'm naked in front of him. He breaks the kiss, his gaze sweeping over me, causing my nipples to furl into tight, sensitive peaks.

"You're so fucking sexy," he growls. Then he stands, shoves our plates aside, and lifts me onto the countertop. I gasp when the cool marble meets my skin, my eyes immediately going to the wall of glass surrounding us.

"If anyone's watching, let them. Let them see how I make you mine," Cole says, and I shudder as the part of me that craves being reckless and free pushes against my restraint.

Then he's pressing me down, and I'm letting him, my heart thundering as his big hands spread my thighs. My eyes are closed, breath spilling from my lips in frantic bursts. Then his mouth is on me, hot and wet, and he eats me like he's a starving man, his tongue spearing into my opening and wringing a gasp from me.

His fingers replace his tongue, which traces a path to my clit, the sensitive bundle of nerves already swollen with need. He flicks it and then sucks it between his teeth. I'm so close, my hips buck against his hold. Just before I lose control, he stops and I cry out with frustration, my eyelids flying open.

Cole is staring down at me, his eyes hot and hungry. Then he picks up the almost empty bottle of wine and tilts it so a small stream trickles over my pussy. I almost shriek at the sensation, but before I can say anything, he's sinfully lapping at the liquid covering me.

I squirm. "God, Cole, that feels so good."

With a hand under my ass, he tilts my hips up, and then the bottle's cool glass brushes against my inner thigh as he pours another trickle over me. This time, with the way he's angled me, I feel it pool at my entrance. His mouth covers me, and he drinks. The thought of what he's doing is such a turn on, and even with no direct stimulation against my clit, my orgasm barrels closer. But it's not quite enough to push me over the edge.

I thrust my fingers into his hair, tugging to get him where I need him the most. With one final flick of his tongue, he moves upward. My breath shudders out of me as he latches onto my clit, sucking it between his lips.

And then the smooth rim of the bottle presses against my entrance and I gasp, shooting almost upright. "Cole?"

"Lie down," he growls, and I obey, collapsing against the bench. The tip of the bottle eases into me and I don't know whether to be embarrassed or aroused. My body decides for me, and my internal muscles clamp down around the neck. The cool hardness of the glass feels incredible inside me, especially when Cole doubles down on my clit.

He thrusts the bottle, but not hard enough to be uncomfortable. Just enough to give me some pressure and friction where I'm craving it. I imagine what we would look like if anyone saw us: me, laid out naked on the countertop with my legs spread, and a shirtless man with his head buried between my thighs, fucking me with his mouth and the neck of a wine bottle.

The mental picture and the physical sensations are enough to catapult me over the edge, and I cry out as my climax hits. My channel clenches around the bottle and my clit pulses against each lash of Cole's tongue. By the time it's over, I'm a sweaty, shuddering mess. Finally Cole stands, pulling the bottle from me. All I can do is lie bonelessly on the countertop and stare up at him as he gives me a dark, sensual smile. He raises the bottle to his lips and tips it up, the strong column of his throat moving as he drinks most of the remaining wine inside it.

His arm slides under my back and tugs me upright, holding the bottle to my lips. "You taste fucking divine," he says.

I open my mouth and let him pour the last drops of wine onto my tongue. He sits down, pulls me onto his lap, and kisses me again so that we're sharing the taste of the wine and me. My body quakes almost as much as my heart and mind. Cole is too much for me. Too much of everything I'm not. And yet the feeling he gives me when I'm with him like this and can let go is addictive.

Too addictive.

The way his mouth claims mine, the possessive grip of his hands on my body—none of it feels casual or temporary. I don't want to move from where I am. I want to stay here, pressed against him like this, without reminding myself that this must end.

But I can't, so I gather myself and pull away. When I try to slide off his lap, he tightens his arms around me. "Where do you think you're going?"

"I should probably go home."

He feathers his lips down my neck. "Stay," he murmurs against my skin.

"What?" I lean back to meet his gaze.

His brow is furrowed, as if he's not sure of what he's saying. "It's late. You should stay."

"You . . . want me to stay the night?"

He doesn't bother to answer my question. "I'll get you one of my shirts to wear." He lifts me off him and disappears down the hallway to his bedroom. I trail behind. He's never asked me to stay before. I never really expected him to. I assumed it was a way to keep the reality of our non-relationship front and center in my mind.

But now . . . now I'm confused. I enter his bedroom and find him rummaging around in a drawer. He turns toward me and holds out a white T-shirt that will be far too large for me but nicer than sleeping in the one I was wearing all evening and will have to wear home tomorrow.

I take it from him, my fingers brushing his, and a little curl of warmth blossoms in my stomach. I do my best to suppress it. I don't want to give in to the temptation of thinking this means something.

And yet . . .

I pull the shirt over my head. It hangs down to mid-thigh, but the material is soft and luxurious. Cole stares at me, the intensity of his gaze heating every inch of my skin. He scrubs his hand over his mouth, then abruptly turns and disappears into the bathroom, coming out carrying a new toothbrush for me to use. We both quickly clean up, and before I know it, he's climbing into his huge bed and holding the covers back for me.

I slide under, but lying there next to him, I'm not sure what to do with myself. Cole doesn't exactly seem like the spooning type, but then he rolls toward me and places his large hand on my stomach, the warmth of his palm seeping through the shirt and relaxing me.

We might not be cuddling, but being here with him like this still feels special. I think I might be smiling as I drift off to sleep.

CHAPTER THIRTY-TWO

COLE

I wake to something hot pressed against my side. My eyes fly open and immediately find the woman curled up next to me, her mass of dark hair draped over my arm, the rest of it partially covering her face. Her long, dark eyelashes flutter against her cheeks as she dreams.

I'm not sure what came over me last night when I asked her to stay. No. That's not true. I know exactly what I was thinking. I was thinking that I liked that she'd cooked for me. I liked that she'd laughed with me. I really liked what she'd let me do to her afterward. Having her with me after a long fucking week of work had felt good. More than good. I hadn't wanted that feeling to go away.

I hadn't wanted *her* to go. And I don't know what the hell to do with that.

I slide myself away from her and out of bed. She makes a little whimper and curls into herself, and I want to crawl right back under the covers, roll her onto her back, and bury my head between her legs. My thoughts are all over the place right now, and I need to focus on something else.

After using the bathroom, I dress in my workout clothes

and head to my personal gym. I spend the next hour pushing my body hard, all to keep myself from thinking about the woman in my bed. The one who keeps working her way further and further under my skin. I force myself to think about my plans for the weekend. Today is our monthly catch-up with Mom, an event which my brothers and I—and Mom as well, I'm sure—dread equally. It's been even worse since Dad's arrest. Mom's doing her usual routine of ignoring anything even slightly unpleasant, while Roman, Tate, and I are there for appearance's sake. As soon as lunch is over, we'll all go our separate ways. Duty done for another month.

Ten minutes later, I put my weights on the rack and turn, stopping when I see the slender form standing in the doorway. My dick stirs at the sight of her in my T-shirt. Her nipples are clearly visible through the white cotton, and all I can think about is getting my mouth on them. Then I notice the way her fingers twist together in front of her. She's uncertain about being here. Probably as uncertain as I am about having her here.

Delilah walks toward me, and I take in the soft sway of her hips. I wait for discomfort to overwhelm me with the urge to rush her out the door. But I just stand there and watch her come closer. Rather than telling her I'll call Jonathan to take her home when she stops in front of me, I step toward her, wrap my hands around her ass, and yank her against me.

Her wide eyes look up at me, and I'm overcome with the need to strip that shirt from her body and fuck her right here on the gym floor. I fist my hand in her hair and tug back her head.

"Cole," she says. "Do you want me to—"

"Do you want to come to lunch with my family today?"

Her lips part and she stares at me. "You want me to spend time with your family?"

It sounds ridiculous when she says it, and I don't know what I was thinking by asking her, but instead of backtracking, I double down. "Yes. Do you have anything planned for today?"

"I was just going to do some work."

"You work too hard," I growl.

She laughs softly. "Like you can talk."

I angle my head toward her, breathing her in. "Feel free to distract me."

She stares up at me, something soft and warm blooming in her eyes. Then she crosses her arms, grasps the hem of her shirt, and tugs it over her head.

I DRIVE Delilah back to her apartment in my Maclaren so she can get changed. When she comes out dressed in a pretty blue sundress and high-heeled sandals, my fingers itch to slide the silky material up her thighs and sink into her. I'd love to take her back to my penthouse and spend all day in bed with her rather than go to this lunch, but appearances are all-important and our monthly family lunch must be maintained—a sign of our solidarity. It's even more important after what Dad did.

I start the engine, pull into traffic, and head toward my family's estate in Westchester County.

We drive in silence for a few minutes, the scenery outside the car window changing from the skyscrapers of Manhattan to leafy suburbs.

Delilah breaks the silence. "Will your brothers wonder why I'm there?"

I glance at her, taking in the furrow between her brows. Considering I'd surprised myself when I invited her, I've no doubt my family will be shocked, but the last thing I want to do is make her feel uncomfortable. "My brothers already know about you."

"I know Tate does, but I didn't realize they both do." She bites her lip. "Won't they think it's strange that I'm with you today?"

Worry laces her voice, and I can't help but feel a twinge of guilt.

"They will," I admit, trying to keep my tone even. "But they won't say anything."

"And what about your mom? You didn't tell her you were bringing me, did you?"

"No." It's better that way. At least she won't have time to sharpen her claws. "Mom will be polite." At least on the surface. I can't imagine her reaction to me bringing a woman to lunch, let alone a woman who works for me. "Just don't expect her to be like your mom. She's not particularly . . . maternal."

At this stage, Delilah's probably wondering why I invited her. I'm not exactly painting an appealing picture of my family. But I can't lie to her either. This won't be a fun family catch-up. Maybe that's why I invited her. Not because I particularly want to expose her to my family, but because I'm not prepared to give up the warmth of her presence in exchange for another cold meeting with them.

Delilah seems to sense my hesitation. "Is everything okay?"

I pause, then decide to tell her the truth. "These lunches aren't exactly enjoyable. It's just something we do to keep up appearances and fulfill our societal obligations. My mother likes to tell her friends that she spends quality time with her sons, and we go along with it because it's good for business if we maintain a façade of family unity. Investors and shareholders like to think there's a close-knit family running the company. But there's no love lost between any of us. Basically, it's just a matter of going through the motions until we can leave."

"I'm sorry," she says, and when I glance at her, sympathy shimmers in her eyes.

I shrug. "It's just the way it is."

"Well, I'll do my best not to make things more uncomfortable."

With the hand that's been resting on the gearshift, I reach over and slide her dress up until I can curve my hand around her bare thigh. "You won't."

Twenty minutes later, I turn up the long gravel driveway. As we reach the end and the main house comes into view, Delilah's mouth drops open. She peers out the window at the white columns flanking the entrance of the sprawling three-story Georgian mansion made of red brick.

She shakes her head in disbelief. "This is where you grew up?"

"When I wasn't in boarding school."

Her eyes widen as she turns to look at me. "I didn't know you went to boarding school. Whereabouts?"

"In New Hampshire."

"Wow. I can't even imagine what that would be like. Although, I guess you had your brothers, at least."

"No, I didn't."

"What do you mean?"

"Roman is five years older than me. By the time I was in high school, he'd started college. Tate went to school in Massachusetts."

"Why did Tate go to a different school?"

279

Now's not the time to get into Tate's situation. "We should probably get inside."

She keeps looking at me for a beat, then gives me an understanding smile. "Okay."

Before she can unlatch her seatbelt and get out, I exit the car and round to her side so I can open her door for her.

I worry she won't wait for me, but she does, accepting my outstretched hand and stepping out gracefully. Her fingers are warm in mine, and I can think of a hundred other things I'd rather be doing with her right now than this. But we're here now, so I guide Delilah up the steps to where Peters is already holding the door for us.

"Good afternoon, Mr. King, ma'am," he says.

I swear my parents chose Peters because he's just as warm and affectionate as either of them. Which is to say, not at all. From his cool greeting, you'd never believe he'd known me since I was a child. Then again, my parents have never encouraged familiarity with any of our staff.

"Afternoon, Peters. Are we eating in the dining room or on the south lawn today?"

"The south lawn, sir."

Delilah looks at me with wide eyes again; however, as we step into the large foyer, she transfers her deer-in-headlights gaze to the surrounding space. "Oh my god," she whispers to herself as her hand flutters up to press against her chest.

I look around, seeing the place the way someone who is unfamiliar might. The foyer boasts twenty-four-foot ceilings, and the pale blond wood floor, white walls, and expansive windows fill the area with light. Directly in front of us, a wide staircase sweeps upward. With all the sun streaming in, the place should feel warm and inviting. But it doesn't. At least, not to me. If I had memories of these rooms filled with love and laughter, it might feel like a family home, but I don't have those memories. I have others.

My eyes go to the closed library door, but I turn away before the scene I witnessed there can play through my head.

We follow Peters to the back of the house, where glass doors lead onto the porch. My brothers are already seated at the table in the middle of the precisely manicured lawn.

Peters opens the door for us and stands to the side to let us pass. I step out, then turn back and see Delilah paused on the threshold. It hits me that this must be intimidating for her. Not thinking too hard about it, I reach out, thread my fingers through hers, and tug her forward. When she comes with no more hesitation, a strange warmth unfurls in my chest. We make our way across the lawn, with Delilah walking on her tiptoes so her heels don't sink into the grass.

Noticing our approach, Tate and Roman look up. I can see their raised brows from here, but I ignore them. A moment later, Mom looks over her shoulder. She stiffens, but I keep moving forward, bringing Delilah with me.

"Cole," Mom says as we draw closer, "I didn't know you were bringing a guest."

Her gaze drops to where my hand is joined with Delilah's, and her lips thin. The intimacy of what I'm doing hits me with a sudden twist of discomfort in my gut. I let go as soon as we reach the table, using the excuse of pulling out Delilah's chair for her. "Mom. This is Delilah."

"Hello, Delilah." Mom runs her silvery-blue eyes over Delilah, then twitches her lips into what's supposed to be a smile.

"It's very nice to meet you, Mrs. King," Delilah says, her own smile far warmer than Mom's.

"Good to see you again, Delilah," Tate says, his lips curved into a smirk.

Roman just nods, his gaze coolly assessing as he watches Delilah sit gracefully in the chair I've pulled out for her. But then, that's the way Roman looks at everyone.

I take a seat between Delilah and Mom, who takes a sip from her teacup and delicately puts it on the saucer. "So, Delilah, what is it you do?"

"I'm an architect."

Mom's blonde eyebrows arch. "An architect? You're very young for that, aren't you?"

"I completed my licensure early."

"Delilah's very talented." Tate throws this in with a sly grin in my direction. "She's working on the new hotel development."

I don't miss the way Mom's eyes narrow. "You work for the company?"

"I work for Elite Architecture. We're contracted to the King Group for the duration of the development."

"I see." Mom picks a bit of lint off the table before leveling me with a cold look I don't acknowledge. I merely reach for the open bottle of wine and fill Delilah's glass, followed by mine.

"Roman and Tate were just telling me how things are going with the development," Mom says. "Apparently, there are some concerns with the investors?"

"They're sitting back and waiting to see if we fail," I respond. "As soon as we show them the final numbers, they'll realize they're going to make more money from us than ever before."

"As long as you don't allow yourself to get distracted," she says, her gaze skimming over Delilah.

Delilah shifts in her seat, then reaches for her wineglass.

"I don't get distracted," I say, ignoring what sounds suspiciously like a muffled snort from Tate. "And besides, the people working for us are the best in the business. I don't have any concerns about them dropping the ball." My eyes meet Delilah's, and she smiles at me.

The arrival of lunch breaks the tension. A troop of servants arrives, carrying plates and placing them in front of each of us. As usual, the food is exquisite and there's a few minutes of silence as we all enjoy our meals. Unfortunately, it doesn't last.

"When did you last speak to your father?" Mom asks.

I share a look with Tate and Roman, and it's Roman who answers. "A few weeks ago. They're still discussing a plea bargain, but he's holding out."

Mom snorts. "He's being stubborn."

"Don't tell me you thought he'd go down without a fight?" Tate asks, amusement coloring his voice. Out of all of us, there's the least love lost between him and Dad, for obvious reasons.

Mom sighs. "Well, hopefully all of this will blow over soon."

I grit my teeth. God forbid anyone or anything disrupt her perfect, careless existence, let alone her husband's arrest. She's more worried about how the women at the country club look at her than the fact that her husband has no respect for her or his family.

The whole thing is a joke—sitting here and having lunch together, pretending we're a happy family that gives a shit about each other. Because that's all it is and all it's ever been—a pretense.

"So, Delilah," Mom starts up again, "is your family from New York?"

Delilah puts down her fork. "No. I grew up in North Carolina. Near Raleigh."

"And what do your parents do, dear?"

"My mom is a hairdresser."

Mom's nostrils flare and her lips purse. I grit my teeth. She's not even trying to hide her horror. "And your father?"

Delilah raises her chin and looks my mother straight in the eyes. "My father's not around."

God, this fucking woman. She's not letting my mother intimidate her for a second. She's not pandering to her or trying to win favor. She's not ashamed of her upbringing. She's proud of who she is, where she comes from, and who she loves. Her defiance is a refreshing change from the status-obsessed world I come from.

I catch Tate's slow grin, and the way he's looking at her pisses me off. I rest my arm on the back of her chair and trail my fingers up the side of her neck. Goose bumps ripple down her arms, and she cuts a glance in my direction. I give her a smile that promises a few good orgasms later, and her cheeks flush.

Mom's expression is pinched. "That must have been . . . difficult."

Delilah shrugs. "Mom worked very hard to give me a good life, and now I hope to do the same for her."

"What do you mean?" Tate asks before I can, and I glare at him.

Delilah smiles in his direction, making my teeth grind again. "I'm saving up so that I can build a house for her. I've already started designing it. It's going to be a surprise."

I didn't know that. But then, I haven't bothered to ask her for many details of her life, have I?

"You're obviously close to your mother," Tate says. "I've

always wondered what that's like." His lips curl, but I'd hardly call what his mouth is doing a smile.

"Uh . . ." Delilah shoots a glance at Mom, who doesn't deign to acknowledge the comment. "Yes, we're very close. It was just the two of us when I was growing up."

"How sweet." Mom sounds like she thinks it's anything but sweet.

Delilah looks around the table, then at me. She still has a smile on her face, but I can see the uncertainty in her eyes. Considering my parents never did anything for us that didn't serve themselves, the fact that my mother is trying to make Delilah feel bad about how she grew up makes red flash across my vision.

I'm about to claim an urgent meeting I'd forgotten about, but Delilah speaks up again. "I may not have grown up in a mansion"—she gestures toward the house behind us —"but my mom showed up for me every single time I needed her. As far as I'm concerned, that means more than anything money can buy."

My mother narrows her gaze on Delilah, who merely picks up her fork and continues eating. Pride rushes through me. Since when has a woman stood up to my mother as directly and sincerely as Delilah just did? And what must it have been like growing up, knowing you had someone who cared about you that way? Someone who would put your needs above theirs. Someone who loved you more than money, power, or themselves.

Roman picks up the conversation, giving Delilah a break from being the focus of the conversation, although Mom's gaze occasionally slides back to her. I have no idea what she's thinking, since her face is frozen as much by lack of discernible emotion as it is by Botox. Roman, Tate, and I run over some numbers for the new project while Mom listens. Delilah tries to make small talk with her, but the replies she receives are cool and short at best. Delilah's increasing discomfort distracts me from talking work with my brothers.

I was an idiot to think my mother would unbend enough to be courteous to a woman who doesn't meet her wealth and power requirements. I should never have put Delilah in this situation. I don't know if I'm angrier at myself or my mother.

It only takes one more curt response from Mom, and I'm done. I push my chair back and stand. "We're going."

Delilah rises as well. "Thank you for lunch, Mrs. King." Her words may be calm, but tension radiates from her. How she manages to be so polite to the woman who has alternated between ignoring her and being borderline rude, I don't know.

Fuck it. I thread my fingers through hers again and look over at Tate and Roman. "I'll see you in the office." Then I look at Mom. "I'll see you next month."

She's staring at me in shock. "But Cole, we haven't—"

Without bothering to wait for her to finish, I tug Delilah after me and we make our way back to the house. As soon as we get inside, I press her against the wall and skim my nose down her neck. "I'm sorry."

Breathing in her sweet scent calms me. As does the way her arms go around me, her hands pressing against my back. "It's okay. It wasn't your fault."

I let out a harsh laugh. "I shouldn't have asked you to come. I know what she's like."

She's silent for a moment, her hands smoothing up and down my tense muscles. "I can't say I enjoyed the experience. But . . ." I pull back to look at her and feel a strange throb behind my sternum as her green eyes meet mine. "I'm glad you wanted me here."

My erection presses hard and heavy against her stomach, and my need to fuck her, to bury myself in her so deeply she'll never get me out, is nearly overwhelming. If I didn't think my mother and brothers might decide to come inside any minute now, I'd strip her naked right here and push my way into her.

Instead, I lead her back through the house. When we get to the foyer, my gaze goes straight to the library door, my fingers tightening around Delilah's.

"What room is that?" She points with her free hand. "And why does it bother you?"

I shoot her a surprised look.

"Both times we've come through here, you kind of glared at it."

Even with my current bad mood, I almost smile. For some reason I don't fully understand, I take her over there and swing the door open.

The too-familiar scent of leather-bound books, polished wood, and a hint of old paper invades my senses.

"Wow," Delilah murmurs. "This is amazing." She walks into the room, heading straight to the nearest bookshelf and running her finger along an embossed spine. "How many of these are first editions?"

"Too many to count." I step alongside her. "It used to be my favorite room in the house when I was younger. I was one of the few people who ever used it."

I sense her turn to me, but I don't look at her. "What stopped it being your favorite?"

When I move past her and make my way to the center of the room, she follows me. It looks exactly as it did back then.

Book-filled shelves line three walls, while the large windows in the fourth wall offer a view of the manicured grounds outside. At one end of the room, a large wooden desk dominates the space, surrounded by leather armchairs and a sofa. "I used to love coming here on rainy days and finding a new book to read."

"I can imagine," she says softly.

"I came down to do some reading one rainy day when I was about nine years old. When I opened the door, I saw Dad was already in here." The unpleasant memory flashes through my mind—my father, reclining in one of the armchairs, shirt open, pants at his ankles, and his head thrown back as a woman's head bobbed up and down between his legs. "He was getting a blow job. From our nanny."

"Oh, god," Delilah says. She moves closer until she's pressed against my side. I look down at the sympathy swimming in her beautiful eyes. "That's awful."

"I was old enough to have a pretty good idea what was going on. Old enough to realize what he was doing was wrong. That there was some kind of betrayal happening." I don't go into detail. I don't tell her I'd stood there, jaw agape, staring as he grabbed her head and shoved her down on him while he groaned. I don't mention how horrified I was or that my face got hot and I had a sudden, shocking urge to cry—something I'd already learned was not acceptable. "I tried to shut the door before he saw me, but I wasn't quick enough." I give a humorless laugh. "He wasn't even embarrassed at being caught. He just grinned and winked at me."

Delilah moves to stand in front of me and slides her arms around my chest. I instinctively wrap my arms around her too. "I'm so sorry," she says. "That must have been so confusing for you."

"I couldn't slam the door quick enough. I worried myself sick about whether I should tell Mom, wondering what she would do if she found out. Eventually, I confessed what I'd seen to Roman, and he told me that Mom already knew and didn't care. Or maybe she cared once, but not enough to disrupt her life. Particularly since she was having her own affairs."

"That's so screwed up," Delilah whispers.

I shake my head to dismiss the memories, not only of what I'd seen Dad doing, but also Roman's disclosure of the truth about our family. I'd known my parents weren't affectionate people, but until Roman spelled it out for me, I hadn't realized it wasn't just because they weren't demonstrative. It was because they didn't love—or even particularly like—each other. Or us.

That was the day I found out the truth about Tate, too. The whole thing had opened my eyes to reality—love is an illusion. As I grew up, it became even clearer. Relationships are basically business deals, children are considered investments, and affection is mostly a façade. In my world, at least.

I clear my throat. "Anyway, the library kind of lost its appeal. I avoided it after that."

"That's understandable," Delilah says, tightening her arms around me. "I'm just sorry your dad was so selfish. That he took something special from you like that."

Driven by instinct and need, I grip her chin and angle her face so I can kiss her. The warmth of her lips and the taste of her mouth drive out any other thoughts.

Her hands roam over my back, and she presses herself against me, sending a wave of heat rolling through me.

I want her again.

Fuck. When don't I want her?

Just having her body against mine eases something inside me that seems like it's been drawn tight for as long as I can remember. I drag my lips along her jaw until I reach the delicate skin by her ear. "Come home with me again tonight."

She doesn't say anything, just nods. Her eyes are hazy, cheeks flushed, mouth swollen from how hard I kissed her. She looks perfect. And suddenly I'm imagining what it might be like to have her with me like this all the time.

My ribs tighten around my lungs. I promised myself I would never get taken in by the illusion. I can't start believing the lie that this can grow and become more—that it can last. That doesn't happen in my world.

What if it can?

I close my eyes and claim her mouth again. I'd be stupid to let those thoughts take root.

What if it's already too late?

CHAPTER THIRTY-THREE

DELILAH

I'm smiling as I initial the latest set of internal plans. I seem to do that a lot lately, smile at nothing. And the reason is about six foot two inches, dark-haired and blue-eyed, with a dick that doesn't quit. I laugh to myself. I really am going off the deep end.

It can't be a bad thing to be so happy that I'm smiling and laughing to myself, can it? As long as I don't let myself forget that this thing Cole and I have won't last forever.

But there's a part of me, the part that watched too many Disney movies when I was little, that can't help but hope that might change. I've noticed a difference in Cole over the last few weeks—since that lunch with his family. A softening. A warmth where once there wasn't. It's like he's slowly peeling away the layers of his coldhearted persona, revealing the man underneath. And as it turns out, I can't get enough of that man.

The sex is still intense. We've done it all over his penthouse, twice in his limo with Cole's hand over my mouth so Jonathan couldn't hear me, and in his office one night when we were working late. Then there are the moments when he seems almost tender—when he holds me in his arms or strokes the hair away from my face and presses soft kisses to my lips.

He's started laughing more too, helped me cook several times, and shared quite a few more bottles of expensive wine with me. On the nights I go home to my apartment, he always kisses me before I leave. But just as often, we end up falling asleep next to each other in his big bed.

I'm still scared to allow myself to get my hopes up, only to be disappointed.

Although I don't think disappointed is the right word anymore.

My phone rings and Cole's name flashes on the screen. A thrill runs through me. I hope he's calling me up to his office so we can see each other today. I haven't seen him since the weekend, and it's Tuesday now. Stupidly, I miss him. I'm supposed to go to his penthouse tomorrow night, but I'd love to see him sooner.

"Hi." My voice comes out breathier than I'd like, but he seems to have that effect on me. And surprisingly, I don't hate it.

"Delilah." His voice is a little brusquer than I'd hoped, but that's him, and I'm learning to accept it.

"Yes. Do you need to see me?" I wince. That came out a little too eagerly.

"I'd like to, but I'm heading into a meeting with the board. I just wanted to let you know that I have to fly to the UK tonight, so I won't be able to see you tomorrow."

"Oh . . ." My stomach drops. "That's . . . okay. Has something happened?"

"The lawyers just informed us the prosecutors are going to offer Dad a final plea bargain. If he rejects it, he's going to trial.

Whatever the result, it's going to have an impact. I'm heading to the UK to prep our international offices and handle whatever concerns our overseas investors might have after the news breaks. Cole and Tate will take care of any issues here."

"Of course. Do you think you'll be okay? You know, with whatever happens?"

He's silent for a moment. "I want to feel bad for him, but I don't doubt for a second that he's guilty, and that makes me realize just how dead our relationship is. He cares more about his mistresses than he's ever cared about his family—and that's not saying much, considering how many mistresses he's had. So I'm returning the favor. I don't care what happens to him. I only care about what it means for the company."

My heart twists painfully. I didn't have a father while growing up, but my mother gave me all the love I ever needed. Cole had two parents and two brothers, yet he didn't have any of the love I did. No wonder he doesn't trust relationships. When has he ever had one worth trusting? When has anyone ever been there for him unconditionally? "Do you know how long you'll be gone for?"

"At this stage, I plan to fly back next Thursday."

Just over a week. I let out a quiet breath. Before Cole, I had no problem being by myself or hanging out with Alex. Even when I was dating Paul and he went away to a symposium for a week, I didn't bat an eyelash. I just took the opportunity to spend more time on the project I was working on. This is different.

My feelings for Cole are different.

"I'll get back late." He interrupts my thoughts. "So make sure you're free Friday."

"I'll see if I can pencil you in." I roll my lips together.

"You will, will you? I assumed you'd be wide open for me on Friday."

"Oh, no." I match his suggestive tone. "I fill up very quickly."

"Fuck." He lets out a groan. "If my meeting wasn't about to start, I'd have you up here and bent over my desk before you could say, 'I'm always open for you, Cole.'"

I laugh, then lower my voice to a purr. "I'm always open for you, Cole."

He curses again. "I have to leave straight after the meeting, but I'll message you when I get a chance."

I sigh. "Okay. Well, have a good flight. And I hope everything goes well."

He says goodbye and I hang up. I get straight back to work, but there's a heaviness in my chest that wasn't there before. I missed him after only a few days. Now it'll be almost two weeks before I see him again.

A few minutes later, my email notification sounds. Clicking it open, I see a message from Samson.

Good afternoon, Miss West,

Mr. King has asked that you not make any plans for this weekend. You are to pack an overnight bag, casual wear only, and a car will pick you up at 8 a.m. Saturday morning.

Kind regards,
Samson

I frown and pick up the phone.

"Hi, Samson," I say, when he answers. "I just got your email, and I was wondering if you could give me more details. Cole didn't say anything about this to me, and I'm not sure what to expect. Can you tell me what kind of event this is for? I'd like to prepare."

"I'm sorry, Miss West. Cole didn't give me any details."

I glance at the clock. "Has he already gone into his meeting?"

"Yes, he has."

"Okay, thank you."

I hang up and stare at the email again. What has Cole arranged? I shoot him a quick message on his phone. It will be off during the meeting, but he'll get it as soon as he finishes.

> Can you tell me what I'll be doing this weekend?

Then I try to put it out of my mind so I can get some work done.

Two hours later my phone buzzes and I grab it, opening the message from Cole.

> Don't overthink it.

What does he mean?
I furiously type back.

> What's to overthink about a vague request to pack a bag and go somewhere unknown?

> Trust me.

I hesitate before I respond. I do trust him, don't I? As disconcerting as it is to go into something blind like this, Cole wouldn't send me anywhere that would make me uncomfortable.

> Okay.

> Good girl. I'll reward you for that when I get home.

> You'd better.

> Have a good flight.

I fight the urge to end my message with something else —something more affectionate. Or to call him just to hear his voice again. I don't want to be needy like that, even though it's becoming harder and harder to fight wanting more with him.

I finish up the rest of the day, trying to force down both my sadness at not seeing him and my curiosity about this weekend. I have the apartment to myself, since Alex is in LA for the whole week, visiting Jaxson. She finally admitted how much she missed him, and he leaped into action, organizing his schedule so he'd have some time to spend with her. I'm sure she's having an amazing time, so even though I wish I could talk to her about Cole, I won't call her. Her time with Jaxson is precious, and I don't want to take away from that by having a long phone conversation.

I eat dinner with a glass of wine in front of the television and then call it an early night. Well, an early night for me, anyway, only working for two hours on my laptop before turning the lights out.

The rest of the week passes quickly. We're nearing deadlines, so the whole team has their heads down as we try to get our plans signed off. Cole has messaged me every day, but we haven't spoken on the phone. I know he's busy, and when he's not in meetings, he's out at various dinners and social events. Though I'm happy he's messaging me so regularly, I wish I could hear his voice. Once or twice I've considered calling him, but every time I pick up my phone, ready to dial his number, I end up putting it down again. If I call him, my voice will betray how much I miss him.

He'll know how I feel.

But now that it's Saturday, and I'm standing outside my building with my overnight bag at my feet, I really wish I'd gotten the chance to talk to him and grill him some more about where I'm going. I meant it when I said I trusted him, though, which is funny. If you'd asked me a few months ago, I would have said he's the last man on earth I'd trust.

Well, except for my father.

Cole's sleek black car pulls up in front of me, and Jonathan gets out with a smile.

"Good morning, Miss West," he says, picking up my bag for me.

"Morning, Jonathan." He opens my door, and when I slide in, he shuts it behind me, then places my bag in the trunk. As soon as he returns to the driver's seat, and before he pulls out into traffic, I lean forward and ask, "I don't suppose you know where I'm going?"

His gaze meets mine in the rearview mirror, the creases at the corners of his eyes revealing his smile. "I'm afraid I don't. Cole just told me to take you to the airfield."

"I'm flying somewhere?"

"Yes, ma'am," he says.

I sink back into the plush leather seat as Jonathan maneuvers the big car into the stream of traffic. I spend the rest of the trip trying to guess where I might be going. Although the thought that Cole might fly me to the UK to see him is nice, it's blatantly unrealistic. I've only packed an overnight bag, and flying to the other side of the world and back for one night seems like a huge waste of resources, even for a billionaire.

If it's work related, surely he would have told me. He could be sending me to a relaxing spa, although that doesn't really seem like Cole's style. Then again, nothing about this really screams "emotionally unavailable billionaire only interested in a no-strings-attached sexual relationship."

I try to distract myself during the flight by reading a romance, but my mind wanders to where I might be going, then to Cole and what's happening between us. My thoughts run in circles until the captain announces we're beginning our descent. The flight was only about an hour and a half, which raises a niggling suspicion in me.

After we land at a small airfield I don't recognize, I descend the stairs, and the scent of the air is so familiar I know my suspicion must be true. Emotions swirl through me, but I hold them in until I know for sure. There's a limo waiting for me, and I laugh to myself that Cole thinks I need a car like this when a normal sedan would do. Hell, an Uber would do. But this is who he is, and my chest floods with warmth because he's organized this for me.

The driver takes my bag with a nod, then holds my door open. Once he's shut it behind me, he places my bag in the trunk, then climbs into the driver's seat. He seems to know where he's going, so I sit back and look out the window. Soon I see familiar sights, and my suspicion is confirmed. I'm smiling so broadly I can feel it in my cheeks as I pull out my phone and tap out a message to Cole.

> Thank you, thank you, thank you!

I'm not expecting a response, and I shove my phone back in my purse, eagerly looking out the window. Happiness buzzes in my veins as we get closer and closer to our destination. When the car pulls up outside the small, single-story house with all the pretty flowers in the front yard, tears well up in my eyes. The driver stops the engine, and I throw the door open and dash up the path.

Mom must have heard the car pull up, because the door opens and she rushes out. "Delilah." Her voice is breathless with shock, but delight wreaths her face.

"Mom!" I wrap my arms around her and breathe in the subtle scent of lilacs that drifts from her skin, the result of the lotion she applies every single morning.

I pull back, scanning her face, which is so like mine. I've always been glad there's hardly any of my father in me. Only the color of my eyes—green to my mother's blue— marks me as his daughter.

"I'm so happy to see you," Mom says. "Why didn't you tell me you were coming?"

I laugh. "I'm happy to be here, and I didn't tell you because I didn't know."

Her brow furrows. "What do you mean?"

"Let's go inside and I'll tell you."

Mom nods, but her gaze goes over my shoulder, a quizzical expression crossing her face.

I glance behind me and see the driver standing there with my bag. He holds it out to me. "Mr. King's instructions are for me to pick you up at three p.m. tomorrow for your return flight."

I take it with a smile. "Thank you."

He nods, then heads back down the path to the car while Mom regards me with raised brows.

"I'll explain," I say.

Her lips quirk. "Let's get you inside, then."

Every time I come home it feels like I've never left. It's been months since I've visited, but the familiar creak of the front door and the smell of freshly cut flowers and furniture polish fills my senses. I breathe in deeply, taking it all in. As always, everything looks the same—the comfortable, well-worn floral couch, the small TV in the corner, the childhood photos of me that adorn the shelves. Warmth and comfort washes over me.

"I still can't believe you're here," Mom says. "Why don't I make us a cup of tea, and you can tell me everything."

"Let me just put my bag in my room and I'll help," I say. My old bedroom is just down the short hallway. After I drop my bag on the familiar single bed, I join Mom in the kitchen. While I fill the kettle, she puts some cookies on a plate in a routine that takes me straight back in time to when it was the two of us living here. On odd occasions, I catch her smiling at me as we move around the kitchen. We sit next to each other on the small couch when we've finished.

After we both take a sip of our tea, Mom smiles at me. "Tell me how you're here and why you didn't know you were coming."

I let out a breath. "Well, I've been seeing someone. Kind of."

Her brows furrow. "Kind of?"

I look down and brush an imaginary speck of lint off my jeans. "It's just casual. And I'm not sure it's going anywhere . . ."

"Why wouldn't it go anywhere? I mean, you're smart, you're beautiful. Why wouldn't any man want to be with you?"

I put my cup on the coffee table and reach for a cookie. "Because he has . . . other priorities."

She frowns. "Like what?"

"His job. He's very focused on that at the moment, and that's okay. He has to be." I hurry to add that last bit, in case it sounds like that upsets me. That's not the issue for me.

"What does he do?"

I really don't want to lie to Mom, but I know what her reaction will be. Still, I might as well get it over and done with.

"He's an executive."

"You're being very vague. What does an executive mean exactly?"

"Well. He's the COO of the King Group."

Mom's eyes narrow slightly. "Isn't that the company you're working for at the moment?"

"Yes."

"But you don't work directly for him, do you?"

I let out a sigh. "I'm still working for Elite, but the King Group is our client and we're working out of their building."

Mom's mouth twists. "Oh, Delilah. Is that a good idea after what happened with Paul? Surely you could get in trouble if anyone finds out. Both of you could."

I wet my lips. "Probably not him, since he's one of the company's owners."

Mom's mouth works but she doesn't say anything for a few seconds. Then it comes out in a rush. "Delilah, you know what men like that are after. The minute they get everything they want from you, they'll bail. They don't want to marry you. They just want to use you until it gets too complicated or someone more suitable comes along."

I reach for her hand and squeeze it. "It's not like that with us, Mom. He's not like Dad. He hasn't lied to me about his intentions or pretended to be in love with me, and I'm not expecting a ring or anything like that."

A furrow appears between her brows. "Then why be with him if you already know he doesn't want a future with you? Why not find a normal man who'll want to settle down and have a family? I know you're too young to think about that right now, but why risk your heart for a man who'll never be interested in more?"

"We're just having fun." Although, that's not quite true anymore. I push down my guilt at not being honest with her. "I've spent so long working so hard. It's nice to let go and enjoy myself for once. And Cole . . . He forces me to do that. I like it. Plus, he's the one who organized for me to fly here this weekend as a surprise."

"Ah. That's who Mr. King is, then?"

I nod and Mom's face softens. "I know how hard you've worked, sweetheart. And how much you've achieved. I want you to have fun. I want you to enjoy your youth. I just don't want you to waste your heart on someone who doesn't deserve it. And men like that . . ." She shakes her head. "Men with power and wealth, they don't live the same way as the rest of us, and they don't care about anyone who isn't in their world."

"Cole's not like that." I pause because again, that's not quite true. "I mean, obviously he lives a different life from most people, but he cares. Otherwise, why would he have sent me here?"

She presses her lips together, her eyes searching mine. Then she lets out a sigh. "You know I don't regret what happened with your father because you are the best thing that ever happened to me, but I don't want you to go through the pain of realizing you've given your heart to someone not worthy of it." One corner of her mouth turns up. "But then, you've got a far better head on your shoulders than I did when I was younger. I let myself get swept up in your dad's charisma and all the attention and excitement of being with someone like him. I just think you should be careful. Okay?"

"I will, Mom, I promise. I know exactly what this is, so I won't be upset when it ends." The lie pinches inside my chest.

Worry still shimmers in her eyes, but she smiles gently. "Well, that's all I can ask for."

LATER THAT NIGHT, I'm lying in bed and finally have time to look at my phone. When I see the message notification, I quickly swipe the screen.

> I'm glad you're happy. I'll think of a way you can show me your gratitude when I get home.

> > I'm very happy. And I've already thought of a way to thank you.

> Is that so? Care to enlighten me?

> > No. It can be a surprise.

> I've got some ideas too.

> > I just bet you do.

> What are you doing now?

> > Mom and I just finished binge-watching Buffy the Vampire Slayer, drinking wine, and eating popcorn.

> Sounds like a blast.

It might not be as glamorous as hanging out on the red carpet or attending VIP events, but it's one of my favorite things to do. You shouldn't knock it until you try it ;)

The three dots blink on the screen, disappear, then reappear again. Why is it taking him so long to reply?

Finally, his message pops up.

I'm always down for spending time with you and a bottle of wine.

Memories shuttle through my brain and heat sweeps over my skin. Not the reaction I need to have when I'm all alone in my childhood bed. Still, I wonder if that's what he was going to say all along, or if he changed his mind halfway through replying. Maybe he planned to say something along the lines of "that sounds like my worst nightmare."

I have to go. I've got an early flight to Berlin tomorrow. Have fun with your mom and I'll see you on Friday.

Good luck with everything.

My finger hovers over the keypad before I give in to the ever-building pressure in my chest and add, "I miss you."

The bubbles appear and disappear, then stop completely. I puff out a breath. I shouldn't have said anything.

I turn out my light and stare up at the dark ceiling, wishing I could take back my words. But a few minutes later, my phone beeps again. I pick it up and read the message with a smile so big I feel it spreading over my face.

I miss you too.

CHAPTER THIRTY-FOUR

COLE

I flick through the television channels, trying to find something to lull my brain toward sleep. After flying back to London from Germany this morning, then having a full day of meetings, I'm struggling to switch off. I've also been waiting for a call, so when my phone rings, I swipe it off the side table. "Did he accept?" I ask without bothering to say hello.

Roman's voice comes out clearly through the phone speaker. "He did," he says, and I let out a silent sigh of relief. "If he admits his guilt and pays a forty-five million dollar fine, his prison sentence will be reduced from twenty years to eight."

"Fuck. Eight years?" We knew they wouldn't go easy on him, not when government contracts were involved, but still . . . As much as I meant it when I told Delilah I didn't care what happened to Dad, I can't imagine how he's feeling right now. Then again, I can't imagine what he was thinking, getting involved in insider trading to begin with. His arrogance convinced him he would never get caught, and look where that's gotten him. Sitting in a damn prison cell for eight years.

"The news will break soon," Roman says. "Do you have a sense of how our investors will take it?"

"There's obviously some concern. A lot of them have adopted a wait-and-see attitude so far. I've been prepping them for a guilty verdict and reassuring them that it won't change anything. That Dad's actions were his and his alone and not a reflection of the King Group's business practices."

"Any talk of withdrawing?"

"There were some rumblings at the start, but I emphasized that even with the change in leadership, we're continuing to operate at expected levels, and that we'll honor all our financial commitments. It seems to have eased concerns. If we can get through the next few weeks with no major setbacks, everyone will relax, and we can finally move on from this."

Roman lets out a heavy sigh. "That's exactly what I was hoping to hear. Not that I had any doubts you'd pull it off."

That glimmer of pride is back, but I shrug it off. "You sound tired. How are things back there?"

"Everyone wants to see progress with the hotel project." He pauses for a beat. "Berrington is pushing for us to bring forward the groundbreaking for the first three hotels."

I frown. "Why? Our current timeline is realistic and exactly what we put forward when we went through the equity financing process."

"I had that conversation with him. I get the sense he's looking for an excuse to pull his investment, but so far, we haven't given him one."

I scrub my hand over my face. "Having a major investor bail right now is the last thing we need. Did he give any indication as to why? The King Group has made him a lot of money over the years."

Roman is silent, thinking, I assume. "It's rumored that he's considering increasing his investment in Steele Enterprises."

"Our profitability and revenue growth projections outstrip Steele Enterprises'. He knows that."

"Agreed. But Steele Enterprises is still performing well in the current market. And Jake Steele is Berrington's cousin by marriage. I wouldn't put it past Steele to use the situation with Dad's arrest to put pressure on that relationship. With Berrington getting closer to retirement, there's a good chance he's putting greater stock in personal relationships than in financial metrics these days."

"He was college buddies with Dad."

"Exactly. But he's not dealing with Dad anymore, is he?" Roman's frustration pours through the phone line.

"I can set up a meeting with him when I get back," I offer.

"I plan to have lunch with him tomorrow. I'll test the waters to see what he's really after, because I don't think he actually cares about the groundbreaking date."

"Okay. Let me know how it goes and if you need me to meet with him."

"Will do." His voice has gone distant, his attention moved elsewhere, but just before I'm about to end the conversation, he comes back. "Can you call Mom? I haven't had a chance to talk to her since Dad took the plea bargain."

Talking to Mom is the last thing I feel like doing. Still, I agree, and then we end the call.

Just as it does every night, the urge to speak to Delilah rises in me. She's gotten under my skin in a way I never thought was possible. I'd much rather talk to her than Mom, but I've made a point to avoid calling her while I've been gone. As if the minute I dial her number because I can't stand not hearing her voice any longer, I won't be able to deny what this thing between us has become.

My fingers move over the screen as I pull up our message history, then scroll back to the one where she told me she missed me. I almost hadn't replied, but the thought of leaving her hanging after she put herself out there like that had sent a stab of pain through me. Not that I would have said it back if it wasn't true. The problem is, it's *too* fucking true.

To distract myself from dwelling on the implications of that, I pull up Mom's number and call it, hitting speaker and putting my phone on the side table. Then I swing my legs over the side of the bed and sit with my elbows resting on my thighs as I wait for her to answer.

"Cole."

I roll my eyes at the lack of warmth in her voice. "Hi, Mom. Have the lawyers been in touch with you about Dad?"

She lets out an impatient sigh. "Of course. Eight years. It's about what the idiot deserves."

"I'm sure he appreciates your sympathy."

"If he wanted my sympathy, he should have restricted himself to buying his whores diamonds instead of trying to set them up for life."

She's not wrong. But it makes me wonder what she's bought the men she's had affairs with over the years. What did she get for Tate's dad?

"Suffice it to say, I'll be serving your father with divorce papers first thing tomorrow."

The news is hardly a surprise. It's not as if their marriage has ever been anything more than a matter of convenience, and my father has just stopped being convenient. It was only a matter of time after Dad was found guilty, or in this case, admitted his guilt. "I'm sure he'll be expecting it."

She sniffs. "He's lucky I held off as long as I did."

"Well, I just wanted to make sure you're okay," I say. "Obviously you are, so, considering it's eleven-thirty p.m. here, I'll say goodbye."

There's a long pause and I glance at my phone to check it's still connected. Hesitation isn't exactly Mom's style. "How are you and your brothers doing with . . . everything?" she finally says.

Now it's my turn to search for words. I don't remember the last time she voluntarily asked any of us how we were doing. I clear my throat. "I'm okay. I've got back-to-back meetings with all our investors over here. I'll have to do some more damage control once the news spreads about Dad's plea bargain. Roman is dealing with some shit from Berrington, but I'm sure he'll handle it. And Tate . . . Well, Tate is Tate. Not much seems to faze him."

"Well, I'm glad you're all doing well, but I should go," she says, and I almost laugh. She's obviously reached the extent of her motherly concern. Which, considering she normally has none, is impressive. "I'm having dinner with the Jeffersons tonight. I'm sure they'll ask about your father, so I'm going to have a glass of wine beforehand."

"Good idea. The Jeffersons are painful at the best of times."

After we say our farewells, I turn the phone in my hands as I stare into the dimly lit room. Having Mom ask about how my brothers and I are doing when there's no one else around to keep up appearances for is unusual, and I'm not sure what it means. Is it just an aberration or is being away from Dad softening her a little? Or is it possible that what Delilah said during our last lunch together made some kind of impact?

I shake my head. I'm obviously reading into it too much. Being around someone as caring as Delilah has me seeing signs of affection in others that aren't really there. For all I know, this was just a one-off because of the recent events with Dad.

But now Delilah's on my mind again. Not that she seems to be off it much these days. I open my phone again and pull up her number. I stare at it, the same debate I've had every night running through my head. It's been six days since I've heard her voice. Only four more days before I'll be back in the US, and she'll be back in my bed. I've made it this long; I can last four more days. My finger hovers over the screen for another moment, ready to close everything down and go to sleep. And then I'm hitting call and leaning back against the headboard as I wait for her to pick up.

"Hi, Cole. I'm so happy you called."

Her soft, sweet voice sends a rush of warmth spreading through me. Fuck, I'm in so much trouble. "How are you?" I ask.

"I'm good. Working hard to get the detailed designs done so they can get signed off by the deadline."

"I'm sure you'll manage it. Don't work too hard. Make sure to take a break."

"Yes, Dad," she teases.

An unexpected grin spreads across my face. "You could at least go with daddy."

She laughs. "I didn't take you as the daddy type."

"You're right. Let's avoid daddy."

"How are you doing, anyway?" she asks.

I rub my hand over my face. "Roman called. Dad took the plea bargain today."

"Oh, Cole. Are you okay?"

I have to stop and think. Am I okay? When Mom asked how I was doing before, I told her about work. I didn't stop to assess how I'm feeling about everything, and I doubt I would have shared it with her regardless. But with Delilah . . .

"I don't know. I feel . . . conflicted. There's never been any love lost between us. I respected him as a businessman, but I didn't love him as a father. And now, any respect I had for him has been destroyed."

"That makes sense. What he did was selfish."

"Exactly. My brothers and I were raised to put the company above everything else. It's our name. Our legacy. It's the only damn thing holding this family together, and he risked it all. For what? For women that weren't his wife. Women he had no connection with other than the physical. I can't reconcile his behavior."

"I guess the only thing I can say is that people are complicated. Don't drive yourself crazy trying to make sense of his behavior. Sometimes you can't. Sometimes you just have to accept that people make selfish decisions all the time without thinking or caring about the consequences for the people they're supposed to love the most. Family should always come first. Maybe that's a lesson your father never truly learned."

She's right. Family was never Dad's priority; it was the wealth and the power he craved. The women were just part of that. Another way to bolster his ego.

"Is your mom okay?"

Trust her to ask, even though Mom was rude to her the only time they've met. "She's divorcing him."

311

"I can't say I'm surprised."

I didn't know how much I needed to hear Delilah's voice until I realize that, for the first time in days, all the tension has left my muscles. I don't want to waste the short time I have to talk to her on the topic of my mom and dad. "Enough about my parents. What are you wearing?"

A laugh bursts out of her, the sound bright and beautiful in this dark room. "You didn't just ask that."

"I did. Are you going to tell me?"

"Mmm, let me see," she purrs seductively down the line, and I love that she knows me well enough to let me change the topic and not press for more. "I'm wearing a sexy set of koala pajama shorts. And a white T-shirt with a stain of indeterminate origin over my left breast."

I grin at the picture she paints, but I lower my voice. "If I was there, I'd rip those koala shorts off you and have my way with you."

"Would you want me to leave my shirt on?"

"Definitely. There's nothing I find sexier than stained white T-shirts."

She laughs again. When she speaks, her voice is soft, and I can hear the smile in it. "I like you like this."

Without even being here, she soothes parts of me I didn't know needed soothing. I tip my head back, close my eyes, and do my best not to let on how her words affect me. "And here I was thinking you like when I tell you to bend over and take my cock."

"That too."

Her breathless tone has me hardening, and I rub my hand over myself. "Are you alone?"

My hopes are dashed when she replies. "No. Alex is here. We're actually just about to have dinner."

"That's a shame. I'll have to take care of this on my own,

then. At least I know exactly what I'll imagine while I stroke myself tonight."

"What's that?"

"You, spread out in front of me in that sexy, stained T-shirt."

She laughs. "The stain really does it for you, huh?"

Before I can answer, I hear Alex telling Delilah that their dinner's ready. We say goodbye, and after I hang up, the silence in the room seems louder than it was before.

I close my eyes and let my head fall back. I have to face the truth. My craving for her isn't fading. It's only growing stronger, even now, with time and distance between us. I need to figure out what the hell I'm going to do about it because at the moment, I feel like I'm standing at the edge of a ravine, one step away from plummeting over the edge.

And I have no fucking idea what I'll find at the bottom.

CHAPTER THIRTY-FIVE

DELILAH

My phone buzzes on my side table, waking me from my sleep. I blink drowsily at the time on my clock. It's after midnight. Who on earth is calling at this time of night?

I pick it up and see Cole's name on the screen. "Hello?"

"Delilah." His deep voice sends a thrill through me, and I immediately perk up.

"Is everything okay? Are you back in New York? I thought I wouldn't hear from you until tomorrow."

"I wanted to see you. Can I come up?"

My pulse speeds up. "You're here? Of course."

I rush to the door and press the button. I look down at myself. Should I change into something sexier? At least this shirt doesn't have a stain on it. Then I shrug. I'm too excited to see him to worry about changing into lingerie.

When the knock comes, I fling the door open and take him in. He's wearing a button-down shirt, with the sleeves rolled up—one of the sexiest looks on a man—but as I smile up at him, it's the dark shadows under his eyes that catch my attention.

I grab his arm and pull him into my apartment. "What are you doing here, Cole? Not that I'm not happy to see you."

He doesn't answer me. Instead, he backs me against the wall and drops his head, his lips brushing against the sensitive spot at the crook of my neck. Goose bumps scatter over my skin, and my nipples harden. Since I'm not wearing a bra, he must be able to feel them pushing against his chest. But for a moment, he just stands there, his fingers curving around my waist, pressing into me, and I run my hands over his biceps, up to his neck, sifting through the hair at the back of his head.

"Are you okay?" I've never seen him like this before.

He lets out a breath and steps back. "It was a long trip. Non-stop meetings with investors who want to be stubborn just for the sake of it." He scrubs his hands over his face. "I'm fucking exhausted."

And he came here instead of going to his comfortable penthouse? A hot rush of emotion hits me. He wanted to see me. I swallow hard. This is the first time he's deliberately shown me this side of him. The one that isn't the unflappable billionaire, focused and in control at all times.

I move closer, cupping his jaw and brushing my thumb over the stubble a day's worth of travel has given him. "My bed isn't anywhere near as big or as comfortable as yours." His brow cocks at that understatement. "But you're more than welcome to join me in it."

His eyes sweep over my face. "I'd like that."

"Okay." I can't stop the smile that pulls at my lips.

"Okay," he repeats. He's still standing there looking down at me, his gaze fixed on mine, so I reach for his hand, twine my fingers through his, and start toward my bedroom.

He follows, but a thought occurs to me, and I look over my shoulder at him.

"Do you need to let Jonathan know?"

He shakes his head. "I sent him home when you buzzed me in."

He was intending to stay the night here when he got here. He's come straight from the airport, intending to stay with me. I shouldn't let something so small mean so much, but I can't help it. It does. It means a lot.

I don't wrap myself around him the way I want to. I just nod and continue leading him to my bedroom.

"Is Alex here?" he asks as we reach my door.

"She's spending the week in LA with Jaxson."

"So we're all alone. What a shame," he drawls, with a crooked smile.

A thrill ricochets through me, but I don't say anything.

I do a speed check of my bedroom as we enter. Thank god I keep it relatively neat, and there aren't bras and underwear scattered all over the place. Not that Cole seems bothered by what my bedroom looks like. He stares at my bed, and I know what he's thinking. I suppress a laugh, dropping his hand and going into the bathroom and returning with a spare toothbrush. "I don't have any clothes that will fit you."

"That's okay." He's already unbuttoning his shirt. "I won't be wearing clothes if I'm in bed with you."

I watch him strip, my gaze wandering over his broad chest and sculpted abs. He drops his pants and boxer briefs, revealing his already half-hard erection, and my stomach clenches in anticipation. He chuckles as he saunters toward me, letting me look my fill before tipping his head down so that I think he's about to kiss me. Instead, he takes the toothbrush from my hand, brushes his lips over my forehead and says, "Thanks, kitten." Then he slaps me on the ass. "Get undressed and get into bed. I'll join you in a minute."

I shake my head at his back as he walks into the bathroom. Relaxed Cole is just as intoxicating as intense Cole.

Doing as he said, I strip off my pajamas, then crawl under the covers, waiting for him to get back. On his return, he pauses at the door, head tipped to the side, taking in the shape of me under the blanket. His gaze travels up to my face and his eyes lock on mine with an intensity that steals my breath. I wish I knew what he was thinking, but I can't read his expression, and before I know it, he's striding across the room, lifting the covers, and sliding into the bed.

"Roll over," he says.

I turn so my back is toward him, and he pulls me against his chest, draping his arm over my waist and pinning me to him. I wait with bated breath for his hand to start roaming, but it doesn't. Instead, he splays it over my stomach and presses a kiss to the top of my head. Barely a handful of seconds later, his breaths deepen and he's sound asleep.

My thoughts whirl around my head. We've never slept together without having sex first. Does this mean he's feeling the same way I am? Hope blooms in my chest, and I lightly trace my fingers over the back of his hand. It's too soon to start imagining a future where we might spend more and more nights curled up like this. Unfortunately, my heart isn't listening to those words of wisdom.

It's too busy beating in time with his.

MY EYES DRIFT OPEN the next morning, the numbers on my bedside clock coming into focus. Five-thirty a.m. What woke me so early? I flash back to last night, remembering Cole falling asleep behind me, and the last of the fog clears from my mind. I roll over and look for him, but apart from me, my bed is empty. Did I only dream him being here? Before disappointment can hit too hard, a noise filters through my bedroom door. I sit up, clutching my blanket to my chest.

Another sound reaches me. Is Cole still here and doing something in the kitchen? I climb out of bed and pull my short, silky robe over my naked body, tying it loosely before heading out of the room.

My feet stall, and my heart does a little flutter in my chest. Cole is standing at the counter with his back to me, wearing just his boxer briefs, while the early morning light illuminates his muscular body. Bowls, spoons, and various ingredients are spread on the surrounding countertop, and he's peering intently at his phone, which is propped against a cookie jar.

He's making breakfast.

Tears prick the backs of my eyes. It's a ridiculous reaction to someone making a meal, but this is Cole. He spent the night in my apartment—just sleeping, not screwing me blind—and now he's doing his best to make what I think might be pancakes. Any resistance to what I'm feeling disintegrates, drifting away like ash on the breeze.

I've fallen for him. Hard.

My heart squeezes painfully in my chest as I watch him try to crack an egg into the bowl, swearing under his breath as bits of shell go with it.

I never thought I could love a man like him, but I do. Because he's not a man like him. No, that doesn't make sense. I give my head a slight shake, trying to sort through the chaotic rush of thoughts and emotions tumbling through me.

Cole is so much more than the cold, arrogant billionaire he shows the world—that he showed *me* when we first met. I labeled and classified him in my head and told myself I had to be careful with my heart around him. Just like Mom should have been careful with my dad. But I've seen the man beneath the façade now. A man who is as real and vulnerable and flawed as anyone else. And yes, a man just as capable of getting eggshell in his pancake batter.

I walk forward as quietly as I can, and he's so absorbed in watching what the person on the screen is doing, he doesn't notice me until I do something I wouldn't have considered a few weeks ago. I slide my arms around his waist and press myself against his back.

He actually jumps. "Fuck. You scared me."

I press my cheek against his warm skin. "Are you making pancakes?"

"Trying to," he grumbles, and I can't help but laugh.

He throws down the spoon and turns in my arms, so that now he has me against his chest. He looks down at me, his brows furrowed. "The guy in the video makes it look so fucking easy. I'm going to call Jonathan and get him to pick up some—"

I shake my head and smile up at him. "No, you're not. We're going to make them together."

His gaze traces over my face, dropping to my mouth, then to the open neck of my robe and back to my eyes. His rapidly growing erection tells me he likes what he sees.

He strokes his thumb over my jaw, his eyes sweeping over my face. "I didn't fuck you last night."

"You were exhausted."

He nods. "I don't sleep with women."

My brows shoot up. "I think you've slept with plenty of women."

He shakes his head, focusing on me again. "I've fucked women. I've never slept with any of them until you."

I run my palm up and down his chest. "I'm glad you came here last night," I say softly. "I'm glad you slept in my bed."

He's still watching me, and the hint of wariness in his eyes hurts my heart a little. He really has no idea how to handle this. Whatever this is now. I reach up and curl my hand around the back of his neck and tug him down to my waiting lips.

My heart does a little twirl when his mouth crushes against mine. I open for him, going up on my tiptoes to give him better access. He might have been too tired to fool around last night, but there's no sign of that exhaustion now. His body is hard against mine, his groan vibrating into my mouth.

He runs his hands over my waist, then grips my ass, his fingers pressing into me, kneading me. Then they slide lower and he's lifting me so I can wrap my legs around him and grind myself against his erection. "I fucking missed you. I missed this."

"Me too," I pant as he walks us back toward my bedroom.

In a demonstration of strength which has my arousal spiraling higher, he lowers me slowly to the bed. Then he stands tall, staring down at me where I lie sprawled on the mattress, my robe barely held to my body by the tie around my waist.

Cole's hungry eyes move over me as a muscle tics in his jaw. He stares at me so long with that inscrutable expression on his face that I start to get nervous.

I sit up, but he shakes his head. "Lie down, Delilah."

The rasp in his voice has me pressing my thighs together, even as I comply.

As soon as I'm flat on my back again, he lifts the end of the tie around my waist and draws it slowly so that the knot falls open. Using his index finger, he flicks each side of my robe to the side, exposing me to the heat of his gaze.

"So fucking gorgeous," he murmurs, as if to himself, and my pulse flutters in my throat. I'm so gone for this man.

I don't have time to dwell on my newly acknowledged feelings, because before I know what's happening, he's gripping me by the thighs and dragging me to the edge of the bed.

"Cole," I gasp, but he ignores me, dropping to his knees and spreading my legs wider.

"Brace yourself, kitten. I'm not stopping until you've come at least three times."

CHAPTER THIRTY-SIX

DELILAH

"I don't know if I—" But I'm too busy moaning as his lips make contact to finish the thought. He's not messing around. Within a few minutes, I'm yanking at his hair as I scream my way through my first orgasm. "Cole, I need you inside me."

He looks up at me, his intense eyes on mine. "Not until you come two more times."

"Cole, oh god." Two long fingers slide into me, stroking and curling, rubbing against my G-spot. My back arches off the bed as I come a second time, my body clenching around his fingers.

"One more," he demands.

But my body knows what he wants now, and I'm already ramping up for another one. When his fingers leave my body, the sudden lack of pressure inside me has me crying out in protest.

"Where do you keep your toys?" he asks.

I blink up at him, my mind hazy. "What?"

"Those toys you're so proud of." One corner of his

mouth quirks up as I groan and cover my eyes with my hand. The mattress next to my shoulder depresses and a big, warm hand closes around my wrist. He pulls my hand away and my gaze locks with his. He's leaning over me, bracing himself on one hand. "Don't get shy on me now. The picture of your beautiful little pussy being fucked by a big, fake cock has been stuck in my head since you first told me about it. Now I want to see it in real life. So tell me where they are."

Even though I'm embarrassed, I'm excited too. My heart thrashes against my rib cage because that's what Cole does to me. He makes me desperate to experience everything he wants to show me. I trust him to make it good for me. I trust him with myself.

"Middle drawer." I point at my side table, and he releases my hand and reaches for it, yanking it open and rummaging around.

I have a few different toys in there—a couple of my favorite dildos and a vibrator or two. Cole finds my biggest dildo and pulls it out. It's flesh colored, realistic, and big—though definitely not as big as him.

"How often do you use this?" he asks.

"Not much anymore."

He holds my gaze. "No?"

I wet my lips and shake my head.

Without looking away, Cole slides the dildo through my slick, already swollen folds. "Why is that?"

"Because—" I gasp as the head of the cock pushes into me.

"Because?" His voice is husky as he eases it out, only to press it smoothly back in.

I swallow hard. "Because I don't need it anymore."

"Why don't you need it anymore, kitten?"

"I have—" He twists it inside me, and I inhale sharply. "I h-have you."

Cole's pupils flare wide, satisfaction etching itself across every line of his face. "That's right. You have me," he says, his voice a dark bass growl. For a heartbeat or ten, our gazes are locked together, and I swear I can see what I feel for him reflected back at me.

Finally, he looks away, his gaze dropping to where I'm stretched around the toy. He's moving faster now, burying the length of it inside me with every stroke. It feels good, but it's not him. "Please, Cole."

He doesn't acknowledge my plea. "Your pussy looks incredible filled with this cock. I could do this for hours."

"I want you." But my hips are moving now, riding the toy as he thrusts it into me. The pressure grows inside me and I'm almost there, but I need more. Something else to tip me over the edge. "Cole. Please. I need you."

"I want to see you come with this inside you. Give me that and I'll give you my cock. Can you do that for me, kitten?" He rolls his thumb over my clit, sending a jagged shard of pleasure through me.

"Yes," I gasp. "Yes."

"Play with your nipples," he demands.

I cup my breasts, running my thumbs over the stiff peaks, then pinch them, sending little shock waves directly to my core.

"Good girl. You're so fucking sexy." Cole's voice is rough with desire, his gaze dropping back to what he's doing between my legs. The stark hunger written on his face as he uses his thumb to massage my clit is enough to shatter me. Cole thrusts the toy into me one more time and I cry out, arching my back as my internal muscles pulse around the intrusion.

My body has barely finished spasming when Cole pulls the toy from me and tosses it on the bed. He kneels between my thighs, his erection so hard it's flush with his stomach. With one hand, he presses it down, his expression almost pained. "Say I can have you bare."

My eyes fly to his. He knows I have an implant, but this is the first time he's ever brought up not using a condom.

"I've never gone without." His tone is almost harsh, but there's a rawness to his expression that reaches right inside me and wraps its fingers around my heart. "I want you with nothing between us. I need . . ." A muscle jumps in his jaw. "I need to feel all of you."

God, I want it too. Badly. With all the ways he's taken me over the last few months, having him want me with nothing between flays my chest wide open. "I want to feel you too. I want to feel everything."

He gives his cock a hard jerk, as if he can't help himself. "You want it? You want me to fill you with my cum?"

I barely have a chance to form the shape of the word yes before he's on me, working his cock into me with shallow thrusts that drive me out of my mind. The minute he's fully seated in me, he drops his forehead to my chest and groans. "Your tight little pussy is so hot. You're going to burn me alive."

His hips flex and we both moan at how good it feels. When he moves again, it's to pull out all the way to the tip, leaving me empty and desperate for him to fill me again. Then he does, with one hard pump, at the same time as his lips find mine. There's a desperation to his movements that has me responding with equal fervor, even though I've already come three times. He licks and bites his way down my neck, then takes a nipple into his mouth, sucking it hard and rhythmically.

Every hard slam of his hips against mine has his pelvis rubbing against my over-sensitized clit, and I'm tightening around him, my body already preparing to throw me into a fourth orgasm. But before it can, he pulls out of me.

"Turn over," he growls.

I do as he asks, scrambling onto my hands and knees, craving him inside me. With one thrust, he claims me again, leaning over me with a hand on my hip, the other pressing between my shoulder blades until my chest is flat on the mattress. He feels huge at this angle, and I pant and moan incoherently.

He slips his finger inside me, alongside his dick, and the sting of the increased stretch causes me to inhale sharply. He doesn't keep it there, though. The next thing I know, he's rubbing that arousal-slicked finger against the tight ring of muscle between my cheeks, and I freeze.

He's touched me here before and even though it still makes me nervous, I know how well he can play my body. I take a breath and relax, earning me a growl of approval that vibrates through every molecule inside me.

His finger presses into me, and I squirm and cry out when he breaches my back channel, slowly sinking it in to the first knuckle. He gently eases it out and back in again, even as his cock continues to stroke languidly into me, until the foreign sensation morphs into pleasurable pressure.

God, what does it say about me that it feels so good that my orgasm surges closer?

He knows. "You like that, kitten? You like my cock in your pussy and my finger in your ass?"

"Y-yes," I manage to get out.

He pushes his finger further in, then pulls it out so he can add another. It's more pressure, and I still again, until I grow accustomed to the sensation. The movement of his hips has slowed now, his cock gliding slowly in and out of me as he concentrates on my behind, twisting his fingers inside me, stretching me.

I wriggle my hips, wanting him to move again, my orgasm hovering just out of reach, but he leans over me, bracing one arm on the mattress so he can whisper in my ear.

"I want to fuck you here, Delilah," he says, with another thrust of his fingers. "I want to claim every single inch of you. Only when I'm buried balls deep in you am I going to let you come again. And believe me, you'll orgasm so hard, you'll milk the cum straight out of me."

My eyes are wide, my throat dry. "I don't know. . . . I've never done that."

"I know," he says, "but you'll do it for me. And you'll love it. I was the first person to have your pussy. I'll be the first person to have you here." His fingers push deeper as he slams his cock into me, and I almost explode right then. Except he stops again, and I cry out in frustration.

"Tell me you want it," he demands. "Beg me to make you come with my cock deep inside your ass."

"God, yes, please. Fuck me in the ass, Cole." I never thought I would hear myself utter those words to anyone. But Cole isn't just anyone. I trust him to make me feel good. If he says I'll come hard, then I believe him. Like he said, I want to share this first with him too.

"Your pussy is dripping. I won't even need lube," Cole says. "I'll go as slow as I can for as long as I can, okay?"

"Okay."

His fingers trace up my spine, and he presses a soft kiss to my shoulder blade, the tenderness of his touch making my heart swell, even as my pulse kicks into high gear with nervous anticipation. He pulls completely out of me, leaving me empty. Before I can voice my protest, he's dipping his fingers into me, gathering my arousal and spreading it up to my behind. I can feel how wet his fingers are, how wet I am, and I shiver at the thought of what's going to happen. When I look over my shoulder, he's stroking his cock, his fist wrapped around the slick shaft.

His eyes meet mine, and my stomach swoops at the look in them. They blaze with heat, but there's something else there too. An intensity of emotion that sends my heart into overdrive just as much as it sets my body on fire. I'm distracted when he presses the blunt head of his erection against me. I hold my breath as his broad crown pushes through the tight ring of my opening, and I whimper as my body clenches around the intrusion.

"Fuck," he growls. "You're so fucking tight. Relax, kitten, let me in."

I try to do as he says, and gradually my muscles loosen. Cole pushes deeper, inch by inch, filling me until I don't think I can take any more. Then he pushes even further and the tension inside me snaps. I let go completely, allowing myself to be taken over by the new sensations coursing through my body.

"That's it, beautiful. You feel amazing." He releases a ragged breath. "You are amazing."

I close my eyes, my heart expanding even more at the emotion I'm sure I can hear in his voice. Moving slowly at first, he lets me adjust to him before he picks up the pace. Once I start moving with him, he wraps one arm around my waist while his other hand finds my clit again, rubbing it with the perfect amount of pressure. He forges deeper into me with each flex of his hips, his tempo picking up until the spark of an orgasm flares to life deep within my core.

The expert movement of his fingers and the relentless

strokes of his cock soon have me panting and begging for more. My whole body trembles. It's something completely new—an intense sensation unlike anything I've ever experienced before.

And Cole knows exactly what he's doing; he teases me until I'm on the brink of orgasm multiple times, then backs off just enough to keep me from falling apart. Each time it seems like he's reaching deeper inside of me, and as my inner walls clench around him, I edge closer and closer to that explosive pleasure.

"Are you going to come for me, Delilah?" he asks.

"Yes. Oh god, yes. I'm so close."

"Good girl." He wraps my hair around his fist and tilts my head back so our eyes meet. "You look so fucking beautiful with my cock in your ass."

A moan falls from my lips at his words. With each labored breath, tension radiates from every sharply defined muscle in his body. His pace picks up until his hips are slapping against me with every thrust, sending shockwaves through my body. I can barely think straight.

Cole works his fingers over my clit, and a completely new sensation rages up inside me—a wildfire of heat and ecstasy. This orgasm is going to be unlike any I've experienced before, and my muscles are already trembling as I approach the point of no return.

When it hits, my body draws tight, and I scream as it ravages through me. I clamp down around Cole's cock, and he curses. Without anything filling my pussy, my inner muscles spasm hard around nothing. A cry of shock flies from my lips when a gush of liquid wets my thighs.

Cole's low groan is almost feral. "That's it, kitten. Fucking soak me." His fingers continue their movement, forcing more spasms, more gushes. "You're perfect, Delilah. So fucking perfect."

The last word is half grunt, half growl as he slams his hips into me one final time. Then he's shouting, his cock swelling and jerking as he unleashes himself inside me.

By the time he's done, I'm a weak, quivering, dripping mess. My limbs go out from underneath me, and I collapse on the bed, Cole coming with me and blanketing my body with his. He pulls out slowly, the sensation sending a shiver down my spine, then slides his arms under me, rolling us so we're lying on our sides, facing each other.

The sheets beneath me are wet, and embarrassment burns my skin. Even though he seemed to enjoy how my body reacted, I made a mess of the bed and of him too. I close my eyes and press my forehead to his chest so I don't have to look him in the eye.

As he strokes a soothing hand up and down my back, a hard knot forms in my chest. My feelings are all tangled up —my feelings for him, about what we just did, about what *I* just did. It's too much.

I try to swallow the sob, but it forces its way out of me.

Cole freezes. "Are you okay? Did I hurt you?"

I shake my head, but another sob is building, so I turn my head from his chest and bury my face into the sheets beneath me.

Cole pushes himself up on the bed, and before I can register what he's doing, he's pulled me up with him and has me cradled in his arms.

He tips my chin up. There's a hard line to his jaw, but his eyes are stormy with emotion. "Did. I. Hurt. You?" he repeats.

I shake my head, and his features relax, the tightness in his shoulders loosening. "Then what's wrong? I'm pretty sure I was reading the signals right, and you enjoyed it." His lips curve up a little, a hint of smugness showing through.

I press my hand over my eyes. "I've never done that before," I mumble.

Like earlier, he takes my wrist and tugs my hand away. His brow is furrowed. "I already know that was your first time doing anal, so I assume you're saying you never squirted before?"

I nod, and a savage smile grows on his face. He tunnels his fingers through my hair and grips it at the back of my head, his eyes piercing into me. "Good. That means I get to claim that first too. The thought of you giving something so incredible to a man like Paul makes me want to tear him to pieces."

I don't know whether to laugh or cry. His gaze softens, his expression becoming almost tender. If tender is a word you could use to describe Cole.

"You have nothing to be embarrassed about, Delilah. Nothing. You are the sexiest woman I've ever met. What we just did? The way you surrender all of yourself to me—the way you trust me to take care of you. Fuck. It's *everything*."

I finally relax, smiling up at him. "It felt amazing." I run my fingers over his stubbled jaw. "Everything you do to me feels incredible. Although . . ." I shift in his lap and wince a little at the ache. "I think I'm going to be reminded of this for a while."

"Good. I want you to remember exactly how much of yourself you've given me." His wicked grin fades, and the intensity of his gaze consumes me, making my heart pound erratically in my chest. He brushes his thumb across my jaw, his eyes dark and serious. "Delilah, I . . ."

My breath stalls as I wait to hear what he's going to say.

His brows draw tightly together, and he swallows.

There's something in his expression I haven't seen before. Something that makes my ribs squeeze tight. For a beat, his eyes drop closed. When they open again, the look is gone, and his smirk is back. "I hate to admit it, but I'll need your help to finish the pancakes. I don't think I can do it on my own."

I laugh, even though it's not what I'm hoping to hear.

But after the way he's claimed every part of me, the things he's said, even the way he's holding me now, I have to believe he feels it.

Exactly the way I do.

CHAPTER THIRTY-SEVEN

COLE

I stare out the window at passing cars, exhaustion clawing at me. Even with my deep sleep last night—which must have been the best I've had in a long time—jet lag woke me up early and now I'm flagging.

Jonathan turns the limo toward my penthouse, and I have to resist the urge to tell him to turn around and take me back to Delilah's apartment. Even though I told her she should take the day off—considering I woke her up late last night and tired her out before her day even started—she insisted on getting ready and going in. She even refused my offer of a lift to the office, telling me to go home and unpack.

I drop my head back and close my eyes, reliving the memory of her underneath me this morning—experiencing again that overwhelming need to claim every part of her. And it wasn't just the desire to be as physically close to her as possible. It was how it felt holding her in my arms afterward. When she cried, my chest had constricted so hard that I'd struggled to breathe. Then the next second, my heart was thundering as she smiled up at me through tear-filled eyes.

I'm so damn addicted to her. I groan and rub my hand over my eyes. No, she's more than an addiction. That's just the excuse I've been giving myself for craving her the way I do.

I almost told her I loved her this morning, but the words lodged themselves in my throat. I never, *never* believed I would want to make that declaration to someone. That I was so close to letting it slip free shook me. I need to figure this out. I need to work out what it means for us going forward, because right now, I'm sailing in uncharted waters with her. All I know is that what I feel for Delilah is far beyond anything I've ever felt for anyone before.

My phone beeps and I pull it from my pocket. It's Roman.

> I need to see you at the office.

> I'm just on my way home. What's this about?

> We need to discuss it in person.

> I'll be there in twenty minutes

I redirect Jonathan to King Plaza, wondering what issue can't wait until this afternoon.

As I enter Roman's executive suite, he's waiting for me on one of his leather couches, a steaming coffee in front of him. I pour myself a cup, since I get the feeling from his expression that I'll need my wits about me, then sit on the couch opposite him. After taking a sip, I ask, "So what's the emergency? I've already given you the details of how everything went."

Roman leans forward, his expression serious. "This is partly related to that." He pauses before continuing.

"Berrington called me yesterday. He came right out and said he's seriously considering withdrawing his investment in the King Group."

"What the fuck?" I put my coffee cup down and scrub my hand over my face. "We're meeting our projected deadlines. Our numbers are good. What's his deal?"

Roman shrugs. "He wants to invest in Steele Enterprises."

"I'll arrange a meeting. Reassure him about our projections."

"It won't help. He was pretty firm with his intentions. He said he wants to put his money into a company that will benefit his family going forward."

I lean back in my chair. "Okay, well, we have options."

"That's why I wanted to talk to you," Roman replies. "Berrington brought up your relationship with Jessica. He mentioned that if our families were closer, it might inspire him to keep his investments in place."

I throw back my head and laugh, but when I notice Roman isn't joining in, I stop. He's not even smiling. "You can't be serious."

Roman's brow furrows. "Of course I'm fucking serious. Getting engaged to Jessica is the quickest and easiest way to get everything back on track. All our investors remain in place, we complete the development on time and within budget, everyone forgets about the situation with Dad, and we can move past all this shit."

"Jessica and I don't have a relationship. I'm not marrying her."

"You haven't officially dated her, but you two have been fucking for years." Roman's eyes narrow. "You don't think Berrington liked seeing the two of you at events together? This alliance makes sense, and it gives him the personal connection he's looking for. Jessica is part of our world. She understands what's required of her. And it's about time you thought about settling down."

"Jessica and I may have fucked, but I have no interest in spending the rest of my life with her. Why don't you marry her?"

Roman scowls. "I've been married once. It's not happening again. And Jessica wants you, not me, and not Tate."

It sinks in that he's serious and my mind immediately goes to Delilah—to the feel of her in my arms this morning, the taste of her on my lips, the way she gives herself to me so trustingly, the look in her eyes when she smiles at me . . .

"What's the problem here?" Roman asks, impatience sharpening his tone. "Jessica is beautiful, we can use her wealth and connections, and you already know you're sexually compatible. What more is there?"

"Having those things didn't work out for you, did it?" I ask.

"This isn't about what did or didn't work for me." He drums his fingers on his knee and scrutinizes me. "Tell me this isn't about your architect."

I stare at him, and my silence must tell him everything he needs to know.

He groans. "She has a pretty face—and apparently a golden pussy. Otherwise you wouldn't be hesitating like this."

My hands clench into fists.

"But you can't honestly tell me you're going to put that ahead of this company, are you? This is our legacy. The King Group is who we are."

I've done a lot for this company, but marrying Jessica is

asking too much. I blow out a breath. "That can't be the only option."

"There might be others, but none that won't negatively impact profits going forward."

"Don't you think we have enough profits?" I growl.

His brows arch. "No, I don't. And we promised our investors Dad's arrest wouldn't affect our bottom line. Breaking that promise is the start of a slippery slope."

I stare at him, going over the options in my head.

Roman leans back in his seat, regarding me with a chilly gaze. "I can't believe you're letting a fling get in your head this way. What the hell are you thinking?"

"I'm thinking that maybe there's more to life than work, money, and fucking," I snap, then pause, taken aback by my own words.

Roman snorts in disdain. "Then you're an idiot. Love is nothing but a fantasy people like to believe in so they can feel better about life. Sure, you can meet someone you're attracted to. The sex is good, your body starts producing chemicals, and suddenly you've conned yourself into believing there's something deeper between the two of you. Then what? You get married, only to find out that when the chemical high wears off, it was all just an illusion. Your pretty new wife starts enjoying spending your money more than fucking you. What you convinced yourself was love turns to indifference. In the end, you're stuck in a loveless marriage like our parents and every other couple we know. You have affair after affair, or you split up and go back to fucking random women anyway. Either way, it turns out the same."

"How very cynical of you," I say through gritted teeth, even though Roman's words have cut straight to the heart of all my doubts. After all, up until recently, that's exactly what I believed. The hollow growing behind my ribs tells me that deep down, I might still believe it.

"Realistic," Roman responds. "Jessica is gorgeous, you know you both enjoy each other physically, and she has money of her own, so she won't be looking to take you for all she can get."

Anger pulses behind my temples. "Delilah isn't a gold digger."

He ignores me. "What you give Jessica is a powerful alliance that elevates her to the top echelons of society. We get her father's commitment to maintain his investment, which protects the one damn thing of any worth this family has going for it. Please don't tell me you'd let that go for something that is completely replaceable. This is the best option we have without compromising the company's financial position, and if that's not motivation enough, then you're not the man I thought you were."

I sit back in my chair. Is Roman right?

"Let me tell you something," he says, and for the first time in a long time, I see something other than aloofness or anger in his gray eyes. Whatever he's about to say, I get the feeling it isn't something he shares often. "When I married Katherine, I'd convinced myself that I loved her—and that she loved me."

Shock courses through me. I had no idea Roman had genuine feelings for Katherine.

"It only took a few months for the lie I was telling myself to fall apart," he continues, his gaze becoming distant. "Whatever we felt at the start, it wasn't love. If it was, it wouldn't have turned to hate so quickly."

I didn't know any of this. I shake my head. At what point did my brothers and I become such fucking strangers? There's a tightness in my chest I haven't felt for a long time.

A sense of loss I'd desensitized myself to years ago when I realized caring about people, and expecting them to care about me, was a fool's game. "Is that why you got divorced? Because you've just finished telling me that love isn't important. Why would hating each other matter?"

He hesitates. "They say that the opposite of love isn't hate, it's indifference. Maybe if all we'd felt for each other was indifference, we might still be married today. But hate is different. Seeing the eyes of the woman I thought knew me better than anyone else filled with loathing, and knowing she saw the same thing every time she looked at me —that was impossible. So learn from my fucking mistakes. Marry the woman you feel indifferent about, and you'll never be disappointed when you realize the truth."

All the warmth that filled me since being with Delilah trickles away at Roman's confession.

He holds my gaze. "However a marriage starts, it always ends up the same way. Better to treat it like the business merger that it is from the beginning and not suffer any disappointment along the way." Is that bitterness in his voice? I don't care enough to think about it at the moment. I'm too busy imagining the light in Delilah's eyes when she looks at me fading away to cold dispassion, just the way my parents always looked at each other. The way they always looked at us. Something barbed twists in my chest, and a dull sound echoes in my head—the final nail being beaten into a coffin.

"Sometimes you have to make tough choices in life— choices that hurt more than they should." Roman pauses, studying my face, and I'm not sure if what flickers through his eyes is sympathy or something else. "Delilah will find someone who'll care for her more than you ever could, and Jessica will never care about you enough to hate you."

"What's the arrangement?" My voice is steady, even as ice coalesces around my heart. As Roman talks about announcements and investment percentages, I clench my eyes shut and let my head drop back on the chair.

I try not to think of Delilah's eyes, her smile, her voice, her laugh.

Because in the end, I'm still the same man I was before I met her.

And I know what I have to do.

CHAPTER THIRTY-EIGHT

DELILAH

The doorbell rings and my heart races—it's a reaction I'm still getting used to. After a quick glance in the mirror to run my fingers through my hair, I open the front door. Butterflies take flight in my stomach and my mouth goes dry when I see Cole.

It's been two days since he was last here. Two days since we made pancakes in my kitchen and ate them as I sat on his lap. He'd called me at work later that day to cancel our original plans for the weekend, telling me there was a situation he had to resolve, so when I got his message an hour ago asking if he could come over, I was excited. I'm finding it harder and harder to be away from him, and I hope this means he feels the same way.

I smile at him, then rise on my toes to press my lips to his.

His hands go to my waist, his fingers curling into my skin, but he doesn't pull me into him the way I'm expecting. I drop down and search his face. His jaw is tense, that familiar muscle twitching in it. Nerves tumble through me, and I swallow. "Do you want to come in?"

He nods and follows me to my small living room. I sit on the couch, but he remains standing, so I jump to my feet again, not wanting to be at a disadvantage. It's exactly the way I used to feel with him, before all this started. Icy dread settles in my chest.

"Delilah . . ." He scrubs his hand over his mouth but doesn't continue. He just stares at me with his lips pressed together.

I know what's coming. My instincts scream it at me with an intensity that rasps anxiety down my nerves. "Just say it." I'm relieved when my voice comes out with only a small tremor I hope he won't notice. "Whatever it is, just say it."

He clears his throat. "I know this is sudden, but it's time we end this."

Even though I know it's coming, pain still lashes across my heart. I try to take a deep breath, but it gets caught in my lungs. "Why? I thought . . . I mean, last time we were together . . ." I can't find the words I need.

"Jessica and I . . ."

My spine snaps straight. "What about Jessica?"

His eyes burn with some unknown emotion as he stares at me.

"What about Jessica?" I demand. "If you're about to do something you know will hurt me, then just do it, for god's sake."

His eyes shutter. "Jessica and I are getting engaged. I wanted to tell you before it's officially announced."

For a second, I can't process his words, my mind and body paralyzed. A heartbeat later, the pain and betrayal hit, burning through every flimsy wall I'd thrown up in preparation.

"What?" My mouth makes the shape of the word, but I

have no breath to force the sound out. I try again. "What do you mean? You told me there was nothing real between you. You told me you weren't sleeping with her anymore. You told me that. You promised."

My head screams at me to stand firm without pleading for him to change his mind. It tells me what I already know: He's serious and not a thing I say will make a difference. It tells me I'll regret begging as soon as he walks out the door. I know all that. But my heart . . . My heart pounds out a rhythm that won't be denied, a pressure to fight for something that it somehow still believes is worthwhile. So I open my mouth and I beg as the tears I can't hold back slide down my cheeks. "Please, Cole. Please don't do this. I thought this was working between us. I thought you were feeling the same—"

He's shaking his head before I even finish speaking. "Don't, Delilah. Don't make this harder than it has to be. This was always going to end, and you know that. We both knew it."

My heart shatters into a thousand pieces. My head might have believed that, but my heart had succumbed to hope a long time ago. My heart, that is just as much of a liar as the man standing in front of me. Was this how my mom felt when my father walked away from her because she—*we* —didn't fit his life?

That thought is enough. I swallow, dash the tears from my cheeks, and give a curt nod. "You can leave now."

His shoulders tense, but he doesn't move. He just stands there, staring at me with his hands clenched at his sides. I don't care if this isn't easy for him. I don't care if he didn't intend to hurt me. He's choosing this—he's choosing *her*—so he can damn well suffer the consequences.

I turn and walk to the door, more traitorous tears

welling over. I let them fall this time. Tonight is the last night I'll allow myself to cry over Cole King. I unlatch the door and hold it open. He still hasn't moved.

"Delilah, I . . ." he says, his voice rasping.

"Get out, Cole. I don't want you in my home anymore. I don't want you in my life. You want us to be over? Then we're over. So get the hell away from me."

His eyes flash, but he jerks into motion. I look away as he approaches, my hand tightening on the door handle, waiting for the moment I can slam it behind him and break apart without him witnessing it.

But he doesn't even give me that. He stops in front of me, and I close my eyes, not wanting to see whatever's visible in his.

The heat of his palm pressing against the side of my face makes me flinch. My lips part as his thumb brushes my cheek, wiping away the tears I can't seem to control. I jerk my head away from him, staring at him, shocked that he would touch me like that. As if he has any right. As if tenderness has any place here.

"I'm sorry," he says, his voice hoarse. And then he's gone.

I shut the door, locking it as if I actually think he'll barge back in and tell me it's all been a terrible mistake. Then I stumble to the living room, curl into a little ball on the couch, and sob.

CHAPTER THIRTY-NINE

DELILAH

Thank god the design phase of the project is almost over. Another two weeks and all the detailed plans will be finalized, then I can get out of here. Not only out of this building, but out of New York. At least temporarily. Possibly permanently.

It's been two weeks since Cole broke my heart. One week since news of the engagement went public. I haven't seen him since he left my apartment. Weekly meetings have been taken over by Tate, much to my relief. Having to sit across a table from Cole right now would be unbearable.

The morning after Cole's visit, I sucked it up and spoke to Paul, notifying him of my intention to take a leave of absence after the final designs have been signed off. As much as I might like to stay through the construction phase, my heart is too sore to allow it. The thought of running into Jessica around the building—or worse, Cole and Jessica together—is too much to bear. Instead, I'm going home to spend some time with Mom and maybe interview with some of the architectural firms in the area.

It's not that I don't love New York and living with Alex,

but I miss my mom, and now with Paul and Cole serving as constant reminders of my bad decisions, it seems like maybe home is where I should be. I may not see Cole anymore, but this building is still filled with his presence.

"Delilah," Paul says, appearing next to my desk.

I put down my pen and swivel in my chair to face him. "How can I help you, Paul?"

He frowns at my terse tone, the way he always does when we speak these days. As if he's surprised I don't want to talk to him any more than I have to.

"You know how I told you a while ago that the King Group had entered our design concepts into the H+ Design Awards?"

I nod.

"Well, the good news is we're now finalists, so we're invited to attend the awards ceremony. It's the weekend before you go on leave, but you're expected to attend as one of the design team."

"I understand," I say. He turns to walk away, but I stop him. "Will . . ." I clear my throat. "Will C—Mr. King be there?"

He knows what I'm asking and doesn't hide the smugness in his expression. "Of course they'll all be attending. And I'm sure Cole will want to show off his lovely new fiancée too."

I don't allow myself to react, knowing that's what he wants. And when I don't, he huffs out a breath and leaves. I turn back to my computer, closing my eyes and letting out a sigh. This is going to be a nightmare.

To make myself feel better, I double-check my flights for home, then pull up the email I received three days ago from a senior partner at Abbott-Bennett, one of the most prestigious architecture firms in Raleigh. I skim over it, gnawing on my lip as I read.

Dear Delilah,

Thank you so much for your expression of interest in our firm. I've had a look over your credentials and achievements, and I must say that I'm very impressed. Since you've said you'll be in the area in a few weeks' time, we'd love to set up a time for you to meet myself and the other partners. If this is of interest to you, please reach out to my executive assistant and organize a date and time that suits you. I've given her your details and she'll be waiting for your call.

I've been delaying making the call. Not because the firm wouldn't be wonderful to work for, but because it feels like I'm running away from New York with my tail between my legs. Even though I love the idea of living closer to Mom, I know a part of my heart will always be here in New York.

Or is it with Cole?

I can't think like that. Cole took my heart and threw it back in my face, choosing instead to be with a woman he told me he has no interest in. He either lied to me back then, or the feelings I imagined he had for me were only in my head. Because there's no way he could marry Jessica if he feels for me what I feel for him.

Felt for him.

The pain rushing through me solidifies my intentions. As soon as I get home this evening, I'll call and arrange an interview time.

"DO I HAVE TO GO?" I moan. It's two weeks later, and my hotel designs have been officially signed off and submitted to the King Group's in-house construction planning team.

In a rare show of appreciation, Cole is hosting an extravagant dinner tonight to celebrate the team's hard work, but I claimed a migraine and came home instead. Paul tried to strong-arm me into attending, but I refused. It's bad enough I have to see Cole tomorrow at this award ceremony. The thought of sitting across a table from him for hours tonight is intolerable.

"Yes, you have to go," Alex says, bringing me back to our current topic of conversation. She gives me a firm look. "Don't let him win. You will walk in there with your head held high like the brave, beautiful, talented woman you are."

I slump back on my bed while she marches to my closet and starts brusquely sorting through my dresses, of which I don't have many appropriate for the occasion. She makes an approving noise and pulls out one, holding it up with an assessing eye. Then she turns and thrusts it toward me.

"You will wear this. You will look stunning. You will make him swallow his tongue. And you will make him regret every single decision he's made in the last month. Hell, maybe in his whole life."

I take the dress and look at her. "What if he doesn't? What if he looks at me, then looks at Jessica and thinks, 'Thank god I made the right choice'?"

Alex comes over, takes the dress out of my hands, and lays it carefully on the bed before wrapping me in her arms.

"It doesn't matter, Dee, because what he thinks is inconsequential. You have so much in front of you, and since he's an asshole and obviously not your person, that means you still have your great love ahead of you. One day you'll meet the man of your dreams and Cole will be a distant memory. He'll be married to that bitch and living a miserable existence." She gives me a fierce smile. "Just hold that in your head, act as if he doesn't affect you, and realize you will get through this and come out stronger on the other side."

My spirits lift and I give her another swift hug. "Thank you so much."

"Anytime, babe." She sits down next to me. "I know this probably isn't the best time, but I've got some good news."

"I can do with some good news, so hit me."

Her smile is bright. "Jaxson called this morning, and he and the guys have decided not to move to LA. They're going to base themselves out of New York."

"Oh my god, Alex. That's fantastic!" This time it's me throwing my arms around her.

Her laugh sounds slightly giddy. "He told me to get my ass in gear and find us some apartments to check out."

I'm so happy for her, I really am, and I make sure to hide just how much my heart is breaking. Even though the pain in my chest is overwhelming at the moment, the smile on Alex's face gives me a glimmer of hope that one day the hurt will ease, and I'll know the same happiness as Alex.

Hopefully that little glimmer is enough to get me through tomorrow.

MY HAND SHAKES as I steal a glass of champagne off the waitress's tray. Well-dressed men and women fill the ballroom, flitting around, talking architecture. At any other time, I'd love to network and discuss the ins and outs of sustainable design, but waiting for the moment when Cole and Jessica make an appearance has me twitchy. I've yet to see them, and any bravado that Alex instilled in me has already begun to drain away.

"Hello, Delilah."

I spin around and frown. "I'm really not interested in talking to you, Paul." I look around. "Where's Philippa?"

He scowls. "We're not together."

I don't feign interest. "What a shame for you."

"Don't be like that," he says, stroking his fingers down my forearm. "She was never you. I don't know what I was thinking."

"I do. You were thinking you could have your cake and eat it too. You were wrong. Now I'd appreciate it if you leave me alone."

"Delilah," he starts, but before he can continue, a large figure slides between us.

My heart jumps when I think it might be Cole, but golden eyes meet mine, not blue.

"I think the lady has made herself clear, don't you?" Tate's cold voice and large presence are enough to intimidate Paul, whose eyes dart between us.

He lets out a bitter laugh. "Wow, were you sleeping with all three brothers, or just the two?"

Tate doesn't move, so it must be his expression that makes Paul shuffle back a step.

"I should be so fucking lucky," he growls. "And you know it, too. Which is why you're trying to worm your way back into her life. You had your chance and you screwed it up, so how about you go sleep it off in the bed you made for yourself."

With one last piercing look, Paul slinks off and Tate turns to me, his lips tilted up in a smile.

I let out a breath. "Thank you."

He shakes his head. "I'm sure you would have handled him yourself. I just don't like his face much."

I laugh and he tilts his head at me. "You know you have awful taste in men, right?"

My heart pangs. "I know." My lower lip trembles before I can stop it, and his eyes drop to it. He reaches up and brushes my hair from my face.

"You deserve better."

I stare at him in confusion. Is he flirting with me?

He grins and leans closer. "Just go with it, beautiful."

His eyes dart over my head and I stiffen, certain of what his wicked smile means. Cole and Jessica are here.

"Why are you doing this?" I murmur.

His gaze meets mine, a serious expression darkening his eyes, somehow making him even more good looking. "Because at one time we actually were brothers."

I don't know the full story behind Cole's relationship with Tate and Roman, but I know enough to understand there's pain there. I put my hand on his arm. "You'll always be brothers. Don't let go of what you have because it's hard. You're all still here. You still have each other."

His eyes search mine for a moment before the mischief sparks back to life. "My brother really is making a mistake."

I shrug, unsure what to say, and he laughs. Then he takes my barely touched champagne from my hand and downs it before placing it on the table behind him.

"Come on," he says, putting his hand on my back and guiding me to the bar. "I need something harder than champagne."

In my peripheral vision, I glimpse a tall, dark-haired form with a statuesque blonde at his side. I deliberately don't look in Cole's direction. He doesn't deserve my attention and I refuse to give it to him, even though I can sense his gaze on me.

"Whiskey?" Tate asks me, and I flash back to the first night I met Cole. My first instinct is to say no, but then I square my shoulders. Maybe I just need to go back to that moment and redo it. Pretend I never went home with Cole.

"Yes, thanks."

He orders, and when we receive our drinks, he turns so he's leaning back against the bar.

I match him. I don't intend to look for Cole, but I'm unable to avoid him because he's directly in my line of sight and staring right at me. His brows are lowered, his lips in a tight line.

Seeing him for the first time in weeks sends a jolt of pain through me, but I refuse to let it show. I stare back as coolly as I can. Our eyes are locked, but I have no idea what's going through his head. I want to look away, but it's as if I'm trapped in his gaze.

Until Jessica breaks his focus. She presses herself against him and he looks down at her, his hand coming to rest on her waist as if on automatic.

Pain punches the air from my lungs and tears blur my vision. Damn him. And damn my stupid emotions. Before I can look away, his gaze is back on me and I know, I just know, he can read the hurt on my face because I didn't have time to school my expression.

I lift my whiskey, throw it back, then gasp and shudder in response. But the burn of the liquid is exactly what I need. I put the empty glass on the bar, ready to excuse myself from Tate's presence, but he stops me before I have a chance by cupping my cheek and sweeping his thumb over my lower lip, then raising it to his mouth. I freeze when his tongue flicks out to taste the drop of whiskey that must have clung there.

He hums in approval.

"W-What—"

"You'd better go," he says. "He's on his way over."

I don't hesitate, spinning and walking away. I'm sick of this, of the two of them and whatever it is they've got going on. Of the games that rich people play with people's emotions. Of feeling hurt all the time.

I'll get tonight over with, and then I'll be done with all of them.

I keep walking as raised voices beat against my back. How dare Cole be pissed off. He has no right. No damn right.

I'm heading for the large balcony when a clawed hand grips my arm. I stop and turn, my eyes narrowing as they meet Jessica's icy glare.

"I know what you're doing," she hisses.

"You don't know anything."

"Trying to play brother against brother. It's a cheap tactic and it won't work. Cole chose me. He was always going to choose me. This world will always be his priority, and unlike you, I'm a part of this world. So just accept it and move on."

My eyes dart over her shoulder to see Cole bearing down on us, a furious expression on his face. Behind him, Tate is adjusting the lapels of his suit, as if Cole had grabbed him there.

I turn back to Jessica and wrench my arm away from her.

"I'm not playing anyone, and if you think I have any interest in being a part of this world, you couldn't be more wrong. I want nothing to do with any of you." My eyes meet

Cole's again, even as I continue to address Jessica. "You're all miserable people living miserable lives, where the only joy you seem to have is playing games with other people's emotions. You're welcome to each other. I'd rather live a real life with real people and real love than dirty myself with whatever it is that passes for relationships in your world."

I spin on my heel and walk to the balcony with my spine straight and my head held high, trying my best to hold back the tears filling my eyes.

I slip out the door and rush to the balustrade, gripping it and leaning out to take a deep breath. Before I can take more than one lungful of the crisp air, a hard body presses against me.

My whole being reacts to his presence, my muscles loosening, my fingers itching to reach back and bury themselves in his hair. But a split second later, my head takes back control.

"Get off me, Cole," I hiss. "Your fiancée is inside, and you don't have the right to touch me anymore."

He doesn't budge, his hands dropping to my hips, his fingers pressing into my flesh while his lips find the crook of my neck.

"I can't do it," he rasps, his hot breath sending goose bumps skittering over my skin. "I can't do it."

"What?" My voice trembles. "What can't you do?"

He doesn't answer, only pulls me tighter against him. "It's not supposed to be this hard. I thought I could do it, but seeing you with him tonight, I can't . . ."

So it was just seeing me with Tate that made him jealous. So damn typical.

I shove back as hard as I can, and he finally gives me enough room to turn around. I meet his gaze, but the blaze in his eyes doesn't electrify me the way it used to. In this moment, looking at his stupidly handsome face drawn tight with tension, I hate him more than I've ever hated anyone in my life. Even my father. At least he never pretended to care about me.

"Well, let me make it easy for you," I say, not recognizing my own voice. "I'm going to walk back into that ballroom. I'm going to listen to the award ceremony. I'm not going to talk to you or Jessica or Tate. I won't even look in your direction. Then, as soon as it's over, I'm going to walk out of here and forget about you, and you're going to do the same, Cole. Because whatever I thought we had was a lie and a joke, and I have no intention of dwelling on it. When I finally meet the man I will love for the rest of my life, you will be a distant memory. Now get out of my way."

His posture is rigid, his face frozen, as if carved from stone. He stares at me, the fire in his eyes dimming until they're blank pools of icy blue. He steps aside and I brush past him into the ballroom, where I proceed to do exactly what I said I would do. I join the Elite team, keep my eyes fixed on the stage, clap as the awards are announced, and even muster a genuine smile when our team receives the award for Sustainable Hotel Design Concept. I do all of it. All except the part where I said I'd forget all about him. It's too hard to forget when my heart is breaking all over again as the truth of my own words rings in my ears.

What I thought he felt for me was a lie—one I was responsible for telling myself.

CHAPTER FORTY

COLE

I slam into Tate's office on Monday morning to find him kicked back in his chair, his feet on his desk as he talks into the phone. This is the first time I've seen him since the awards ceremony, which he disappeared from while I was still doing my best to keep Delilah in my view at all times. Then he up and flew his personal airplane to Napa Valley for the rest of the weekend and refused to answer my calls.

His brows rise at my precipitous entry. "Something's just come up," he says to whoever's on the other end of the phone. "I'll have to call you back."

He hangs up as I stalk toward his desk, then pisses me off by grinning and folding his arms behind his head. "To what do I owe the honor, big brother?"

I fist my hands, pressing them hard onto his desk as I lean over it. "What the fuck are you playing at?"

He pretends confusion. "What are you talking about?"

"You had your hands on her."

He taps his finger against his lips. "I've had my hands on lots of women. I mean, just last night I—"

"I don't give a fuck what you were getting up to last

night. I'm talking about Saturday night. You had your hands. On. Delilah."

"Oh, that's right. You know, I can see the appeal. She really is gorgeous, isn't she? All those curves, and that mouth. The things I could do—"

"Shut the fuck up!" I roar. "I don't want you anywhere near her. If you touch her again, I will end you."

The way his brows rise makes me realize how unhinged I sound. About as unhinged as I feel.

Seeing Delilah looking so fucking beautiful and real while I was forced to stand next to Jessica for appearance's sake had made me a little crazy. When Tate brushed his thumb across her lower lip, I'd almost crushed the glass of champagne I held in my hand.

Jessica had called out after me as I stalked over there, but in that moment, I hadn't given a fuck about my fiancée. The only thing that had thrummed in my veins over and over again was that Delilah was mine.

But of course, she wasn't mine, as she'd pointed out a few minutes later on the balcony. The ice in her eyes when she told me she wanted to forget I existed had been the reminder I needed. Whatever was between us—*had* been between us—would die just as surely as it did for everyone. Better to see that coolness in her gaze now before I did something stupid like tie us together and condemn us to a lifetime of regret.

That didn't stop me from being furious with my little brother. He has always been a man whore, but he's never gone after a woman I've slept with. It's an unwritten rule that all three of us have stuck to over the years. What he did with Delilah is unacceptable.

"Why all the fuss?" he asks, as if he doesn't notice that I'm about to launch myself across the desk at him. "You're about to be married. Why should you care about one of the many women you used to sleep with?"

My nostrils flare. "She's not—" Although it must be obvious from my actions that she's far more than that, I cut myself off before I can admit the truth. The fury suddenly leaves me, and I drop into one of the leather chairs facing his desk.

I scrub my hands over my face. "Fuck."

When I look at him again, there's an expression of curiosity on his face. "I've never seen you like this before."

I let out a harsh laugh. "You haven't been around me enough to see me in any particular way."

He nods. "Fair point. But if I had been around you more, would I have seen you like this before?"

I shake my head, and he leans forward.

"So what is it about this woman that has you all jealous and possessive when one of the most beautiful women in New York is wearing your ring on her finger?"

The reminder of the huge rock I'd given Jessica a couple of weeks ago has my stomach clenching. It was expensive, gaudy, and ostentatious, and Jessica had loved it. Mainly because she'd sent the details of the ring she wanted to Samson, and I hadn't cared enough to look for something myself. In fact, I'd sent him out to buy it for me.

Tate appears genuinely curious about what's on my mind, but I'm at a loss for how to explain it to him. Even if I knew, I'm not sure I want to share my feelings with him. Despite being brothers and working in the same building, we barely see each other. Not until our father's arrest six months ago, anyway. Since then, we've spent more time together than we have in the past ten years.

"Do you remember how we used to play hide and seek

whenever Mom and Dad were out of the house?" I surprise myself by asking.

Tate sits back in his chair, caught off guard. "I remember. You two could never find me."

"That's because you were small and could hide in places we couldn't reach."

His lips curve up, and for a moment, I catch a glimpse of the little boy I used to play with. A dull ache throbs in my chest. "When did we stop being friends?" The question slips out before I can stop it.

His smile fades. "Were we ever really friends?"

I'm taken aback by his response. Doesn't he remember? He and I were closer in age than me and Roman, so we naturally gravitated toward each other. "I thought we were."

He nods, but his expression grows distant. It's rare to see my youngest brother looking so pensive, and I find myself leaning forward. "Remember that time you hid in the heating vent so you could leap out at old Mrs. Jenkins when she was folding the laundry? She almost had a heart attack."

The pensive expression vanishes, replaced by his familiar smirk. "Fuck. I was an asshole."

I chuckle. "We all were."

It hits me suddenly. I can't point my finger at any one thing that caused the distance between us as kids, but perhaps dwelling on the why isn't as important as working out a way to bridge that gap now. If my time with Delilah taught me anything, it's that life may not be perfect but having even one person who shows up for you when you need them can make everything better.

Our parents won't ever be those people, and there's no way my future wife will be. But maybe, just maybe, Tate and I can be that for each other.

"Would you like to grab a drink tonight?" I ask.

His eyes widen a little, and he rubs his chin. "I'm game. But only if you answer one question for me."

I narrow my gaze, but what do I have to lose? I nod. "Go ahead."

"You've never had a problem telling Roman no before. Why did you go along with this marriage arrangement?"

Something flippant hovers on my tongue, but I can't bring myself to say it. Trivializing what I'm doing feels like a disservice to Delilah. So I tell him the truth. "That whole thing about 'it's better to have loved and lost than never to have loved at all' is bullshit. Believing you have something special and then seeing it disappear in front of your eyes is far worse. If I'm going to end up in a loveless marriage, I'd rather not start off with the illusion that it's more."

He seems to understand. "You won't miss what you never had."

"Exactly." Except, even as I say it, I know it might be too late for me. I've had Delilah now, and I don't know if the memory of the warmth in her smile and the heat of her touch will ever fade or if I'll carry around this ache in my chest for the rest of my days.

"I'm sorry I messed with you on Saturday," Tate says, knocking me out of my reverie.

"Why did you?" Even with our new truce, I'm not sure I won't punch him if he says something I don't like about Delilah.

"Because I liked you better when you were with her. You look too much like our father with Jessica on your arm."

I wince. "You don't pull any punches, do you?"

He raises his brows. "Do you want me to?"

"No. It will be nice to have one person I can rely on to tell me the truth."

A slow grin crosses his face and out of nowhere, a surge of affection hits me. "You may live to regret that," he says.

I push myself to my feet. "I'm sure I'll start regretting it as soon as I leave this room."

His chuckle follows me out of the office, and as I walk back to mine, I feel the slightest lightening in my chest for the first time since I told Delilah I was marrying Jessica. It's bittersweet, though, because I'm not sure the possibility of a better relationship with my brother would have been possible without Delilah.

The lightness doesn't last. As I take a seat behind my desk, a wave of regret hits me. Even when she's not with me, she's making my life better.

But I haven't done the same for her.

And now I'll never get the chance.

CHAPTER FORTY-ONE

DELILAH

Mom hands me a steaming cup of tea. I lift it to my lips and breathe in the soothing peppermint scent as she sits down next to me. Tonight is my first night back at home, and although I'm happy to see Mom, my heart still aches. It seems ridiculous. How can I mourn something that was never real to begin with? And yet, I do. If it's this hard for me, I can't imagine how Mom must have felt when my dad walked away from her, especially since she was pregnant with me.

Mom places a comforting hand on my back. "How are you doing, sweetheart?"

There's no point in lying. "I just feel sad all the time. And angry. I'm angry too. But mostly sad and embarrassed." I look down, a lump forming in my throat.

She gently rubs my back. "You have every right to be angry and sad. That's normal when any relationship ends. But why are you embarrassed?"

"I should have known better. I did know better, but I did it anyway. Got involved with a rich man and fell in love. I did everything you warned me against doing."

Mom sighs and brushes some hair off my face. "Warning someone when it comes to matters of the heart never works. I should know. My parents warned me enough." She laughs softly. "And they were right. And they were wrong, too. Because look what I got." She smiles at me, love shining in her eyes.

I can't help but smile back, and I lean into her, laying my head on her shoulder. "I love you too."

"Don't let one selfish man harden your heart, sweetheart. There will be others. Men who will love you for all that you are. And then that one special man who steals your heart and refuses to let it go."

"That wasn't the case for you, though, Mom," I say softly.

"Well," she says, "I had more love than I needed with my little snuggle bug." She smiles, using the childhood nickname she used to call me.

I laugh through my tears. "I haven't been a snuggle bug for a while."

Mom strokes my hair. "You'll always be my snuggle bug. And besides, it's not like I've ruled out meeting someone. I'm just not putting any pressure on myself. If it happens, it happens."

I let out a breath. "I'm glad I came home."

"I'm always glad to have you home. You know that," Mom says. "But make sure it's because you want to be here, not because you're scared. Be brave. Choose to live your life despite the people who might try to drag you down."

"I will, Mom. I have some time to think about what I want to do, and I have that meeting with Anderson-Bennet next week. I'll see how that goes, and then I can make a choice."

"That's all I ask. Don't give up your dreams because of a man."

"I won't." I hug her tightly, and she holds me close. Then I let out a breath and lean back against the couch, taking another sip of peppermint tea. I think about what I just said, and I wonder if my dreams might have changed. Going back to working so hard and never letting myself go enough to really enjoy life doesn't sound so appealing anymore. I guess if Cole has given me anything, he's given me a new perspective. I want to make Mom happy, but I know she won't want me to do it at the expense of my own happiness.

"Come on," I say. "We didn't get to finish our Buffy marathon last time I was here. Now we'll have plenty of time."

She settles back in the seat next to me as I get the episode queued up. No matter how my heart has been broken, I'll always have Mom.

I rest my head on her shoulder again, and she reaches for my hand, holding it tight.

"SO, you're currently working in New York." The elegant, dark-haired woman looks over the top of her glasses at me. "Can you tell me why you're considering leaving?"

I cross my legs and glance at the three partners of Anderson-Bennet. "I've loved working with Elite over the last year, but I realized how much I miss being near family. I guess I just got homesick."

She smiles warmly. "I know that feeling. I worked in New York for two years before moving home. It can be a big, lonely city."

Something pinches in my chest. "Yes, it can."

She nods and looks back at my résumé. "Honestly, everything I see here is perfect. We'd be foolish not to take you on, particularly considering your recent work with the King Group. We don't have many people with your qualifications and experience knocking down our door."

"Thank you."

She taps a fingernail on the desk. "You only need to consider whether you'll really be happy downscaling your work. We don't have a lot of billion-dollar companies on our books, and there's a chance you might get bored. Take some time to think about it, maybe two weeks, and then call us back with your decision."

I smile and nod. "Thank you, I'll do that."

After saying our farewells, I leave the office and get in my rental. If I move back here, I'll have to buy a car. I curl my fingers around the steering wheel and take a deep breath. I'm so conflicted. I love working in New York, but I miss Mom, and with everything that's happened with Paul and Cole, the comfort of home is pulling at my heart now.

I have three more weeks of leave after this one, so at least I'll have time to think about it before I make a decision. Hopefully when my heart has healed a little and my head is clearer.

Though I've got a horrible feeling it will take more than three weeks for the pain in my heart to ease.

I shift the car into gear and head home.

CHAPTER FORTY-TWO

COLE

I lean on the balcony railing with a whiskey in my hand. Just like the night Roman called with news about Dad's arrest, my eyes are drawn to King Plaza, visible in the distance from my penthouse the way it was from the hotel. And the same as that night, the lights are on in Roman's office. My fingers tighten around the cut-crystal glass as the weight of my thoughts presses down on me.

Is any of it worth it? The late nights, the drive to succeed, the constant pursuit of wealth and power. Is this really all there is? My brothers and I may have the best of everything, but does that make it a life worth living?

Ice cubes clink against the glass as I sip the whiskey, closing my eyes so I can focus on the smooth burn as it goes down rather than the hollow that resides in my chest—the one that's been there since the day I walked away from Delilah.

"Cole?" Jessica's voice interrupts my thoughts, and I grit my teeth. Giving her a key to my apartment was a mistake, but it was the compromise I made after she threw a tantrum when I refused to let her move in. I'd told her that could wait until after the wedding. A smirk tugs at my lips as I remember the look on her face when I said I was a traditionalist and didn't believe in living in sin.

She was not happy.

Still, her having a key is almost worse since I can never predict when she'll make an appearance.

I head back inside to deal with her.

She's just coming down the hallway from my bedroom, obviously having checked there first. When she sees me with whiskey in hand, a feline smile of satisfaction crosses her face.

She slows her walk, her hips beginning to swing as she slips the straps of her dress off her shoulders. I keep my gaze on her face, completely uninterested in what she's offering. Not while I still have Delilah's memory in my head.

Jessica comes to a stop a few feet in front of me, her smile slipping as I raise a brow. "Come on, Cole," she says, a frustrated whine creeping into her voice. "Don't be like that. We had some good times before she came along."

Her dress pools at her feet and she looks up at me with a pout as she runs her fingers over her breasts.

I clench my teeth and look over her shoulder at the black mirror of my massive wall-mounted television. Even as I keep my gaze fixed on the screen, the room almost seems to recede away from me, as if the walls of my apartment are drawing back, the space around me growing bigger and emptier with every breath I take.

My ribs constrict so hard they trap the air in my lungs while my heart hammers an erratic and painful rhythm in my chest. Fuck. I'd think this was a damn panic attack if I didn't know better. It's the truth ripping its way into my consciousness. This is it. This is my future. A big empty apartment filled with all the luxuries money can buy and two empty fucking people with empty hearts rattling around inside it.

Because that's what Jessica and I are. Empty fucking people. We're the definition of the walking dead. Strutting around with our wealth and our power, pretending to live when we have huge fucking voids in our chests where our hearts are meant to beat.

Me, my brothers, my parents—we're empty people living in empty houses. I've no doubt Jessica's the same. We've grown up knowing nothing but the scramble to get to the top of the pile and then the struggle to stay there, no matter what the cost. We never let ourselves admit the payoff isn't worth the price, because once we admit that, what the fuck are we left with?

Is that what I want? A replica of my parents' soulless marriage, raising my children the way I was raised.

I've seen firsthand what the alternative is—I've felt it. Delilah wasn't an illusion. She was real, I had her, then I threw her away. Memories of her touch, her laughter, her warmth flood my mind, and I can't ignore it any longer. When I was with her, she filled every hollow part of me, made me feel whole for the first time in as long as I can remember. She made my life better, and I want to be the man who does that for her. I *need* to be that man.

I focus on Jessica again. "I can't do this." Then I shake my head because that's not the truth of it. "I won't do this."

Something brittle crosses her face. "Don't be ridiculous."

I look her straight in the eye. "I don't want this. And I don't think you do either."

She scoffs. "Why wouldn't I want this? The two of us make perfect sense. I've known we'd get married since the first time you fucked me. You're mine, Cole. You always have been, no matter who else you've been with. I've just been waiting for the right time for us to make it official."

"Is that really what you want? A sham of a marriage? A man who doesn't love you?"

She looks genuinely bewildered. "What does love have to do with anything?"

"You really want to go through life not caring about me and having me not care about you?"

She flicks her hair over her shoulder and shrugs. "That's the way it is. You know that. My parents have a perfectly successful marriage and so did yours until your dad got careless."

Got careless? Jesus. I turn away from her. She's not going to get it. Just like I didn't for far too long. Maybe you can't until you experience the alternative.

"Come on, Cole," she says. "I'm happy to do whatever you want to do once we're married." Her arms wrap around me from behind, her breasts pressing against my back. "You know you'd get bored with her anyway. You and me, we're the same. We know what we want and what we have to do to get it. You get me pregnant, give Dad an heir and a spare to keep him happy, and then you can do what you want, and I can do what I want. You can fuck anyone you choose. Hell, after you get me pregnant, you can track her down and fuck her until she's out of your system. Just be discreet, for god's sake, and whatever you do, don't get her pregnant. The last thing we want is to deal with rumors of a bastard running around."

She's managed to insult Delilah and my brother in one go. I pull away from her. "You're as cold as fucking ice, aren't you?"

She laughs. "And you're exactly the same. She was in love with you, and you broke her heart because your business and your money mean more to you than she ever would. So don't stand there and judge me."

The truth of her words cuts deep and my jaw clenches.

Jessica doesn't read the signs. She tips her head down and looks up at me through her lashes. "We're made for each other, Cole. Now stop messing around and come and make your future wife happy."

I step closer and bend down to murmur in her ear. "That's exactly what I plan to do." Then I turn and leave.

CHAPTER FORTY-THREE

COLE

I walk into Roman's office without knocking. He looks up at me, surprise lighting his eyes for a brief second before he shuts it down and leans back in his chair. "To what do I owe this pleasure so early on a Monday morning?"

I stride to the leather seats in front of his desk and drop into one, stretching out my legs and crossing them at the ankle. "It's over."

One dark brow rises. "What's over?"

"Jessica. Me. I'm done."

His eyes narrow and he leans forward. "She has a ring on her finger."

"She can keep it or sell it. Whatever she wants. But it no longer represents a commitment from me to her."

"Jesus Christ, Cole," Roman snaps, and it almost feels good to see the anger on his face instead of that implacable indifference. "We had an agreement, for fuck's sake. When did you speak to her? It might not be too late to turn this around."

"I spoke to her last night. And it is too late, because I will walk away from this company before I marry her."

I see the closest thing to shock on his face that I've seen since we were kids. "You can't seriously tell me you're so repelled by Jessica that you'd give up your shares in this company to avoid marrying her."

"It's not Jessica."

"Then what the fuck is it?"

"It's Delilah."

Roman explodes out of his seat, planting his hands on his desk and leaning over it to stare me down. "No. You are not risking this company for a woman you had a fling with."

I smooth down my tie, far calmer than him in this moment. "It's funny," I say. "When something is right, when you know deep down that it's right, nothing else matters. Not money. Not power. Nothing." He stares at me as if I'm crazy. "I don't expect you to understand. Hell, if you'd said the same thing to me six months ago, I'd have thought you were crazy. But Delilah changed all of that. She changed me. And there's no going back, even if I can't convince her to give me another chance. I don't want to walk away from the King Group, because this is our company and I want to be a part of its future. Maybe there's even some hope for this family going forward. But I will trade it all for more time with her."

Deep creases form in his forehead. "So you're willing to end up with nothing?"

"Even if I walk away, I'll be far from destitute, but if you're talking about me having no part of this company, then yes, that's a sacrifice I'm willing to make. But it would be good if that weren't the case. I think if you, me, and Tate sit down, we can figure out a way to salvage Berrington's investment that doesn't rely on me marrying Jessica. He's a smart man. He might want to think he has a personal stake in a company, he might be happy pandering to his daughter to get it, but first and foremost, he's a businessman, and he'll listen to what we have to say."

Roman regards me with steely eyes for a moment, then sits down again.

He drums his fingers on his desk with a look of consideration on his face. I wait patiently for his response. "I don't pretend to understand your position," he eventually says, "but I don't want to lose you. If you're determined, then let's get this sorted out."

My shoulders relax as he picks up his phone. "Tate, do you have a moment to come to my office?" He listens. "Good. See you in a minute."

He hangs up, then steeples his fingers under his chin as he scrutinizes me, something that almost looks like amusement flickering in his eyes. "You have hope for this family, huh?"

My lips tug up, but I shrug casually as the door swings open and Tate walks in. "It's never too late," I say.

"What's it never too late for?" he asks, making his way to the chair next to me.

"Second chances." I might be answering his question, but it's dark hair and green eyes I see.

Tate eyes me curiously, then turns his attention to Roman. "What do you want to talk about?"

I focus on my brothers. The three of us are going to work this out, and then I'm going for Delilah. I'm getting her back, and I don't care what it takes.

CHAPTER FORTY-FOUR

COLE

The driver pulls up, and I sit there for a moment, taking in the house that Delilah grew up in. It's small, but the front yard is well maintained, with flowers and shrubs planted in beds around the front porch.

It's funny. I can't imagine growing up here, but I can picture Delilah as a child as clear as day, running through the sprinklers during the heat of summer, kneeling side by side with her mother as they planted flowers, helping her mom carry the groceries up the porch steps. Simple things. Things she might have taken for granted. Things I'd give anything to have experienced because maybe it would be easier for me to know how to be with her. How to give her what she needs.

I tell the driver to wait for me further down the street, then I climb out of the car. I'm wearing a suit, which may have been a mistake in hindsight, but it's too late now.

I stride to the front door, wondering if anyone will be home. If Delilah is even staying here. I assumed she would, but I don't know for sure. I'll find out soon.

I knock and wait. When footsteps sound on the other

side of the door, my heart pounds against my ribs, hoping I'll get to see her again for the first time in far too long. But when the door opens, it's not her. Although, if I were to guess what Delilah will look like in twenty years or so, this would be what I would imagine.

She's petite, dark-haired, and with the same cat-like eyes as her daughter, although hers are blue. Does Delilah get those green eyes from her father? The man that rejected her in favor of his wealth and position—just like I did.

I push that thought aside. I need to focus.

The woman looking up at me purses her lips and crosses her arms. She obviously knows exactly who I am, and she is not impressed. "Delilah isn't here, so you can get back on that private jet I'm sure you flew in on and fly right back home again."

Getting past Delilah's mom will be the first challenge, but not one I plan to back down from. "Sorry, ma'am. I can't do that."

She narrows her eyes. "And why is that? You have everything you need back in New York. Your fancy penthouse, your fancy cars, all your money. Your *fiancée*. Leave my daughter alone and let her get over you in peace."

Sharing my feelings with a stranger is normally the last thing I would do, but now's not the time to hold back. "I don't have a fiancée, and I definitely don't have everything I need. Because I need Delilah. I need her, and without her, everything else is meaningless."

She studies me, a line forming between her brows. Then she steps back. "If you won't leave, you might as well come in."

A silent breath rushes out of me, and I step over the threshold, taking in the well-worn furniture and the small, functional kitchen off to the side. Bright throw pillows on the couch and sketches of flowers on the wall give it a cozy, lived-in feel.

"Would you like tea or coffee?" she says.

"Just some water, thank you," I reply.

"I only have tap water." Her chin is raised as if she thinks I'll make a fuss over her lack of anything fancier.

I smile. "Tap water is fine."

The corners of her lips give a faint twitch, and I take that as a win.

She goes to the kitchen and returns with a glass, which she sets on a coaster on the small wooden coffee table. Assuming that's an invitation to sit, I do, and she settles in the armchair opposite me.

I've been in a lot of high-pressure meetings with very powerful people, but I don't think I've ever sweated more than I am under the piercing gaze of Delilah's mom. It's the look of a mother who wants nothing more than to protect her child. It's a look I never got to see growing up, but I like that Delilah did. I like knowing that even without her father in the picture, she knew she was loved and protected.

I want to be the person who loves and protects her now. I haven't done a good job so far, but I'm going to change that.

"Okay. Let me hear it," she says. I frown, and Delilah's mom shakes her head. "What are you hoping to achieve by coming here, Mr. King?"

"It's Cole," I say, and she nods, but her stony façade doesn't change, and she doesn't offer her name in exchange. I let out a breath. Hopefully she'll hear the honesty in my voice. "I made a mistake. I hurt her, and there is no acceptable excuse for what I did. I don't know if I can make it right or if Delilah can find it in her heart to forgive me, but I'm going to try anyway. I want to give her everything she's ever wanted. Everything she's ever dreamed of. I want to know what it's like to wake up with her every morning and go to sleep with her every night. I want a life of loving her. I'm not sure what it will take to show her I'll never make the mistake of leaving her ever again, but that's what I'm here to figure out."

During my speech, her face softens, and by the time I finish, I swear there's the glimmer of a smile on her face. "Well, you're here, and that's a good first step. Can I ask what happened to the woman you were planning to marry? Did you leave her brokenhearted too?"

That's a loaded question if ever I heard one. "You have to understand, Ms. West—"

"Beth," she says, and my hopes rise a little higher.

"Beth," I acknowledge before continuing. "You have to understand that marriage isn't about love in my world. It's about alliances. It's about trading power and influence. I never loved Jessica, and I can guarantee she never loved me. Her feelings might have been hurt when I broke it off, but more likely her ego and definitely not her heart."

"So why did you agree to it in the first place? You must have known Delilah had feelings for you and that your decision would hurt her."

A trickle of sweat makes its way down my back. I'm not painting myself in the best light here, but there's nothing to do but forge on. "Because I believed love wasn't important for people like me. I thought it was the one thing we didn't get to have."

She watches me intently. "Are you saying you believe differently now?"

I picture Delilah making me grilled cheese in my barely used kitchen. I picture her with her face lit up as she talked about her designs. I remember how she stood up to my mother without even blinking. I see her smile and hear her laugh and remember the silk of her skin and the sound of her gasps.

I look her mother right in the eye. "Now I believe love is there if you look for it, regardless of who you are, and if you're lucky enough to find it, you hold on to it with everything you have. I think the only people who don't deserve love are those who refuse to believe in it, even when it's right there in front of them."

A slow smile breaks across her face. "Well then," she says, softly. "Delilah never did do things by half."

I'm not exactly sure what she means, but the smile she gives me makes me think I've convinced her I'm here for the right reasons.

"Of course, that's the easy part," she says. "Now you have to convince her. Do you have a plan for that? Or are you going to wing it the way you just did?"

I grimace. "To be honest, I haven't thought past getting to see her again."

There's a noise outside, and she looks toward the front door. "Well, I think you're going to get your chance."

CHAPTER FORTY-FIVE

DELILAH

I park Mom's battered old car in the driveway and collect the groceries from the back seat before carrying them up the path to the house. Before I can put the key in the lock, the door opens, and I smile at Mom. "I got all the ingredients you wanted, and I picked up some ice cream for dessert. Do you—" I stop when I notice the serious expression on her face. "Is everything okay?"

She reaches to take the bags from my hands. "Cole's here."

My heart almost stops. "What?"

"He's here. But it's up to you if he stays."

I throttle the feeling of betrayal that swells in my chest —Mom wouldn't have let him in if he hadn't given her a good enough reason. I just don't have a clue what that could be.

I draw in a long breath, then another one, my heart beating a rapid tattoo in my chest. Mom gives me a reassuring smile, nods toward the small living room, then heads for the kitchen with the groceries.

He's standing, watching me as I approach, and my

breath catches in my throat at the sight of him. I don't know why he's here. I don't know why he isn't back in New York with Jessica. I'm torn between drinking him in and wanting to walk straight past him into my bedroom.

But my mom didn't raise a coward, so I stop in front of him and look up. He's just as gorgeous as I remember. What I don't remember is the drawn look to his face, and the glimmer of desperation in his gaze.

"Delilah," he says, and just my name spoken in that deep, velvety voice makes me tremble.

I don't beat around the bush. "Does Jessica know you're here?"

If I expect him to flinch or act evasive, I'm disappointed. He holds my gaze steadily. "I don't care if she does or not. I ended it with her."

My traitorous heart leaps at that news before I remember that he still traded me in for a woman who's part of his world. That he stood in front of me and told me he planned to marry someone else, meaning he never felt for me what I felt for him. I stand firm. "Why are you here, Cole? I'm pretty sure I said everything I had to say to you at the awards night."

His eyes bore into me. "You did. And you had every right to say all of it. I . . ." For the first time, he looks uncertain, his eyes flicking away as he rubs his hand over his chin. "I fucked up more than I thought it was possible to fuck up. I put my company first. I put myself first. I hurt you in a way I never imagined I could hurt someone because I never believed someone could feel about me the way you did."

My resolve wavers, but I can't let down my guard. He's hurt me once, and there's nothing to stop him from doing it again when his position, his status, and his need to hold on to his wealth and power require it of him. "Is that an apology?" I ask.

His brow creases a little, his hands coming up as if he wants to grip my arms and pull me toward him. Thankfully, he doesn't make contact, letting them fall back to his side. "Not enough of one. I'm sorry, Delilah. I'm sorry for all of it —every bit of pain I caused you. But I'm here to make it right. I'm here to win you back."

"Win me back?" I shake my head. "Cole, there is no winning me back. I may not have said the words, but I was offering you my heart. I stood there in front of you, begging you not to leave me, and you walked away and put a ring on Jessica's finger. I'm sorry things didn't work out for you two, but that doesn't mean you get to come running back to me to pass the time until the next society princess comes along to share your crown."

Icy fire flashes in his eyes. "That isn't what this is."

"Then what is it?"

He takes a step forward, his voice lowering. "The only reason I got engaged to Jessica was for the King Group. The minute I realized what a mistake I was making, I ended it." He reaches for me again, and for a moment I weaken, letting him cup my jaw. His gaze sears into me. "I never fucking touched her, kitten. You need to know that. I couldn't bear the thought."

I hate the surge of relief that hits me at his words. It shouldn't matter. It *doesn't* matter. I step back and his hand drops.

He doesn't let that deter him, though. "I want another chance to be the man you need, Delilah."

"No." Tears fill my eyes and I shake my head. "I already gave you a second chance. I'm sick of having to give everyone a second chance. My father was given all the chances in the world to be in my life. I gave Paul a second chance and look where that got me. I shouldn't have to give everyone more than one chance to love me."

"Delilah—"

"I want you to leave." I ignore the way my voice trembles.

"No, Delilah. Just let me—"

I turn my back on him and walk to the front door, opening it and standing there, waiting for him to leave. For a moment, I think he won't. That he'll force me to face him again. To listen to the words that my heart will try too desperately to cling to. Because I want to believe him. I want it so much that the longing threatens to choke me. But I can't. I can't believe him.

Then his presence looms behind me. "You're right. You shouldn't need to give me another chance, because I should have realized what I had before I lost you. But I'm going to fix this. I'm going to fix us."

"There is no us, Cole." Exhaustion leaches through my veins, and I need him to go.

He ducks his head so he can meet my gaze with unwavering eyes. "There'll be an us in my heart forever, Delilah. Even if there isn't in yours anymore. I'm not leaving until I've done everything in my power to convince you that you'll never have to give anyone else a second chance again. I'll be the last chance you'll ever need to take."

He turns and strides down the path without looking back, although he glances at Mom's rusty car as he passes. It's lucky he doesn't turn, because if he had, he might have seen the way my legs went weak at his words. He might have seen the tears that sprang to my eyes with the almost overwhelming urge to reach for him. To bury my face in his chest and believe him.

But I'm too hurt, and my heart is too scarred to open for him again so easily.

He says he'll stay until he convinces me there's still an us, but I bet he'll be gone as soon as he's needed in New York.

And then I'll know.

I'll know exactly what I'm worth to Cole King.

THE NEXT EVENING, I return home after my jog, my feet stuttering to a halt as I pull out my earphones.

What the hell?

My first thought is that Cole's back, having driven himself this time, but I know that's not it. The shiny red car in the driveway is brand new. It doesn't even look like it was driven here. It looks like someone picked it up from the car lot and dropped it in front of Mom's garage where her car normally sits.

I walk up the path and let myself into the house, spotting his dark head straight away. He's sitting on the couch, the same place as yesterday, and Mom's sitting opposite him, serenely sipping a cup of tea.

I take a deep breath, then drop my keys on the sideboard. "Please tell me that's your car outside." I direct the comment to Cole.

He stands immediately, his deep blue eyes raking over me in a way that still has the power to make my heart flutter. He looks from me to my mom, who's sitting back in her chair, watching me with a tiny smile that I don't understand. She should be the last person encouraging Cole. She knows exactly how reckless men like him are with the hearts that are given to them.

"It's your mother's," Cole says.

"You bought it for her." It's a statement, not a question, because of course he did.

"The other one seemed like it was on its last legs."

My gaze goes to Mom. "I'm assuming you didn't accept it."

She laughs. "Of course not. I thanked Cole but told him I don't accept cars from strangers, no matter how rich they might be. We're just waiting for the dealership to pick it up again."

I return my glare to Cole. "I can't believe you bought a car."

"He also bought a plot of land," Mom says calmly.

My gaze ping-pongs between her and Cole. "What?"

"For my dream house that you're apparently designing for me." Her smile is soft. "I'd like to see the plan sometime."

"I—Of course. I just wanted to be closer to affording it before I told you. I'm not quite there yet, and we definitely don't need the land yet." I pin Cole with my stare, not sure if I'm more annoyed at him for buying land or spilling my secret.

"It's a good plot," he says. "It's on the river. I thought you could put in a boat dock—"

I let out a slightly hysterical laugh. "A boat dock? Cole, Mom's not rich. I'm not rich. We're not going to spend our weekends on a boat, sipping champagne. That's your life, not ours. And if Mom doesn't want a car from you, I can guarantee she doesn't want an expensive plot of land."

Mom stands and brushes down her skirt. "I might give you two a moment alone."

"Don't worry, Mom," I say. "Cole's just leaving."

I stare at him until he clenches his jaw, nods, and turns

to Mom. "Thank you for the tea, Beth." For the first time I notice the empty teacup on the coffee table in front of him, and something warm flutters to life in my belly at the thought of Cole and my mom drinking tea and talking. That feeling doesn't bear looking at too closely right now.

"It was my pleasure, Cole. And thank you for your thoughtful gifts. I hope you understand why I can't accept them."

A smile pulls at the corners of his lips. "I do now." He inclines his head to her. "I'll see you next time."

"Next time?" I question, but Mom merely smiles benignly as Cole moves toward me.

"We need to talk outside," I say.

He follows me onto the porch, and I close the front door behind us before whirling on him. "I can't believe you thought you could buy your way back into my life. And using my mother to do it. You should know I don't want your money, Cole. Stop throwing it around and thinking it's going to fix things."

"I'm not throwing it around," he says, his voice pitched low. "I'm not trying to buy your heart back. It's worth far more than I have."

A lick of warmth spreads through me. Why does he keep saying such sweet things? "Then why did you think turning up here with a new car and a plot of land would win you any favors?"

His eyes darken. "Because it's the only thing I can offer you—the only thing I can give you that you need."

I stare at him, then shake my head, sadness welling up in my chest. "No. It's not, Cole. I don't need your money or what it can buy me. A relationship isn't supposed to be transactional that way. It's about being with someone because you can't imagine not being with them. It's about sharing your heart and soul with someone, knowing they see you for who you really are—that they understand you in a way no one else can."

His jaw is tight as he watches me. "Okay," he says.

That wasn't what I was expecting. "Okay?"

He nods, steps closer, and reaches up to brush a strand of hair off my face. "I'll do better next time."

"Next time?" I say weakly. "I thought you'd have to go back to New York soon."

"I don't need New York. I need you."

He says it so simply that my heart almost bursts free from the prison I've put it in, but I manage to hold firm. I want to believe. I want it so much I'm practically vibrating with the need to throw myself into his arms. But words are meaningless, and I don't know if I can trust his.

He reads my indecision and takes a step back. "The truck will be here to pick up the car soon."

"Okay," I whisper.

His lips tip up at the corners a little. "I'm not giving up, Delilah." It's all he says before he turns and walks down the path toward the driver and car waiting for him. I don't stay to watch him get in and drive away, too scared I'll suddenly cave and run after him.

I go back into the house and find Mom in the kitchen, washing up the teacups. I slump against the counter and bury my face in my hands, tears threatening to spill. "What am I going to do, Mom? He thinks using his money is the way to prove he cares, but that just shows he doesn't know me at all." I pause, my voice trembling. "If he doesn't understand something so fundamental about me, how can he possibly feel the way he says he does?"

Mom dries her hands on a dishcloth, then rubs her hand

up and down my back. "I think you might need to look at it differently."

"What do you mean?"

"He was using his money, that's true, and it's not how he should try to win you back. But you have to remember, that's all he knows. It's how he's lived his life, and it's not always easy to change that way of thinking. And . . ." Mom pauses for a moment, her expression turning soft. "He knows you, Delilah. It might not look that way on the face of it, but he knows you."

I should be surprised that Mom's defending Cole, but somehow, I'm not. "What do you mean?"

She strokes my hand. "What do you care about?"

I shake my head, bewildered.

"For better or worse, you've driven yourself so hard all your life. Why is that?"

I swallow past the lump in my throat. "Because I want to give you a better life." I admit it, saying the words to her for the first time. "The life stolen from you when you got pregnant with me. I want you to be happy and have nice things—" I suck in a sharp breath.

Mom nods, her love for me shining in her eyes as she smooths a strand of hair away from my wet cheek. "If he was just throwing his money around, he would have used it to buy you jewelry or fancy clothes you don't want. He would have bought *you* a car. He wasn't using his money to impress you. He was using it to give you something you care deeply about."

Tears blur my vision at the truth of what she's saying.

"I think you should give him a chance, Delilah. If I didn't believe he was truly sorry and that he cares about you, I'd never say it. But he does care. A lot. He just hasn't quite figured out the best way to show you yet."

"Mom," I whisper, hope warring with pain in my chest. "He hurt me so badly."

She wraps her arms around me. "I know, sweetheart. I know he did. And I know I've spent your life telling you to be cautious with men—with giving them your body and your heart—because I didn't want you to go through the same pain I did with your dad. But that doesn't mean I don't want you to experience great love, and you'll never know if Cole could be that for you if you don't take a chance. From what you've told me, he didn't have much love growing up, so maybe he doesn't know how to express that part of himself. But he's trying, Delilah. It might take him some practice, and it might take you to show him the way, but I can't think of anyone better to show him how to love with his whole heart than you."

I lay my head on her shoulder and let myself cry silently for a few minutes, and then I pull myself together and wipe my eyes. "I don't even know where he's staying. I didn't ask. What if he doesn't come back?"

She brushes away a tear I missed. "If he doesn't, then it will just prove you were right and his heart wasn't in it. But I don't think you have to worry about that. I think you'll see him sooner rather than later." She squeezes my hand. "Okay?"

"Okay."

And it's that hope that I hold on to as I lie in bed, trying to fall asleep that night. Maybe, just maybe, there's a chance for Cole and me after all.

CHAPTER FORTY-SIX

COLE

I pull up outside Delilah's mom's house and shift the car into park. Since I plan to be here for the foreseeable future, it makes sense for me to rent a car rather than relying on a driver all the time.

The sunset sends warm beams of light through the window as I sit and consider what my next steps will be. I have to recalibrate. Buying things for Delilah's mom was a mistake. She doesn't need my money. Give Delilah a few more years, and she'll be able to buy those things for her mom herself.

Unfortunately, I haven't come up with another plan yet. Everything I think of involves money in some way. So for now, I'll just keep showing up. Being near Delilah, even if she hasn't forgiven me, is far better than spending hours alone in my hotel room. And maybe something will come to me when I see her.

I lock the car and make my way up the path that's already become so familiar. When I knock on the door, there's no answer, although Beth's battered old car sits in the driveway. I walk around to the side of the house and peer over the fence. "Hello?"

Delilah's mom pops her head around the corner. "Oh, Cole. I'm back here, honey."

I pause at the term of endearment. Sure, I've had women call me that before, when they were trying to be cute or seductive, and it never did a thing for me. But hearing it from Delilah's mom, spoken with an undercurrent of what seems to be genuine affection, tightens my chest.

I unlatch the gate and make my way to the backyard, where I find Beth kneeling by a small vegetable patch. I'm struck by a sudden vision: Delilah in the backyard of a house she's designed just for us, digging up carrots she's grown herself, maybe with a little doppelgänger of her own helping her, just the way I'm sure she would have helped her mom. Pain pierces my chest. It's something I never would have imagined wanting before, and now the thought of not having it feels like an unbearable loss.

"Delilah will be back in about half an hour," Beth says, shading her eyes against the lowering sun as she looks up at me. "She went to pick up the ingredients for dinner."

"She's hard to catch," I say.

"She always does better when she's busy."

I nod at the vegetable patch. "What are you growing?"

She points them out as she names them. "Green beans, squash, carrots, zucchini, and cucumbers."

"That's quite impressive."

She shrugs as she sinks a trowel into the dirt. "It's a good way to save some money on groceries."

I wince internally. That's not something I've ever had to think about. Suddenly I'm ashamed to be standing above her in my designer clothes. "Can I help?"

She squints one eye at me. "You'll get dirty."

"That's okay." It's not like I can't afford a new suit.

A grin spreads across her face. "Okay, then. Kneel here next to me, and I'll put you to work."

I do as she says, and she hands me a little spade.

"Just dig holes a couple of inches deep and about this far apart"—she gestures at the holes she's already dug—"and I'll start putting the seeds in."

I dig into the soft dirt. "What are we planting?"

"Beets."

"Beets, huh? Not my favorite."

"Maybe you have to try them prepared the right way."

I chuckle. "Maybe."

We chat for a while, and then I hear the back door open and look up in time to see Delilah walk out. She stops in her tracks when she sees me. What thoughts are running around behind those pretty green eyes when she looks at me?

"Hi," she says softly. "You came back."

"Of course." Didn't she believe me when I said I wasn't going anywhere?

"And you're helping Mom plant beets?"

I glance down at my fingers wrapped around the spade. "It appears so."

She walks down the steps toward us, and she's so fucking gorgeous that it's suddenly hard to take a breath.

"Delilah, do you mind finishing this off while I get dinner started?" Beth says, and when I glance at her, she gives me a subtle wink.

My lips tilt up in response, and then she's standing and brushing the dirt off her knees, and handing her trowel to Delilah, who sinks down next to me.

The scent of sunshine and wildflowers invades my

senses. All I want to do is to pull her to me and kiss her, but I doubt she'd appreciate that.

"This is something I never thought I'd see," she says, and when I look at her profile, the corner of her mouth is turned up in a smile.

"Me either. You'll have to take a photo and send it to my brothers."

She's silent for a moment, dropping seeds into the holes I'm digging. "Do they know where you are?"

"I told them I was coming to try to get you back at the same time I told them I wouldn't marry Jessica."

"Were they okay with it?"

I laugh. "I didn't really give them a choice. We just had to find a way to secure Berrington's investment that doesn't involve his daughter."

"And what way is that?"

"We've given him first right of refusal on any international commercial properties we develop for the next ten years."

I sense rather than see her turn to look at me. "That seems like a good deal for him."

"It is. It's not something we'd normally consider offering anyone."

"And your brothers didn't have a problem with that?"

I face her then. "There was an intense discussion, but once they realized how serious I was, they came through."

Her eyes brighten. "They showed up for you."

I nod. "Maybe there's hope for my brothers and me after all."

"I'm happy for you, Cole."

Her words ring with sincerity, and I can't resist the urge to touch her any longer. I grip her hand firmly, pulling her to her feet, then gently brush my thumb over her cheek. "I enjoy talking to you like this, Delilah," I say softly. "I like being in the house where you grew up. But I want to make it crystal clear why I'm here. I'm here for you. I want a future with you. I'm not just looking for a casual fling or your friendship. I want all of you, heart, body, and soul. The only future I can envision now is one with you by my side. And I know I fucked up with the car and the—"

She shakes her head and I stop.

"You didn't mess up, Cole," she says softly, her voice filled with emotion. "Those weren't gifts that Mom and I could accept, but the fact that you wanted to take care of her . . ." She swallows, and it's there, shimmering in her eyes —the look that makes me feel alive the way nothing else does. A smile trembles on her lips. "It took me a moment to see it, but it means more to me than anything else. It showed me that you know my heart. And it showed me yours." Her hand comes to rest on my chest, right over the wildly beating organ. "And I really, really like what I see."

Relief floods through me, and without thinking, I step forward, sinking the fingers of one hand into her soft hair and curving them around the back of her neck so I can pull her closer to me. "I like what I see too," I murmur.

"Is that so?" Her voice is barely above a whisper.

"Yes. In fact, I don't just like what I see. I love what I see."

She wets her lips, her eyes locked on mine. "You do?"

"I love it," I say, hoping she can hear the sincerity in my voice. "I love what I see so much that I don't think I can live without seeing it anymore." My eyes drift over her face, drinking in every detail.

Her breath turns uneven. "I had the impression you didn't believe in love."

"I didn't believe in much of anything until I met you," I

admit. "You showed me what love looks like, how it feels. There's no going back now."

"Did I show you how to hold on to it?" Her question hangs in the air, uncertainty threaded through it.

I know what she's asking, and I trace her lower lip with my thumb. "Delilah, I will never let you go again. It's not an option for me. Before you, my life was empty—*I* was empty —and I didn't even know it. I can't go back to that. I won't. And I'm not just saying that because I need you to forgive me and love me again. I mean it. I will *always* mean it. I won't let anything come between us. Not money, not my company, nothing. You are the most important thing to me. You've changed everything, and I can't imagine going back to the way I was before, thinking wealth and power were enough to make me happy. It's you, Delilah. You're what makes me happy."

Her eyes glisten, even as the corners of her mouth lift in a smile so full of joy that I swear the heart I once thought was cold and dead is going to smash its way through my chest. She tips her head to the side, her long dark hair tumbling over her shoulder. "I never knew you were so poetic."

"What can I say? You bring out the best in me."

Her lips part and she goes up on her toes. Sensing her intention, I twist my hand in her hair to stop her from closing the distance between our lips. Because I need her to know without any doubt. I keep my gaze fixed on hers. "I love you, Delilah. It took me too long to admit it to myself, and not because I didn't feel it—fuck, it was because I was feeling too much of everything I'd never felt before. But now that I've said it, I don't plan to stop. Maybe one day, if you forgive me, you'll be able to say it ba—"

She doesn't let me finish, her hands framing my face. "I

love you, Cole. I never stopped, as much as I wanted to. And I won't make you wait for me to say it, because I've already forgiven you." And right there, in her mother's garden, with the setting sun bathing her in golden light, she kisses me.

I let her take the lead for a few seconds, reveling in a moment where I can taste her again. Then I take over, reclaiming her mouth the way I intend to reclaim her body later. My hands roam over her curves, dropping to her ass so I can pull her flush against me. She moans into my mouth, her hands twisting in my shirt as if she never wants to let go. And I plan to make sure she doesn't. Because I won't. I'm never leaving her side again. I had everything I wanted when I was growing up, but not the thing I needed most. Now that I have it, I'll cherish it as if it's the most valuable thing in the world. Because it is.

She is.

And I'll spend every damn day from here on out proving it to her.

EPILOGUE
DELILAH

Mom reaches over the table and squeezes my hand. "I could get used to this."

I look around at the restaurant we're dining in tonight. It's fancy, even by Cole's standards, and although he and I eat in fancy restaurants quite often, we also cook at home a lot now. Cole has turned out to be quite the promising home chef. Late-night grilled cheese is still our favorite, and we need it a lot to keep our energy up.

But tonight is a special occasion—Mom's birthday. Cole sent his private jet to pick her up and fly her to New York for the weekend. We're putting her up in one of Cole's hotel suites, all expenses paid. I think we're all grateful for that bit of privacy during her visit. Cole insists on giving me multiple orgasms every night, and he doesn't like it when I'm quiet. I don't think any of us want to be traumatized by my mom having to listen to that.

Speaking of Cole, I look around for him. A few minutes ago, he'd excused himself to make a call, and gone outside. I was surprised he'd left in the middle of Mom's birthday dinner for work, but I know he wouldn't leave for something that wasn't important.

Across from me, Mom's smile freezes, her gaze fixed on something over my shoulder.

I turn to look at what's caught her attention and my heart sinks.

You have got to be kidding me.

It's been years since I last saw my father. As far as I know, he spends most of his time in Europe with his family. So how can he possibly be here now?

I turn back to Mom. "I can't believe it. Are you okay? Do you want to leave?"

"Just ignore him." Mom focuses on me and shakes her head. "It's all he deserves."

She's right. I smile and she returns it. She looks lovely tonight. I hope that when I'm her age, nineteen years from now, I'm as elegant and beautiful as she is.

"I have something for you when we get back to the house," I say. "Another present."

Her brows shoot up. "But you've already given me so much."

Cole and I spoiled her because we could. Sometimes throwing money around is just as satisfying as you might think, and seeing Mom's face light up with each gift brought me so much joy.

The sudden tightening of Mom's expression is the only warning I have before *he* steps up next to our table. I look up at my father and then at Mom, who takes a determined spoonful of her dessert.

"Beth, you're looking good," he says, then clears his throat. "Delilah, you look lovely."

My eyes widen. The gall of this man. He cannot seriously think this is an appropriate time and place to approach the woman he abandoned and the child he never acknowledged.

"Thank you, Ted," Mom replies, finally deigning to look up at him. "Is there some reason you've come over here?" I'm so proud of her composure.

For a moment he looks uncomfortable. But only for a moment. "I saw that you're dining with Cole King tonight," he says, and it all becomes clear.

"Yes." I wait for him to turn his attention to me. "Cole is my boyfriend. But I'm sure you know that already."

He doesn't even look ashamed. I don't think men like him know what shame feels like. If I ever thought Cole was arrogant and entitled, I was wrong. The epitome of those two things is standing right here in front of me.

"I had heard the rumors. Congratulations. That's quite the coup," my father—*Ted*—says.

I shake my head. How do you even respond to a comment like that?

Mom puts her spoon down with a clink. "Is there something you wanted?"

"I know we haven't always had the best relationship, Beth, and I want to apologize for that. I was under a lot of pressure back when . . . everything happened. My parents would have disowned me for getting a girl pregnant." He looks at me again. "That wasn't fair to you, Delilah. And I'd like to make it up to you if you'll let me."

"Make what up?" Cole's voice comes from behind me, and I turn in my seat to look up at him. He's focused on my father, though. While he looks completely calm, I can sense the cold anger rolling off him.

Oblivious, Ted extends his hand, a broad smile on his face. "Cole. Ted Barrett. CEO of Apex Industries."

"I know who you are." Cole doesn't take his hand.

After a few seconds of leaving it hanging in midair, my father drops it. Undeterred, he forges right ahead. "I've been wanting to meet you. I have some fantastic investment opportunities I think you'll be—"

"You don't," Cole says.

My father stops, obviously confused. "Sorry?"

"You don't have any investment opportunities I'd be interested in, because you no longer own the majority share of your company. The King Group does."

All the blood leaves my father's face. "What?"

"Your company has been having difficulties for a while now—mismanagement, apparently. Your shares are at the lowest price they've been for a decade. I saw you come in, and I decided now was the right time to make the call. So no, you don't have some investments for me. You *are* an investment. And unfortunately for you, as of"—Cole checks his watch—"ten minutes ago, you're no longer CEO of Apex Industries. My brothers and I will appoint one of our own people to take over first thing tomorrow."

My father stares at Cole with an expression I'm not sure I've ever seen on anyone's face before. "Y-You can't be serious. That's . . . That's preposterous—"

Cole turns his back on him. "Are we all done, ladies?"

Mom stands in one graceful movement, and I follow her lead. "Yes, thank you, Cole," she says. "The meal was delicious."

He gives her the smile I love to see. One filled with the easy affection that has grown between them over the eight months Cole and I have officially been together. It warms my heart to see him receive the type of maternal care he never received growing up. To be short, she mothers him and the big, bad billionaire that he is eats it up.

We make our way past Ted, who is pulling his phone

out of his pocket and frantically tapping the screen. He'll find out soon enough that Cole isn't bluffing. When my man takes my hand in his, I look up at him, meeting his warm gaze, and mouth *thank you* behind my mother's back.

He bends down and brushes his lips against mine. "Sometimes having money and power is a good thing."

I smile and run my fingers over the five o'clock shadow on his cheeks. He just can't help himself. As much as he wouldn't confirm it, I still believe he was responsible for Philippa and Paul being gone from New York when I got back from my leave eight months ago. Apparently, Philippa had made a sudden decision to return to the UK, and Paul had been sent to the Hong Kong office for three years. It may not sound like a punishment, but everyone in the office knows that while he's out of New York, his chance of promotion to partner is next to none.

Regardless of why they were gone, I can't say I was disappointed not to have to see either of them.

We make our way out of the restaurant and into the car already waiting for us. As Jonathan pulls into traffic and heads toward the penthouse, I watch Cole and my mom chatting easily together. *How did I get so lucky?*

When we arrive, I get Mom settled on the couch with a glass of red, then rush to our bedroom to get her last gift. Cole follows me, and before I can pick up the rolled-up sheet of paper from where I left it on the bed, he wraps his arms around me from behind and pulls me to him.

"Have I told you tonight how damn sexy you look?" His hot breath whispers against my ear.

I laugh softly. "Just once or twice."

"About half a dozen more times and it will almost be enough." He brushes his lips against my jaw.

"Who knew you'd turn out to be such a charmer?"

His hand slides down my thigh and up again, bringing the hem of my dress with it. "Maybe I just want to get in your panties."

I tip my head forward to give his mouth access to the nape of my neck. "Oh, you definitely want to get in my panties."

"I can have you coming in two minutes." His voice is rough with desire.

"Cole," I gasp. I can feel him pressing hot and hard against my back, and it's a fight to stop his hand's journey, but even with him, I have my limits. Screwing each other's brains out while my mother waits for us in the lounge room is a boundary I'm not willing to cross.

I turn in his arms. "We can't. But I promise I'll make it up to you later."

"I'm going to hold you to that." The rasp in his voice has heat pooling low in my core. "Because the minute your mom leaves, the only words that will be coming out of your mouth are *yes, Cole*. Now practice saying them for me."

His hand roams lower and his fingers rub over me, making me moan. I give him what he wants. "Yes, Cole."

He growls in satisfaction and releases me. I take a deep breath and try to compose myself, then pick up the gift and follow him out of the room.

When I give Mom the plans for her house, she cries happy tears. I tell her I can make any changes she wants, but she says she loves the design, that it's perfect. Not too big and not too small. It has everything I ever remember her mentioning. A little library of her own, a beautifully fitted-out kitchen, a mudroom and a sunroom, and a covered patio where she can sit and look over her vegetable garden. And two guest rooms for visitors.

One more celebratory glass of wine later, Cole calls for

Jonathan, and with promises to meet up tomorrow for breakfast, we say good night. I go down with Mom to make sure she gets into the car safely while Cole stays upstairs to tidy up.

He must have been waiting for me, because as soon as I walk back in the front door, he grabs me and spins me so my chest is pressed against the wall. His big body against mine makes my heart thunder as always, and I let out a little moan of encouragement.

"Remember what you promised me?" he asks, and it takes my mind a moment to register.

I close my eyes and smile. "Yes, Cole."

"Good. That's all I want to hear from you until I tell you otherwise. Okay?"

"Yes, Cole."

"Good girl." His voice is pitched so low, I shiver in anticipation.

His hands slide under my dress and into my panties, finding my slick core straight away. I get the feeling he's too impatient to take this slow. He'll make me come quick and hard so that he can drag out my next orgasm until he has me screaming his name.

With the fingers of one hand sinking into me and the other cupping my breast and pinching my nipple, he has me reaching my peak in record time.

"Let me hear you," he says, and I give him what he wants.

"Yes, Cole. Yes, yes, *yes*."

My body explodes with my climax, my ass pushing back against his rock-hard cock as I writhe on his hand. When I'm finally finished and sagging against the wall, Cole nuzzles my neck. "Stay where you are, don't move a muscle, and remember what you promised."

I nod, and he steps back, the air cool on my sweat-slicked back. I keep my palms and my forehead against the wall like he commanded and wait to find out what he wants from me next.

There's a brush of knuckles down my spine, and then, "Turn around."

I bite my lower lip in anticipation of what's coming, and I turn, only to gasp when my eyes drop and I see him on one knee. He's holding out a turquoise ring box, with the most beautiful diamond engagement ring shimmering against the satin material inside.

"Delilah," he says as my heart flings itself against my rib cage. "I love you in a way I didn't know was even possible. From the moment you sat down next to me in that bar, you've made me feel things I've never felt before. Every time I think I can't love you more, you prove me wrong. Being with you makes me want to be a better man. The kind of man who can be a good husband and"—he takes a deep breath, his grip on the ring box tightening—"a good father."

My heart squeezes tight at the flash of vulnerability in his eyes. For a man who had no good parental role models, the fact that he wants to try to be better for his own children —for the children *we* might have one day—floods my chest with indescribable warmth.

"I want to spend the rest of my life showing you how much I love you." Cole's voice becomes deeper, rougher. "I need to know I can make every one of your days happy. So please, kitten, marry me. Be my wife and let me show you just how incredible our lives can be together." His brows lower, his eyes glittering with intensity. "And don't forget what you promised."

I can't help it. I laugh. Because of course he would stack

the deck in his favor that way. He planned it out perfectly, and god, I love him. I love him so much it hurts. I sink to my knees in front of him, gently move the hand holding the ring box out of the way, and slide into his arms. He wraps them around me, even though his brow is furrowed and he's obviously wondering why I haven't answered him yet. But in this moment—a moment I could never have dreamed of happening a year ago and now can't imagine not happening—I just want to be as close to him as physically possible.

I brush my lips across his and breathe the words.

"Yes, Cole."

THE END

ALSO BY L. M. DALGLEISH

Fractured Rock Star Series

Fractured Hearts

Fractured Dreams

Fractured Trust

Fractured Kiss

Box Set

Fractured: The Fractured Rock Star Romance Complete Four Book Series

Crossfire Rock Stars

The Promises We Make

Empty Kingdom

Coldhearted King

Novellas

Wishing for Always

Part of the multi-author Silver Linings Series.

KEEP IN TOUCH

Join my mailing list at www.lmdalgleish.com/newsletter for news and updates, as well as to be the first to hear about new releases, sales, and giveaways. Or you can follow me on Facebook, Goodreads, Instagram, or Bookbub for pre-order and new-release alerts.

My Facebook reader group, L.M. Dalgleish's Fractured Heroes Reader Haven, is where I post teasers, update you on my current work in progress, let you know about new releases and giveaways, and just generally chat.

Links:
Facebook.com/DalgleishAuthor
Instagram.com/lmdalgleishauthor
TikTok.com/@authorlmdalgleish
Goodreads.com/author/show/20465571.
L_M_Dalgleish
BookBub.com/authors/l-m-dalgleish

ABOUT THE AUTHOR

L. M. Dalgleish is a lifelong book lover whose passion for romance novels began in the long, sleepless nights following the birth of her first baby. Two more babies later and she's still in love with strong heroines and the heroes who love them.

She lives in Canberra, Australia, with her husband, three kids, a fluffy black cat, and a fluffy white dog. In her spare time, she enjoys hanging out with her family, reading, eating too much pasta, and watching horror movies.